THE BOMB-MONGER'S DAUGHTER

Borgo Press Books by RORY BARNES

The Bomb-Monger's Daughter: A Modern Novel
The Dragon Raft: A Young Adult Novel
Human's Burden: A Science Fiction Novel (with Damien
    Broderick)
I'm Dying Here: A Comedy of Bad Manners (with Damien
    Broderick)
Space Junk: A Science Fiction Novel
Valencies: A Science Fiction Novel (with Damien Broderick)
Zones: A Science Fiction Novel (with Damien Broderick)

THE BOMB-MONGER'S DAUGHTER

A MODERN NOVEL

RORY BARNES

THE BORGO PRESS

MMXIII

THE BOMB-MONGER'S DAUGHTER

FIRST BORGO PRESS EDITION

Published by Wildside Press LLC

www.wildsidebooks.com

For the gregarious solipsists of
Château Despair, with love.

And with heartfelt thanks to Heather
and Dave Datta, wizards of the scanner.

CONTENTS

THE TAVERNA
NOTEBOOKS

Regardless of what the cops think, I think he's dead.

There is now no possibility that van Niekerk is alive and well and hiding in South America or anywhere else. I am convinced of this. Still, I suppose it is Scotland Yard's job to go on looking for him, to keep the file open. My job is to come to terms with the fact of his death, a fact I will no longer permit myself to doubt.

Van Niekerk hasn't been kidnapped and held to ransom, nor has he engineered his own disappearance. He hasn't made off with the money from the Hong Kong bank, despite the millions of dollars that are missing. I think the bastard is dead. I know the bastard is dead. Dead as a bloody doornail. It's my bet that he's somewhere in a shallow grave with his throat cut; or in the Thames in concrete boots. I'm not going to mope around waiting for him to ring me; and I'm damned if I'll dance attendance on the postman in case a letter should arrive addressed in his handwriting. I'm through with all that. And why should I worry anyway? I had severed all connections with him six months before it happened, hadn't I? I'd made it very clear I never wanted to hear from him again. See if I care about the "mystery" of van Niekerk's disappearance.

Well, of course I bloody care. That's why I'm writing in this exercise book. I care because I loved my father. Loved and hated him both. That's why part of me wants him at the bottom of the fucking Thames and the other part of me wants him hiding in

Rio de Janeiro. I am his daughter after all.

Initially, like the police and the newspapers, I thought he had been kidnapped. It was a reasonable theory. My father was absurdly rich—fat pickings for any enterprising kidnapper. But as hope faded, as the kidnap theory became less and less tenable with every new day on which the ransom demand failed to appear, I, like everybody else, began to suspect straight murder. The man had enemies; no doubt about that. What shady merchant-banker, arms-dealer, and swindler doesn't? And van Niekerk was all three and a few other things besides.

But then the Hong Kong bank collapsed and all that money was found to be missing from its already depleted assets. And when the other two partners suddenly disappeared with the same baffling lack of clues as van Niekerk, the conclusion was obvious—all three had got out from under just in time. And the press soon cemented that theory with their Insights and their Exclusives and their In-Depth Probes. Never had a fan been hit by so much shit. Helicopters, automatic rifles, howitzers, ammunition, the Brazilians, that Doctor Schmit chap, false bills of sale, "swing" transactions, the CIA, the South Africans. And that was just the Hong Kong bank, not even a major part of van Niekerk's financial empire. But the Insighters and the Probers soon got to work on the rest; as did the Companies Squad and the Fraud Squad with slightly more rigour and a bit less fuss. And it all came crashing down around our ears. But not around van Niekerk's ears. He wasn't there.

So when all this was happening, I thought, I found myself wanting to think, that van Niekerk had got out just in time. After all, in a much smaller way, he had had a financial empire go bust on him once before. He must have learnt something in the fifteen years since the New Delhi débâcle, if only when to run.

That's what I thought then. But I don't any more. My father is dead.

My mother, of course, never had any doubts at all. She was happy to proclaim van Niekerk's demise from the moment he disappeared. A few days after the bank collapsed, Detective-Inspector Michaels of the Yard flew to France to interview Jennifer. It was a doomed mission; my mother had only seen her ex-husband on a couple of brief occasions since their divorce nine years previously and there was nothing serious she could tell the detective. Still, she made him welcome, offered him the hospitality of her decrepit château, a good lunch under the beech trees, and an hour-and-a-half's diatribe about van Niekerk's appalling personality problems. You see the poor man was a victim of his own anally retentive character, itself a legacy of his puritanical Afrikaner upbringing. He had been a hoarder, Pieter. He had always been trying to make more and more money by any possible means, until finally he had been quite unable to keep his pathological cravings within decent bounds. If only he had taken my mother's advice years ago and had himself properly psychoanalyzed he would never have come to this sticky end.

What end, exactly, the detective wanted to know.

Well it was obvious really, wasn't it? The Third World, the *misérables* of the earth, had finally become fed up with Pieter's continual meddling in their wars of liberation and internecine struggles: all that gun-running, sanctions-breaking, all that sort of thing. They had cooked his goose once and for all, the *misérables*, done for him with a quick assassination job. Simple as that. The detective made a few notes in his neat hand, closed his notebook and drove his hired car back to Charles de Gaulle for a late flight to Gatwick.

A day or two later a Paris newspaper sent a reporter to interview Jennifer. She told him the same things she'd told Michaels, although she had probably worked on the story a bit by then. A clipping of the resulting article was sent to me in Liverpool, but by the time I received it Jennifer's views on her ex-husband were already appearing in the English papers. A spiritualist in Nottingham had written to Jennifer with the news that she was in contact with someone from the other side who knew my father. Van Niekerk, it seemed, was anxious to contact my mother and to reveal to her the whereabouts of (a) his mortal remains, and (b) a secret cache of gold bars. For a small consideration, communication with the deceased could be arranged. As the spiritualist had also made my father's wishes known to one of the yellower evening papers, and as the paper had rung my mother in France seeking her reactions, Jennifer was able to inform the world at large of her absolute faith in the old crone's powers and to assure interested parties that, as soon as the gold was unearthed, she would found a retirement home for broken-down horses, the home to be named after her ex-husband. In life, you see, Pieter had always been fond of animals as his frequent visits to Ascot and Newmarket had borne eloquent testimony.

The cynical may doubt the sincerity of my mother's declared belief in van Niekerk's death. What is not in doubt is her belief that wherever he was—on the other side or on this—her previous husband was reading the daily papers.

But if Jennifer was able to contemplate van Niekerk's disappearance and possible death with a facetious equanimity, it was more than I was able to do. It is still more than I am able to do. At the time of writing, my father's continued absence finds me caught between wildly fluctuating moods of anxiety and relief, depression and dull acceptance. But this, I suppose, is to be expected. My mother might have seen little of van Niekerk in recent years, but until just over a year ago, I used to stay with him in Kensington for a few days every couple of months. I remained a dutiful daughter and, I must admit, a loving one. Although, loving in no way precludes hating.

But I will come to my own part in the story in good time. I will start with Jennifer, who has known her own share of anxiety and depression, and perhaps beneath whose flippant reactions to van Niekerk's disappearance there may be feelings akin to my own. I will go back to 1950, eleven years after Jennifer was born, ten years before she gave birth to me.

* * * * * *

The present queen's mother once had a few words with my mother. I'm not sure what the old biddy was doing at Jennifer's school, but there she was, standing on the grass of the playing-fields like a mighty oak in front of this line of little bobbing Brownies drawn up for her inspection. We have a photograph on the back of which my late grandmother's fussy handwriting proclaims: "Her Majesty the Queen graciously speaking to Jennifer Goldstein, Thursday the fifth of July, 1950." The precise content of this gracious conversation isn't recorded, but there is Jennifer in the line of sturdy little English girls, a cat among the pigeons, or perhaps I should say a pigeon among the cats, smiling at the queen, who smiles back warmly, even graciously at the little girl in front of her. Jennifer's Brownie uniform is a size too large. This emphasises rather than hides the insubstantiality of the limbs it covers. Jennifer is thin. She is not yet emaciated. The anorexia nervosa hasn't yet turned her into a living skeleton, but there's not much of her. Her face, however, is very pretty, even with stumpy little plaits sticking from the sides of her head like handles. The photograph clearly shows the high cheek bones and wide-set eyes that would later, in their mature form, regard with considerable sensuality anyone who glanced at the back cover of one of her novels. That photo, the one on her books, that bloody photo haunted my adolescence. Some children are said to grow-up in their parents' shadows. I grew-up in the shadow of a dust-jacket.

I'm tempted to say the dust-jacket shows unbridled lust, but it is saved from that by a hint of sleepy reserve, a suspicion of world-weariness. Kilminster took the dust-jacket photo in the garden of the Clapham flat. He and Jennifer had been fucking all afternoon. That's what bridles the lust a trifle: Jennifer is shagged-out, post-coitally exhausted.

But I'm running ahead of my story. In the other photograph, the 1950 one, Jennifer smiles at the queen, but her smile has a nervous energy whose source is in the slightness of her body, the uncertainty of her place in the file of stolid native-born children. It may have been the anxious, refugee quality of the little girl that attracted Her Majesty, calling up a simple desire to allay the anxiety of the outsider. And in those days Jennifer's anxiety was intense. I know this from things she has told me about her childhood and from a number of scenes in her novels in which she has made use of that feeling of not belonging, of not being quite certain of one's acceptance. At the time she secretly feared she would be forced to leave the school to which the Brownie circle belonged. Her fears were undoubtedly groundless and could have been dispelled by any intelligent adult she might have confided in; but Jennifer did not seek the confidence of adults and she had only one close friend of her own age. She was aware that her mother had had a difficult time arranging for her admission to the school, that it had taken a good deal of argument to persuade the headmistress that someone not of the Anglican faith would be a welcome addition. Jennifer had joined the school during the final year of the war when the bombs, doodlebugs and V2s were falling on London in one last spiteful shower. It was only because the majority of the girls had decamped en masse at the beginning of the war to the school's temporary location in a large house in Buckinghamshire that there had been the possibility of admittance to the small day school that continued to operate in London. Now, after five years of peace, Jennifer knew that demand was again exceeding supply. There were waiting lists; fully-ticketed, tithe-paying Anglicans were being forced to send their daughters elsewhere. Jennifer feared that the pressure of numbers would force her dismissal.

It is hard for me to estimate the effect of that school on my mother; the whole ambiance of the place must have been so different to anything I have ever encountered, either in London or, later, in France. And again it is hard to really understand what it must have been like growing up with my grandparents for mother and father, and with my uncle for a brother. I only vaguely remember my grandparents, but I have often stayed with my uncle and aunt and experienced family life as they live it, solid and bourgeois. But I have experienced it forearmed as it were by my own fairly odd background: family life as I have lived it with my mother and her various husbands. To come to terms with what it must have been like for Jennifer, trapped in that post-wartime world of parents and school, with no escape and no outside standpoint from which to view things, I will have to adopt my mother's own trick: story-telling, the creation of fiction from incomplete sources. What follows, then, is based on the memories of that time that Jennifer has shared with me, my knowledge of the participants and, ironically, Jennifer's own fictional treatment of her childhood.

My grandmother gave as her ostensible reason for choosing an Anglican school for her daughter the flat statement that the school's bomb shelters were the best in London. We may doubt the completeness of this explanation, but not its obvious force. By the time Jennifer came to be enrolled in the school, two houses in every seven had been affected by enemy action. On her way to school with her friend Tamar, the only other Jew to have been admitted, she had often seen the results of the previous night's air raids: the piles of rubble, charred timbers, water-soaked possessions, and barricades. The conversations on the bus would be dour, phlegmatic. "A Heinkel come down over Hammersmith," a man would say to his neighbour, "still with a full load; unexploded five hundred pounders all over the place, our Harry's been picking them up with the squad." Jennifer and Tamar would sway in the crowded bus as it rounded a corner, their satchels under their arms or clasped between their ankles, on their way, through a gap-toothed city, where people died at night to the dull crump of bombs and the chatter of ack-ack batteries, to St James's School for Girls where hats had to be worn with the brim turned *up*, where gloves were required when the gels were outside the school grounds and where, at morning assemblies, the school sang hymns about England's green and pleasant land. Still if the school were Anglican it was not oppressively religious; the easy assumption that church-going in moderation was civilised, a bit of a bore, but part of life, suited most of Jennifer's teachers and fellow pupils.

In the assemblies, Jennifer and Tamar sang the hymns and gazed at the floor during the mumbling of the Lord's Prayer, as did everyone else. "Our Father which art in heaven Hello be thy name...." It was not until she was nine that, chancing upon a written version of the prayer, Jennifer learnt with an unwarranted degree of alarm that Christians do not address their god in this way.

"He's not called Hello, he's called Hallowed."

"No he's not," Tamar said, "he's called God. Hallowed means they look up to him."

"Oh."

When she was ten Jennifer was picked for the junior hockey team and then quietly dropped. She sat on a bench in the dark wooden changing rooms, looking at her plimsolls, listening to the dull clunking of the ball against the curved sticks of the players and the hearty bellowing of the games mistress, a loud, jovial woman called Mrs Blanchard. She was cold, but did not bother to put on her cardigan. She shivered, trying to increase the sensation, to feel colder still. She held her jaws so that her teeth were a hair's breadth apart, listening for the rattle. The already gloomy changing room was momentarily darkened still further as Mrs Blanchard entered.

"Ah, there you are Jennifer dear, not catching cold, I hope!" Mrs Blanchard sat down on the bench beside the girl. "It's a terrible pity, but can't be helped. Just one of those crosses we are sent to bear. But the team does have to play on Saturday mornings you know. Never mind, can't be helped. Have you thought about netball; they only play on Wednesdays. Silly of us to have made the mistake in the first place, we just didn't think, you see!"

"Oh," Jennifer said. She didn't see.

"Well come along," Mrs Blanchard said, "No use sitting around moping, you'll catch your death."

Jennifer burst into tears. She cried helplessly, without hope, letting the tears run down her cheeks. Beside her Mrs Blanchard said, "There, there, girl. No need for the waterworks, it's not the end of the world you know."

Jennifer wanted to throw herself against the games mistress, to be folded against her large breasts, to be held, lost in the folds of the older woman's tunic, held safe. And next to her she sensed Mrs Blanchard turning, as if to embrace her, but all the games mistress did was pat her bowed shoulders as one might pat a dog or try to cure a coughing fit.

"Come on, Jennifer, buck up," Mrs Blanchard said, but with some of the heartiness gone from her voice. Confronted by one of those rare occasions where robust common sense fails to carry the day, the games mistress was lost—not for words, but for tone of voice. "There, there," she said quietly, "there, there." But if her voice had softened, the pats on Jennifer's heaving shoulders increased in tempo, heartiness of voice being replaced by heartiness of gesture. Jennifer cried and sniffled, seeing through her tears her thin ankles in their white socks and the black canvas of her plimsolls against the hard grey concrete of the changing room floor.

"There, there," Mrs Blanchard said, "what's the matter, dear?"

"I don't know," Jennifer managed between sobs, "I don't know."

"Well, if you don't know, there's not much use in crying about it, is there, eh?" Mrs Blanchard said, making one last attempt to bring common sense into play, patting Jennifer all the harder. Jennifer continued to cry, wiping the back of her hand across her face in a gesture that merely spread the tears more evenly. The thumping on her shoulders stopped. Beside her, Mrs Blanchard was suddenly a mass of purpose and decision. The games mistress stood up, darting a hand into the pocket of her tunic. "Here, dear, use my handkerchief."

Jennifer took the proffered handkerchief and buried her face in it, embracing the square foot of cotton as if it were alive. She sensed Mrs Blanchard leaving the changing room. From outside, her voice back to full pitch, the games mistress could be heard calling across the playing field for Tamar. Jennifer stifled her sobbing, wiping the tears and her nose with the handkerchief. She heard Tamar arrive, slightly out of breath.

"Yes, miss?" Mrs Blanchard's reply was indistinct. "No, miss, I don't think so," Tamar said.

"Well, go in and see her, there's a dear."

Tamar entered and took Mrs Blanchard's place on the bench. She moved closer to her friend, taking one of her hands in hers, saying nothing.

Later, as they walked from the bus stop to the corner at which they usually stood and talked before parting, Tamar said, "She must think you spend every Saturday in the synagogue."

"But we hardly ever go."

"Well, tell her then."

"I can't."

"Well, I'll tell her for you."

"No, don't," Jennifer was suddenly desperate, "don't tell her."

"Why not? You want to be on the team."

"No I don't. I don't want to be on the team. Don't tell her, please."

"Oh, all right, dummy," Tamar said, "be mad if you want to. See if I care."

The two girls walked in silence to their corner, but instead of standing talking, they remained just long enough for Jennifer to clutch both her friend's hands and plead, "You won't tell her, will you?"

"If you say so. I don't care."

"Cross your heart and hope to die."

"Cross my heart and hope to die."

Jennifer turned and ran home. She could no more have upset Mrs Blanchard's preconceptions than she could have stopped biting her nails.

I used to bite my nails too. Once Jennifer let my father paint my stubby little fingers with some vile gunk called Mandarin Lady, a preparation which, according to the label, contained the ancient herb wormwood, but which was also guaranteed to be non-injurious to health, a statement that bore the imprimatur of one Dr Phelps M.B.B.Chir. Jesus I loathed Dr bloody Phelps. I still loath Phelps. If ever I meet him, I will be very injurious to his health. I've never really forgiven Jennifer for allowing van Niekerk to put the stuff on my fingers. She could have stopped him, she could have come to my rescue as I twisted and screamed, my wrist caught in my father's hand, my fist clenched shut while he tried, with his other hand, both to hold the bottle with its little brush and to force my fingers apart. I won in the end, of course. I hid the bottle. I smashed the replacement bottle. I kept my fingers well and truly bitten down to the quick until I was eleven when I decided they didn't look very nice and so let them grow. I did it of my own accord. Cold turkey. I could give up smoking tomorrow. Just like that. Only as I've never smoked in my life, the exercise is denied me. This is straying from the point a bit, which at the moment is meant to be Jennifer's child-hood, not mine; but, as I say, I'm working from incomplete sources. In trying to think my way into Jennifer's world I find I am using bits and pieces of mine. That Mrs Blanchard lady, for instance, was a P.T. instructor at the school I went to in Putney during our 'poor' period. I've no idea if there was anyone like her at Jennifer's school, although I'm sure there easily could have been. They are pretty common, those big, beefy, hearty, hockey-playing women. Boadicea was probably one.

Anyway, like me, Jennifer bit her nails. I know this because she has told me so on a number of occasions. But I'm not sure what, if anything, my grandparents did about the habit. As I remember them, they were a nice, if doddery, old couple. You'd think they would have produced nice, normal children. What they produced, my grandparents, was Jennifer and Simon, who grew up a bit twisted. Well, let's say they had a few problems, of which Jennifer's chronic refusal to eat anything was one. Some sort of explanation is necessary—a Mandarin Lady explana-tion will do as well as any other that I can imagine. Perhaps I'm about to mix slander with falsehood in a scurrilous defamation of my grandparents' memory, but I don't think so. The little scenario I have in mind feels right to me.

Jennifer began to bite her nails during her first week at St James's. She was six years old. It was the last year of the war. Jennifer's mother painted her daughter's finger-nails with a clear liquid that came in a pretty blue bottle and was called Mandarin Lady. The bottle stood on a shelf above the bathroom basin. Jennifer sat in the lukewarm bath that her mother had recently vacated and loathed the bottle. The bath was filled to twice the depth of the line that her father had painted around the inside of the tub at the patriotic height of five inches. If two people used the water, her mother argued, twice as much was permissible. Jennifer twisted her legs within the confines of the bath, bringing one skinny foot towards her straining head. Her teeth closed on the nail of her big toe. With a click they met and her toe-nail began to split. Three more bites and a sickle moon of nail detached itself. She spat it into the water and watched it float for a few seconds, held by the soapy grey water, before it sank out of sight. She brought her foot back to her mouth, feeling the strain in the muscles of her thigh and torso that both hurt and was all her own. She took another sickle moon from the same toe, biting as close to the quick as she could force her teeth.

As Jennifer's fingernails grew, her toenails receded. Where she had bitten her toenails back to the raw flesh, her shoes rubbed and chafed. One evening her mother came into the bathroom where Jennifer stood wrapped in a towel, her naked feet exposed. She twisted them into the meagre cover of the worn bath-mat, curling her toes under like a chimpanzee.

"Jennifer, you disappoint me."

My grandmother painted my mother's toe-nails with Mandarin Lady. My mother stopped eating. At dinner, Jennifer played with her food, pushing the woody wartime carrots from one side of the plate to the other. Her brother finished his and said, "If you don't want them, give them to me."

Jennifer began to push her plate across the table, but her father ordered her to eat them herself. She refused. Her parents cajoled, threatened, pleaded—to no effect. Finally, under intense pressure, she managed to get a forkful of carrots into her mouth. Then another and another. With her mouth full of carrots she set about swallowing. A rush of saliva rose to meet the descending vegetables. Her stomach heaved. A violent spray of carrots and saliva splattered the table and her brother. "I say, Jen!" Simon said.

Simon went to a boarding school in the country. He spoke like that, Simon. He said things like "I say, Jen!" with the appalling public school accent he still uses today. In those days he had to be dissuaded from calling his parents Mater and Pater. So there he sat opposite Jennifer, with carrot and spit all over his face. Jennifer started to giggle and then to laugh. She laughed hysterically. By which I mean she was actually in hysterics. It wasn't funny. Jennifer wasn't laughing at anything funny. Her father became very angry. He'd grown those carrots himself. Jennifer laughed. Her father shouted; he ordered her from the room. She disappeared with alacrity to the safe foodless haven of her bed under the Morrison table. The others finished their meal in a silence punctuated by my grandfather's occasional remarks that there was a war on and that prisoners of war would dance for joy at the sight of carrots like those. Through two closed doors came the sound of Jennifer laughing under her steel table, although her laughter turned to crying, real crying, before she was silent.

There she lay, cold and empty, with her face buried in the pillow; yet she saw herself from the other side of the room. The table obscured the bed, yet she saw through the green baize cover scattered with her school books, pens, and ink bottle; through the half-inch of steel plate, to the girl lying diagonally across the checkered counterpane. She wore grey woollen stockings that had been darned on both heels, a mauve skirt rucked up to expose half her thighs and a black cardigan. Her hair against the pillow was dark brown, the colour of well-lacquered furniture. Her wrists and hands were very white. In the cold reaches of her disembodied understanding, Jennifer saw that the figure on the bed was beautiful. The elegance of the slight curves that defined her calves and thighs, the slim wrists, and her hands with their long delicate fingers that were as perfect as the stems of flowers. She watched a vast rubbery woman enter the room and bend stiffly from the waist, straining to contort the masses of flesh, peer briefly at the prone beautiful girl, and then straighten up to announce to the green surface of the Morrison table, "You shouldn't upset your father so. Jennifer, you have been very bad, very ungrateful. It isn't easy to make ends meet these days. Your father works very hard to provide for you. He grew those carrots himself. He could have given them to the night-fighters, but he chose to give them to you instead. He loves you very much, Jennifer. We both do, you know that. But you have been very ungrateful, very selfish. You have hurt your father a great deal."

The enormous woman stared down at the Morrison table as if she too were possessed of the ability to penetrate its surface. Jennifer knew she was faking, knew that nothing met the woman's gaze but the green cloth and the scattered books, that the beautiful girl on the bed was inviolate in her steel world. The enormous woman continued her speech, "But we don't want to believe that you are really like that. We don't want to believe that our daughter, whom we have brought up with love and kindness, is really in her heart of hearts a selfish, wilful, disobedient, little girl. We know you are not really like that, Jennifer. You do very well at school. Your father is always pleased to read your reports; he says they are much better than his were when he was your age, but you know how hard things were for him then. Even now, with this terrible war, you are having things very much your own way, young lady. You should be grateful that your father is at home. Most of the girls at your school have fathers who are away fighting. Many of them have lost their fathers for ever. Your father's work in London is very important to the war effort, just as important as the work of a soldier or a fighter pilot, and we are lucky to be able to stand beside him...."

The enormous lady's words became indistinct, they boomed and echoed around the room, sounding like the distant crump of bombs, as senseless and as formless. The thin, beautiful girl on the bed lay in her own world, knowing that the rumbling words couldn't touch her, that she could not even hear them. Jennifer marvelled at the beautiful girl's strength, at her immunity, at her magic, charmed safety. And she knew the secret, the magic spell. The rumbling died and the enormous woman once again bent slowly to peer under the table through which she could not see, but her bending was far more painful, far more grotesque than it had been the first time, for during the rumbling of the formless words, she had grown and swollen as though fed on the words themselves, so that now the act of bending required the compression and extension of huge masses of flesh. By some miracle the woman brought her face below the level of the table. She stretched a bloated arm towards the beautiful girl's leg, tugging, hopelessly, ineffectually at that which was beyond touching. The woman released the leg, straightened to her full height. There was another brief rumbling and she left the room, closing the door.

Jennifer awoke sometime in the night. She was lying, still fully dressed, across her bed. Through the thick wire mesh that enclosed three sides of the Morrison table she could see the outlines of the legs of her chair, of the armchair that stood in the corner of the room, and the lower shelves of her bookcase. Bright moonlight flooded the room from the bay window whose blackout curtains had not been drawn. She lay trying to identify the books in the shelves by their shapes and sizes and her knowledge of where they were normally kept. Content, secure in her new knowledge, she dozed until awakened by the sirens that signalled the coming of the bombs and of her brother.

Simon slept upstairs in his own bedroom, but during raids came downstairs to share Jennifer's bed. She heard him tramping down, heard the door open and shut and heard his automatic, sleepy, "Shove over, Jen." Simon disliked cold sheets; regardless of which side of the bed Jennifer was sleeping on, he attempted to push her to the other, the better to enjoy the warmth of the place she had vacated. He fumbled his way under the table, reaching out to determine his sister's whereabouts.

"Aren't you in bed?"

"No."

"Why not?"

"Why should I be?"

"It's bloody freezing, Jen."

"I'm not cold."

Simon's hand touched hers. "You're like ice.... You've still got your clothes on."

"So what?"

"I don't know, suit yourself. Just let me get in, will you?"

Simon organised himself into bed. He always slept in his dressing gown and with socks on his feet. The socks, or his feet, or both, smelt. They smelt of Simon and they smelt of his boarding school. All Simon's clothes had his name sown onto them. His handkerchiefs had his name sown onto them. The sirens ceased. There was a minute or two of silence followed by the sound of aircraft overhead.

"Ours," said Simon.

"I know."

"Spitfires."

Very far away ack-ack guns began firing.

"The docks," Simon said, "Isle of Dogs probably."

The crump of bombs began to mix with the ack-ack chatter. Simon said, "You got the old man into a terrible bait at dinner. I thought he'd throttle you."

Jennifer said nothing. Simon started a long account of a boy called Grearson who had been nearly throttled by a master at his school. Jennifer hated Simon's school; little seemed to happen there except thrashing and throttling and ragging and fagging and something called Saturday mornings. But, apart from the prodigious feats of the RAF, nothing else informed Simon's conversation. It appeared that on the occasion in question, Grearson's antics during a latin lesson had so enraged the master concerned—someone called Old Soames-Prichard—that he had bodily lifted Grearson from his seat by his neck. Grearson had turned red and then blue, his eyes had begun to bulge. Simon admired Grearson for being able to enrage Old Soames-Prichard to the degree necessary to induce this feat. He also admired Old Soames-Prichard for possessing the manly qualities necessary for its performance.

Once Simon had brought Grearson home for a long weekend. Jennifer and her parents called him Thomas, but Simon only called him Grearson and was called Goldstein in return. Jennifer slept in Simon's room upstairs, it being understood that in the event of a raid she would share her parents' bed under their Morrison table. Simon and Grearson took over her room. On the first evening of the visit Jennifer entered her own room to pick up the book she had been reading. She entered without knocking, thinking the boys to be elsewhere. Both boys were in the room, both in their pyjamas, the bottom halves of which they had pulled down in order to inspect each other's buttocks. Their buttocks were striped with blue and yellow bruises. Grearson pulled up his pyjama trousers with the speed of a conjurer. His face, with all its spots, turned bright red. Simon was slower to react, less embarrassed.

"I say, Jen," he said, "Fair play."

Jennifer withdrew.

Later, when she was alone with Simon, she said, "Who did that to your bottom?"

"Old Soames-Prichard. Carrington and Hamble got it too. Grearson got twice as many because he was the ringleader. You should have seen Old Soames-Prichard, he was wild. The man was ropeable."

Simon went on to describe the beatings in some detail. Jennifer loathed Old Soames-Prichard. Simon's admiration knew no bounds. In the history of human threshing machines it was clear there had never been a hero of quite his stature, his powers bordered on the super-human. That it was Simon's own buttocks that had been the proving ground for these powers seemed of little account.

A bomb exploded much nearer.

"Five hundred pounder," Simon said.

"Our Harry's been picking them up with the squad," Jennifer said.

"What?"

"Nothing."

"Daft," Simon said. "Stop rattling your teeth. You're not in a funk are you?"

Jennifer clamped her mouth shut to stop her teeth chattering.

Simon said, "You're shivering like a leaf. Get into bed, I can't hear properly with you shivering away."

Jennifer slowly climbed into bed in her clothes. Her brother said, "This pillow smells of carrots."

"Let's send it to the night fighters." Brother and sister giggled.

* * * * * * *

There are a number of things wrong with the above account, if account is not too pretentious a word for an exercise in pure hype. At the end of the war Jennifer was only six. The way she developed in my little story you'd think she was at least ten, maybe twelve. Although all through her childhood Jennifer ate very little, the real period of self-imposed starvation occurred between her fifteenth and eighteenth birthdays. It was during this time that the distortions of self-image—in which she came to see her own pitiful skinniness as beautiful and ordinary people's bodies as utterly monstrous—took place. I've got a lot of my grandmother's dialogue wrong; she wouldn't really have talked like that. Oh well, I try, I try. The thing is, as I've said before, the scene feels right. I've got the tensions right, the psychological mechanisms or whatever it is that gives veracity to stories of this kind. I understand Jennifer better for having written about her like that. And it's understanding, not misunderstanding. Back to the story.

* * * * * * *

When Jennifer was eleven (when she really was eleven, in

the year of Grace 1950, when she had that gracious conversation with Her Majesty) a lean, rangy man in a dog collar arrived to give the girls in Jennifer's class instruction. They were all to be confirmed in their membership of the Church of England at the completion of the course. Jennifer and Tamar were excused. They walked backwards and forwards under the elms at the end of the playing field, sometimes glancing towards the windows of the room in which the cleric was initiating their classmates into the mysteries of their sure, established faith. The cleric's name was Canon Carstairs; he had been in the army and had been wounded at Dunkerque. He walked with a limp, supporting himself with an ivory handled stick.

"What do you think he's telling them?" Jennifer said.

"Oh, all about extreme unction and all that."

"What's extreme unction?"

"It's what soldiers get when they're dying. They go to heaven if they get it. Christians that is."

"What's it look like?"

"It comes in a bottle. A little bottle, it's a sort of oil or something. It's something like...."

Tamar wasn't quite sure what it was like. She had seen a film at the cinema in which a priest of some kind did something with a little bottle on the field of battle. She was prepared to guess that the bottle contained unction. Jennifer thought of the little blue bottle of Mandarin Lady, she thought of Canon Carstairs painting the toenails of dying soldiers on the beach at Dunkerque. The soldiers arrived at the entrance to heaven where God allowed those with long nails through the gate. Those who had not received their extreme unction from Canon Carstairs had bitten their nails back to the raw flesh. God turned them away. They wandered around outside the walls of heaven, lost, not knowing what was happening inside. The soldiers wanted to know what was going on. It wasn't so much that they thought the people in heaven to be happier than they themselves were, rather they felt excluded, they felt they were missing out on the strange rites and practices that went with admission to heaven.

One of the soldiers on the outside had been very unlucky indeed. He had been on the beach at Dunkerque with Canon Carstairs when he had been hit by a shell. The shell blew both his feet off.

Canon Carstairs raced across the beach to the dying soldier, tugging his bottle of Mandarin Lady from his tunic pocket. But he could not find the soldier's feet. The soldier lay on the beach slowly dying. Canon Carstairs ran around like a terrier looking for a thrown stick.

"I think they're over there," the soldier called, pointing with his arm. Canon Carstairs ran to where the soldier pointed but could not find the missing feet. "I'm dying," called the soldier in despair.

"Hang on, old man," yelled Canon Carstairs, "we'll have them in a jiffy. We're all in this together, you know."

The soldier lay back on the beach with a low groan; Canon Carstairs ran faster and faster, this way and that, but nowhere were the soldier's feet to be found. All around him the beach was littered with bits of seaweed and driftwood; often he thought he saw the feet in their big army boots, but when he ran up to them they changed to seaweed. "Please hurry," groaned the soldier.

"Hang on," shouted Canon Carstairs, "we'll find them soon."

The beach was now deserted and night was falling fast. One last brave little pleasure steamer waited at the water's edge. The pilot of the brave little pleasure steamer was waving to Canon Carstairs to come on board. "We're leaving," called the pilot, "we can't wait any longer."

"Hold on!" yelled the Canon. "Just one more minute."

"I'm dying," groaned the soldier.

"Come on," shouted the pilot, "bring the soldier with you."

"I've got to find his feet first," shouted Canon Carstairs, "it's no good without his feet."

Canon Carstairs ran faster and faster around the darkening beach. The pilot of the brave little pleasure steamer prepared to leave without him.

Suddenly, there were the feet in their boots, standing neatly together on the sand. The Canon pounced on them; he raced across the sand to the dying soldier. "I've got them, I've got them," he yelled.

"I'm dying," groaned the soldier.

"Last chance!" shouted the pilot, "I'm leaving now."

Desperately Canon Carstairs picked up the soldier, holding him over one shoulder. He stooped to pick up the feet in their boots and managed to get hold of both of them by their laces. He lumbered down to the water's edge. Wading through the little waves he managed to get both himself and the soldier into the brave little pleasure steamer. Apart from the pilot they were the only ones on board. The pilot put out to sea.

"Quickly, quickly," groaned the dying soldier, "Extreme unction."

"Hang on old man," muttered Canon Carstairs tearing at the laces of the boots, racing against time to get the feet out before it was too late.

Just then a shell landed on the deck. It couldn't have been a very big shell because it didn't do any damage, but it exploded with a bang that knocked Canon Carstairs sideways across the deck. He realised he had injured his own leg quite badly. Then he lost consciousness.

When the Canon came to, his first thought was for the soldier. The soldier lay very still on the brave little pleasure steamer's gently heaving deck.

"It's too late," said the pilot. "He died while you were asleep."

"Oh dear," said Canon Carstairs sadly, "we were in it together, you know."

The pilot turned round from the helm. He looked gravely at Canon Carstairs sprawled on the deck. "I think you will need this from now on," he said, handing the canon a walking stick with an ivory handle.

When the soldier awoke he was being carried along piggy-back by a friend of his called Grearson. They were passing through a forest of elm trees.

"Put me down, Grearson," said the soldier.

"You've got no feet," Grearson said.

After a while they arrived at the gate of heaven. God was standing at the gate. "Well, let's have a look," he said, "Don't stand around moping."

Grearson placed the footless soldier on the ground and bent to remove his own boots; his socks had little tags with his name sewn onto them. He presented his feet, which smelt strongly of boys' boarding school, for inspection by God. The toe-nails were large and curled over at the ends.

"Good work, Grearson," God said. "Canon Carstairs keeping you up to the mark is he? In you go."

The footless soldier watched his friend, Grearson, pass through the gate of heaven. He looked up at God.

"Well," said God, "what do you want?"

"I want to enter the kingdom of heaven," said the soldier, "but I haven't any feet."

"I can see that," God said.

"Canon Carstairs found them, but he got hit by a shell."

"Can't be helped," said God. "It's a cross we are sent to bear, it's just one of those things."

"But can't you make an exception?" asked the soldier.

"Sorry, but without feet there is no possibility of extreme unction, and without extreme unction you can't come in."

Sadly the soldier bumped his way over the grass of the playing fields that surrounded the kingdom of heaven, towards the elms. In the forest he met others who had died without extreme unction. They gazed from the trees towards the high walls of heaven. "What do they do in there?" they asked each other, but no one knew. The soldiers walked backwards and forwards under the elms, talking and casting glances at the high walls. The soldier without feet sat on the grass under a tree by himself, feeling doubly alone. Just then he heard the cantering of hooves. A dazzling white unicorn pranced through the trees. Sitting on the unicorn's back was a beautiful girl.

The soldier had never seen anyone so beautiful, for the girl was very thin and her brown hair shone like the polish on his bookcase at home. Her eyes were as green as emeralds and her arms were as slender as the stalks of flowers. She smiled gravely down at the poor footless soldier. The soldier fell instantly in love with the girl.

"Do not be sad," said the girl, "There is nothing in heaven that you could want. Heaven is not what it seems. Nothing happens behind those walls, but throttlings and thrashings and ragging and fagging and it is always Saturday morning."

"But my friend Grearson...."

"You will have to forget poor Grearson," the girl said. "He is getting it now from Old Soames-Prichard and that will be his lot for ever and a day."

The soldier shed a tear for Grearson, for he had been a loyal friend who had carried him on his back right to the gate of heaven itself, and then, when the slim, beautiful girl looked deeply into his eyes and smiled her grave, beautiful smile, he forgot him completely. The girl slid from the back of the unicorn, landing on the grass beside the soldier as lightly as thistle-down. She took the soldier's hand in hers.

"I am Princess Jennifer," she said, "and this is my faithful steed, Tamarand."

The unicorn lowered its head to nuzzle the poor soldier, being careful not to spike him with its horn.

"I live far from here in my castle by the lake," Princess Jennifer said. "In my castle there is an old silversmith, wise in the ways of his craft and of the magic of the wild woods and the gloomy mountains. Come to my castle and he will fashion you a pair of silver feet that will be the envy of all who see them and at night you shall dance with me in the Great Hall."

"Fair Princess Jennifer," the footless soldier replied, "I would if I could, but your castle is far from here and I cannot walk."

"I shall walk," the princess replied. "Tamarand will carry you."

The unicorn knelt by the soldier who climbed upon its back as best he could. The princess called to the other soldiers who had been denied the false pleasures of the kingdom of heaven and together they formed a merry band which set off behind the princess and her faithful steed for the castle by the lake. And all the livelong day as the birds sang and the hawthorn blossomed on the bough, the poor footless soldier beheld the slim form of the beautiful princess who walked at the unicorn's head.

* * * * * * *

That idiot Leclercq invited Jennifer to my school once. He thought it would do us good to be talked to by a real writer. So Jennifer turned up and talked to us about *Mixed Blessing* which had just been translated into French. In the English version the story contains the notorious altar-wine gaff, but that had been edited out of *Les Bénédictions contradictoires*. Since the story is all about faith, doubt, sin, God, and priests, Jennifer thought it would be just the thing for our literature class. Catholicism has a pretty firm grip on our part of Oise.

There is virtually no autobiographical element in *Mixed Blessing*. The story concerns a young boy caught between the simple Roman Catholic faith of his mother and the anguished, complex atheism of his father. If anything, the story is biography, being based closely on the experiences of James Kilminster. All of it, that is, except for the scene where Allen (the Kilminster figure in the story) walks under the elm trees on the driveway to the seminary in which his mother wants him to train for the priesthood. Allen experiences a feeling of alienation from some vague and unobtainable certainty. The strength of Jennifer's story lies, ironically, in the very feebleness of the feeling she manages to evoke. Allen somehow knows that his uncertainty cannot be dignified by calling it a Doubt, that it generates no possibility of experiencing the Dark Night of the Soul. There is to be no wild turning from God only to be saved by a blinding revelation of His Amazing Grace. For Allen there is to be no divine ecstasy in the bosom of Christ as reward for the travails of forty days and forty nights in some wilderness of the spirit. Such saving as Allen's soul is to be granted will be a fairly mundane, ordinary, run-of-the-mill, suburban affair. This drives

Allen into a fit of pique. The lad wants to be a proper Catholic, the fit stuff of priesthood. It occurs to him that his mini-doubts, uncertainties, failures of faith are basically Protestant, the sorts of things that any old member of a red-brick Methodist church on a street corner in some Midlands housing estate might experience. In a hopeless attempt to increase the intensity of his feelings, to soup up his doubts into Doubts, Allen deliberately rails against God, calling him names, blaspheming, swearing, trying vainly to say the Lord's Prayer backwards, daring God to strike him down or save him, one thing or the other. God, of course, isn't fooled for a minute and sends (if you want to read divine intervention into the story—Jennifer leaves it up to the reader) a kindly old priest, who comes down from the seminary to see what on earth is the matter with this idiot child yelling and shouting and waving his arms about in the driveway. The moment Allen sees the priest he freezes, blushes with embarrassment and tries to pretend he is rehearsing a part for a play. The old priest starts to draw the boy into conversation, and as the two walk up and down the drive of the seminary Allen explains his longing, his feeling of being outside both the sure, unquestioning faith of his mother and the anguish of his father. It is this feeling that my mother evokes so well in the story. Kilminster says this is the only bit that she didn't get from him, that it comes straight from her own experience; that for Allen's mother's simple faith one should read the easy Anglicanism of Jennifer's school, and for the father's complex suffering, the Judaism of her parents' household. According to Kilminster, Allen's longing to be included as he walks under the elms of the seminary driveway is Jennifer's longing to be accepted and included that she felt walking with Tamar under the elms at the bottom of the school's playing fields. There are obvious difficulties with this reading of the story. My feeling is that Jennifer's longing was more intense, her feeling of alienation far greater than Allen's. What I think she did in *Mixed Blessing* was transubstantiate her intense experiences through the medium of Kilminster's general lukewarm feebleness into the body and soul of the fictional Allen. There is more of Allen in Kilminster than he would like to believe.

So Jennifer turned up to talk to us about the story. I wasn't really looking forward to the visit. I don't think children in general like having their parents visit their schools whatever the reason. School is not part of the parents' domain; they ought to keep out, stay in their proper network of relationships. But in this case it was inevitable and I didn't object all that strongly; I was quite resigned to it. Jennifer entered the room and everyone stood up, as was customary when strangers visited our class-rooms. I stood up automatically and felt a complete idiot for doing so—fancy standing just because your mother has entered the room—but then I could hardly have stayed sitting down. I was relieved to see that Jennifer was not too eccentrically dressed, although I'm sure that most of my classmates would have died of embarrassment had their own mothers appeared at school wearing elastic-sided pony boots, jeans, roll-neck jersey and one of those inside-out sheepskin jackets from Afghanistan with the embroidery worn to shreds. We all sat down and our teacher went through the expected rigmarole about how lucky we were to have Anasuya's mother, Mme Saintenoy, who writes under the *nom de plume* Jennifer Kilminster, with us to discuss her story, *Les Bénédictions contradictoires*, etc. etc. etc. Jennifer was, by now, quite used to all this literary lionising. The French are even better at it than the English, but Jennifer can stack on a concerned-writer-talks-to-intelligent-and-sensi-tive-audience act any time she wants to. But she doesn't always want to. It's when she feels bored with the whole performance that she deliberately accentuates her eccentricities, says things for no better reason than their shock value. I know that one of the reasons I am so fond of my mother, one enduring strand of my love for her, is just this oh-bugger-it-let's-jolt-this-lot-out-of-their-complacency streak in her makeup. But you (whoever you are, I'll discuss you in a minute) must remember that I was then seventeen, had lived in France for four years, and that the school in question was deep in the heart of rural, Catholic Oise, where a Protestant is a rarity, let alone an eccentric English Jew with two surnames, neither of which is the same as her daughter's. So I sat at my desk feeling slightly uncomfortable, watching my mother go through the motions of being a minor literary personage.

Jennifer talked to us for a while about the implications of the story. She stressed that, as she saw it, the importance of Allen's feelings lay in their lack of intensity and his impotent realisation of this lack. She down-played the religious aspects, they were just a vehicle for the exploration of Allen's psychology, his place in the world. Instead of religion, Jennifer argued, she could have used love, sexual passion, political ambition, some sort of artistic expression, whatever. The whole religious thing was just a device, a gimmick if you like. I know this upset a few members of the class. None of my close friends gave much thought to religion, but there was one clique of three girls and a couple of boys, individually, who were in the grip of an adolescent religious fervour of one sort or another. I'd told Jennifer about them the previous week. "Poor bastards," she'd said, "they're probably just sex-starved." It was possibly with this conversation in mind that she had decided to dwell on the inconsequence of the religious content of the story. For the budding mystics and saints in the class this was a bit disturbing. I knew from earlier discussion that one or two of them had read a degree of spiritual, maybe even theological, complexity into *Mixed Blessing*. They hadn't really expected the author to equate the whole lot with activities such as screwing. But I, for one, was quite happy for Jennifer to do this, I wasn't that hypersensitive to the feelings of my peers.

Jennifer performed for about twenty minutes, and it was a good performance. She spoke with an honest common sense that was at considerable variance with the way most French intellectuals carry on. Her language was free from jargon, she didn't patronise us because we were only school kids, she was often very speculative in tone. She seemed to be inviting us to join her in an exploration of the story; she made virtually no reference to the fact that she was the author of it; certainly made no attempt to give her words extra authority because of this. She sat on the edge of the teacher's desk, relaxed, serious, and friendly. Her French is good, with very few stilted or odd constructions (although her accent is entirely English-educated London, I suppose you'd call it). So, as I say, it was a good performance; just how good, only I knew. Jennifer actually has very firm ideas about her fiction; she, and she alone, understands the motivations of her characters, the symbolic significance of elements of the story, the correct interpretation and weight to be given to any action or twist of plot. She regards literary criticism as the most spurious of academic disciplines. Departments of literature in universities are staffed entirely by frauds and charlatans who couldn't write a coherent laundry list, let alone a novel or play, and yet who have no trouble extracting vast amounts of taxpayers' money to concoct spurious fantasies about the works of real writers most of whom are starving or working themselves to death at menial tasks. There is a drawer in Jennifer's workroom in which, among other things, she stuffs the photocopies of the reviews of her books that her publishers send her. Some of these she has obviously read, or at least glanced at. They tend to have words like RUBBISH or GIBBERISH scrawled across them in black biro. So there was, then, this trifling discrepancy between her performance in our classroom and the sort of literary discussion we occasionally had over the dinner table at home.

Jennifer ceased talking, turned to our teacher and said, "Perhaps I'd better stop preaching now, so that we can have a discussion."

That old pedant, Leclercq, called for questions. After a short pause a boy raised his hand, Leclercq nodded to him, and he stood up and began, "Madame...."

Jennifer said, "Look, please don't stand up. I get nervous when people stand up to talk to me. I feel as if they are picking a fight."

There were a few restrained laughs at this. The boy sat down and began again, "Madame, do you find in your writing that structure pre-supposes form, or do the characters exist in their own right?" (Or some bilge like that.)

"I'm sorry, I don't think I understand the question."

The boy began a long reformulation of his question. It was as unintelligible as the first version. His name was Jean de France and he fancied himself as the class intellectual. At one point in his ravings he said, "...as Althusser has put it...."

Jennifer cut him off with, "I'm sorry, I can't understand a word Althusser writes, he's got the literary style of a tin of treacle. God alone knows what his ideas are about."

Leclercq broke in with, "I think perhaps the discussion should concentrate on Mme Saintenoy's actual story. We can perhaps leave general philosophical questions to a later date."

There followed a few routine questions about *Mixed Blessing* which Jennifer dealt with in her routine way, that is by giving the clear impression that she was hearing them for the first time, that she was actually considering her answers as she gave them. I had noticed that one of the religious girls, a very short, plain girl called Paulette, was becoming more and more agitated, shifting constantly in her seat, fidgeting. Finally she raised her hand. Jennifer nodded to her.

"Madame, do you think your story is irreligious?" she said with a rush.

"No," Jennifer said. "Do you think so?"

"Madame, you say that Allen's problems could be explored through art or political ambition or...or love. You say that it is not important to you that he cannot find true spiritual oneness with his creator. When...when...he leaves the priesthood, it is to become a worker in a biscuit factory.... Do you think it is better to make biscuits than serve the Almighty?"

During her question Paulette had become increasingly agitated, distressed. She had finished in a torrent of words that was almost unintelligible. Jennifer was quiet for a moment, then she said very gently, "Do you think the story is irreligious?"

Paulette said, "Madame, I thought that the story showed the

dangers of taking the Lord's work lightly, of not trying with all one's heart and soul to do His bidding. I thought...I thought it was an object lesson...a parable."

"Then that is a good way to read the story."

"But, Madame, you have said that religion does not matter."

"Well, it doesn't matter to me. But that's no reason why it shouldn't matter to you."

"But, Madame, you wrote the story."

"Look...err...what's your name?"

"Paulette Duprey."

"Look, Paulette, my opinions about my stories or novels are no more important than anyone else's. Once a writer has written a story it is in the public domain. It is just so many words on paper. Anyone can have ideas about these words. There is nothing special about the writer's ideas themselves. The ideas can be judged good or bad according to how well they seem to explain the story, how well they make sense. If you think my ideas make sense, you should accept them. If they seem wrong to you, you should reject them. Maybe I have not understood the story properly. Maybe my critical insights are at fault."

Leclercq murmured, "Madame is being too modest."

Jennifer turned to him, speaking more forcefully than she had done to Paulette, but still very seriously, very earnestly. "No, I am not being modest. That is my position on all writing; I believe this of all writers of fiction...that they do not have a privileged position from which to pronounce on their own work. Often indeed, writers are very bad literary critics. Look at the faculties of the universities; how many good writers are there in the departments of literature? Very few. I believe this is so because writers know best how to write, not how to criticise. It is best that they leave criticism to those who are most fitted to do it, to academics."

At this point Jennifer's eye caught my own. I mouthed the words *lying hound* at her. She didn't flicker an eyelid. I looked at Leclercq and then at Paulette. They both seemed vaguely relieved, but disappointed; they clearly wanted an authoritative version of the story—what was the point of having the author to speak to you if her words were worth no more than anybody else's? The lesson was drawing to a close; Leclercq looked at me.

"But we have heard nothing from Anasuya. Perhaps you would like to ask the last question."

I don't know why he did this. Maybe he wished to re-emphasise the uniqueness of this lesson, to salvage some of the privilege that Jennifer had been at such pains to deny. It is possible that he foresaw the day when I too would be a well-known writer (even then I had a reputation for literary ability and many people just assumed that I would want to follow in Jennifer's footsteps if I could only make the grade). Perhaps he wished to be able to recall in his dotage the great debate between Jennifer Kilminster and Anasuya Tamar van Niekerk that raged in his very classroom.

I said, "No, not really. There's nothing I can think of about the story that I haven't already discussed with my mother."

"And these discussions have left you with no issues that you would like to take up again with your mother? There is nothing you would like to share with us by way of debate?"

"No, not that I can think of."

I had the uncomfortable feeling of being stared at by too many eyes. The whole room wanted me to say something. Jennifer was smiling that amused, quizzical smile, like the one on the back of her books. She said in English, "Go on, Ansu, give them what they want."

I said in French, "Jennifer I know your story back to front. I've known it for eight years."

I had only just taken to calling her Jennifer at home, and still often called her Mummy; at that time, more often than not. By deliberately using her name in class I suppose I was trying to assert my independence, my right not to be called upon to perform the tricks Leclercq and the rest of the class wanted from me. But I realised as I said it that I'd also called my mother *vous* (*votre nouvelle*). I doubt that anybody in the class picked this up, or if they did, found it remarkable. Some of them would probably have called one of their own parents *vous* in similar circumstances. One poor girl, I knew for a fact, never called her parents anything else, even at home. But Jennifer obviously found it remarkable and it obviously amused her; she replied very formally, calling *me vous*.

"You aren't usually so reticent in your comments about my writing." She then explained in a stage whisper to Leclercq, "I think she's just being loyal; she really thinks *Les Bénédictions contradictoires* is fourth-rate pulp, but she's too polite to say so."

There were a few gasps from those who believed Jennifer to be talking seriously, a few laughs from those of my friends who knew her to be joking, and a number of nervous titters from the majority who didn't know what to think.

Leclercq said, "Madame, she can't think that. She surely knows *Les Bénédictions* to be a work of great literature."

This was a nervous over-reaction on his part. He wasn't a complete dolt, he knew the difference between a good, competent, modern short story and great literature. But once he'd said it, the words were out. Jennifer, highly amused, turned back to me.

"Do you," she said, still calling me *vous*, "know great literature when you read it?"

She was laughing as she spoke and the laughter robbed the words of their aggression. But still, I'd had enough of the situation. I had to call a halt by saying something. What I did say surprised me as I was saying it. I'm still not clear about the psychology of my decision. I have privately coined the phrase 'third-rail-syndrome'. As anyone familiar with London knows, the Underground works on a system in which the electricity is carried by a third rail in between the two ordinary rails along which the wheels run. One can walk along the platform looking down at this third deadly rail sitting there gleaming like the other two. It would be the easiest thing in the world to hop down onto the floor of the tunnel and touch the rail. The rail fascinates me; I always stand well back from the edge of the platform, just to put distance between the rail and myself. I imagine touching the rail. Poof! One dead girl. Of course I've never come anywhere near touching the rail, but this desire to touch what one most fears seems to be part of my make-up. (Other people's too. Kilminster says he once tried to look down the barrels of a loaded shotgun with his fingers on the triggers.) As I have said, I began the lesson with some vague fear that Jennifer would say or do something outrageous, just for the hell of it. I would have thought that I would have done anything to avoid the possibility of her doing so, but what I now said—calling her *tu* consistently—was, "All right, I'll ask you a question about this work of great literature. In your reply to Marcel you said something about the times having changed since you wrote the story, you said social mores had changed in a way that allows writers more freedom of expression, can you tell us how you would write the story today?"

This was asking for it. Jennifer had once shown me the rough draft of *Mixed Blessing*. In 1971 she initially wrote the story much as I imagine she would write it today; it was full of blasphemy and swear words. For obvious reasons she cut these out in the fair copy she submitted for publication.

"Well," Jennifer said, "I don't suppose I'd change much of the action. It would be more a matter of being able to be more honest, more explicit in some of the scenes. Today one can show directly, what, eight years ago, one had to hint at. For example, I say in the story that Allen railed against God, that he blasphemed and swore. I don't actually write down in direct speech what he said."

I could sense the rise in tension around me. Leclercq was managing to hide his discomfort under a blanket of high seriousness. Jennifer went on, very serious herself, considering her words. "Of course there is no point in filling up a story with a whole lot of obscenity in order to simply shock, although"—and here she looked very grave—"many modern writers seem to me to be doing just that. No," she said with conviction, "you don't produce great literature that way."

Leclercq, slightly less uncomfortable, nodded sagely in assent. "But there are times and places when to do so is intrinsically desirable within the confines of the story itself, when to do so is, as the English law courts put it, a matter of literary merit. Now let us look at the scene outside the seminary. I think a great deal could be learnt about Allen from the words he would use. His act, railing against God, is not something that he habitually does. He is forcing himself to do so, his motivation comes from a muddled, adolescent self-hatred. All this, I think, could be very clearly shown by putting in direct speech what he would actually say."

Jennifer paused for a moment, she was very sober, very adult. "Now what would he actually say?"

I glanced at Leclercq, the poor man was probably wetting his pants.

"It would be quite wrong to show Allen swearing away with all the fluency of a seasoned trooper on the field of battle."

"*Oh, mais oui.*"

"On the other hand we should not show him as having no more imagination than a five-year-old who has discovered that some words can quickly gain the attention of adults, but who has no idea what they mean. No, Allen is feeble, but not that feeble. He has an imagination."

The tension was rising, Jennifer was building to the punch line beautifully. Nothing in her manner, not a flicker of an eyelid, betrayed anything but serious, intelligent, reasoned concern for literary verity. But the punch line, when it came, was extraordinarily infantile. I was embarrassed at the time; I'm still embarrassed. It embarrasses me to write it down in this exercise-book.

"I think Allen would say something like"—and here she suddenly switched to English—"'God, you are a silly old fart and I'm sick of eating your stringy son every Sunday. Pitooee!'"—back to French: "I don't know; something like that. I'm sorry my control of French idiom is not good enough to put it in your own language, but I'm sure Anasuya can help if you don't understand."

The tension collapsed in a mad buzz. The linguistic abilities in the room covered a wide range; I suppose two or three students understood pretty well what Jennifer had said. Another two or three had a good idea. The rest were at sea, including Leclercq, who, I knew for a fact, had virtually no English at all. Someone nudged me from behind.

"What did she say?"

"Nothing much," I said, shrugging.

Leclercq was looking at me. I contrived to give the impression that Jennifer had said nothing out of the ordinary. And, in fact, of course, what she had said bore no relation to the 1971 rough draft at all. In that version, Allen really had sworn like a seasoned trooper. I felt both relieved and let down that Jennifer hadn't given a full-bore translation of the original text. Leclercq regained the floor, thanked Madame for giving up her valuable time, expressed appreciation of all we had gained and so on and so forth, the bell rang, and we all trooped out to lunch. During this meal, with no help or hindrance from me, it became irreversibly fixed in the school's folk lore that Anasuya's mother had spent an entire lesson mouthing obscenities and oaths.

The thing about Jennifer is that she is genuine. Her tact (as with Paulette) is genuine; her gauche lack of tact (as with the silly bit of half-baked blasphemy) is genuine too. She's not entirely consistent or indeed stable, my beloved mother, but at any one time she's quite genuine. One more quick anecdote: Jennifer was once removed from the guest list of the British Embassy in Paris after she had told the first secretary (a dark, Mediterranean-looking man with a thoroughly incongruous upper class, double-barrelled English surname and accent to match) that he was even more of a wog than she was. This at some official dinner or other. My mother is the only European Jew I know who regularly refers to herself as a wog. My mother is the only person I know who regularly refers to herself as a wog.

* * * * * * *

I suppose I really ought to get back to 1950 and the eleven-year-old Jennifer walking with Tamar under the elms and fantasising about the footless soldier and the princess, but there might be some point in my making explicit exactly what this whole story is about. I should say who I am and what are the circumstances under which I am writing.

My name is Anasuya Tamar. I was born in New Delhi in 1960, the only child of Jennifer van Niekerk née Goldstein, aspiring writer, and Pieter van Niekerk, entrepreneur, importer-exporter, economist, "adviser" to the World Bank, currency speculator, and crook. Until a year ago I had that ugly Afrikaner surname as well, but I legally dropped it in favour of my middle name, Tamar, which is now my surname. (Incidentally, if my first name looks odd on paper, it is quite easy to pronounce, two ordinary English names with a "ya" on the end; Anasuya, Anna-Sue-ya. The diminutive is even easier; Ansu, Ann-Sue. I love my name, it's the most beautiful combination of syllables possible in any language. It's the only word of Hindi I know.) When I was six the Indian government very sensibly deported my father, or rather refused to renew his visa on the grounds that he was South African, a nationality not overly well regarded in those parts. The real reason was much more complicated and concerned the bribing of the wrong members of Congress with the wrong amounts of black money at the wrong time, and the possibility of a scandal which would have involved various high government officials. I don't know all the details. My parents returned to London, where, two years later, Jennifer left van Niekerk to live with and then marry a refugee from a Catholic seminary, James Kilminster. That marriage lasted four years. In 1974 Jennifer met and married the French journalist Jean-Claude Saintenoy and went to live in the rundown château he had inherited from his grandparents (his parents had more sense than to try to live in it). From that point Jennifer's household consisted of herself, Jean-Claude, me, Jean-Claude's two children by his previous marriage, Philippe and Silvie, and eventually my half-brother, Bernard. To this can be added a changing population of au-pairs, hippies, reformed dope-fiends, *marginaux*, and visitors, among whom Kilminster and his current lady friend are often included. At one stage last summer we counted twenty people in residence; in winter the numbers are usually lower, especially if Philippe and Silvie are staying with their mother in Paris.

Under the terms of Jennifer's divorce from van Niekerk, that man had legal right of "access" to me, his daughter. It was only after a good deal of unpleasant legal wrangling that Jennifer was allowed to take me to France at all. I continued seeing my father from time to time, staying with him in Kensington or in expensive hotels in the South of France. When I was just twenty I decided, under emotionally taxing circumstances, not to see any more of my father. Six months later he disappeared.

The police are still looking for him. I hope they find him. Or maybe I don't. The man is loathsome in many ways, but he is my father and my feelings for him are complicated and often confused. This, I suppose, is the real reason I am writing this account, story, semi-novel, call it what you will. I wish to become clear in my own head about my father, my mother, Kilminster and myself.

That in essence is me, but who are you? To whom is this story addressed? When I started it, I thought I was simply engaged in talking to myself. But I am my mother's daughter; I have already had stories published in university magazines; I once wrote a long feature article for one of

Jean-Claude's papers, comparing my French school with one in Bury St Edmunds to which some of us had gone on an exchange visit. (The food in English schools would poison a dog.) I find I cannot write for long without imagining the response my words will evoke when read by some vaguely conceived, reasonably intelligent person, The Reader, that every writer seems to have in their head. So I am writing as if for publication, although at the same time trying to be honest with myself about the events I recall or try to imagine. In other words, the criterion I am using is did it happen, could it have happened like this? Not, does it work well as part of the story, as fiction? So perhaps this narrative will appear jerky at times, lack the smooth plausibility of a proper novel. Too bad. If you want a smooth, well-wrought plot, you can always pick up a real novel. Try one of Jennifer's if you like. *The Tides of Winter* isn't bad. Stay away from *The Testament of Michelle Jacob* though; that has so many holes in its structure it's more like a sieve than a novel. Enough of this.

When my father disappeared I had completed my first year at university in Liverpool, but had suspended my education in favour of a temporary job designing exhibitions. I had had an inconclusive love affair with a West Indian cripple called Joseph and I found the publicity and uncertainty that van Niekerk's vanishing act produced upsetting. I was ready for a holiday. Kilminster—who teaches physics in Liverpool—was going on study leave. Instead of putting up at some university or research institute he had decided to spend six months on the most remote Greek island he could find, taking with him a carload of books, papers, photocopies, and a fairly flash and complicated electronic calculator. He said he had more than enough to think about without having to rabbit on to other physicists all day. I was moaning to him in a restaurant just before he was due to leave, telling him how much I envied him, how depressed I was, *fishing* in other words. He bit. I accepted his offer in two seconds flat. We spent three or four days buying books and copying articles, loaded up the car, and left for France. We spent a drunken weekend with Jennifer and Jean-Claude discussing the Mystery of van Niekerk's Disappearance and left one morning, me at the wheel, Kilminster holding his head and groaning. We were half way to Italy before his hangover even started to abate. I don't drink. I felt fine. Four days later we were on the ferry to the island. We took rooms over a taverna on the eastern shore. And this is where I'm writing now. Kilminster sits in his room, playing with his calculator, staring at the ceiling, scribbling. I sit in mine, filling up blue exercise books with this narrative.

One last thing. It might help in understanding this story if the relative ages of the participants are taken note of. Very roughly speaking there is a decade between each character and the next. i.e. when Jennifer married Kilminster I was ten, Kilminster about twenty, Jennifer about thirty, and Pieter van Niekerk about forty. So Kilminster found himself with a mother and daughter who were almost equidistant from him in age (actually I'm three months *closer* to him than Jennifer) and a very jealous ex-husband who was twice his age. Poor K, and fresh out of a monastery. Back to the elms.

* * * * * * *

Jennifer told her story about Canon Carstairs to Tamar, who listened gravely.

"I don't want to be a horse."

"A unicorn. And it's called Tamarand."

"Sounds like Tamar to me."

"Well anyway it's a magic unicorn who can turn into a princess as well."

Together the girls finished the story. Princess Jennifer married the footless soldier (now equipped with silver feet). Princess Tamar married one of the other soldiers and would sometimes turn back into a unicorn to give him rides. Everyone lived very happily in the castle and there was constant merrymaking. The happy band of soldiers, under the old silversmith's instruction, built a magic aeroplane with gossamer wings and on midsummer's night they flew over the forest to heaven and bombed it to smithereens, putting an end to the horrible things that went on there. A number of inmates survived the bombing, having been warned of the raid by a sweet dove of peace sent by Princess Jennifer with a message, on the strength of which they secretly built themselves Morrison tables. Among those to escape was Grearson, who made his way to the castle where he received a warm welcome from his old friend the footless soldier and a magic potion from the old silversmith which cured his smelly feet for ever.

"And then they had an enormous feast," Tamar said, "with hogsheads roasted on spits and wine in silver goblets."

"No," Jennifer said, "there is no need for a feast, because in the castle no one ever gets hungry because of a magic spell that only Princess Jennifer knows about."

This bit of the story disappointed Tamar, who couldn't see the point of such a spell, especially when there was no lack of roast hogsheads in the castle. Better to eat, drink, and be merry. But Jennifer was insistent, very insistent, that there was no eating done in the castle. It wasn't necessary and no one *wanted* to eat.

"It's my story anyway," she said fiercely.

"Oh, all right," Tamar said, startled at her friend's vehemence, but vowing to herself that in her version of the story there was feasting in the Great Hall every night.

* * * * * * *

All this stuff—footless soldiers, bombing raids on heaven, unicorns—was later, much later, to become the basis of Jennifer's story, *Fable*. In its mature form the story doesn't really work. It is too self-conscious, the surreal bits are not clearly focused enough. I've done a better job with my recreation of the source material; there's a fine lightness of touch in what I've just written that allows the fantastic elements to appear in all their clean-limbed absurdity. I don't know about you, but the mental picture I have when I imagine Carstairs running around the beach is wholly Dali. The beach is as clean as a starched khaki table-cloth. I he soldier, the cleric, and the feet are arranged formally upon the sand under a brooding grey and silver sky, the brave little pleasure craft is very far away at the water's edge, the small figure of the pilot points out to sea like an Old Testament prophet. I wish I could paint sometimes. I have no real talent in that direction. I can do passable sketches of buildings, that's about all.

It is late at night. I've been writing all day and my eyes are tired. Also my brain. I need sleep. Tomorrow I'll write about something simple, something that I can remember perfectly easily without having to invent whole sections, something that won't overtax my neurones. But for the moment, sleep. Sleep it is a precious thing beloved from pole to pole. Goodnight.

* * * * * *

Good morning.

My mother encouraged me to masturbate.

Written down like that the statement looks a bit puerile, something you might find on a lavatory wall. Still, it's true, so there is no need to suppress it. Two or three years before I lost my virginity—two or three years before I took to fucking—I knew more about the mysteries of female orgasm than some women I've met know about it five years after the great event. When I say Jennifer encouraged me, all she really did was make it pretty clear in the course of various conversations that if she sleeps alone for more than a couple of consecutive nights she wanks, that she thinks people who don't do likewise are a bit odd and that this applies to virgin schoolgirls as well as anybody else.

I agree with her entirely.

I can't really remember when I started. It was before we moved to France, sometime during those Clapham years. Perhaps I would have done it anyway, without any tacit 'permission' or whatever from Jennifer. In retrospect it certainly seems unthinkable that I wouldn't have taken it up, but all the literature, all the hard evidence, indicates that not all that many women do masturbate, and very few of those who do started when they were virgins. Be that as it may, I took to the whole exercise as a duck to water. At first, as far as I can remember, it was just pleasurable, comforting—I suppose a sort of advanced thumb-sucking. My first orgasm happened quite unexpectedly; I was just curled up in bed wanking dreamily and suddenly these warm, loving shudders washed over me like tides. I tried again but with no results. In the morning though, I came twice.

I came twice the first time I ever fucked a man. Rare, I'm told, but I expected nothing less.

"Are you sure you've never done this before?" he asked.

"I've had lots of practice," I said.

"You've been reading your mother's novels again," he said.

"She told me you said that to her."

"Did I? Maybe I did. She has that Spiros character say it in *The Crooked River*."

I went in at the deep end in a long clean dive. No mucking around with water-wings, no mucking around at all. Not that I hadn't already experienced a bit of mucking around by others.

At school I had joined Amnesty International. We met at lunchtime and, sometimes, after school, in one of the cafés or at Paul's house. Paul was my maths teacher; twenty-two or twenty-three, bearded, posters of Ché and Fidel on the walls of his flat. He didn't like the countryside, he didn't like teaching in Oise, he wanted to go back to Paris. He sometimes referred to the wastes of Oise as Siberia. Actually there are times in winter when the wind cuts across the open fields, driving the snow into the ditches and against the sides of farm buildings, when the landscape is so bleak, so inhospitable and desolate that it could well be some Russian steppe. There are very few animals around our part of Oise as almost all the fields are used solely for crops. So there are no fences to break up the landscape, just fields cultivated hard up to the sides of the roads. There are a few woods and a large state forest some ten kilometres away, but on the roads from school to the château, these appear only as dark clumps on the skyline, emphasising, if anything, the openness of the fields around them. There is a crossroads in the middle of this openness, unrelieved by any trace of habitation, just two stop signs and two priority signs and a crucifix in one of the fields. Around the base of the crucifix someone has planted four or five small fir trees, which, from a distance appear as hooded figures, monks or grieving women, gathered at the base of the cross. Christ looks down on them, emaciated, cold, without hope; his side pierced by the lance, the thorns around his head bristling like broken glass. The Christ figure has been carved from wood and painted. The paint is faded, but blood still runs in dark lines from the lance and thorns, and from the nails in his hands and feet. In summer, when the fields around him are green or golden, when the sky behind him is blue or white with high clouds, he looks quaint, folk art. You could sell him quite profitably in any of those expensive shops in Albemarle Street or the Avenue de Suffren which specialise in icons and suchlike. But in winter, when there is snow on the fields and the evening comes at five o'clock and the sky is unrelieved in its greyness, he looks so alone and desolate I could cry. At the time I'm talking about, I rode my mobylette to and from school most days. I would chug up to the crossroads, stop at the stop sign if I felt inclined, or veer right without stopping if I did not. The flics are fierce about stop signs around our way; they can be found lurking beside the most remote and minor road junctions, but there is nowhere for them to hide at this particular crossroads, even Christ and his circle of hooded figures can give them no shelter. It was here, in the insubstantial lee of Christ, an hour or two after dark, with the wind driving the snow across the beams of the van's headlights, with the ridges of cold earth in the ploughed fields standing hard and black against the snow that Paul made his intense declaration of love for me.

There had been a meeting of Amnesty at his flat that evening after school. It had been a working meeting, not a talking one. We had sat around writing letters to presidents and ministers of justice in one dictatorship or another, requesting clemency, legal review, news of the whereabouts of, release, commutation, and so forth for various prisoners of conscience. Polite, pleading letters to fascists and torturers. *Your Excellency, I am writing to you out of a deep concern for....* There were eight or nine of us at the meeting; Paul, the other teacher with whom he shared the flat, me and half a dozen of my fellow students. Coffee was brewed at intervals, a bottle of wine circulated. When the meeting broke up I invited Paul to dinner at the château. I had an ulterior motive, but I made it plain.

"If you come to dinner, I can put my mobylette in the back of your van."

"So that is the only reason you ask me, to save yourself the ride."

"No, it's because you are charming and delightful and witty and intelligent and...."

"And what?"

I was going to say, "and you are impressed by the château I live in, the fact that my step-father is a well-known journalist and my mother a writer whom you find sexy." But Paul was an intense, serious young man and the French don't find remarks like that funny at the best of times, especially if they are true, which in this case they were. So I said, "Oh, and generally sexy," which, given the company and the fact that he was my teacher and I a sixteen-year-old virgin schoolgirl, was a bit risqué, a bit de trop, and a bit gauche, but not wildly so. Old Leclercq would not have approved, but we were well clear of his ambience.

So I rang the château, told whoever answered to expect an extra person for dinner, and left the flat with the others to manhandle my mobylette into the back of Paul's van. The van was one of those small, rudimentary Deux Chevaux, with two tubular steel seats with canvas upholstery bolted to the floor in front and nothing at all in the back. It had no heater and no radio and little in the way of suspension or shock absorbers. Paul drove it too fast. We roared out of town and began the desolate traverse to the château. The bare, ploughed fields veered in the headlights, the snow lying in long ragged strips like frozen waves.

"It's like the Retreat from Moscow," Paul said.

"And in the rue St Jacques they are arguing in the cafes, plotting revolution in the bars, and downing cognac while reading *Liberation*."

"I really must get a job in Paris," Paul said with conviction.

"Having served your exile in Siberia."

"Exactly, Anasuya, that's exactly what it is like, this place,

Siberia."

"So you've said before."

"Well it is, isn't it? Look!" He gestured at the landscape beyond the windscreen. He was so humourless, so earnest.

"I suppose it is a bit bleak," I said.

Paul started a long monologue about Paris which included nostalgic references to the events of sixty-eight. (He must have been about fourteen or fifteen in sixty-eight, one or two years younger than I was then.) I liked Paul, he was a good teacher, he was serious and dedicated, he read a lot, would talk about what he read at length, was always trying to interest others in Amnesty or some other cause, but he was so lacking in self-awareness, so utterly humourless. He wore circular gold-rimmed spectacles like Trotsky.

We arrived at the crossroads. He stopped at the stop sign although there was nothing in sight at all. I thought for a moment he was unsure of the direction. "Left," I said.

But he put his hand on my knee and said earnestly, "Did you mean what you said back at the flat?"

"What?"

"When I asked you why you were inviting me to dinner."

I had to think for a few seconds to recall what the hell it was I had said, I almost burst out laughing—he was so intense. There wasn't much light in the car itself, but little highlights of fire ran around the gold rims of his glasses when he moved his head. I couldn't actually see his eyes. He was genuinely expecting an answer. I looked along the beams of the headlights, Christ stared gloomily down at the humanoid trees at his feet. I said, "Oh, of course, I meant what I said. You are all those things aren't you?"

"I love you very much, Anasuya."

The grip on my knee turned to a squeeze of sorts (I was wearing woollen tights, corduroy jeans, and a long duffle coat; he had gloves on). I said, "That's all right; impressionable young teachers often get crushes on their mature students."

I thought this was rather good; a neat reversal of the normal cliché. I thought I'd *sell* it to Jennifer. We had been playing a game at home that involved bargaining good lines, scenes we'd experienced, dialogue overheard in shops etc. for a slice of the advances on her novels. If Jennifer fancied what she was given, she'd record it in the commonplace book in which she keeps notes for possible stories. If the item had been sold to her, she'd record the name of the seller and the agreed price. If it ever appeared in print, she paid up. On her last novel I'd earned twenty-five francs. It was all funny money, of course. I spent the twenty-five francs on a bottle of wine which the rest of them drank one evening making the appropriate comments. They'd even forced a sip or two of the stuff down my throat. It tasted vile. If I worked on the impressionable-young-teacher remark, gave it a bit of background, I reckoned it would be worth at least three or four francs. Paul said, "You aren't like the others. I don't regard you as a student."

This was becoming a bit serious. I was only sixteen after all. I said "What do you want to do?"

"I don't know."

"I don't know either."

There was a moment of silence. I felt a trifle absurd sitting in this tin van in the middle of nowhere with Christ glooming away in the limelight and Paul being intense and earnest and hopelessly indecisive. The car was starting to smell of petrol. There had been no way of securing my mobylette in an upright position, so we had simply lain it on its side. I turned around.

"I think my tank's leaking."

"Then we shouldn't smoke."

"I don't."

"Neither do I."

"Dinner will be almost ready, let's go."

"Anasuya, will you sleep with me?"

"Of course."

I'd said it. I'd said it nonchalantly, without thinking, with the blasé insouciance that the situation demanded. My heart, as they say, was in my mouth a second later. The whole situation had the emotional charge of a refrigerator.

"Let's go, Paul, I'm freezing."

Paul leant over to kiss me. Which was only reasonable, I suppose; I'd just freely consented to screw him. We kissed, leaning over the gap between the two seats, where the handbrake was. Paul's glasses got in the way. But the kiss was warming, friendly, reassuring, even if it had no sexual dimension at all. We broke and Paul let in the clutch and we drove away. I realised he must have had his foot on the peddle the whole time, that the car had been in gear. So I'd done it. Given up virginity. I'd been planning to take the step for at least a year. I'd made half-hearted feints at some of my friends, some of whom I knew to be already no strangers to the act, some of whom were undoubtedly still in my own sorry condition, but one or other of us had always drawn away, turned the suggestion into a joke, danced backwards behind a nervous sophistication to which we had no right. In fantasy, with my finger on my clitoris, I'd tried out the whole bunch. Kilminster and Jean-Claude as well, although I'd turned Jean-Claude into Kilminster halfway through the proceedings. But Paul simply had not featured. With a slight unease, I realised I was committed to screwing someone with whom I'd never imagined the act. It didn't seem quite right, like performing a part in a play for which one hadn't learnt the lines. But still, I was going to do it. I was going to putter along these roads in the morning, no longer a virgin, knowing what it was all about. And I was quite fond of Paul, no doubt about that, I liked him well enough. And he'd presumably be quite good at it, wouldn't fumble about, which was probably more than most of my coevals from school would have been able to manage. Paul said, "We could take a hotel room in Paris next weekend."

"Be buggered we could," I said in English.

"*Pardon?*"

"You can sleep in my bed tonight."

"But. In your own house. Your mother...."

"Jennifer won't mind. You've read her books, you know what she's like. If anything, she'll be amused."

"It wouldn't seem right."

"It will seem right enough. We don't have to advertise the fact. We can wait until they've gone to bed. Or you can come up to my room to…I don't know…help me with my homework or something."

Actually this was a reasonable point. I would really have preferred Jennifer et al not to have guessed what was going on, at least until morning. There are limits to intra-familial intimacy.

"Are you sure she doesn't mind you, err.…"

"Fucking *à la maison*. No she doesn't. She's not that sort of hypocrite. Neither is Jean-Claude."

It struck me from the tense he'd used (present continuous, I believe it's called) that Paul was unaware he was going to be the first. I decided not to tell him, partly because, given his unease, the knowledge would probably have forced him to back down altogether, and partly because I really didn't want him to know—in one sense this was to be a private experience—and, of course, there was an element of straight pride, if I'd given him the impression I was an old hand at the game, I didn't want to suddenly reveal myself as a complete tyro.

"Are you on the pill?"

"Yes," I lied.

I actually owned three packets of the pill—had done so for almost a year. Once, during one of my more serious exercises in nervous sophistication, I had taken the things for a month, but had felt such a fraud when I'd finished the packet to no effect that I'd not started another. As for the lie, it didn't matter, my period had finished the previous day, I was as safe as houses, and I was now totally committed to screwing Paul. I sensed increasing unease on his part, I hoped this wouldn't turn into actual disinclination.

"Do you really love me, Paul?"

"I haven't been able to think about anything else for weeks."

"Really?" I was actually quite astonished by this bit of information—there was obviously some element of melodramatic overstatement—but Paul wasn't one for wild claims and he was too serious to joke.

"Really," he said, "I notice what you are wearing, who you talk to, who you have lunch with; sometimes I walk along a corridor on the off-chance that you'll be there."

"How nice." I said, just slightly alarmed.

Paul swung the car into the château's drive and, under my instruction, backed it up to the shed in which I kept the mobylette. This was some distance from the main building. I wanted to kiss him properly, without the restraining confines of the Deux Chevaux's seats. Once we'd unloaded the mobylette, I did this. Paul was responsive but tense—*Jesus, just who is the virgin around here?*

Dinner was quite a merry affair. Jean-Claude was leaving for Togo the next day to cover the trial of some captured mercenaries. It was to be one of those well-conducted show trials with the mercenaries being shot at the end of it. All Jean-Claude's expenses were to be paid by the Togo government. There was considerable discussion about the type of fruit then in season in Togo. Jennifer impressed on Jean-Claude the necessity of bringing back as much fruit as possible—mangoes and guavas especially—since there was little to be had in the local shops at the time. She flirted with Paul, but more to make him feel at home than for any other reason. Paul brightened up a bit, became less tense. The rest of them drank slightly more than normal as a way of giving Jean-Claude a send-off. We were eating duck Normandy which Little Jim, one of the reformed dope fiends then in residence, had cooked. At least we all were except Silvie, who had the ritual meal of bacon and eggs instead. We eat quite well at the château and a lot of the geese, rabbits, chickens, and ducks are grown on the place. They invariably get adopted by the smaller children whose job it is to feed them. They give them names and pet them and refuse to eat them when their time comes, so the bacon and eggs meal gets served up automatically to whoever once loved and cared for the present meal. Jean-Claude once tried to impose a moratorium on giving the animals names. Without names, he argued, they'd be less like family when we came to eat them. It was a good idea, but it didn't work; the children gave them secret names. So names were again declared permissible. Silvie's ducks had been called Grasshopper and Aurélia, they were delicious. I sat between Silvie and Little Jim, watching Paul across the table. He was really quite attractive. And he really did deserve a job back in Paris.

The meal finished, we washed up, sat around drinking coffee and cognac, and talking. Someone put on a record. The children did their homework lying on the carpet in front of the fire. After a while Jean-Claude announced he was going to bed. Jennifer went with him. Little Jim disappeared with the au pair, Caroline. The children declared themselves bored with homework and went off to watch television. Paul and I remained. We sat on either side of the fire like two old crones.

"Come and help me with my homework," I said.

My room was as cold as ice. The radiator is normally turned off during the day. I turned it on, but it would take time for the room to become warm. I sat on the bed. Paul took a pace forwards and then backwards. My room is actually quite small, although it has a sort of ante-room (cupboard might be a better word) with a wash basin and bidet, which is useful for pissing in.

"Are you sure your mother won't mind?"

"What's it to do with her? Stop worrying, come here."

It had become clear to me that if anything was to develop from this scene, I would have to be pretty firm with Paul. He sat on the bed next to me. I took off his Trotskyite glasses and laid them on my table. We kissed. After a while he thawed out. He lay over me, his hand under the various layers of my clothing.

"Let's get into bed," I said.

"I don't have any pyjamas," Paul said.

"Eh?" I said.

"I don't have any pyjamas," Paul said.

"You don't need them."

"I can't sleep without them."

"Oh, all right then, I'll lend you a pair of mine; they're a bit small, but they'll fit."

Paul disengaged himself. He seemed to want me to find the pyjamas immediately. Looking back on the scene now, it is obvious that I should have given up the whole exercise there and then, or else dragged Paul into bed; more or less ripped the clothes from him. But I was sixteen, inexperienced, and more than slightly bewildered. I wanted to appear blasé and sophisticated, and the easiest way to do that was to fall in with Paul's wishes as if they were perfectly normal, as if young men invariably borrowed my pyjamas prior to screwing with me. I found him the largest pair I could and gave them to him. He disappeared into the ante-room, half-closing the door. This was insane. I undressed and got into bed, naked. Paul returned, looking like a tramp with his forearms and ankles exceeding the limits of the pyjamas by at least fifteen centimetres. He got into bed beside me. What happened next is hard to describe and I'm still not sure I understand the psychology of it all. We rolled around, fumbling and kissing. I couldn't get Paul to take off his pyjamas. He wouldn't screw me. He wasn't impotent, although he didn't seem to appreciate my ascertaining this. He kept rolling away to face the wall.

"Let's make love," I said eventually.

"No," Paul said.

"Why not?"

He said nothing.

"Why not, Paul?"

"Because I don't want to, that's why not."

"Please, Paul."

"No."

I did nothing for a while; I didn't really sulk, I didn't really fume with anger, although there were elements of those emotions in the way I felt. I was basically bewildered, confused. I didn't know what was going on. I didn't know what I ought to be feeling.

"Paul, talk to me."

Silence.

"Please, Paul. Please talk to me."

"What do you want me to say?"

"Tell me what's wrong. Have I done anything wrong?"

"No."

"Well, why can't we make love?"

"Stop nagging me!" he shouted at the wall, "Stop going on and on and on. You're like an old shrew. Nag, nag, nag."

I should have become angry myself. I should have thrown him out of bed, but I was so startled by the fury of his outburst, so unsure of what was happening that I did nothing.

"Go to sleep," he said.

I lay next to his hard back and shoulders, miserable. I heard the children come upstairs from the television room. Their footsteps faded down the corridor to their own room. I wanted to go after them, to sit on a bed and chatter about anything at all, to kiss them goodnight. But I couldn't leave the hard, angry presence in my own bed. I watched the branches of the tree outside my window. They were illuminated faintly by light coming from one of the other rooms of the château; Jennifer and Jean-Claude's probably. Whoever's light it was, it went out. There was nothing but blackness beyond the glass. I thought perhaps that what words had failed to do, touching might achieve. Slowly, as tenderly as I could, I put an arm around Paul. With my right arm over his shoulder, I tried to slide my left arm under his neck, thus to enfold him. He was hard, unresponsive. Dead weight. Like the time I had tried to move my father after Jennifer had knocked him unconscious with the glass ashtray. I was still wearing some bracelets on my wrist which must have caught in his hair, or grazed his ear or something. He started up, turning roughly towards me.

"Stop pestering me, Anasuya. Go to sleep."

Those last three words were spoken like a true schoolteacher, they carried an assumption of legitimate authority. That did it.

"Don't you tell me to go to sleep or not. This is my bed. I'll do what I like in it. If you don't like it, get out."

"You're a stuck-up bitch, Anasuya, a rich, superior, stuck-up bitch."

"Then what are you doing here? Tell me that. In the car you told me you loved me, that you couldn't think about anything else. Now what? I'm a stuck-up bitch and you won't screw me."

He started to turn away again. I hit him. Rather feebly, I must admit, I wasn't in a very good position to land a blow, but I hit him. He turned back to face me; I didn't recognise him, he was angry and trapped. I realised he was as bewildered as I was. He really had no idea what was happening.

"I must have been mad," Paul said.

"So must I," I said and turned my back to him. After a while I slept. A cold, angry sleep.

I woke sometime before dawn and put my arms around Paul. He accepted my embrace like a child. Nothing else happened. In the morning we both went down to breakfast. I felt a fraud.

But breakfast was fairly rushed; Jennifer was driving Jean-Claude to Orly and they were running late. Jean-Claude was anxious about catching the plane, he kept pacing about, calling to Jennifer to hurry. We all kissed good-bye. Jennifer kissed Paul particularly warmly. Modern mother being friendly with daughter's first lover. Jesus wept!

I wept, puttering past Jesus on my mobylette. Paul had offered to drive me and the mobylette to his place. But I refused. I wanted to be alone and the ride to school was the only chance I'd get. So I chugged through the snowy fields, a virgin yet, and my tears clouded my vision. But in winter it's easy to cry when riding a mobylette, even with one's eyes protected by goggles.

I saw Paul around the school during the next couple of days, but not to speak to, although I actually learnt the rudiments of parabolic change over a small increment from him in a maths lesson. After school on the third day he took me to one of the town's cafés. He apologised over a café crème and said he didn't understand what had happened. It was a real apology, at heart he was decent and warm. I said I didn't understand either and not to worry about it. We remained friends. Of sorts. Put it down to experience.

But it happened again. Not with Paul, with René, one of the members of my immediate group of friends. It was with René that I'd played one of the elaborate pseudo-sophisticated games of flirtation six months previously. This time I was deadly serious. I suggested we spend a weekend in Paris, that we sleep on the floor of Jean-Claude's office in the rue St Marc. People often do this, there are a few sleeping bags and a couple of blow-up rubber mattresses in a cupboard for just this purpose. I can't be bothered describing the whole scene over again. There were differences between this one and the one with Paul, but not many or profound ones. I was very upset when I returned to the château on Sunday night.

Kilminster was there, unaccompanied. Jean-Claude was in Brussels and not expected back until Monday night. Perhaps this is why Kilminster had come over by himself. I don't know; he often spends time with Jennifer. I didn't care. I was miserable and upset. Even Kilminster's unexpected presence did little to lighten my feelings, and, of all the people I know, his sudden appearance should have dispelled whatever depression I was feeling. We ate a gloomy dinner—maybe it wasn't gloomy, the others might have been enjoying themselves, but in retrospect it certainly appears funereal to me. After dinner, Jennifer and Kilminster went for a walk. It was early spring by then; properly clothed, post-prandial walks were quite possible. I went to my room and lay on my bed, staring at the ceiling, wondering what was the matter with me. Why did ordinary, red-blooded, heterosexual men behave like that when I tried to sleep with them? Angrily I told myself that there was nothing the matter with me, it was them. I had enough wit and self-respect to be able to tell myself this. But at heart I wasn't sure. I looked around my room and hated it. The posters, the pictures, the books, the mogul miniature from our house in New Delhi. The whole lot yelled fraud at me. Young intellectual on the threshold of womanhood, with her paperback copies of Lessing and Fannon and Elias and

Soyinka and Clavel and Jennifer Kilminster and old uncle Tom Cobleigh and all. Fraud! It's the room of a poor little school kid who can't get a fuck. I heard my mother and Kilminster return from their walk, their footsteps crunching on the gravel of the drive. Kilminster said something I could not catch, Jennifer laughed and there was a slight irregularity in the sound of crunching gravel. I knew—I could picture exactly—what had happened. Without actually stopping walking, Jennifer had thrown her arms around Kilminster, kissing him and pushing him slightly sideways at the same time. Jennifer now said something about which they both laughed. The door opened below my window and they entered the house. I was more miserable than ever.

Half an hour later Silvie came to my room. "Jennifer says to come downstairs and be sociable."

"I don't want to be."

"All right."

Silvie didn't care at all, she was just the messenger. I couldn't face sitting around by the fire trying to enter into whatever conversation was proceeding. I was utterly lonely. I ran to the top of the stairs and shouted down to Silvie's retreating head, "Tell Jennifer and James to come up here for a minute."

"All right."

I could have told her to inform the company I was about to leap out of the window and she would have said, "All right."

My mother and Kilminster arrived. Not only had they brought their brandy glasses, they'd brought the bottle.

"What's up with you?" Kilminster demanded.

He lowered himself onto the bed by my side. Jennifer sat on my other side. The three of us regarded the opposite wall like the see-no-evil-hear-no-evil-speak-no-evil monkeys.

"I'm a virgin."

"What?"

"But Jennifer said...."

"Jennifer got it wrong."

"But, Ansu, you told me...."

"I lied to you, Mummy. I'm not lying now. I'm a virgin. I ought to know if I am or not."

"She probably does," Kilminster slowly informed Jennifer.

I told them the whole story. Jennifer muttered things like, "The bastards!"

"My daughter!", "Upsetting my daughter…." All Kilminster said was "Frogs," in a tone of voice that indicated he'd heard the same gloomy story dozens of times. He can be a right little chauvinist when he wants to. When I'd finished Jennifer said, "Darling, why didn't you tell me before?"

"Why should I?"

"I *am* your mother."

"I know you're my bloody mother, for Christ's sake. I'm your daughter. I'm also Anna out of the *Tides* of bloody *Winter*."

"I wouldn't have written about…."

"You write about everything. But that's not the point. That's not the point at all…."

I was almost crying. Jennifer started to say something, but Kilminster cut in with, "Jennifer, love, belt up."

He put his arm around me. Jennifer did too. Kilminster tried to force some brandy on me, making encouraging woofing noises like a St Bernard who'd just found a dying climber. They had been drinking from those big balloon glasses you warm in your hands so that the smell of the brandy gets stuck in the balloon (the fumes, the bouquet, whatever it is brandy has). Kilminster got the mouth of the balloon over my nose. The stink of the brandy hit me like a slap. I sneezed violently, spluttering the stuff all over the bed, myself and Kilminster.

"Jesus Christ," Jennifer said.

"Steady on, old girl, I say, steady on," Kilminster intoned like a country parson on a run-away donkey. By now I was laughing and crying simultaneously. Jennifer stood up yawning exaggeratedly.

"Well, there's only one thing for it. You'd better borrow one of my husbands. I don't want to see either of you till tomorrow."

She kissed us both in quick succession and left the room.

It took me a few seconds to understand what she'd said. I was still laughing and crying too much to respond to anything very quickly. I looked at Kilminster. He looked at me and shrugged his shoulders. One arm was still around me, he moved his hand to the back of my neck and massaged me for a few seconds.

"You're as tense as a steel cable. Lie down."

I lay on my stomach, my head in the pillows. Kilminster massaged my shoulders and back.

"Do you want to?"

"Yes," I muttered into the pillow.

I was wearing a V-neck sweater over a corduroy shirt. Kilminster undid the buttons of my shirt sleeves.

"Sit up."

I sat up and he peeled both sweater and shirt over my head in one smooth motion.

That will do. You can imagine the rest.

The time has come to change gears. I'm going to do a hard-bitten, real-life cop shop drama. My interview with

Detective-Inspector Michaels of the Yard.

Talking to Michaels was an odd experience, at once simple, demanding, unreal and then, eventually, exhilarating. I can remember walking away from the Lyme Street station after I'd seen him to his train, almost floating, buoyed up with the relief from tension. In the confused sea of depression and lethargy that was my world in those first weeks after my father's disappearance, the interview with Michaels stands out as an island of purpose and life. Although, during it, I never once lost the feeling I was an actress on the set of some dramatized thriller. I'd read it all before; you could wrap the scene in glossy paper covers and call it a rattling good yarn.

Michaels appeared to be the cop assigned to doing the rounds of van Niekerk's family. After Jennifer had given him lunch under the château's beech trees, he left for Paris. A day later he was back in London where he must have talked at length with my father's present wife, a fool of a woman called Bernadette. Then he rang me, suggesting he came to Liverpool; we could meet either at my place or the offices of the Liverpool CID. I don't much like the fuzz. Most of my dealings with them have been in connection with my shoplifting activities, and the Merseyside constabulary weren't very polite the time I abandoned my Mercedes either. But obviously I had to see this Michaels man, and as for once I would be voluntarily helping the police with their enquiries, I decided to make his acquaintance in the police station itself, to experience the dubious delights of entering the place as an honest citizen. It is not far from Huskisson Street to the police headquarters, so I walked there through the bombed-out, boarded-up Georgian elegance of Liverpool 8, passing through the shadow of the absurd cathedral, where it squats— all ten million tons of soul-crushing stone—like a suet pudding above the city, and then down the hill through the Chinese streets to the river. The brand new police building is just across the road from the docks. It looks like a police building: brown walls with brown-tinted windows that allow those on the inside to look out and those on the outside to see nothing but their own reflections or the reflections of other buildings and the sky. Urban renewal breathing back life into the desolate ruins of the Merseyside dockland. Well yes…Mussolini would have approved.

A nice young constable escorted me to a clean, modern interview room on the fourth floor and then left me alone. From the brown windows there was a fine prospect of docks, silted up, decaying, the warehouses and bond stores—even as I watched—falling to the wrecker's ball and chain. The Mersey lay, brown and muddy, in the middle distance. On the skyline the refineries and towers of the Wirral were half obscured by the early summer haze. The Birkenhead ferry was leaving its wharf. In a courtyard immediately below me, a number of marked and unmarked police cars were parked neatly in bays. The room I was standing in held a table with a telephone, a number of functional chairs, and two comfortable easy chairs. The floor was covered with a beige carpet laid in squares— carpet tiles I think they are called. From the rest of the building came muffled sounds of typewriters and footsteps. I returned to my contemplation of the Birkenhead ferry which was now churning across the river in a straight line, but with the whole boat skewed sideways to compensate for the current.

> To stand and be still to the Birkenhead drill
> Is a damned tough bullet to chew.

Kipling said that, but he wasn't talking about cooling your heels in the offices of the Criminal Investigation Department. The door opened and I turned to shake hands with a man in his mid-forties.

Michaels was well dressed in a charcoal grey suit, blue and white striped shirt with discreet gold cuff-links, short black hair greying at the temples. He wore glasses with solid black frames.

"Miss Tamar, isn't it?"

The interrogative tone related more to the surname itself than my identity.

"That's right. I stopped using my father's name almost a year ago."

"Ah, I see," he said affably, as if I had just enlightened him on a particularly baffling part of the case. He must have known perfectly well about my name-change and its reasons; that idiot Bernadette would have rattled on about it for hours. She rattles on for hours about anything to anybody.

"Won't you sit down," Michaels said.

He had that pleasant nondescript voice that is called BBC or Received Pronunciation. He could have been an executive in a publishing house or an established firm of wine importers— something solid and respectable but not wildly profitable. We each sat on a functional chair.

"You might as well sit in one of the comfortable ones," Michaels said, "I would too, only I'll probably need to take notes—with your permission, of course—and I'll need this to lean on." He patted the table beside him and then took a thin notebook and fountain pen from the inside pocket of his jacket, laying them on the table.

"Would you like some tea, coffee?"

"Tea would be fine."

Michaels pressed a buzzer on the table and the door opened a few seconds later to reveal the constable who had shown me in. "If we could have some tea, please," Michaels said.

"Certainly, sir."

I suppressed a violent urge to say, 'Weak with lemon, Jeeves.' This was meant to be a fucking police station, not a vicarage. Perhaps the man was trying to repay the hospitality my mother and that dimwit Bernadette had extended to him.

The door closed and Michaels said, "All this must be very upsetting to you." He spoke conversationally, warmly, but with a professional gravity.

"It is. More than I would have imagined."

"I gather from the present Mrs van Niekerk that you hadn't seen much of your father lately."

"No, I'd more or less severed all connections. But it is still very disturbing."

"Well, of course, it must be...." Michaels allowed his sentence to trail off into unspoken understanding.

"Do you have any idea what's happened to him?" I said.

"Very little I'm afraid. Your mother seems quite convinced that...."

"Jennifer isn't convinced at all...that's just the line she's taking. She probably thinks Daddy is sitting pretty somewhere reading all about himself in the papers."

"Did your father wear driving gloves as a rule?"

"Why?"

"We found his car, as you know. There were no fingerprints or palm prints on the steering wheel, which would be suspicious if your father normally drove bare-handed."

"He often wore gloves if he was driving one of his vintage cars, but...."

"It was his Rover that we found."

"Nothing wrong with the heater?"

"No. It was functional and was set at half."

"Then that is very suspicious. Daddy wouldn't have been wearing gloves. I'd say he has been kidnapped by someone who hijacked his car with him in it, someone who knocked him unconscious and then drove to Fulham or wherever, wearing gloves."

I looked at the notebook lying under the detective's hand on the table; its owner appeared little inclined to record my theory. Very, very dryly Michaels said, "You have your mother's capacity for conviction."

"Sorry. I shouldn't be facetious. It's only a way of coping. I have been very depressed lately."

There was a knock on the door and the constable entered with a tray of tea things and biscuits. Michaels busied himself pouring tea. When we both had cups in our hands, he said, "We are trying to gain as full a picture of your father as possible. As we have no real leads at the moment, this is all we can do. For all the fuss in the papers, we are still very much in the dark about his disappearance."

"I understand."

"Can you tell me as much as you can about your father. Tell me what sort of person he is." Michaels unscrewed the cap of his pen and selected a fresh page in the notebook.

"I don't know," I said, "It's hard to begin."

Michaels said nothing. To fill up the silence, I said, "My father is very rich, as you know. I suppose he is hard and ruthless as all self-made businessmen are. He is also very generous. He is generous in a possessive and totally unrealistic way. That is really why I broke with him. He wanted to own me by giving me things. He gave me everything I wanted and lots that I didn't want. Do you know about the cars he gave me?"

"The present Mrs van Niekerk did mention something," here Michaels allowed himself a small smile, "She said you have a police record over one of them."

"I tried to abandon it in the street. That's illegal apparently."

"I'm afraid it is."

"I have a feeling that in some ways my father is a romantic. Maybe that's the wrong word, in some ways he lives in a fantasy world.... Look, I don't really know very much about my father's business activities. I knew a lot of them were suspect, of course, but all this stuff in the papers about helicopters and howitzers and bombs for the Brazilians, that's all news to me. It's a bit of a shock, I'd never really seen myself as a bomb-monger's daughter before. Sorry, I'm rambling. What I'm trying to say, is that I'm sure a lot of my father's penchant for the underworld, for contact with criminals and crooks, is romantic.... Do you know Dino Torri?"

"Well, I don't exactly *know* him."

"But you've heard of him in a professional way?"

"Yes."

"Well, my father knew Dino Torri. *Knows* Dino Torri, although he says he wishes he had never met him. And Torri isn't a banker or financier, he's not a crooked capitalist like Daddy, he's a petty crim, a crook. Daddy doesn't *have* to know people like Torri; he doesn't have to frequent gambling clubs and race-tracks and associate with night-club owners and so on. The whole demi-monde thing isn't because he can't make money legitimately, or, you know, make it by sitting in a well-appointed office with secretaries and telex machines like any ordinary capitalist. The other side of his operations is just for the romance, the danger, the...I don't know...the excitement, the power. Am I making sense?"

"Have you met Dino Torri?"

"I met him in a night-club once. I was there with my father. Torri kept reminding my father about how they had been good friends back in the old days, when we lived in Putney. My father was quite put out, almost afraid. As soon as Torri returned to the bar he insisted we leave. Just as we were standing up Torri sent us a round of drinks, but my father refused it."

"Was Mrs van Niekerk with you on this occasion?"

"Yes."

"Ah!" Michaels said and wrote something in his notebook for

the first time.

"Why?" I said.

"She mentioned a 'very shady character' but had forgotten his name."

"Bernadette's a twit."

Michaels smiled, took off his glasses, polished them, and returned them to his nose. I'm sure his glasses had been quite clean to begin with.

"Tell me about Mrs van Niekerk."

"I just have; she's a twit. That more or less sums her up."

"Why do you think your father married her?"

"God knows."

Michaels was silent, waiting for more. I said, "My father is getting old. He won't admit it. He likes to have the company of young women. That's one of the reasons he is so fond of me. He liked to be seen in public with me, in restaurants and clubs. I think he married Bernadette so that he would have an attractive, well-dressed young woman on tap whenever he felt like appearing in some fashionable nightspot."

"Why did Mrs van Niekerk marry your father?"

"For his money. I don't know. Maybe that's unfair. I don't like her because she's a fool, so I've always told myself and the rest of my family that she married him for his money, but I've no proof. Hell, I'm sure she hasn't…I'm sure she hasn't arranged my father's disappearance or anything like that. She's too stupid for one thing—you've met her, you know what she's like. For another, my father gave her all she needed, just like he used to give me all I needed."

Michaels wrote something in his notebook.

"Look," I said, "Do you think my father is dead? Do you think he has been murdered?"

"We really have no leads. We don't even have theories. He has just disappeared. It is possible that the arms deals and the bank in Hong Kong collapsing have something to do with it, but my friends in the Companies Squad are of the opinion that if he hadn't disappeared the deals would have gone through and the bank would not have collapsed. The causal relation works in the wrong way. That's confidential, of course."

"Don't worry. I'm not Jennifer."

"What do you think, do you think he is alive?"

"I don't know. I don't know. I just don't think he'd disappear without leaving a note. But then he might. The whole fantasy world, demi-monde thing I was talking about might lead him to arrange a totally inexplicable disappearance—you know, do a Stonehouse. Your friends in the Companies Squad might be wrong, he might have foreseen the disintegration of his financial empire. It happened before, after all, years ago in India. That's the real reason he was deported, being South African had nothing to do with it."

"Is your father ever violent?"

"What?"

"Sorry, I didn't mean to upset you. It's just this process of trying to get a complete picture of the man. Many of these demi-monde types, as you call them, are violent at times. If your father was attracted to their society...."

"Well, he might be attracted to it, but.... Look, he can be moved to violence, I suppose. He slapped my mother about a bit, but only as part of domestic quarrels in which she threw things at him. And the last time I saw him, we had a fight, a physical one. It started as an argument and then when I tried to walk out of the room he grabbed hold of me. I hit out at him and he hit back. All he tried to do initially was physically prevent me leaving the room, but I struck the first blow. I'd say he was about as violent as I am."

"How violent are you?"

"I can be hot-tempered."

"And your father's temper?"

"It can be hot too, but it takes a lot more to excite him. He's more in control; but when the control goes, then he's probably far more unreasonable, blind, than I would be. You know, the more you screw the safety valve down, the bigger the explosion in the end."

"Before you broke off relations with your father, did he mention anyone who might have an interest in doing him harm?"

"No, not that I can think of. He had the normal rich businessman's fear of all the revolutionary groups around the place. He believed his world to be under attack from liberation armies, urban guerrillas, hijackers, the IRA, and people like that. At least that's how I always saw him. But now it appears he was running guns to South America and places.... Look, I know most arms merchants are totally amoral, they'll sell to anybody, they'll sell to both sides in the same war if they possibly can. But my father wasn't actually selling the guns, just doing the illegal banking transactions. I don't think Daddy would do that for both sides. I think my father's bomb-mongering was probably quite moral by his own standards. I'd be willing to bet a week's wages that if all these investigations turn up evidence about more arms deals, they'll all be to...to dictators, governments, upholders of the status quo. I'm sure my father would never help guerrilla movements, whatever the profit involved. He hated those sorts of political organizations. Hated them."

After a moment's silence, during which, to my surprise, Michaels interrupted the neat column of handwriting in his notebook by doodling a picture of a flower. He said, "And yet Dino Torri and his friends are hardly known for their firm moral stand."

"No, but they are in a completely different category from the urban guerrilla movements. There was something conservative, reactionary, about my father's penchant for the world of fixed horse-races and protection rackets, Soho-type crime. Illegal actions for private profit were civilised, they didn't attack the system, they supported it."

"You talk of your father in the past tense."

"Do I? Well, this was before I broke contact with him, I suppose he still thinks these things. If he's still alive."

"Did he ever mention any political groups in particular who may have had it in for him?"

At this point I laughed, sat forward in my chair, smiling. I had rather been running off at the mouth. Michaels was being a very sympathetic listener. I had to keep reminding myself he was a cop.

"Jennifer's theory! The wretched of the earth have cooked his goose once and for all, quote unquote."

"You don't give it much credit? Your father never mentioned...."

"Oh, he mentioned them all the time. He'd say things like, 'These lunatics in Italy who have kidnapped Moro....' He'd never dignify them with names, never call them the Red Brigades or whatever."

"Was he afraid of being kidnapped himself?"

"If he was he never mentioned it to me. But he was very conscious of 'security'. That house in Kensington is like a fortress. There are alarms on all the windows and doors. There is an automatic lock on the front gate and a loudspeaker device—but you know that, you've been there. I think he had a gun, I'm not sure."

"Why aren't you sure?"

"I was there one night when he was out with Bernadette. When they came home, I embraced my father to kiss him. I put my arm around his waist and felt something hard and metallic in his pocket. I said, 'What's this, a gun?', not expecting it to be anything of the sort, and my father pulled away from my embrace very quickly and said something about a tin of cigars he'd been given. But he didn't produce them, didn't take whatever it was out of his pocket. And it hadn't felt like a cigar tin to me. Do you think he's been kidnapped?"

"That was our immediate suspicion after we'd found the car. But that was three weeks ago, and no demand for ransom has been received. It is starting to become very unlikely."

"Would you, the police, know for certain if a ransom demand had been made?"

"How do you mean?"

"He has all these international contacts. He is on the boards of various firms in Switzerland and South Africa and Hong

Kong. Would they necessarily tell you if they had received a ransom demand?"

"No, not necessarily. It's possible that someone is paying for your father's release at this moment, but I wouldn't pin too many hopes on it."

There was a long pause during which Michaels appeared lost in thought. I decided to allow him to be the first to speak. I watched him draw another little flower in his notebook. They can be very pleasant, these urbane Scotland Yard types; not a bit like the thugs of the Special Patrol Group or the insecure, inadequate bullies who harass shoplifters and demonstrators. I read somewhere that there is a tendency for criminals and policemen to have one Y chromosome too many. That's the reason they become criminals and/or cops. I looked at Michaels sitting quietly on the hard, functional chair; the little flower lay under his pen like a Bewick woodcut illustrating a treatise on natural history. Michaels had a firm, almost italic, hand. You can't tell by looking, of course, but I would have thought he had a sporting chance of having a normal chromosome count. I was feeling quite pleased with the way the interview was proceeding. If Michaels hadn't been a cop, I would have been happy to get to know him better. Behind his head I could see the Mersey flowing ruffled and polluted. The Isle of Man steamer was swinging away from the shore, being picked up by the current and shoved downstream towards the sea like a scapegoat. Maybe it would sink in the spiritual desert of the Irish Channel. God knows, the fat tax exiles and leather-jacketed motorcyclists on board would be providing a full ballast of sin and crime.

The silence in the room continued for ages. Eventually, to break it, I said, "I'm not being very helpful, am I?"

Michaels brought himself out of his brown study. "No, no. You are, you're being very helpful. What do you know about Rasta Action?"

"Who?"

"The Rastafarian Action Group Against Fascism—Rasta Action."

"Never heard of them."

"In your father's desk we found a number of cheques from the joint account you had with him. They had all been made out to political groups of one sort or another. Rasta Action was one of them; you'd tried to send three thousand...."

"Oh, Christ, one of those. I tried to send money to dozens of bodies like that. My father stopped the cheques."

"I know."

"After one of those fights with my father—I think it was over South Africa—I wrote cheques to every anti-apartheid, anti-racist group whose address I could find."

"So you, yourself, have had no contact with them? With any of these groups?"

"No. Or at least only with Amnesty. Was there a cheque for Amnesty International?"

"Not that I can remember."

"Good, that must have got through. I think I sent them twenty-five thousand quid."

"The other groups can't have been very pleased."

"How do you mean?"

"The groups like Rasta Action were probably not very pleased when their cheques bounced. They might have seen them as, shall we say, jokes in rather poor taste."

"Oh Jesus, you don't think one of these groups has...has kidnapped or murdered my father out of spite over a bounced cheque?"

"I think you had better tell me as much as you can about your fight with your father over South Africa."

Michaels had become very serious. I said, "There isn't much to tell. It had become apparent to me that my father had a lot of dealings with South Africa, that some of his firms had been dealing with Rhodesia while the sanctions had still been in force. We had an argument over this."

"How had it become apparent?"

"Just for fun once I looked him up in *Who's Who*. I was in the reference section of the university library and *Who's Who* was on the shelf in front of my eyes. So I looked him up. I'm in it too; next to his name it says 1d, that's me, one daughter. Amongst other things, my father is shown as being on the boards of some of those companies that were exposed in the *Guardian* for sanction breaking. Then there are his South African holdings, diamond mines and the like. When I started the argument with him, he happily told me about all manner of other connections he has with Pretoria. He was quite open, perfectly candid, about it all. Which infuriated me. I stormed out in a rage, drove straight back to Liverpool and wrote out all those cheques. I was very tired at the time. I was also very upset over my half-brother's broken back. It was a stupid thing to do. I was just hitting out at my father in the first available way, using his money for purposes that would hurt him. But do you really think one of those groups I sent cheques to might have decided to take action against Daddy on the strength of it?"

"Your cheques would certainly have brought his name to their attention."

"Jesus, Jesus," I said, "Who were they exactly?"

"Who?"

"Those political groups. They were just names in the classified columns of left-wing magazines as far as I was concerned."

"I don't think any of them were really hard core urban guerrilla organisations. Those sort don't usually advertise for funds, even in the most radical publications."

"That's true, I suppose."

Again there was one of those silences. This time I let Michaels break it.

"How does your father view James Kilminster?"

"James? He hates him."

"With reason?"

"No. Yes. Not really. Kilminster more or less took my mother away from him. From under his nose in effect. My father has never forgiven him for that. And I went with my mother, of course. We both went to live with Kilminster in Clapham."

"And you are still friendly with him?"

"Very. He teaches here now. In Liverpool."

"How does your father view your friendship?"

"Hates it. He thinks Kilminster is 'evil'—that's the word he uses."

"And how does Dr Kilminster view your father?"

"Well…it's hard to say. He obviously has no love for him, but, in a sense, he's the winner—he's retained both my mother's friendship and mine. So he doesn't have to hate my father or anything like that. He has no need for hate. I doubt that he's ever hated anybody seriously; a sort of amused contempt is as far as Kilminster will allow himself to go."

"But you'd say your father was capable of holding strong hatreds over long periods of time? That it was part of his nature to harbour feelings of intense dislike?"

"I suppose so. Yes. Although James is the only person I know about who is the recipient of these feelings. It's a pity in a way that it is my father who has disappeared and not Kilminster; if James had suddenly vanished I would have suspected my father of foul play immediately."

"But not the other way round?"

"What? James kidnapping my father?" I almost giggled. "Kilminster couldn't kidnap a cat."

Michaels smiled again; it hadn't been a serious question.

He said, "And in between your break with your father and his disappearance, did he make contact with you, or try to?"

I told him about the letters and phone calls. How I hadn't responded. I told him about Bernadette's flying visit of reconciliation. I even told him about the stage-managed reception that my household had given Bernadette. He smiled, he'd obviously got poor bloody Bernadette's version of those events a few days earlier. Then we went over much of the ground we'd already covered. Sometime after midday Michaels said,

"Well, Miss Tamar, you've been a great help. I think we now have a much clearer picture of your father than before." He looked at his watch. "I still have a bit over an hour before my train, may I take you to lunch, I think you've earned it."

"Certainly," I said. I was actually feeling quite hungry.

"There is a canteen here, but if you know of any moderately priced restaurant nearby, I'm sure it would be more congenial."

We left the building and walked a couple of blocks through the lunchtime crowds to a small Italian restaurant I'd eaten in a few times with Kilminster. I ordered lasagne and Michaels póllo cacciatóre. He seemed disappointed that I wouldn't join him in drinking a bottle of chianti, but ordered a half one for himself. We chatted amicably for a while. Michaels was married, his wife was deputy headmistress at a primary school, he had two sons, one at university reading law, the other in the navy. I complained about being foreign and hence denied an education, but described my job at the museum. There was a lull while the waiter cleared the plates and we both ordered zabaglione. Then Michaels said, "Please don't answer, if you don't want to—this has no bearing on the investigation—but if we do find your father, or if he turns up by himself, do you think you'll establish contact with him again?"

"I don't know," I said, "I find that I'm very affected by his disappearance. It has come as a real shock to me. I think of nothing else for hours on end. I haven't been able to sleep very well. I jump every time the phone rings. So he clearly still means a great deal to me—is emotionally very significant. In some ways, obviously, cutting myself off from him was an act of aggression on my part. I was trying to punish him for trying to own me, buy me, possess me. And that isn't a very useful action or motivation; I'd like to think I was capable of overcoming it. Maybe subconsciously, even at the time I was reacting so strongly to him, I planned the break to be only temporary. But, at other times I think that all this concern is just a hangover from my love for him when I was a child. When I was small I really did love him, and he loved me. I think he loved me for what I was, without wanting to own me or buy me. It was only after my mother took me away from him that he started trying to buy me back. And when I think that, it seems that even if my father did turn up tomorrow, there'd be no point in going back to him. What do you think I should do?"

"That's not really a question I can answer. I've never even met your father. But surely you could establish some sort of limited contact?"

"*I* could, but I doubt that he could. If I arranged to see him for lunch once every six months, I would just be twisting the knife, throwing the fact that I still no longer cared for him in his face."

The waiter brought the zabaglione. When he had left us, I said to Michaels, "Look, sometimes I feel I know exactly what my father has done and why. It's an insane theory, but sometimes it seems totally plausible, knowing my father as I do."

"Well please tell me," Michaels said, "I'm in the market for theories, I've got none of my own."

"Sometimes I think Daddy has engineered his own disappearance for no other reason than to win me back. He must have known that I'd feel as I do about his disappearance, that if he suddenly reappeared I'd probably fall into his arms. I know that sounds cruel and mad. I mean if it's true, it's insanely cruel to that Bernadette woman, unless she were in on the secret as well, which is impossible because she wouldn't have the acting ability. But it's the sort of cloak and dagger exercise in personal relations that my father would naturally engage in. He might be having a month's holiday in some out-of-the-way hotel. If what you say about the bank collapsing not being related to Daddy's disappearance is true, then there's no reason why he couldn't have just decided to lie low for a bit. Now that there's all this trouble, he might not be able to surface again...but he couldn't have foreseen that.... I'm sometimes sure he will reappear unannounced here, in Liverpool, probably just walk up to me in the street, or be waiting outside the museum one day after work. I can just see him doing it. I can see him being kind and consoling and jolly; telling me he had no idea his little holiday would have affected me so deeply, that had he known, he would have let me in on the secret, that it was all the fault of our little disagreement, but that all that is over now, isn't it? I can almost feel his arms around my shoulders. And half of me wants this to be true. And half of me says that if he really has played that sort of trick, then he is the most unfeeling, cruel bastard possible and I could kill him...."

I searched in my pockets for a handkerchief, which wasn't easy because I was wearing tight jeans and the chairs in the restaurant had arms.

"Here," Michaels said, "Use mine, it's quite clean."

I dabbed at my eyes with the policeman's immaculately white handkerchief. "Sorry," I said, handing it back. "Of course, most of that's wish-fulfilment. It's a way of trying to tell myself he's still alive. But it also seems right, it seems the sort of thing he'd do, the sort of game he'd play. Daddy's attachment to me really is strong, he loves me more than anyone, more than he ever loved Mummy, more, far more, than he loves Bernadette. And, and...I love him, under everything I feel for him, I love him... excuse me, please."

I stood up, clumsily knocking over my chair. Other diners in the place looked up from their meals and conversations. I walked quickly to the back of the room. In the lavatory I looked at myself in the mirror, my eyes were puffy and red, my hair straggled down the sides of my face.

"Well, well," I said to my reflection, "Who'd have believed it possible?"

Back in the restaurant Michaels was very considerate. He told me he understood how I must feel, but could he ask me just one more question?

"Yes, of course, go ahead. I'm over crying now. Ask me anything."

"If your father were playing this sort of game, have you any idea where he might go? Did he have any favourite hotels, holiday resorts?"

I tried to remember all the places I knew my father regarded as civilised watering holes. Michaels wrote them down in his notebook.

"But he flies around all over the place. He'd have a thousand boltholes to go to. He might be in Rio de Janeiro for all I know.

Or, of course, he might be here, in Liverpool. If he wanted to surprise me, if he wanted to watch my reactions to his disappearance, he might be living in the flashest hotel in town. I don't know. Look, don't take all this too seriously; it's just the wild imaginings of a twenty-year-old girl."

"In my job, it is often wild imaginings that give us the lead we are looking for. The rest is mainly hard slog, of course. I'd be a fool not to take your ideas seriously. You haven't touched your zabaglione."

"Oh," I said, looking down at the glass. I picked up a spoon and ate slowly and in silence. Michaels was lost in thought.

I walked with the detective as far as the station. At the entrance he shook my hand, thanked me for my help and gave me his card insisting that I rang him at home or at Scotland Yard the moment anything happened.

"It would be foolish of me to promise anything," he said, "But everything possible is being done; I'm sure we will solve this case no matter what it is that has happened to your father."

"Thank you," I said.

As I say, I floated away from the station. The museum is just across the square, but I decided not to go to work that afternoon. I sat in the weak sunlight for a while and then walked aimlessly about reading the inscriptions on the statues of civic dignitaries. Then I found a phone box and rang Kilminster at the university.

"James? I've just finished with the fuzz."

"How did it go?"

"Fine. Excellent. Michaels was quite pleasant. I even had lunch with him. They don't seem to know anything."

"No. Well, I don't suppose they would. Can you meet me at six, here?"

"Surely. Have you company at the moment?"

"A couple of students."

"Anybody I know?"

"Creighton McFarlane for one."

"Send him my love. See you."

"See you."

As I put the phone down I could hear Kilminster saying, "Anasuya sends her love...."

Poor old McFarlane, God knows what he made of that. He's one of Kilminster's dreary young Ph.D. students. He has a dreary young Ph.D. student's wife called April or May or June or some damn name stolen from the calendar. Half the trouble with Kilminster is that he's a physicist and as such is lumbered with other physicists for students and colleagues.

I once acted as hostess at a dinner party he gave for a whole collection of them; one of those duty parties given to repay the social debts accumulated by unwisely attending other like functions. The whole shooting match would have bored the back leg off a camel.

"And which do you prefer, Anasuya, life in England or France?"

"I dunno, they're different."

"We often go to the South of France for our holidays. A little village outside Aix-en-Provence, St. Zacharie. Do you know it?"

"I know the area."

"Of course it's so good for the children's French."

"They don't speak French in Provence."

Look of blank incomprehension, followed by dawning and nervous comprehension, leading to, "Oh I'm sure it's not what you call French, not the Parisian sort, but...." And so on and so on. Boring conversation matched only by my own appalling arrogance and bitchiness. Anyway, what's wrong with Provençal? I've got nothing against dialect. I live in Liverpool, don't I? For choice. What do people think Scouse is, if not dialect? But I'm getting away from the story.

As I said to Michaels, my father could be violent, but so could my mother. Once, when I was small, she threw a solid glass ashtray at van Niekerk, knocking him instantly and deeply unconscious. I thought she'd killed him. The scene is one of the most vivid in the whole rag-bag of my memory. I'll describe it in all its gory detail later, but for the moment I think I'll concentrate on my mother's marriage. I'm sure an understanding of my parents' feelings for each other is necessary in order to come to terms with van Niekerk's disappearance. Why on earth did Jennifer marry Pieter van Niekerk?

* * * * * *

Her own explanation: that he was the first person to offer, that he had plenty of money and that he provided a chance to leave home, must have some veracity. But I'm sure there was more to it than that. In 1957 when Jennifer met her future husband, she was eighteen and weighed slightly over seven stone. Van Niekerk was twenty-eight and slightly overweight. Jennifer was a student of art at St Martins and a patient of Dr Hilda Glick, psychoanalyst. Van Niekerk was some sort of executive in a firm of importers/exporters, but was talking of branching out on his own—possibly going overseas to Djakarta or Delhi or some other place that sounded a lot more romantic than Golders Green. They met at a party in St John's Wood to which Jennifer had gone with Simon and Tamar. It was at about this time that Simon had, as the saying goes, started courting Tamar. I'm not sure who gave the party or what sort of party it was. Kilminster is no help, of course; I asked him yesterday what he knew about my parents' meeting.

"Dunno. I never discussed the early days of her marriage with Jennifer. I didn't want to know about it. The less I knew about van Niekerk the better. I think it had a lot to do with food, she was dead skinny in those days. I think van Niekerk fed her. You know, like he used to feed the *Après Fin* lot later on. The man was a bit twisted over food."

Kilminster was drinking ouzo in a small cloudy glass. He took a sip, plonked the glass on the table, and said, "Your best bet would be to write a scene in which van Niekerk is popping tasty little morsels into Jennifer's mouth. Like a seagull with its young." And here he did a passable imitation of a small seagull stretching its gullet for a fish. He dropped a sardine from the plate in front of him into his own mouth. Whole. Gulp. He reached quickly for the ouzo.

I know that at one stage in their courtship Jennifer and van Niekerk, together with Simon and Tamar, spent a weekend in King's Lynn. I think the theory was that Jennifer would act as a sort of chaperone for her brother and best friend. Van Niekerk's checking into the same hotel was kept a secret. What follows is a reconstruction, based on these few facts. God knows what validity it has.

* * * * * * *

Van Niekerk met the other three at the station. He had driven up from London by himself in his 1920 Duesenberg Straight Eight Tourer something or other. The object of the weekend— its focus—was a race-meeting at Newmarket that afternoon. Van Niekerk drove them all to the pub into which they had booked. The Stag's Head, three stars, AA and RAC signs prominently displayed, mentioned in the *Good Food Guide*. The two girls were to share a room. Simon had one of his own, as did van Niekerk. Everyone checked in openly under their own names; there were no improprieties involved, these would come with the midnight flits, the surreptitious re-alignment of sleeping arrangements once the hotel's corridors were sufficiently deserted to make this possible. It had been mooted that cheap wedding rings be bought so that the two couples could enter the hotel as if married, but the girls' parents had taken a lively interest in the weekend—Tamar's parents had themselves once stayed in this very hotel and knew it to be reputable—and the possibility of a phone call from London asking for Miss Goldstein or Miss Goodman was not to be discounted. As it was, Jennifer was at pains to ask the proprietress if her room was close to her brother's, establishing at once the nature of her relationship to Simon.

"On the same floor, Miss Goldstein. Across the corridor."

"Oh good, it will be just like home."

"Terence will show you to your rooms now. Lunch is at twelve forty-five."

Once inside their room, with their suitcases open upon the low slatted table and Terence dismissed with a shilling for his pains, the two girls collapsed into each other's arms giggling.

"We've done it, we've done it," Tamar said, "We're having a real live dirty weekend."

"How frightfully, frightfully spiffing!" Jennifer said, only half parodying the role she was playing.

The two girls explored the confines of the hotel room. They bounced experimentally on each of the beds, opened the dark wooden wardrobe, turned on the taps above the wash basin. From the window they could see the hotel's lawns and part of a glassed-in terrace; beyond the lawns were high banks of rhododendron bushes and beyond them a line of willows and the river. The red roof of the hotel's boatshed showed through its surrounding trees. The sun shone warmly. The girls unpacked their clothes. Tamar for some reason cleaned her teeth. The mirror image of Jennifer's face appeared behind her shoulder, painting her lips with lipstick. That done, she blew Tamar a kiss. Tamar took the brush from her mouth and said, "Oh, Princess Jennifer, you are too, too divine. Will you marry me?"

"What will you give me?"

"A ride on my unicorn."

The girls laugh, impressed by their own wit. Tamar rinses her mouth with water while Jennifer experimentally ties a rayon scarf around her throat.

"What's Simon actually like?" Jennifer asks.

"Like?"

"In bed."

"You ought to know. All those nights under the Morrison table."

"Phew! His feet. Do they still smell?"

"Horrible."

Again the girls dissolve into conspiratorial giggles. Perhaps *giggles* is the wrong word, but one can hardly call their laughter *stentorian* either. There is a suppressed confidentiality about it. In some ways one feels that the real intimacies of this weekend are being played out here, between the two girls. Whatever may take place after midnight, when the girls have swapped each other's company for that of Simon and van Niekerk, it will not be as easy, as unselfconscious and playful as the present exchanges. In watching this scene, creating it on paper out of the few facts and plentiful imagination at my disposal, I am at once slightly scornful and slightly envious of my mother and her friend. I have simply never had a giggling intimacy with anyone, even Jennifer herself. The friends of my own sex whom I made at school—both in London and Oise—were always girls I could easily dominate. I didn't really share intimacies with them. Indeed I often went out of my way to hide what I was really feeling. I certainly went out of my way to hide the real nature of the households I lived in, the eccentricities of my parents and their friends. I didn't want people to know that my father was absurdly rich, that Kilminster and my mother were often in bed when I came home from school, and later in France, that I had so much money I didn't know what to do with it, and that the love of my life was my mother's second husband. And then, of course, I was foreign. There is a song by Flanders and Swann in which they sing,

> It's not that they're wicked
> Or naturally bad,
> It's knowing they're foreign
> That makes them so mad.

I have always known I was foreign. I was foreign in India where I was born. I was foreign in Putney, foreign in Clapham, foreign in Oise, so very foreign in Liverpool that they wouldn't educate me, and I'm certainly foreign on this island in the Aegean. Sometimes I'm tempted to fill in forms, *Nationality: Foreign*. And I think this foreignness has always prevented me from experiencing the sort of closeness that I am now creating in this scene. Had Jennifer had another child in India, given me a sister or brother with roughly the same experiences, things might have been different.

So here are Jennifer and Tamar, for all their Jewishness-in-a-yok-society, celebrating a common fund of experiences and values, in this strange hotel room they are thoroughly at home with each other. And they are, I suppose, thoroughly at home with the world represented by the hotel. Jennifer, certainly, belongs in this hotel room in a manner in which she never belonged to St James's School for Girls. When I was describing her feelings of alienation from that school, I said that Jennifer as a child never sought the confidence of adults. Now I'm describing her and Tamar as young adults being quite childishly intimate with each other. Perhaps there is some sort of progression here—from lonely, anxious child to not-quite-so-anxious, young adult—achieved by a *regression* of sorts. Listen to the next bit of dialogue:

"How long is his willy?" Jennifer asks.

Tamar holds her two index fingers about six inches apart like a fisherman telling a modest one-that-got-away story.

"And Pieter's?"

Jennifer makes the same gesture. The two girls bring their outstretched fingers together like gunfighters at very close range, each one slowly widening the distance measured by her own fingers as they do so. Tamar suddenly increases the gap between her fingers to the full width of her arms. Jennifer follows suit. The two girls stand facing each other, their arms outstretched. They join hands and begin a slow dance. There is a knock on the door.

* * * * * *

In his room Simon exchanges the tweed jacket and tie he had been wearing on the train for a reefer jacket and cravat. He is twenty-one, a third-year medical student at Guys. He has spent the last two weeks slowly dissecting the forearm of a corpse known to him, and the other three students with whom he works, as Fred. He looks at himself in the mirror and is pleased with what he sees. He has a thin, handsome face with a lock of black hair that constantly "threatens" to fall into his eyes. He uses hair-cream to allay the threat, but sparingly. He now places his comb, hair-brush, bottle of hair-cream, shaving lotion, safety razor, cuff-links and shaving brush on the dresser near the wash basin. He transfers his wallet from the pocket of his tweed jacket to that of his reefer, checking its contents as he does so. He is fairly sure that he has enough money to hold his own with van Niekerk, or to at least put up a decent show. Van Niekerk, of course, is six or seven years older, and had left the University of Leiden some five years previously. Simon values his friendship with van Niekerk, heartily approves of van Niekerk's friend-ship with his sister, but secretly wonders just how much of van Niekerk's friendship for *him* is a product of his being Jennifer's brother. Simon is both impressed by, and slightly resentful of, van Niekerk's considerable wealth, his vintage Duesenberg, his knowledge of food, wine, London nightspots, his extensive circle of contacts in worlds into which he, Simon, has never penetrated, and, of course, his flat in Maida Vale. Van Niekerk's flat has its uses. Simon made love—as he would put it—in the flat, twice in the previous week. Once to Tamar and once to a certain Juliet, a friend of van Niekerk's. Tamar does not know about Juliet. Juliet had listened with apparent absorption and interest to a long recital of Tamar's virtues: her sweetness of nature, her sense of fun, her warmth, and passion. Juliet had been most sympathetic to Simon's frustration at the prospect of at least another four or five years of student life, housemanship, and national service before being able to marry Tamar. She had then suddenly taken Simon's penis in her mouth and sucked. Simon had been startled, had only just prevented himself from pulling Juliet's head away from his groin and had then lain back to enjoy the experience, wondering vaguely if it was polite to ejaculate in Juliet's mouth. Should he tap her on the shoulder to warn her? A premature climax saved him the necessity of finding an answer. Now, wandering around the confines of his hotel room, Simon checks the plentiful supply of condoms in his wallet and wonders if he should initiate Tamar into the art so recently demonstrated by the experienced Juliet. The previous night, alone in his own bed, the prospect of being sucked by Tamar had appealed considerably, at least it had up to the point at which he reached under his pillow for the handkerchief he kept there in the interests of nighttime comfort. Then he hadn't been so sure, as he isn't now. Tamar after all, is Tamar, not Juliet. Simon glances at himself in the mirror, suddenly spins on his heel and draws an imaginary gun from the waistband of his trousers, firing straight at his own image. This also is something he did last week, only on that occasion he practised the manoeuvre with a real gun, van Niekerk's gun.

He had found the gun while snooping around his friend's bedroom. He had been alone in the Maida Vale flat waiting for the arrival of Tamar. Out of curiosity Simon had tried the drawers in van Niekerk's desk. They had all been locked. The papers on top of the desk were impressive but boring. They related to stocks and shares.

There were two personal letters, but they were from South Africa and written in Afrikaans. So Simon made his way to van Niekerk's bedroom and tried the drawers there. None of them were locked, but the only thing of interest was the gun. It lay, covered by a few handkerchiefs, in the top drawer of the dressing table. There were also a few boxes of ammunition. Simon had taken it out, turned it over gingerly in his hands, found a catch which, when pushed, clicked forward to hide the word 'Safe'. He'd hastily pushed back the catch to reveal the word again and checked the magazine and breech. He had a working knowledge of sturdy service revolvers from his time in his school's cadet corps, but this slim, black, all-metal machine with its magazine in the handle had an exotic, sinister appeal quite unlike anything associated with the heavy objects he had discharged on the school's rifle range while Old Soames-Prichard (Old *Major* Soames-Prichard, as he became on Wednesday afternoons with the donning of his uniform) had barked, "Arm straight from the shoulder, Goldstein. Focus on the target, not the bloody gun, boy!"

Convinced that van Niekerk's gun was empty, Simon had tucked it into his belt and performed the quick draw manoeuvre in front of the bedroom mirror. He had then stalked through the flat as quietly as possible, appearing suddenly in doorways, flattening himself against walls, once diving for cover behind the sofa. A small army of mobsters, Russian agents, blackmailers, Germans, and other shadowy types in raincoats died silently, one by one, under his deadly fire. *Twice* he saved Bulldog Drummond's life by out-gunning whoever it is necessary to outgun in order to achieve this feat. When Tamar rang the doorbell, he slid smoothly to van Niekerk's bedroom, wiped his fingerprints from the gun's butt with his handkerchief, and replaced it where he had found it, all with the practised stealth of the trained MI5 operative. Seconds later Tamar was in his arms. She found him almost breathless in his passion. The couple made love in the spare bedroom almost immediately. Simon said not a word. Tamar came for the first time in her life.

In the hotel bedroom Simon decides against teaching Tamar the arts of the wily Juliet. He makes his way across the corridor and knocks on the girls' door.

And what of van Niekerk himself? How did he spend that half-hour before lunch?

"Scratching his arse probably." (Dr James Kilminster).

Weil he might have done; he was human after all. But not for half an hour at a stretch.

Van Niekerk checked his reflection in the mirror, dabbed a small amount of eau de Cologne on his face, thumbed through the contents of his wallet, scratched his arse, and left the room. At the hotel's desk he exchanged a ten shilling note for five florins and secreted himself in one of the three dark-panelled telephone booths in the lobby.

"Dino? Pieter. I'm in Kings Lynn...that's right. We're motoring over after lunch...be there with plenty of time. What's the word...? Sounds as if it might be worth fifty, don't think I'll go any higher myself. Want me to put any on for you? Certainly.... If you hear anything new in the next hour and a half give me a ring here.... Yes, that's right. Same to you."

Van Niekerk extracted a slim notebook from a pocket inside his jacket, took the gold-topped pencil from its spine, and made a number of calculations, inscribing the figures in a neat, minute hand. Obviously satisfied, he returned the book to his pocket and left the booth for the bar. When the other three joined him twenty minutes later, van Niekerk was just finishing his whisky and affably declining the offer of another from a man in a hound's-tooth suit who had been telling him about salmon fishing in Canada. It is now twelve forty-five and the group make their way to the dining room.

The dining room is dark-panelled, has a dark, patterned carpet, and is furnished with heavily lacquered sideboards and chairs. The tables cannot be seen under their white cloths. In winter the room would be gloomy, but on a sunny summer's day such as this one, the two sets of bay windows provide more than enough light. On one wall is a series of water colours of the lake district, the heavy gilt frames contrasting badly with the insubstantial pictures of water and heather-covered mountains they encompass. On the opposite wall, Royalty is gathered in force: the present queen and her husband and the queen's mother and father. Her father's portrait has black crêpe bands across the four corners.

"About time they took the old boy down isn't it?" Simon says as the four people settle themselves at their table.

Jennifer twists in her chair to stare at the wall behind her.

"I met that one once," she says to van Niekerk.

"Liz?"

"No, her mother. She decorated me for devotion to duty in the Brownies."

"Have you a medal to prove it?"

"No, we've got pictures though. Me and her, having a gracious conversation."

"They have too," Tamar says, "All over the house."

Van Niekerk says to Simon, "You'll have to take me home one day, I'd like to see the native hearth."

It is understood that it would be quite acceptable for Simon to arrive home with a gentile gentleman friend, not so for Jennifer. Jennifer's parents know nothing of her friendship with van Niekerk.

Lunch proceeds. Van Niekerk orders the wine, a light hock. He advises knowingly on the food. Other guests glance occasionally at the four young people, looking up from their own meals whenever a peal of laughter rings clearly over the subdued conversations and clacking of nickel-plated cutlery. One old couple, sitting at an adjacent table attempt to eavesdrop, but are thwarted by the habit all four young people adopt of delivering the significant portions of their conversation in titillating *sotto voce* asides. Jennifer allows her knee to rub against van Niekerk's. Van Niekerk answers the pressure and at one point his hand strays (beneath the adequate camouflage of the tablecloth) to the short split in the side of Jennifer's skirt. His fingers slide over the nylon of her stockings, negotiating a knee, and reaching a point half-way up a slim thigh, before the gathering folds of the tweed skirt make further progress impossible. He transfers his attention to the opposite thigh, tracing a line slowly back to the other knee. During this manoeuvre, Jennifer betrays not a trace of awareness, but continues a conversation with Tamar. Van Niekerk is listening with attention to something Simon is saying.

It is a pleasing tableau: the four are all good-looking in their individual ways; although it is true that one of the girls is so slim as to be very nearly emaciated, but then the obvious sensuousness of her smile seems to rob her of any beanstalk qualities. When all four leave the room after quickly finishing their sweets and without waiting for coffee, the other diners experience a momentary pang of envy. Perhaps they too would like to be in the vintage car that, moments later, crunches round the hotel's gravel drive and disappears into the fens.

At Newmarket van Niekerk paid only scant attention to the first three races. Before the fourth he said to Simon, "I think we should lay a fiver on this one."

It was a figure of speech. What van Niekerk had in mind was laying fifty pounds of his own money and fifty pounds of Dino's money on the race. But Simon said, "We are not all rich colonials you know, Pieter. Some of us are poor medical students. And I don't really gamble as a rule. But I'll bet ten shillings for Tamar. It would be a pity to come all this way and not bet anything at all."

Simon led the way to the enclosure where the horses were being led around by their grooms. The only one to know anything about horses was van Niekerk who watched them closely, but said nothing. The two girls chatted happily about which horse they most liked the look of, going mainly on the colourings. Simon, realising that anything he said would betray his total ignorance, said nothing. Eventually Tamar said, "Number seven. Obviously a winner."

"Excellent," Simon said, "Number seven it is, although if you win I'll expect you to buy me a glass of champagne."

"I wouldn't," van Niekerk said.

"Wouldn't what, darling?" Jennifer said.

"Wouldn't bet on number seven."

"Well you bet on something else, Simon can put ten bob on seven for Tamar and with luck at least one of us will win."

Van Niekerk shrugged and the group began to walk away from the enclosure. Once clear of the crowd van Niekerk said, "I'd strongly advise betting on number four."

"Which one was that?" Jennifer asked.

"Trojan's Lament, the bay gelding."

"The one with the blue saddle-cloth?"

"Yes."

Both girls said, "That won't win."

Van Niekerk shrugged, saying, "That's what I'm betting on. Simon's bet is Simon's choice."

"I'm entirely in Tamar's hands," Simon said as gallantly as

possible.

"Simon, if you bet on that mouldy horse I won't accept the winnings."

"You won't have to," Jennifer said, "That horse couldn't win a donkey race."

"As you wish, as you wish," Simon said airily. Whatever happened, his attitude proclaimed, he, Simon, had no emotional stake in the race one way or the other. The bet was only for the fun of it, a small token of homage to his mistress.

By now they had reached the betting circle. A small crowd jostled around the couple of dozen bookmakers and their touts. The girls hung back as Simon and van Niekerk pressed forward to make their bets. Van Niekerk said to Simon, "Put ten bob on number seven for Tamar, but put a fiver for yourself on Trojan's Lament."

Simon had estimated that after the necessary hotel bills had been reckoned for, a fiver was about all he had left over to take care of the incidentals over the rest of the weekend. Jennifer, he knew, had some money she would lend him if he asked her; but he did not wish to borrow from his sister if he could help it. It did not occur to him that Tamar herself should pay for anything, and although van Niekerk would certainly lend him as much as he wanted with perfect grace, Simon wished very strongly to avoid that option. He was already very much the junior partner in this weekend.

"I'm really not the gambling type," he said to van Niekerk, "I think I'll pass on this one."

"Foolish, foolish."

"You seem very sure it'll win."

"It *could* lose," van Niekerk said from the corner of his mouth with all the conviction of a professional cartographer admitting that the earth *could* be flat.

Simon was tempted. But he was no fool. The two men had reached the bookkeeper.

"Ten bob on seven," Simon said.

"Win or place?"

"Err…both."

"Ten bob each way?"

"Yes."

"That'll be a quid then."

Simon exchanged a green pound note for the betting slips. He watched van Niekerk place his bet—extracting a five pound note from his wallet and then, in rapid succession, nineteen more five pound notes. Van Niekerk was betting a hundred pounds. Simon glanced at the odds on the bookkeeper's board. Fourteen to one. Fourteen hundred pounds. One thousand four hundred quid. His yearly allowance was only a little over four hundred pounds. If he placed a fiver on the bloody horse he'd be up seventy pounds. If it won.

The two men joined Jennifer and Tamar and began the stroll back to the stands. Simon ceremoniously handed the slips to Tamar.

"But there are two bets."

"Thought I'd give you a chance."

* * * * * * *

I suppose at this point I should write a cliff-hanging, heart-stopping description of the race, with a maddening wait at the end while the judges decide on the basis of a photograph between number four and number seven.

Bugger that. I want to get this scene written by this evening, when Kilminster and I and everybody else on the island are going to a wedding down by the port. Anyway, what I'm writing is all very interesting, but it hasn't yet started to tell us why Jennifer married my father, which was my initial aim.

* * * * * * *

Van Niekerk's horse won by a mile. Number seven limped home second last.

"So it comes to pass, old boy," van Niekerk said to Simon.

"Never mind, darling," Tamar said to him, "I love you all the same."

"It was your choice."

"But your money, my sweet."

Tamar kissed Simon on the cheek. "I love you passionately," she whispered.

Simon wished to be allowed to lose his pound with manly nonchalance, not to be consoled, however lovingly, by Tamar. Van Niekerk was already striding off to collect his winnings. Simon said, "I'll go with Pieter, he might need a bodyguard."

But, as well as the wish to free himself momentarily from the company of the two women, Simon also wished to watch van Niekerk receive his winnings; he just wanted to observe the process, see the money counted out. He stood back from the small knot of people around the bookmaker. Van Niekerk was affable with the bookmaker, who muttered some equally affable remarks about winning it all back on the next race, with the flick-snap, flick-snap of blue five pound notes seeming never to cease between his fingers.

Was van Niekerk carrying his gun? Van Niekerk rejoined Simon. "Only half of it's mine," he said.

Simon was momentarily confused. He thought at first that this was some obscure way of van Niekerk offering to share his winnings.

"Don't be silly," he said.

"No. Fifty pounds of that bet was Dino's."

"Oh. I see. Who's Dino?"

"Many things to many people. You should meet him one day. To me he's a useful source of information about horses."

Simon wondered how van Niekerk had interpreted his 'Don't be silly' remark. He wished with an absurd intensity that his friend hadn't understood it. He said, "Has Dino given you any more information?"

"Afraid not."

Which put an end to visions of Simon also being the recipient of a flick-snapping stream of blue five pound notes.

* * * * * * *

In bed that night with Tamar, Simon said, "I worry about Pieter and Jennifer sometimes."

In a mild way he surprised himself with this remark, he hadn't really questioned the assumption that van Niekerk was excellent for his sister before.

"Why?"

"Oh, I don't know. She is only eighteen after all."

"So am I."

"But you're with me.... Look, van Niekerk bet fifty pounds of his own money and fifty pounds of someone else's—some odd character called Dino—on that race."

"Good for him. He can take us all out to dinner in London. But what's that got to do with Jennifer?"

"I don't think he's really her type—he's not really part of her world. He has a gun."

"A gun?"

"I found it by accident in his flat the other day."

"Well, he's a colonial isn't he? They have guns out there. Everybody does, they use them for shooting elephants and tigers and things."

"Not pistols. It was one of those little black guns, the sort you hold in one hand."

"Maybe he has it for self-protection."

"That's just it. I don't know that it's...well, I don't know... it's...."

"Simon, darling, you're completely incoherent."

"I don't know that the sort of person who needs a gun for self-protection is the sort of person with whom Jennifer should be spending her time."

"Don't worry. He probably never uses it. Never carries it around with him. The thing about Pieter is that he's good for Jennifer."

"How do you mean good?"

"He gets her to eat. She's been eating like a horse all weekend if you haven't noticed."

"That's true, I suppose."

"She's happy with him. She's relaxed with him. She laughs a lot when she's with him, and she eats. Just watch her at breakfast."

Tamar and Simon made love again.

* * * * * * *

In van Niekerk's bed, Jennifer said, "Do you think my brother and Tamar should get married?"

"Why do you ask? Are they thinking of it?"

"No, not that I know of."

This was untrue. Jennifer and Tamar had discussed marriage at length. Jennifer had little doubt that Tamar could persuade Simon to take his place beside her under the canopy if she wanted to. She wasn't so sure about her possibilities with van Niekerk.

"They're both very young," van Niekerk said.

"No younger than me, at least Tamar isn't."

"That's true, but you're with me."

The remark seemed to be a bit of a non sequitur, but Jennifer didn't say anything. She and van Niekerk made love again.

* * * * * * *

By six o'clock Jennifer was back in the other bed in the room she shared with Tamar. Both girls woke at eight. For an hour they talked.

"Simon says Pieter's got a gun."

"I know. He uses it for shooting rats."

"Rats? There are no rats in Maida Vale."

"That's what I told him. He said there are more kinds of rats than those who eat cheese."

Tamar laughed. "How perfectly sinister. Do you love him Jennifer?"

"Oh passionately, with all my heart."

"Be serious."

"I am."

"Simon is worried about you and Pieter. He thinks Pieter is not really your type."

"Oh Simon," Jennifer said dismissively of her brother, and then, speaking of her friend's lover, "Simon's sweet. Do you really love him?"

"I think so."

* * * * * *

I'll do one more scene from this weekend.

On the Sunday all four drove in van Niekerk's car to Aldeburgh on the Suffolk coast. They took with them a hamper prepared by the hotel's kitchen staff: cold turkey with a pot of cranberry sauce, pressed ham, cucumber sandwiches, hock, soda water, a bottle of champagne—that sort of stuff. They parked the car in the main street and dawdled around the town, being critical of the Tudor and Jacobean architecture, paying threepence admission to the town's half-timbered meeting house and then making their way to the waterfront to look over the steep sloping pebble beach to the sea. It was a clear, still day. At the water's edge, the sea just managed to grind a few pebbles against one another.

Tamar said, "Ah, the wine-dark sea."

Jennifer said, "Ah, the salt-estranging, wine-dark sea."

"Ah, the gong-tormented, salt-estranging, wine-dark sea."

"Ah, the dragon-haunted, gong-tormented, salt-estranging sea."

"You left out wine-dark. I win."

They all returned to the car and drove for a mile or so along the breakwater that runs endlessly between the sea and the marshes. Half a mile away, across the marshes, the waters of the river Alde glinted in the sun. A wide cumbersome boat with red sails furled along its boom, puttered slowly up stream. Van Niekerk stopped the car and the two couples strolled on, arm-in-arm, towards the squat bulk of a Martello tower. This they circumnavigated, making a number of rather laboured remarks about stately, plump Buck Mulligan before returning slowly to the car. Van Niekerk untied the hamper from the Duesenberg's luggage rack—a sort of shelf projecting from the stern of the car—and together the four people made their way to a level piece of dry, tussocky grass on the inland side of the breakwater. Jennifer spread the travelling rug and the picnic commenced. The conversation was languid, as befitted the drowsy warmth of the day.

"Life should always be like this," Tamar said.

"Pieter dearest, peel me a grape," Jennifer said with the husky insouciance of a pampered courtesan.

With a bit of difficulty and some laughter and remarks about dead men's eyeballs, van Niekerk removed the skin from a single grape.

"Princess, your word is my command," he said, holding the grape in the air about two feet above Jennifer's head.

Jennifer leant back, lifting her head, closing her eyes against the sun and opening her mouth to receive the grape.

We may surmise that, once the damn grape had been dropped into her mouth, she choked, sat forward suddenly, needing to be thumped on the back and offered a quick glass of soda water in much the same way as Kilminster needed his ouzo the other day after he'd tried the same trick with a sardine. But let's not. Let's freeze the picture there, just before the dropping of the grape. Hold it for a few moments and then draw slowly away, allowing the picture to become grainy, pointillist and ultimately impressionistic, fixed like one of those Seurat paintings of people by the Seine. In this picture we have all that is necessary for an understanding of why Jennifer married van Niekerk. (And just to push this device to its limits—in the as-yet-unrealised choking scene we have the correlative of why the marriage so quickly went sour.)

The slim, pretty girl leans back in the warmth and sunlight, resting her weight on her arms stretched behind her. She is wearing a white blouse, open at the throat, a light off-white linen jacket is almost sliding from her shoulders. She wears a tweed skirt and sandals, but no stockings. Her hair is dark brown and hangs just below the level of her shoulder blades. Her skin is smooth, light brown from the summer. As she leans back, smiling a warm, blind-eyed answer to the sun and the lover she knows to be leaning over her, it is her throat that is peculiarly vulnerable and sensual at the same time. And the gesture itself shows a happiness which is in no way diminished by the possibility that it may also contain smugness and self-regard. Her lover, who suspends the single peeled grape above her mouth, also wears a white shirt, but his throat is half covered by a dark blue foulard. He has a long straight nose and light auburn hair and his face also shows happiness which is in no way diminished by the possibility that this young girl, whose seduction and sexual initiation he embarked upon more or less as an amusement, is coming to mean far, far more to him than he would have been able to predict three months previously. If he now wants wholly to possess what he once wished only to sample, it is no matter, for Jennifer wishes to be wholly possessed—at least to the point of being married and given somewhere to live other than her parents' home.

So we draw back slightly, bringing the other two people into the tableau. Simon kneels with one hand on Tamar's shoulder. Tamar has tilted her head to entrap the hand between her shoulder and ear. There are smiles that will turn to laughter the moment the grape drops. All four await the falling of the grape. But by now we are so far distant from the scene that we cannot tell what happens. The people on the travelling rug are only blurred dobs of colour; above them the long line of the break-water divides the earth from the high blue sky. The silhouette of the Duesenberg Straight Eight Tourer something or other lies like a heraldic beast on a bicoloured flag. Slightly menacing.

* * * * * * *

Writing!

I'm not Jennifer's daughter for nothing.

I showed the above to Kilminster who was recovering from last night's wedding, sitting with his head in his hands on the balcony outside my room. Retzina, ouzo, and dancing in circles—they have their price.

"What's a fowl yard?"

"Foul*ard*. Generally, a sort of cloth. Specifically, a cravat made out of same."

"Nothing to do with chicken shit?"

"Fuck off."

"Make me some coffee, Ansu. I'll do the same for you one day."

"I've only once had a hangover in my life."

"Then you'll know what it's like."

I made the poor bastard a glass of coffee on the paraffin stove we use for heat, hot water, and stinking the place up. When he'd drunk it, he said, "Why don't you have them all running in slow motion through a forest of mighty oaks with the girls' hair streaming out behind them in the sunlight that slants through the trees...that sort of thing?"

"Oh, don't worry about the ending. That was just a way of rounding it off, bringing in your seagull-with-young scene. Do you think I've caught the relationships? Do you think their weekend might have gone like that?"

"There's something wrong with the girls' dialogue. I don't think they would have spoken that way."

"You think I've made them a bit too twitterpated? That Jennifer would never have said, 'How long is his willy?'"

"In a word, yes."

"In two words, you're wrong. She described that scene to me once: her and Tamar comparing the lengths of Simon and van Niekerk's dicks. I don't think it was that weekend, but it could have been. Look, they were both eighteen, it was 1957. That's how they spoke. That was the sort of thing they said to each other. They still do sometimes, you ought to hear Jennifer yacking to Tamar on the phone. And in the nineteen-fifties they 'made love', fucking wasn't invented until the sixties."

"I still don't like it."

"Look, there was an odd mixture of childishness and adulthood about that generation—well the middle-class bit of it. All the giggling and comparing lengths of pricks went on in the bedrooms, behind the scenes. As soon as they hit the dining room they were as composed and mature as they could present themselves, even if they were laughing away and having a high old time of it. They were well dressed. They didn't swear. They observed the proprieties. Imagine a group of eighteen-year-olds in a hotel today. Lounging about, scratching their arses—not in the bedrooms, but in the damn dining room. Omigod!"

"Yes, well...."

Kilminster still isn't convinced. He likes to think of Jennifer as never having been an ingénue, as always having had the general wit and precision that she had when he first met her. He's wrong, maybe I'll be able to educate him.

Although in one respect the dear little pedant has been able to educate me. The phrase "ten bob each way" does not indicate the expenditure of one pound. God knows why, but it doesn't.

* * * * * * *

The rest of the dual courtship and marriage can be sketched in fairly quickly.

Six months later Tamar found she was pregnant. She married Simon forthwith according to the full rights of the Golders Green synagogue. I don't think any of the four parents were particularly surprised, or particularly upset by this occurrence. It was generally considered a good match.

Three months later Jennifer said she was pregnant. Perhaps she was, perhaps the few nasty scenes at home that followed the discovery of her liaison with van Niekerk were not the cause of the cessation of menstruation that is a normal symptom of anorexia; perhaps the particularly heavy period she experienced not long after becoming Mrs van Niekerk was a spontaneous abortion. Possible. Jennifer and Pieter were married according to the full rights of the Caxton Hall registry office. Quite a few odd people were present. It was not generally considered a good match in Golders Green. Nor, apparently, was it so regarded in the Kruger National Park.

* * * * * * *

As soon as I was licensed to drive, my father gave me a Mercedes-Benz sports car. It was an absurd thing to do. The car was expensive, ostentatious, impractical, capable of speeds wildly in excess both of the legal limit and my own inclinations. Two people could sit in it in complete luxury; three people found themselves in conditions of over-crowding far worse than those experienced by six people in the family's Renault. I soon found I couldn't drive the Mercedes anywhere without people staring at me. As I didn't drive it at all fast almost anybody else on the road could overtake me. And thousands did. The experience of being overtaken by grinning loons in clapped-out Citroen vans became depressingly familiar. Usually the vans remained alongside far longer than was necessary, which on the narrow roads around our place is nerve-wracking and dangerous. The flics waved me down all the time, mainly to eye off the car. My friends were at first envious, delighted to be taken for rides or allowed to drive it, but soon began to make remarks about rich bitch heiresses and ruling-class decadence. I was eighteen, halfway through my last year at the *lycée*. I drove it to school a couple of times, but felt so embarrassed by it, by the remarks, not only of my fellow-students, but of my teachers as well, that I never took it there again. But the damage was done, everybody knew I owned it. Although, I suppose, everyone would have known I owned it sooner or later, even if I had never taken it to school, or even driven it to town, or driven it anywhere. I could have let it rot in the garage to the same effect. As it was, that's where it stayed most of the time. I continued to ride my mobylette to school, but the experience had now lost most of its joy. That half-hour journey, chugging through the fields and half-dozen villages between the château and school, performed twice a day, had been one of the most important parts of my life. I was quite alone, I had time to think, there was a serene purpose to the ride, an easy familiarity about it all. Every bump in the road, bad corner, tree, Christ and his grieving women, barn, house, and farm were known to me in a way that was comforting, reassuring. I knew this landscape, was part of it. The figure of a schoolgirl chugging through it in the morning, getting stuck behind a tractor-drawn trailer of manure, waving to a farm-hand she knows, *belongs*. A mobylette is part of our landscape, *my* landscape. A ridiculous kraut sports car is not. Simple as that.

On my way home I would often stop in the village nearest the château to buy bread or milk if I knew we needed it. I would pull off the road onto the little triangle of dirt and grass where the men play *boules*, kick the footrest down, walk into the boulangerie, be addressed by name, would address Monsieur or Madame Roux by name, chat for a while, leave the shop, and chug away, the loaves sticking up from the saddle bag or strapped across the pannier, after the fashion of French women everywhere who do their shopping by mobylette. I wasn't a local, I was believed to be English, known to be bourgeois, the vast and broken down mansion I lived in was referred to as "le château" in a manner that sometimes made the quotation marks as audible as the phrase itself, but I was accepted, liked.

I still was, of course. And I could still go shopping in the village on my mobylette. Often did. But it had all started to look phony—a sort of deliberate slumming. Everyone, the farm-hand I sometimes waved to, Monsieur and Madame Roux, everyone at school, knew I could actually be driving the Merc if I wished. It wouldn't have been so bad in summer, but the Merc was delivered just as autumn was ending. Winter set in, it rained often, the wind blew across the ploughed fields. I would arrive at the *lycée*, park my mobylette with the others, enter the centrally heated corridors and, in the cloakroom, take off such outer garments as I was wearing and stand, warming my hands, by the radiators. Usually there were two or three others there who had ridden to school on mobylette or bicycle. We would curse the weather, kiss each other's frozen cheeks, joke about the soft life lived by those who came by bus or walked the few hundred metres from their homes in town. Once, not long after I'd been given the car, I did this—following the old patterns. There had been a slight rain and my woollen gloves were damp. I arranged them between the cast iron pipes of the radiator, held my hands to my face and blew on them, stamping my feet.

"Your heater broken down?" Paulette said.

I thought for a moment this was a normal joke, a suggestion that we ought to have heaters attached to the jumped-up bicycles we rode. But then I realised the remark was more pointed.

"It's more fun on a mobylette."

"Fun!" Paulette said in a tone that carried scorn, incredulity, and envy.

We both left the cloakroom together and as we were walking through the jostling corridors we were passed by René and Jean who, between them, had just bought an old car, a Fiat I think. They nodded to Paulette, but not to me. And it was with René that I'd spent that absurd, painful, and yet utterly intimate night on the floor of Jean-Claude's office in the rue St. Marc.

There is a record by Joan Baez on which she sings a song about the silkies of the Hebrides who come out of the sea, turning into men as they do so, and who, on land, father children to ordinary mortal women. If the child is a boy the father will return when he is grown to take him back to the sea to become a silkie himself. In the song that Baez sings are these words,

> And he has taken a purse of gold.
> And he has placed it upon her knee,
> Saying 'give to me my little young son
> And take thee of thy nurse's fee.'

I played this record a lot in those days. I felt for the mother of the child, of course, but also for the boy. What would it feel like to be brought up among ordinary people and then to be purchased back into an alien submarine world at the whim of one's father? The bloody Merc sat in the shed in which I also kept my mobylette like the purse of gold that had robbed me of my normal relations with my friends and even, to some extent, my family.

I'd known van Niekerk was planning to give me a car—it was to be a delayed birthday present. I rang him the day I passed my test. The Merc arrived two days later. Two junior executive types from some company in Paris that my father owned, or was the director of, arrived one evening in the Merc and another car. The other car was larger, immaculately polished, expensive, but obviously not nearly as expensive as the sports car.

"Who the fuck are this lot?" Jennifer said when they drew up in the yard—we were all sitting around in the kitchen eating bread and jam at the time.

"No friends of mine," Jean-Claude said, "See what they want will you, Philippe."

Philippe met them at the kitchen door.

"Mademoiselle van Niekerk?" one of them inquired.

Philippe nodded to me. I stood up, my mouth full of bread and jam. Swallowing hard I walked over to the door. "Monsieur?"

"Mademoiselle, a present from your father." He handed me a set of keys. I looked at them for a second, realised they were obviously the keys of my expected car and said, "Thanks very much, but where's the car?"

"Voila, mademoiselle!" the man said, standing aside and indicating the sports car with a melodramatic flourish.

"That?" I said.

"Oh for fuck's sake!" Jennifer said behind me.

"That's meant to be my car?" I said.

"But of course, mademoiselle," the executive type said. He was hugely enjoying himself. "It is not to your liking. The colour perhaps?"

"This is just the sort of idiot bloody game Pieter would play," Jennifer said, coming to the door and brushing past me. She walked over to the Mercedes and stalked round it once. She said to the executive, "How much does this damn thing cost?"

"Ah, madame, I'm sure it is of no moment. Monsieur van Niekerk can surely afford it."

"I don't doubt for a second that van Niekerk can surely afford a whole fleet of these bloody things. It's just a stupid present to give a child, that's all."

The executive turned to me. "Perhaps mademoiselle van Niekerk is no longer a child."

"It's not the sort of car I'd expected," I said lamely.

"It will *eat* petrol," Jennifer said, "There is an energy crisis, you know." This was the first time in my life I'd heard my mother express any concern over the energy crisis. "And it will cost the bloody earth in upkeep, petrol, insurance...."

"Ah, madame, do not worry," the executive said, producing a wad of papers and manuals and log books from a thin briefcase. "We have opened an account at the Mercedes garage in town; all the bills will come automatically to our company, mademoiselle van Niekerk will not have to pay for a thing."

"Jesus Christ," Jennifer said.

Everyone else from the château had come out and was standing around. The executive said, "Perhaps Mademoiselle would like to take her car for a short drive?"

I looked dubiously at the controls. They were nothing like the Renault's. "I wouldn't know how," I said.

"Then perhaps, if you would permit me to accompany you, I could be of assistance. It is really quite easy to drive."

I opened the driver's door and got in. The executive opened the passenger door, but then suddenly thought better of it. He said to Jennifer, "But, madame, perhaps you would like to come too? I will sit in the back, I can easily show mademoiselle van Niekerk all she needs to know from there."

"Monsieur, Jews do not ride around in Mercedes-Benz cars."

This was news to me. In India, I knew for a fact, van Niekerk had owned a large Mercedes; Jennifer had gone everywhere in it. The announcement stopped the executive though. For a second he stood immobile, holding the door. Then he said very understandingly, as if expressing condolences at a bereavement, "Ah, well, if madame has those feelings, I quite understand...."

He was beginning to seat himself in the car when Philippe said, "I'll come, then. I'm not Jewish."

"But of course," the man said getting out again. There then followed a slight hiatus. I couldn't see either of their faces from where I was sitting, but it was obvious from the postures of the lower halves of their bodies that they held differing expectations. Philippe was waiting for the executive to climb into the narrow back compartment of the car, the executive was waiting for Philippe to perform this feat. Philippe later claimed that he had been quite aware of this, that he knew the executive expected him to sit in the back. My feeling is that he was just acting out of a loutish unawareness of the proprieties; he'd heard the man offer to sit in the back for Jennifer and it hadn't occurred to him that in this case the same gallantry didn't apply. After a few seconds the man said, rather testily, *"Après vous...."*

Philippe climbed into the back seat, or shelf as it, in fact, was. The executive finally seated himself next to me. After a certain amount of elementary instruction, I drove off. I swung the car slowly around on the gravel courtyard, its headlights picking out the members of the household and the other executive who stood silently to one side of the group. He had not said a word. He hadn't even been introduced, which is odd for the French, who spend half their time introducing themselves and each other. I hoped somebody would remember to invite him inside. I had a vision of him still being in exactly the same spot when we returned, like one of those trees with its shadow painted on the ground in *Marienbad*. Just as we were drawing away from the château and the man was explaining about selecting second gear, Jennifer shouted, "Oi! Stop!"

I stalled the car. I looked back to where I could just see my mother opening the boot of the Renault which was parked under the trees. She lifted a large wicker basket filled with empty bottles from the car and walked over to us. The executive pressed a button and his window retracted.

"Madame?"

"Here, you might as well do something useful on this joy ride, you can fill these."

"What?"

"With water. There's a spring. My daughter knows where it is."

"But of course, madame, delighted."

The man opened his door again and Jennifer passed the basket into the car. With a bit of leaning and shoving we managed to pass if between the two of us to Philippe in the back. It was too large to fit neatly on the shelf beside Philippe, so we eventually arranged it, tilted at an angle, in the centre of the car, wedged between the back window and the two front seats. Philippe sat sideways, his legs under the suspended basket, his head a few centimetres from my left ear. We drove away, the bottles clanking when I changed gear.

Jennifer, of course, claims she had foreseen the results of giving us the bottles, that she had given them to us to deliberately provoke the ensuing disaster. I no more believe her than I do Philippe. We often collect water from the spring; it's a considerable improvement on the stuff that comes out of the taps. The spring itself is about a quarter of an hour's drive from the château, but the last ten minutes are along a bumpy, unmade road. Cart track would be a better description. So I took a longer route, wishing to learn a bit more about the car before trying the rough stuff. Things became quite jolly in the car. I introduced Philippe and myself to the man. His name was Henri Boufflet, he was third in command of the company's Paris office and a great admirer of my father. I crunched the gears a few times, stalled on a couple of occasions, turned on the wipers when I wanted to dim the dashboard lights and generally gave Henri considerable scope for instructing me. Philippe, too, proved a mine of opinionated adolescent advice. He's two years younger than I am and at that time had a bad case of pimples. I was almost beginning to like the car, to feel the pride of possession. It would allow me far more freedom of movement than the mobylette; I could transport my friends, I could visit Paris and London much more easily than I had been able to do when dependent on trains. Henri began to give me a potted history of the Mercedes company and a list of its recent achievements in the Monte-Carlo rally, the Grand Prix, and other motoring events. If I was interested in visiting Le Mans with him, I only had to give the office a ring. The telephone number was on the insurance papers of the car. The car itself, he ought to explain, was actually the property of the company. It was all mine to use as I wished, of course, but for various reasons of sound business it was officially a company car. No one, well no one in the business world, actually owned their cars these days. Even my father himself—and Henri Boufflet was well acquainted with the contents of van Niekerk's Kensington garage, splendid cars the lot of them, especially the Bentley—didn't own a single car! Even the vintage models were company cars.

"Well, fancy that," Philippe said behind my left ear.

I turned the car onto the cart track. Although the surface was rough, the track itself was reasonably level. There was a thin line of unworn grass in the middle, but no danger of scraping the Mercedes's underside. Between the two walls of trees I drove steadily, but slowly up the track. It was now quite dark.

"We must beware of wolves," Henri said.

The track rose gently for about a kilometre, emerging from the forest at one point to traverse a small field of corn before plunging back into the trees. It levelled out for a few hundred metres and then began the descent. The spring is on the side of a nondescript hill and has been enclosed by a low stone wall. Water spills over a lip in the wall in a thin stream that allows one to fill bottles easily. I brought the car to a halt with its headlights illuminating the spring.

As we filled the bottles, Henri became quite jovial. He clearly wasn't the country type; he didn't know where to put his feet in the mud and running water below the spring and he flicked ineffectually at the bottoms of his trousers a few times, but he was in a mood for the adventure of it all. Philippe left us to the task in hand and sat in the driver's seat. I heard the windscreen wipers start. The lights changed to low beam and went out.

"Hey, stop wrecking my car," I yelled.

The turning lights came on, intermittently flooding the scene in a pale yellow glow. The horn sounded, the radio burst into a loud rendition of the evening's news, changed to an equally loud piece of bubble-gum music which died suddenly as the lights came on again and the electric motors that worked the windows whined into life.

"Don't touch the brakes or gear-stick," Henri shouted.

"I'm not stupid," Philippe muttered audibly.

Henri passed me the last bottle, saying, "I think we should relieve your brother of his command, mademoiselle."

"Anasuya."

"Anasuya."

Fitting the basket of the now full bottles into the car proved harder than before. Henri initially tried to fit it into the boot, but the basket was too big and the bottles could not be placed in by themselves as many of them had no corks and had to be kept upright. Eventually, we fitted ourselves in much as before and I drove off. In order to turn around, it was necessary to drive on half a kilometre to the bottom of the hill, where one could turn into a field.

The water from the spring flows down a ditch at the side of the road and crosses the road itself at this point in a slowly flowing stream. *Ford* is too grand a word. I hit the stream faster than I intended, some muddy water splattered onto the windscreen.

"Yee ha!" Philippe yelled as if we had just stormed a mighty river.

"Careful," Henri said.

I brought the car to a halt and then slowly turned it to face the track into the field. There is a gate into the field itself, but set back far enough to allow a car to perform an easy three-point turn. Beside the track is a ditch into which the spring water flows after crossing the road. Behind me Philippe said, "We better clean the windscreen."

He insinuated his arm between me and the door and flicked a switch on the dashboard. The windscreen was instantly covered with a thin coating of mud which the wiper arms then rubbed vigorously into the glass.

"*Merde*," Philippe said, "we need the washer, hang on...."

He flicked a couple of switches. The light inside the car came on, the headlights went out. I couldn't see anything beyond the glass, but as I'd stopped the car completely by this time I wasn't overly worried.

"Cut it out, for Christ's sake, Philippe," I said. I was half annoyed, half amused. I love Philippe, he's a lout and a lunatic and completely barbaric.

"Just a minute, I'll have it clean in a second."

"You're an utter maniac, Philippe...."

Philippe was by this time playing the scene for all it was worth. Like me, he believed that with the car stationary nothing could happen. He began punching buttons and flicking switches with complete abandon. The heater fan started, the radio burst into life again, the hazard lights began to flash.

"Hang on a bit, all we need is the bloody washer."

"Stop it, boy!" Henri said with authority.

"Where the fuck's that knob?"

Suddenly there was a piercing scream from under the bonnet. It rose rapidly through half a dozen octaves and just as rapidly descended. All the riot waggons in Paris were hidden under the damn thing.

"Christ!" I yelled.

"For all your furniture and household goods, *Monsieur Meuble* is at your call...." The radio yelled above the siren.

"Shit," Philippe shouted, "what the fuck's gone wrong?"

By this time he had both arms around the back of my seat and was leaning half over my shoulder scrabbling at the dashboard with all ten fingers like a crazed concert pianist.

"Stop it, boy!" Henri leant over from the passenger seat and attempted to wrest Philippe's fingers from the controls. I was squashed between the pair of them, two pairs of fighting hands more or less in my lap.

"Buzz off," Philippe shouted.

"So give *Monsieur Meuble* a ring on 276 980342...."

"Let go, bugger you!"

"Stop struggling, you little fool."

Henri now had a firm grip on one of Philippe's wrists. Philippe was wildly fending off Henri's attempts to secure the other wrist, while still managing to flick the odd switch or two. The headlights came on again. The siren continued its ear-splitting scream. The wipers kept grinding mud into the windscreen. Henri made a conclusive grab at Philippe's free wrist, knocking my thigh as he did so. My foot slipped from the clutch pedal. The car shot forward. Through the haze of mud on the window I saw the five bars of the gate coming towards us. I jerked the wheel round while slamming my foot on the brake. The car stalled, but continued to slide slowly into the ditch. The sound of a headlight splintering came dully through the screaming of the siren and the gibbering of the radio. The shock was minimal, but sufficient to tip half a dozen bottles of spring water into the front of the car. They landed on Henri, prone, as he more or less was, across the gap between the two seats. Henri swore, released Philippe's wrists and sat upright. He started to rub the back of his neck where a bottle had hit him.

"Turn it off," I yelled, "Turn that fucking thing off!"

Henri leaned forward again, located a switch somewhere under the dashboard and extinguished the screaming. I found the radio switch and turned that off as well. The total silence in the car was broken after a few seconds by Philippe saying in English, "You great fuckwit, you great mongoloid loon."

The phrases were Jennifer's. At that time they were about the only English words he knew. He hasn't much of a flair for languages, old Philippe. He said them again.

"Be quiet!" snapped Henri.

"You did it, I saw you do it," Philippe said, "You knocked my sister's foot off the pedal. Now look what's happened. The car's a write-off."

Henri flung open his door and stepped angrily into the night.

"Jesus, Philippe, did you have to?"

"If it hadn't been for him...."

"I know, I know, but if it hadn't been for you also...."

"Sorry. I don't think there's all that much wrong with the car. Just a headlight probably."

"I've only had it an hour."

"Never mind, Jennifer will be pleased."

"That's true," I said, "I think we ought to get out."

Because of the way the car was angled into the ditch, I could only open my door a few centimetres. I clambered clumsily to the passenger door. Philippe extracted himself from the back, upsetting a few more bottles as he did so. Henri seemed to have disappeared. After a few minutes he materialised out of the gloom. I think he had started to walk back to the château, but then thought better of it. It was some distance and I doubt that he could have remembered the way. Maybe he was frightened of van Niekerk, or wolves. Maybe I'm doing him an injustice, perhaps he'd just gone for a stroll to cool down.

Removing the car from the ditch took about half an hour. We pushed it and pulled it, stuffed twigs and leaves under its wildly spinning wheels. Henri and Philippe swore at each other. Philippe made a number of helpful suggestions. Henri's suit was completely wrecked. A few more bottles of water were spilt. Both outside and inside the car became covered in mud. When we eventually got it free, Henri insisted on driving. I didn't object. Apart from my giving directions we drove home in silence, although at one point I did ask, "What is that siren thing?"

"Burglar alarm."

Jennifer was not only pleased, she was delighted. She turned on all the château's outside lights and walked around the battered car as if it were a Christmas cake.

"Don't ever clean it, Anasuya. Don't ever clean it."

* * * * * * *

It was at about this time that I inherited, was given, the Bottomless Pit as my joint bank account with my father became known. Up until I was fifteen, van Niekerk sent cheques every now and then to Jennifer for my upkeep or maintenance or whatever the word is—those two make me sound like a house or a machine. When I was fifteen, Jennifer told him to send the money directly to me. I opened a bank account and regularly deposited and withdrew whatever sums were appropriate. Then, one time when I was visiting van Niekerk in London, he said, "Anasuya, all this sending of cheques is fairly silly. It would be simpler for us both if we had a joint account."

I couldn't really see the logic of this, but I didn't object. So I became one of the signatories to an account with a Paris bank. The cheques had both our names printed on them. In theory van Niekerk could have used this account as well, could have withdrawn from it. All he did, I'm sure, was deposit as much as was required to cover my withdrawals. The statements were sent to his address, I never saw them. The result was that van Niekerk had a record of how much I'd withdrawn and I had no idea how much was in the account.

"But what if there isn't enough and the cheque bounces?"

"Anasuya, that simply could not happen. Don't worry about it. No reasonable expenditure of yours could break the account. And all your expenditures are reasonable. You lead a quite frugal life, if you don't mind me saying so. Now you're almost grown up, now you are a young woman, you should think more about living in the style that you can easily afford. What are you going to do between leaving school and going to university?"

"Just relax. Read, write, paint my room, read some proper novels for a change, not the Great Literature we have to study for the *bac*. I'll come to London at some stage."

"Why don't you come to New York? I'll be there for a few weeks in June."

"I'd rather see you in London. I don't particularly want to go to New York."

I didn't either. The idea appalled. I had more than enough to occupy me in France and England without going to that violent, strange, and forbidding city.

But I was still worried about the bank account. I *needed* to know how much was in it. Even if there was bound to be more than I could possibly spend. The idea of just signing cheques, even cheques for fifty francs, against a totally unspecified hoard in a strange Paris bank unsettled me. I moaned about this to Jean-Claude.

"If your father says your cheques can't bounce, I'm sure they can't. Even if there isn't enough in the account to cover a cheque, I'm sure the bank manager has a standing order to transfer money into it from one of van Niekerk's other accounts. The man must have dozens of them. Any cheque of yours would ultimately draw on his whole financial empire. Don't worry."

It sounds preposterous to grizzle about having too much money, but the point is this: I was now denied absolutely the experience of drawing up a budget of any kind. I couldn't genuinely make a decision to buy x instead of y, since I could buy both x and y and p, q, and r as well. If I went to the record shop in town with my friends after school, participation in that thoroughly normal scene, rifling through the racks of records, requesting the playing of dozens of different tracks from dozens of different discs as part of the slow elimination of all but one contender for the scarce resources of adolescence, was something I could not take part in. I could buy anything in the shop. I could buy the shop. If I wished to give my friends presents, there was nothing to stop me. Of course I would have been too embarrassed to attempt buying presents on other than socially acceptable occasions like birthdays and Christmas. But it was also embarrassing for me to be in places such as record shops at a time when my friends were deciding on their purchases.

I couldn't really take part in the conversation. My friends preferred to go shopping without me. I preferred to go shopping without them. I took to carrying very small amounts of change. If we went to a café, my deliberately induced penury might force me genuinely to choose between another coffee or a brioche. As it was, I think my general rate of expenditure declined with the acquisition of the Bottomless Pit. It may have been this phenomenon which, in part, caused van Niekerk to give me the Merc. It might have been a way of forcing my hand. I don't know, it's a theory.

The only people I really enjoyed shopping with were Jennifer and Philippe. They stole. I stole too. I know that the psychology of shop lifting is complicated. A lot of shop-lifters are well off middle-class women who do not really need what they steal. Their motive is said to be lack of love. If the world will not give them what they desire, they will take it for themselves. It does not detract from this explanation that what they really want is love and what they steal are clothes, luxuries, and food. What they steal *symbolises* love. Well, that's a theory too. We were taught it in slightly more detail in Psychology I at the University of Liverpool. It might be true of some people, it certainly wasn't true for the three of us. The one thing we all were was loved. Philippe stole because he wanted whatever it was he stole, really needed it. There was nothing arbitrary about his choices. Jennifer stole because she resented the high cost of living in France. It is more expensive to live in France than it is in England, wildly more expensive than Italy or Greece, let alone India. Jennifer regarded this as unreasonable. An item stolen was a blow for reason. She resented paying. I stole because it was unreasonable that I could have anything I wanted without effort. I resented not paying. By stealing, by risking detection and apprehension and possible conviction, I was paying for what I stole: the goods were being obtained at some cost.

We were a merry and quite successful band of shoplifters, although we were caught every now and then of course.

* * * * * * *

I have been trying to think my way into Jennifer's mind at the time when we lived in New Delhi. I was six when we were deported (or, rather, when van Niekerk was deported; I suppose Jennifer and I could have stayed) and I have only fairly hazy memories of my early childhood. Indeed, I'm not really sure how much is memory and how much is pseudo-memory, the result of the stories I've been told, the albums of photographs we still have, and the two or three times I have read Jennifer's *The Tides of Winter*. Certainly some of the 'memories' I have are a bit like photographs, fixed scenes: our house seen from the garden, my ayah teaching me to sew, Jennifer and van Niekerk fighting about something at the dinner table, the bundi painting of Krishna and the cowherds that hung in an alcove beside Jennifer's writing table. I remember being taken to watch the Presidential Bodyguard playing polo: a dusty field surrounded by thorn bushes, horses and men milling around waving long wooden hammers at each other, a marquee set up on the sidelines, and the tinny voice of a loudspeaker saying unintelligible things; van Niekerk storming up to Sarojini, my ayah, demanding 'Where's memsahib?' and Sarojini saying, 'I don't know, sahib' and Daddy shouting, 'You know well enough, damn you!' and storming off; dust.

Then a scene, I suppose it must have been at the same time, of Jennifer and an officer of the Bodyguard appearing on horseback from one of the paths that led away from the polo field and Daddy rushing at the officer, trying to pull him off the horse, a lot of commotion, two polo players galloping up, and then Daddy being held back by some men, blood on his cheek, Sarojini quickly leading me away, but not before I'd seen Jennifer's face—proud, defiant, sadistic. But how much of that is real memory? I remember very clearly realising that the officer was Jennifer's lover, but at four-and-a-half or five, or however old I was then, I wouldn't have known what a lover was. And Jennifer has subsequently described the incident to me in considerable detail, and, of course, made use of it in an altered form in her Mutiny novel, *Pig Fat and Chapatties* (she's good at titles, my mother). Every damn European writer who lives any length of time in India ends up writing a Mutiny novel, just as any Indian writer worth his salt has a crack at the great Partition novel. Jennifer was no exception to the general rule.

But the point I have to come to terms with about our life in India is that we were not a very pretty family. I cannot feel at all sympathetic to these three characters, Mr and Mrs van Niekerk and their snotty little daughter, living their affluent neo-colonialist lives amongst the poverty and squalor and beauty of the real India. Jennifer is reasonably good at languages, but in the seven years she was there she probably learnt no more than three dozen Hindi words. I certainly didn't learn any more myself, and it is impossible to *stop* a child learning a language unless you prevent her from playing with the people who speak it. Some of our servants spoke only Hindi, but then I didn't play with the servants or their children, except for Sarojini and she had a *degree* in English Literature from the University of Bombay or somewhere (which was considerably more education than that possessed by Memsahib van Niekerk, aspiring author, for whom she worked). I have a few of these 'memories' of mine of Indian India. Mainly they are things seen from the windows of our car: street scenes, bullock carts, people on bicycles, the fields of Rajasthan covered with vivid yellow flowers (mustard? rape? saffron?), the body of a dead cow being eaten by vultures (you couldn't see the cow at all, nor the heads of the vultures, just a grey, seething mound of wings). It distresses me that I know so little about the land of my birth, that for the first six formative years of my life I lived in a type of cultural vacuum, isolated by money and language from the people amongst whom I was born. All I have inherited from India is my given name.

But of course I wasn't born among Indians. I was born among wealthy ex-patriots in a British hospital attached to the British High Commission. The Indians in the circles my parents moved in were all westernised to the nth degree, they wore western

clothes, spoke Oxbridge English, sent their children to imitation British public schools or packed them off to England itself
to attend the real things (which are now, of course, pale shades
of their Indian imitators), they drank whisky from Scotland and
wine from France and exploited their servants far more than
the Europeans did. I wasn't isolated by money or language
from these people. All this bleeding-heart liberal regret about
not having known India proper is something I have acquired
long after we were deported. At the time I no more regarded the
India of our servants as my country than I did the moon. And in
caste-ridden India our servants were probably closer socially to
us than they were to a landless Harijan peasant. But I wouldn't
even have known what a landless Harijan peasant was; the low
mud villages and the figures by the side of the road were less
interesting, less delightful, to my childish eye than the waving
fields of mustard flowers. There is one scene of rural India that I
remember, though. It is this: we were driving somewhere (being
driven by our chauffeur that is) and were passing a group of
villagers on the road. The car was almost at a standstill, the
road being blocked by bullock carts and people, our driver was
blasting away with the horn, the people were ignoring us. I
noticed a girl of about my own age—thin, wearing a faded and
tattered sari, bare feet of course—in charge of a thin cow or
bullock. As I watched, the animal lifted its tail to defecate. The
girl darted towards the beast, managing to catch the dung before
it hit the ground. She began patting the dung into a manageable
lump. Our car moved on. I noticed that Jennifer had seen the
girl's actions as well.

"Mummy, why did she do that?"

"Oh, I don't know, darling, the Indians just do things like
that."

"But why, it's dirty."

"Yes, but they don't mind so much."

"But why did she do it?"

"I don't know. Ask Daddy."

Daddy was sitting beside her, but she often told me to ask

him things like that. Van Niekerk, of course, had heard her, but he usually waited for me to actually formulate the question, which seemed reasonable to me, polite in a way. I said, "Why did she catch the cow's poo?"

"I don't know. Ask Venu."

I was sitting next to the driver who was taking no notice of the conversation, but exercising the Mercedes' horn on two cyclists who were weaving about near the centre of the road.

"Venu, why did she do it?"

"What, miss?"

"The little girl. Why did she catch the poo?"

"I don't know, miss."

"Oh come on," Daddy said, half crossly, half joking, "you know everything about India."

"Yes, sahib," Venu said and was silent.

"Well, why did she do it, then?"

"To make fire, sahib."

"What?" I said.

"They burn it, miss."

"Why?" I said.

"I don't know, miss."

"Oh, for Christ's sake, Venu," Jennifer said, "Do you have to answer 'I don't know'" (imitation Indian accent) "to every question you're asked?"

"No, memsahib."

"Well, why do they burn it then?"

"For cooking, memsahib."

"So they gather the cow dung in order to burn it as fuel for cooking purposes?"

"Yes, memsahib."

"Good. Now do you understand, Anasuya?"

"Yes," I said.

The thing to note is that this whole idiot conversation could have been forestalled in the first place had Jennifer decided to tell me herself. No one can be quite that estranged from the way of life of a country they are living in not to know such commonplace information as the fact that cow dung is a major source of fuel. But this conversation is typical of the whole setup at the time (and if my memory of the incident is at fault and I haven't got it down quite right, this sort of conversation went on endlessly). We were all constantly proclaiming complete ignorance of all the mundane and boring things that constituted the other person's world, so any demand for an explanation was likely to be shifted sideways. It was a case of using ignorance as a major form of aggression. The other trick we all used (the mirror image of the ignorance one) was knowing better than the speaker what the speaker really meant.

"I'm too tired to go out this evening," Jennifer would say.

"What your mother means," van Niekerk would say to me, "is that she can't be *bothered* to go out this evening."

"What Daddy means is he wants to drag me out to some damn cocktail party and if I won't go he's going to become extremely unpleasant."

"Jennifer, do you have to be so aggressive," van Niekerk would say aggressively.

"See," Jennifer would say to me with exaggerated resignation, "he's starting already."

"Do you have to bring the child into this?"

"It hurts him," Jennifer would say to me, "that you see him as he really is. He would like you to think of him as the perfect daddy who never says a cross word to anybody."

"I would like you to stop using the child as a way of attacking me."

"Mummy doesn't really mean it," I would say anxiously, trying to patch things up, "She really wants to go to the party only she has a headache."

"No," Jennifer would contradict, "Mummy really means it, Mummy can't be bothered going to this dreary party because she is fed up to the back teeth with Daddy's bloody parties and Daddy's bloody friends. She wants to stay in her own home and play her own piano and write her own letters."

"She really wants to go out and visit her own friends, the

soldiers."

"Pieter, do you mind not parading your sickening jealousy quite so blatantly in front of Anasuya?"

"Ha! You don't like the truth, do you?" Daddy would say and leave the room.

Jennifer would stamp around, slamming open the lid of the piano, playing a few notes, standing up, rooting through the piles of sheet music for some piece, slamming the lid shut, and then walking over to hug me silently for a long time. I would cuddle into her embrace.

"Daddy doesn't really mean it," I would say.

"I wish he didn't, darling, but he does."

Pretty nasty stuff, all told. We none of us look very appealing, not the sort of people you'd want to know. I can remember a conversation in our kitchen in Putney not long after Kilminster had moved in. We were sitting around late one night eating toast covered with some very odd jam that Kilminster's mother had sent him.

"So," Jennifer said, "do you like it here, James?"

"Yes, of course," Kilminster mumbled through the toast.

"You wouldn't always have liked us. Well, you certainly wouldn't have liked *me*, say three years ago.... God I was awful. I've changed though, I'm almost human now. But if I do anything really obnoxious you must tell me. Promise?"

Kilminster looked a bit startled. I can remember being a bit startled myself. At that age it hadn't really occurred to me that adults could change; Jennifer's airy assurance that she had once been awful was a little disturbing. Maybe she would become awful again. I looked at Kilminster. He blushed slightly; he was only nineteen, fresh out of a seminary, and this was his landlady talking to him, a married woman with a nine-year-old daughter.

"I'm sure you wouldn't do anything…err…obnoxious."

"I wouldn't bet on it if I were you. You should have known me in India. I was vain, self-centred, a social snob, vile to the servants. Actually she wasn't all that much better." Jennifer gestured towards me with a piece of toast. "You should have heard her ordering the servants around. You wait till you read the story I'm doing at the moment, it's all there."

And indeed it is all there. The short story she was then working on eventually grew into her novel, *The Tides of Winter*, in which there is a fairly nasty mixed-up little girl called Anna. *Tides* contains a scene in which Anna, aged four, is taunting an old gardener. The old gardener plants a flower, Anna stamps on it giggling with pleasure; he plants another, Anna stamps on that; the gardener remonstrates with her softly in Hindi. Anna understands no Hindi, she starts a chant of 'silly old man, silly old man', the gardener takes another seedling from the box and plants it; Anna, giggling, stamps on it. The gardener decides on passive resistance. Slowly he stands up (he is very old), bends down again, and picks up the box of seedlings. He begins to walk across the lawn to the servants' quarters carrying the box. Anna seeing the source of her fun disappearing, grabs at the box, knocking it to the ground. The gardener bends slowly to pick up the spilt seedlings, Anna rushes in and stamps wildly on the lot. (Right little bitch, eh? Want to box her ears? Well Anna was me.)

In Jennifer's book, Anna's mother then appears. She slaps the child quite violently and yells and screams at the gardener. "Look! Just look at this!" pointing to the smashed flowers on the lawn.

In response to this obvious command the gardener looks at the flowers at his feet. "Just look at them!" The gardener looks even harder.

Anna's mother marches across to the flower bed. "Oh, Christ! Look, just look at what you've let her do. They're ruined, absolutely ruined. As if it isn't hard enough to get anything to grow in this bloody climate as it is. Just look at this."

The gardener moves as quickly as he can towards the flowerbed to fulfil these further injunctions to look, but before he can get there Anna's mother waves him away. "God, you people are hopeless," she declares, walking back to the house. "You can't even control a four-year-old child. No wonder the country is in such a mess." (Want to box Anna's mother's ears as well? That's Jennifer.)

What isn't in Tides is the information that Anna's mother (read Anasuya's mother, read Jennifer) had watched the entire scene from its inception from behind the blinds of her bedroom window. She wished to see what her daughter and the gardener would actually do. As for the flowers—poof!—who cares? Her husband had lots of money and it's unlikely that they cost more than the glass of smuggled malt whisky she was sipping.

In fairness to Jennifer I had better add that she did try to instruct the servants not to bow to my every imperious command. They were told not to pick up things that I dropped or left lying around, they were told to insist that I tidied my own room, put my own toys away. It was a good try, but doomed to a canute-like failure. If it is possible to instruct a Hindu cook or sweeper to order the sahib's child around, it was beyond Jennifer's ability to do so. Even by Sarojini, who was as high-class Brahmin as it's possible to get, I was never actually made to do anything. I loved Sarojini and, as far as I can remember, co-operated with her in most things, but if I wanted my own way badly enough, there was no question but that I should get it. The only time I ever really bowed to authority in those first years of my life, was when Jennifer stood over me, out-gunning me.

I don't want to excuse the way Jennifer or I acted in those days, in many respects we were obnoxious. But I think, curiously enough, the whole Indian experience was somehow good for Jennifer; she left India a far stronger person than she had been when she arrived. Her whole childhood had been spent under the thumbs of her parents and brother. Whatever sense of self she had, it was not one in which she was powerful, capable of influencing her own life and the lives of others around her. There was no way in which she could get people to do what she wished, either by order or suggestion. And, having escaped from her family into the arms of van Niekerk, she probably found herself almost as powerless. Then, suddenly, she was transported to a situation in which eight or nine people were at her bidding; in which, by virtue of the power of her money alone, she was able to command. So command she did, in the worst traditions of the now defunct Raj, in a capricious, sometimes bullying, sometimes patronising, often gratuitous manner. (Well, that may be putting it a bit strongly. At times she was quite friendly, warm even, towards her servants. I think the key word is capricious; at any one time the attitude she adopted was a product of her own half-understood moods, not something intrinsic to the situation itself). So in this odd, quite unpleasant way, Jennifer became powerful, possessed of a sense of her own effectiveness. That this effectiveness was the product of a monstrously hierarchical social setting is regrettable, but it was still effectiveness, something she had not experienced before.

Life in India is very much to do with hierarchies. Caste has been officially abolished, the forty-something divisions of the Raj's Order of Precedence—Viceroy at the top, inspectors of drains at the bottom—have been given the boot, but it takes more than laws and decrees to change social custom. I've developed a theory that explains the fascination the Mutiny holds for English writers. It was a time when the hierarchies cracked, the lower orders rebelled. Although the Mutiny was well over a century ago, it is quite easy for English writers with some experience of India to project themselves back to that time. Social relations were Victorian, military, and hierarchical and, since the Indian content of Mutiny novels is always to do with the sepoys who remained more or less soldiers in the mould they had been forced into by the Raj, it is not necessary to know very much about India *per se*. Even the best English writers say very little about Indian village life or society in general. This is true of Paul Scott, J. G. Farrell, and poor old John Masters; it is certainly true of my mother. To see what I mean, look at a proper Indian novel, a Partition novel, one to do with what it means to be a Hindu or a Sikh or Moslem. There is no way that any of the writers I've mentioned could have produced Kushwant Singh's Train to Pakistan even though at least two of them are better writers than Singh. They wouldn't know enough about village life to start with, and anyway their preoccupations are quite different to Singh's.

My mother's novel, *Pig Fat and Chapatties*, is probably her meanest, most uncharitable book. If the people in it have any endearing traits at all, they are of the blustering buffoon type, the jovial old codger who really doesn't know what's happening sort. The British, especially the British women, are depicted as narrow-minded, obsessive, insensitive, and capable only of a jingoistic patriotism and automatic loyalty to a series of shibboleths (Empire, Flag, Queen, Regiment, Home) that proves useful only in blinding them to reality right up to their grisly deaths. In a sense the women in the book are stronger characters than the men, but only because their prejudices are stronger. The sepoys are possessed of a mixture of Hindu fatalism, respect for caste, British-imposed military structures, capacity for thoughtless action, and a mystical unawareness of what their own mutiny is all about (or should be all about). The novel, needless to say, appeared to a very mixed reception. A lot of reviewers and people in my mother's circle of friends didn't like it simply because all the characters were so nasty.

"But really, Jennifer," I can remember Tamar saying, "who'd want to know these people?"

"I knew them all in Delhi."

"But did you *want* to know them? If it hadn't been your book I wouldn't have read more than thirty pages."

"How often do you read novels these days?"

"Often enough, Jennifer, often enough."

The book was attacked from the right as being entirely insensitive to the subtleties of the British presence in India, of missing the mutually supportive aspects of the relationships between the English and the natives, and among the English themselves; it was attacked for being in effect a caricature. And while this might have been conservative criticism, some of it was quite effective and obviously written by old geezers who knew a lot more about India than Jennifer. The Left loved the way Jennifer had handled the British, but weren't very happy about what she'd done with the Indians, but usually for pretty spurious reasons (one loon seemed to think the Mutiny was a full-blown war of independence conducted with a view to introducing socialism and worker's participation). I think Jennifer's hatred of book reviewers stemmed from this time. She herself was firmly convinced that *Pig Fat* was brilliant. She doesn't think this anymore, but she still regards her first novel as one of her most significant. It's easy to see why. Or it's easy for me to see why.

She wrote the book in a period of intense self-doubt, at a time when she was reacting to everything she had been in India. It was a case of the lady protesting too much. We are all, I suppose, hypersensitive to the same negative aspects of other people's characters that we have only just managed to suppress in ourselves. Jennifer has worked this into a complex and quite subtle way of coming to terms with herself. If you ever want to know what Jennifer is really worried about in relation to herself, all you have to do is note what she is most vehemently accusing other people of. The difference between Jennifer and most people being that in her case she sometimes invents actions and motives which suit her needs and gratuitously ascribes them to the other party. The process can be a bit annoying in real life, but it has its uses as a source of her fiction. What she was saying in *Pig Fat* was, 'Look at these people, I am aware of their faults and vices, hence I cannot be like them. This book is written from an outsider's viewpoint. I am not part of what I describe.' But of course she was, or had been. And the book is really a working through, a coming to terms with, an attempt to make explicit and understand, whole sections of her personality, while at the same time rejecting them. Looked at in this light, the novel is a powerful document. But still, while it might work as a journal of unacknowledged self-discovery, it doesn't work very well as fiction. For as Tamar said, who wants to know? What *Pig Fat* needs is its sequel, the account of what the author then did with herself, what replaced all the negative aspects. In a sense *The Tides of Winter* is this sequel. It was written straight after *Pig Fat*, indeed it was started on the day the other novel was finished. Some parts of it, for example the flower-stamping scene I've mentioned, are redolent of the mean, capricious behaviour of the British in *Pig Fat*. But *Tides* is an altogether more subtle book; Jennifer's characters are more rounded, more complex and far more ambiguous. The book's standpoint has a far greater humanism. And while it is true that its author still didn't understand much more about India or Indians, one of the most powerful incidents in the book concerns an Indian woman who has run away from her husband to London.

The husband is a politician who has been made a member of the upper house by the Prime Minister a short time before this event. The Prime Minister calls the husband into her office and berates him for allowing his wife to leave; he hasn't been granted the high honour of a parliamentary position just to bring the party into disrepute by the scandal of his domestic life. He is despatched to London to retrieve his wife. After some torrid scenes in the house of an English friend in which Sujatha, his wife, has sought refuge, the politician succeeds in persuading her to return to India with him. Once back in India Sujatha becomes desperately unhappy and attempts to kill herself, but fails. She writes a long, agonised letter to her friend in London. The English woman flies to Delhi and the two of them embark on a train trip to southern India. One evening in the train, the women fall into conversation with a wealthy landowner who attacks the role played by the Congress Party in land reform. There is an argument about what the rest of the population thinks about these land reform measures. To test their theories, the two women leave the first-class compart-ment in which they are travelling and engage the occupants of a second-class compartment in discussion. This done, they move to a third-class compartment. The two women have been drinking steadily since the early afternoon and have taken a bottle of brandy with them from which they take sizable slugs between compartments. By the time they alight from the third-class carriage at a station in order to walk back to their own compartment, they are both quite drunk. "Of course," Sujatha says, "we should do this properly, find out what the real people think." She gestures towards the roof of the train where those too poor to travel inside are sitting. Egging each other on, the women climb up to the roof. The station master remonstrates with them and threatens to prevent the train leaving the station, but the women are adamant that they won't come down. Finally the train continues on its way with the women on the roof. The other roof-sitters display a mixture of curiosity and indifference to the women. Attempts to engage in serious conversation about land reform fail completely, so for a while the two women sit silently watching the countryside sliding past them—the fields, villages, temples, and the silver belt of the river, all very still in the moonlight. This stillness and the apparent emptiness of the countryside contrasts dramatically with the clanking, snorting train and its human cargo. The women pass the bottle between each other until it is drained. Sujatha then makes one last attempt at completing her survey of opinions. An old man unwinds the cloth from his face and speaks half a dozen resigned sentences to her in Tamil.

"What did he say?"

"He says everything is an illusion. Mrs Ghandi is an illusion, land reform is an illusion, the Congress Party is an illusion, New Delhi is an illusion. None of them exist."

The train rounds a curve and the smoke is wafted back from the stack along the roof of the train. The old man re-wraps his cloth around his face and retreats into silence. The women decide to climb down the rungs at the end of the carriage to the exposed footplates that link it to the next carriage. They stand up drunkenly and begin the descent. Sujatha slips and falls. It is not clear to her companion whether she has fallen beside the train or under it. In desperation the English woman climbs down to the footplate, gains access to the crowded third-class carriage and tries wildly to locate the emergency chain. There isn't one. She cannot make herself understood. In desperation she opens a door and jumps out. The train is probably only travelling at twenty-five miles an hour. The ground hits her with a jolt and she tumbles down a small embankment, breaking an arm and suffering slight concussion. She is found half an hour later by her friend who has survived with only cuts, abrasions, and bruises.

After a certain amount of not very convincing black comedy involving attempts to organise some sleepy villagers into giving these two shambling, semi-delirious, tattered apparitions succour for the night, the women find themselves in the cabin of a truck being taken to the nearest town with a doctor.

"Of course," Sujatha says, "he was right, that old man."

"What old man?"

"On top of the train. It all is an illusion. Mrs Ghandi, New Delhi, my husband, your husband, marriage, children, illusion, all illusion. None of it exists."

"At the moment only my arm exists."

From that point on the novel details the women's ultimately successful attempts to leave their husbands. At various times both women resort to the stratagem of declaring their husbands to be illusions. In a way it is an ultimate refinement of the igno-rance-as-aggression trick.

"You will *not* desert me. You will *not* make a fool of me in front of my party colleagues," Sujatha's husband storms at her.

"But you do not exist. The party does not exist," Sujatha blandly replies, looking straight through him.

Obviously there are limits to the thesis that if you declare something non-existent it will go away, but the technique has its uses, as Jennifer found when she finally organised herself into breaking with my father. It was that experience which provided much of the source material for *The Tides of Winter* of course. (Incidentally, the genesis of the train story was a trip Jennifer once took with her closest Delhi friend, Anasuya—the other of her friends after whom I was named—to Madras. They did sample the political opinions of the first-, second- and third-class carriages while mildly drunk, but never went anywhere near the roof and certainly never fell off the train. The all-is-illusion remarks were made by a middle-aged man with a retarded daughter in the third-class carriage.)

But all this has been a preamble to scenes I now wish to describe in some detail: Jennifer's leaving van Niekerk for the delights of life lived with James Kilminster, failed seminarian and student of physics.

* * * * * * *

When we returned to England, van Niekerk bought a house in Putney. It wasn't a very big house and it wasn't in a very fashionable street. The Indian débâcle had cost van Niekerk a lot of money. I think the Indians confiscated all his funds and possessions in that country, and the World Bank dropped him like a hot potato. So for a few years we were, relatively speaking, poor. From eight servants we were suddenly down to Mrs O'Grady who came three mornings a week, her migraine permitting. Jennifer had to re-learn the art of cooking. I was instructed in the mysteries of bed-making. And, of course, Jennifer had to learn not to play the Delhi memsahib to Mrs O'Grady. Then there was the famous fight between van Niekerk and Jennifer about the school I was to attend. Van Niekerk wanted me to go to some reasonably cheapo private concern. Jennifer declared for the local government primary school. I don't think this was only a matter of economy on her part (she's never had much idea about money anyway) but part of the beginning of her turning away from all that being a memsahib had entailed. She actually thought it would be good for me to go to the state school.

"For God's sake, Pieter," she yelled at van Niekerk, "If you can't afford to send your daughter to a proper paid-up, upper-class boarding school in the country with ponies and lacrosse and half-terms when the gel's maters and paters arrive in their splendid Rollses and Bentleys, if you can't afford that, at least allow her the benefit of going to a real school with real people for teachers and pupils, not some seedy, genteel, just-keeping-our-head-above-water refugee camp for the daughters of

Conservative county councillors. God in heaven, I'll bet in that bloody place you want to send her to, the girls still wear gloves, like I had to do at St bloody James's. And do you know why? No? Well I'll tell you. It's not only so that they look different from the hoi polloi and general riff-raff when travelling upon the public omnibuses, not only that at all. It's because in that godforsaken place they can't afford to run up a heating bill in winter, so the poor bloody girls just have to wear their gloves inside the school as well as out. Understand? It's so they don't get chilblains on their poor little blue-with-cold fingers."

"Jennifer, you are being ridiculous."

"Like hell I am. I know those sorts of schools. I grew up here, remember, I went to school in London myself. Things might have been different in the Kruger National Park, but here in England the only thing colder than charity is the lower middle-classes. Poor, mean, hyper-respectable, sour, twisted...."

"All right, Jennifer. All right! I'll send Anasuya to one of those places in the country with ponies and lacrosse. I don't know where I'll find the money, but...."

"Like hell you'll send her to the country. The poor child's only seven. She's staying here with me, as part of the family. I'm Jewish, remember. Not some cold-as-ice yok. The bloody goyim might send their children to boarding schools to be rid of them for three quarters of the year, but not me, I'm a schmaltzy Golders Green yid, and my daughter stays here. Christ! Why do the bloody goyim have children if all they can do with them is consign them to those prisons they call schools? Eh? You tell me, you're a Dutch Reformed Holy Roller or something, you understand your own kind. Go on, tell me, I want to know, I'm genuinely interested. Why do the Christians send their children to boarding schools?"

"Your parents sent your brother to a Christian boarding school."

"And look what happened to him. He's turned out more twisted, colder, greedier, screwed-up, repressed than even you. And that's saying something. Do you have any idea what went on in that place they sent Simon to? Nothing but throttlings and thrashings...."

"I've read your little fairy story...."

"...raggings and faggings and Saturday Mornings."

"I just don't think Anasuya would be very happy in this primary school place of yours. And we've no idea what the standards are like, at least if we send her to The Grange we'll have some guarantee...."

"Pieter," Jennifer said very slowly, "The Grange, or whatever you call it, doesn't exist."

"Oh for god's sake, Jennifer."

"It doesn't exist, Pieter, it's an illusion. We couldn't send Anasuya there even if we wanted to, which we don't."

"Jennifer, I was there yesterday morning. I spoke to the Headmistress."

"No you didn't. You might have *thought* you were, but you weren't."

"Is it possible to ever have a serious conversation with you these days?"

"It couldn't exist, Pieter. It would have to be in a museum to exist. With a name like The Grange it sounds more like some sort of hotel. Perhaps that's what it is, perhaps you were in a hotel yesterday. Talking to your mistress. Not a headmistress at all, a real mistress, your mistress...."

My father hit my mother across her face with the flat of his hand. Very violently. Jennifer spun round under the impact, falling sideways from the chair she was sitting in. Van Niekerk shouted something at her in Afrikaans, grabbed her by the hair, pulled her to her feet and again hit her face. Jennifer lurched a couple of steps towards a small writing table in the corner of the room. She leant on the table with both arms, dazed totally. I ran to her, putting my own arms around her. She showed no signs of registering my presence. I turned my head to look at my father. He stood across the room, very white, breathing very hard. I thought he might be going to hit Jennifer again.

"Don't, Daddy," I whimpered, "Don't, Daddy, Mummy

didn't mean it."

Jennifer slowly stood up; she had her back to van Niekerk. For a few moments there was no sound in the room except the harsh rasping of my parents' breathing. Slowly, almost abstractedly, Jennifer disengaged my arms from around her waist and pushed me a couple of feet to one side. Van Niekerk began to say something. There was a heavy glass ashtray on the table in front of Jennifer—an ugly, square thing with a hemi-spherical depression in the centre, half-full of cigarette butts.

I believe that most things thrown in domestic arguments miss, that some fairly powerful inhibition comes into play which prevents effective aim regardless of the intensity of passion felt by the thrower. Jennifer's range would have been about six feet. She did not miss.

The ashtray flew straight to van Niekerk's head. He lifted a hand to ward off the blow, but the missile brushed his fingers aside, striking him above the right eye. He fell over backwards, banging his head on the wall. He came to rest in the typical drunken bum position—half slumped against the wall, his legs sticking straight in front of him, his back curved forwards, his head lolling towards his chest. I ran across the room, throwing myself onto him. "Daddy, Daddy!"

He fell over sideways to lie on his side, twisted around by the skirting board, inert, blood dripping down his face.

"Mummy, Mummy. Is he dead? Please say he's not dead, Mummy, please."

"I don't know," Jennifer said wearily, "I don't know."

She walked over to us and stood looking down for a few seconds. "No, he's not dead, he's still breathing."

She left the room and I heard her being sick in the kitchen. There was the sound of taps being run. I left my father and went into the kitchen. The air smelt of vomit. Jennifer was splashing cold water from the steadily running tap straight onto her face. She buried her head in a dish cloth for a few seconds and then sat on a chair gingerly massaging her cheeks with her fingers.

"God, god, god," she said hopelessly. And then again, "God,

god, god." She spoke in a type of chant, in descending half-tones. She looked like a little girl: rocking, crooning to comfort herself. I stood beside her, embracing her. She put her arms around me, resting her head against my shoulder like a child, and together we rocked gently to Jennifer's descending call to god. After a couple of minutes she said, "Go and have a look at him."

I left my mother's embrace to look at my father. He hadn't moved. I checked to see that he was still breathing. The blood had stopped flowing and the area above his eye had started to swell. The unnatural position in which he lay looked uncomfortable; I didn't want him to wake up like that. I tried to move him, but he was too heavy. I returned to Jennifer in the kitchen.

"Daddy's all right," I said, "But I don't think he's very comfortable."

Jennifer grinned a funny, rueful, sad grin and said, "No, I don't suppose he is very comfortable."

"Come and help me, Mummy."

I returned to my father and after half a minute Jennifer joined me. Without saying a word she helped me pull him away from the wall, turn him flat on his back and place a cushion under his head. I was startled to feel how heavy he was, how unmanageable the dead weight of his limbs was when we moved them. We both stood beside him, looking down like mourners at a graveside. It was now evening and the room was filling with shadows; some light came through the door to the kitchen and a few feeble rays came through the window from the street light outside. Van Niekerk began to stir, he moaned a little, but didn't open his eyes.

"He's waking up, Mummy."

"Yeah, he's waking up all right. I think we should go."

"No, Mummy, stay."

Jennifer's manner changed completely. She strode from the room to reappear a few seconds later struggling into her coat, holding a padded anorak of mine in one hand.

"Put this on," she commanded.

"No, Mummy, stay. Daddy's waking up."

"Come on, Anasuya. Do as you're told for Christ's sake." Her voice was hard, urgent.

I started to struggle into my anorak, but van Niekerk groaned again and without a word Jennifer took me by the hand and led me roughly out of the house. She marched down the darkening street, I ran along beside her, finally getting both arms into the anorak.

"Where are we going?"

"To Tamar's."

"What about Daddy?"

"He'll be all right. I think he might want to be alone for a bit."

We found a taxi in Roehampton village and Jennifer gave Tamar and Simon's Chelsea address. In the taxi Jennifer was silent, tense. She kept drumming her fingers on her knees, oblivious to my presence. I sat in the corner of the seat, looking at Jennifer and then out at the traffic. There were crowds of home-bound commuters in Putney High Street, the pubs had opened for the evening and I glanced into one through an opening door: light, warmth, a crush of people. The back of the taxi was bleak and cold. We crossed the river and I looked upstream towards Hammersmith, the water was black and ruffled, flecked with the lights of factories and warehouses, a tug or barge or something was coming downstream, its wake fanning out behind it, navigation lights glinting. Jennifer suddenly remembered her daughter's presence.

"Come to me," she said softly.

I edged across the seat into her embrace. "What about Daddy?" I said.

"Daddy doesn't exist."

"Is he dead?"

"Yes. No. No, of course he's not dead. He was just knocked out, that's all."

Her hands searched for mine, found them and held them. Speaking carefully, choosing her words, Jennifer said, "I'm sorry you had to see all this, Ansu. It's not the sort of thing someone your age should witness. You mustn't worry about Daddy, he'll be all right. Do you understand?"

"Yes," I said.

"We'll just go to Tamar's for a while until we work out what we are going to do. Is that all right?"

"Yes," I said.

Tamar and Simon lived in one of those vast complexes of expensive flats off the Chelsea Road, the sort with their own gardens and driveways. The taxi drove around the semi-circular drive until we located the right entrance. Jennifer had no money. She told the driver we'd be back in a few minutes to pay him.

"That's all right, missus," the driver said, "I'll come up with you."

"Oh Christ! If you're so suspicious, keep the child as hostage. Anasuya, stay here a minute, keep this gentleman company." Jennifer strode into the entrance and was lost from sight.

"Charming. Bloody charming," the driver said. He hadn't sounded suspicious to me; he'd sounded as if he really wanted to help, or perhaps he'd envisaged a bigger tip for seeing us to the door.

I said, "Mummy is very upset."

"I can see that, love," he said patiently.

"You mustn't mind what she says. She doesn't mean it."

"In this trade we get it all, love. Don't worry about it." He lit a cigarette and then said quite conversationally, "She had a bit of a tiff wiv your dad, then?"

"What?"

"You know, your mum and your dad been fighting?"

"Yes."

"Who won then?"

"What?"

"Who got the better of it, who come out on top?"

"Mummy hit Daddy with the ashtray."

"Did she just," the driver chuckled to himself and then said to me, "She looked a right tough one, your mum. I thought to meself soon as I saw you in the Village like, I thought, hello

Charlie me lad, here comes a tough one. Your old man hit back did he?"

"Mummy knocked Daddy out, but he is going to be all right. He must be awake by now. He's better now."

"Bugger me. Beg your pardon." The driver whistled quietly.

Tamar appeared from the entrance, fumbling with her purse. She paid the driver who drove off, saying "Keep yer end up, love."

Tamar hugged me and we silently entered the building and rode in the lift to her flat. Jennifer was sitting on the sofa, a large glass in her hand. A bottle of brandy stood on the glass-topped table at her feet. Simon was pacing up and down the length of the living room. I sat down beside Jennifer. Simon ceased pacing long enough to give me a perfunctory kiss before saying to Jennifer. "Well if you won't let me phone, I had better go and see him."

"Leave him be, Simon. He'll be all right."

"No, I'll go over and take a look at him. I am a doctor you know."

"Yes, Simon, I had grasped that fact."

"And Pieter is my brother-in-law."

"I am aware of that also."

"Then I'll slip over to Putney, won't take a minute."

Simon started for the door, his mind made up. Jennifer twisted around on the sofa to shout at her brother's retreating back, "Don't you dare bring him back here, do you understand, Simon. Don't you dare bring him back here."

Tamar appeared with another glass, poured herself a slug from the brandy bottle, asked me did I want a glass of milk or anything and, when I said I didn't, packed me off to play with my cousins in one of the further reaches of the flat. I didn't really know my cousins very well at that time. I'd met them occasionally on trips back to England with my parents, but apart from a holiday in Scotland when I was about four, I hadn't spent much time with them. Jennifer had always been a trifle dismissive whenever their names came up in conversation—*empty-headed* and *simpering* were the words I'd most frequently heard her use.

"Poor Tamar, fancy being the mother of those two. Still if she will go and marry someone like my brother, what can she expect."

They had awful names: Randolph and Samantha. Jennifer had once said that if Grearson had been blessed with a first name it would have been Randolph. His sister would have been called Samantha.

"But," I can remember saying, "Grearson must have a first name. Everyone has a first name. You said he was called Thomas or something."

"We only called him that to be polite, darling. We made it up. Really his full name is Grearson. Grearson pure and simple."

I can remember thinking my mother mad. I knew the difference between real people and those who appeared in the stories she sometimes told me at bedtime. I knew there had been a real Grearson as well as the made-up Grearson whose dubious adventures in heaven and hell entertained, delighted and sometimes frightened me, but did Jennifer?

I found my cousins and their au pair, Ingrid, playing in their remarkably well-stocked playroom. I eyed the assorted toys, meccano sets, dolls-houses, bikes, trikes, easels, and so forth with considerable suspicion, having recently become aware that everything left lying around has to be put away. Was it all worth it? Worth it or not, I was soon playing with complete absorption an elaborate board game that involved sinking vast amounts of enemy shipping. Tamar had to call us three times before we dragged ourselves away from the board to eat.

We all sat around the kitchen table eating one of those high teas that looks like breakfast: scrambled eggs, toast, jam, bowls of cereals. We children drank some sort of chocolate concoction; Jennifer and Tamar, brandy; Ingrid, as befitted someone in her position half-way between the adults and children, both. Jennifer now appeared very happy, ebullient. She laughed a lot. Tamar laughed with her. They indulged in a number of hilarious whispered asides. We children chattered and laughed, Ingrid told a story about losing her way when she first came to London, parodying her own broken English to heighten the effect. It was all very jolly. Obviously, in Jennifer's case, a lot of the jollity was manic rather than joyous, a bright bubble that could burst at any tick of the clock. I think I must have genuinely suppressed what I'd experienced earlier in the evening—at least on the surface of consciousness I was decidedly enjoying myself.

The sound of the front door opening and Simon letting himself in intruded during a lull in the conversation. Jennifer glanced quickly at Tamar, but Tamar just shrugged and said something to Ingrid about pulling up another chair. A few seconds later Simon appeared in the door. He said something quickly and hurriedly that nobody caught—we were all still chattering.

"What?" Tamar said.

"He can't remember anything," Simon said slightly more loudly, but just as quickly, "I found him reading his diary, trying to work out which day it is."

"But he's all right, is he?" Tamar asked.

Before Simon could reply, van Niekerk himself appeared in the doorway behind him. A large piece of sticking plaster covered half his forehead. He looked a bit confused, but quite friendly.

"Hello, Tamar," he said over Simon's shoulder.

"Oh, hello, Pieter," Tamar said.

"Simon!" Jennifer exclaimed.

"He wanted to come," muttered Simon, edging into the room to let my father past. Van Niekerk shuffled into the kitchen, looked around, saw Jennifer and myself, smiled a cheerful, if dazed, smile and said, "Hello, darling. Hello, Anasuya."

Jennifer said nothing. She sat as if made of stone. I said, "Daddy!"

"Hello Anasuya," my father said again.

He looked at Randolph and Samantha, appeared to recognise them, but obviously could not bring their names to mind. "Oh, err, hello you two," he said vaguely, and then to Ingrid, "And, err, hello, how are you?"

"I'm fine, thanks," Ingrid said to van Niekerk, whom she'd never seen before in her life.

There was a moment of general confusion while chairs were found and extra places laid. Ingrid started to scramble more eggs. Simon sat down next to Jennifer who hissed something fierce under her breath. Simon tried to explain quietly, but was interrupted by van Niekerk saying to Jennifer, "I seem to have hit my head. I can't remember how. I'm…err…I'm a bit fuzzy at the moment."

"Yes," Jennifer said.

"The err, the good doctor found me. He says I've got slight concussion. I should take things quietly for a day or two. I might remember how it happened, or I might not. He says only time will tell. That's right, isn't it Simon?"

"Yes, yes," Simon said, "You'll get back all your long-term memories soon enough, nothing to worry about there. It's the short-term stuff that's dicey. What you were doing just before the, ah, the blow; the previous ten minutes, that sort of time lapse. Short-term memory is quite different from long term, completely different part of the brain, different neural circuits, in fact the whole manner in which the information is stored is quite…."

"Shut up, Simon," Jennifer said. "Look, Pieter, you were knocked unconscious by me. I threw that big glass ashtray at you."

"Oh," van Niekerk said, as if struggling to see the point of a crossword clue, "Oh, I see. That explains it, then."

He looked around the silent table, embarrassed by his own confusion, muttered, "Yes, yes, of course, that would explain it," and returned to eating the scrambled eggs that Ingrid had laid silently before him. The meal continued in virtual silence; my father looked neither angry nor resentful, just dazed and bewildered. In a matter of minutes we children were despatched back to the playroom. We continued sinking enemy shipping. Samantha said, "I think uncle Pieter is funny."

"Chap got hit on the head by a cricket ball last term,"

Randolph said, "Couldn't remember a thing about it."

"I'm buying two more anti-submarine planes," I said.

Ingrid appeared and organised us for bed. When we were ready, we all trooped into the living room where the adults were sitting talking. They all had glasses of brandy or some other booze, except for my father who seemed to be drinking milk. They formed a subdued, but not particularly tense, group. Samantha and I did the rounds, kissing everyone and saying good night. Jennifer held me for a few seconds longer than usual saying, "You're my absolutely most favourite Ansu in all the world." Randolph kissed his mother and aunt and rather formally shook hands with his father and uncle. I suppressed a fit of giggles and glanced at Samantha, but she didn't appear to think anything untoward was happening. Off we went to bed. A spare one had been made up for me in Samantha's room. We lay in the dark talking in hushed tones to each other about nothing very important.

I have a vague memory of Jennifer materialising in the middle of the night, whispering, "Move over, darling," and climbing into bed with me. I felt my mother's arms around me, snuggled into them and returned to sleep. In the morning she wasn't there. Perhaps I dreamt that bit.

Jennifer and I stayed at Tamar's for three or four days. There was a certain amount of coming and going; van Niekerk put in regular appearances and he and my mother would lock themselves away in one of the flat's many rooms, to reappear either tight-lipped or smiling tentatively. I wasn't party to any of these negotiating sessions and it was only years later that Jennifer told me what had gone on. Roughly speaking, she had agreed to return to him if he gave up his mistress, was nicer to her, and allowed her to have the final say in such matters as which school I was to attend. One of the reasons she gave to herself for returning to van Niekerk was that this was in the best interests of her daughter, me. "God I was weak!" she said to me that evening in France when we discussed the whole scene. "I should have left him there and then. After all those torrid scenes, after braining the bastard, I just went crawling back. Half the trouble was that he couldn't remember the fight. I'd knocked all the anger out of him, he became quite reasonable. And I was insecure, financially insecure. I wouldn't have known how to go about looking for a job; all those years in Delhi had left me with an appetite for money and no clue about how it was to be made. And then there was you. I suppose I really did feel that you needed him, that you would be better off with two parents than one. I don't think it was only a rationalisation on my part."

I remember this conversation well. It took place in the bath. Jennifer had her feet under my bum. She wriggled her right foot, stabbing me with her big toe.

"It was all your fault," she said, "If you hadn't been so fond of him, I'd have been strong enough to leave then."

"Jennifer, be fair, I was only seven."

"Still he hadn't been very good to you as a father."

"How good had you been as a mother? Didn't I spend most of my time with Sarojini?"

"Maybe I wasn't ideal either."

So we went back to the dark Putney house. I was sad to leave Tamar's, I liked the feeling that there were always a number of people around, I'd never lived in a house with only two other people in my life. In India nobody lives in a house with only a couple of others, neither the rich nor the poor. My room in the Putney house had a bay window that overlooked the grounds of St Mary's Rehabilitation Hospital. This place, Jennifer insisted, was the artificial knee capital of the world. She might have been exaggerating a bit, but there was no shortage of legless and armless people hobbling and tottering around the hospital gardens.

In a sort of yard, quite literally under my bedroom window, were a few low utilitarian buildings roofed with that grey corrugated asbestos stuff that is now considered so dangerous to health. These were the hospital's workshops; a constant banging and hammering and the buzz of electric drills came from them. At lunchtime the workers would come out to sit in the sun or kick a football around. At times, men in white dustcoats would walk purposefully across the yard, two or three artificial limbs under each arm. There was one, a young man of about twenty, who would sometimes wave up to me, where I sat in the window. Sometimes he'd wave an artificial arm or leg, its hinges and moving parts parodying the movements of his own perfectly normal limbs.

I was sent, needless to report, to the local government primary school, where, at the beginning at least, I was far from happy. My teacher was Mrs McKenzie, a Scot. I couldn't understand a word she said.

* * * * * * *

I remember the next two years of my life very well. They were dreary. I grew to tolerate my school. Jennifer and van Niekerk bickered interminably, but, as far as I know, never erupted into real violence again. Van Niekerk nearly made a fortune on a number of occasions, but his dealings never quite paid off. I suspect that it was during this time that he became genuinely criminal in his approach to high finance, that it was the failure of his legal or semilegal plans that gave him the push in the direction of the arms-dealing and sanctions-breaking that was to entertain the readers of the daily papers after his disappearance ten years later. But I could be wrong.

During these years Jennifer wrote a few short stories in a dilatory, almost neurotic fashion, and started the novel that was later to appear as *Pig Fat and Chapatties*. I was an ordinary little London school girl, no more, no less.

Not long after my ninth birthday, Jennifer decided she would enrol for a degree.

"You don't need a degree, Jennifer."

"I'll decide what I need."

"We are not going to remain poor for long. That I can guarantee."

"So you keep saying, Pieter, so you keep saying...."

"The moment the Swiss company is incorporated and Deitzinger establishes a reserve fund...."

"I don't give a fuck about reserve funds or Deitzinger or Swiss cheese with holes in it. I don't give a fuck about our 'poverty'. It's my mind, Pieter, my mind."

"There's nothing wrong with your mind, Jennifer. Filling it up with school books won't improve it, you can learn more from real life."

"My sanity, god damn you van Niekerk, I'm talking about my sanity."

"The University of London is not a health clinic. If there was anything wrong with your sanity, which there isn't, you could go to a psychiatrist."

"I've *been* to one of those, if you'll remember. Dear old Dr Hilda Glick. She warned me against marrying a father-figure."

And so it went on. No ashtrays thrown, but no mention of the real feelings and fears either. Jennifer, of course, believed that a degree would give her the economic freedom necessary for leaving van Niekerk. Van Niekerk believed exactly the same thing. My parents had seldom been so closely of one mind. As it was, events moved far faster than the three-year minimum it would have taken Jennifer to complete a degree. By the end of her second term she had effectively dropped out. It was at the University of London though that we met Kilminster.

I say we because apparently I was there as well as Jennifer, although I can't remember the occasion myself. Jennifer dragged me around quite a few dreary places that summer, the admissions office of the university must have been one of them. Kilminster says he remembers the whole thing very well; I've pumped him for as many details as possible. He keeps raving away about the dead egg.

"It was one of those baleful eggs. You know, the ones that stare at you, stone-dead but still malevolent. Stop laughing Ansu, you know the ones. Actually they reconstitute them so that they never end. One great endless egg."

"What?"

"They take thousands and thousands of ordinary eggs, separate the yolks from the whites and then hard-boil them while forcing them through these concentric tubes. So what you get is one long sausage of a hard-boiled egg-yolk in the middle, white on the outside. That's why you never get a slice of veal and ham pie with the end of an egg in it; you always get what looks like the middle of an egg. Which it is in a way, but not an ordinary egg, an endless egg."

"James, are you being serious?"

"I'm just telling you about the egg. The egg is very important to your story, symbolic in a way."

"I think you are trying to pull another altar wine gaff; just because you fooled Jennifer doesn't mean you can fool me."

"Have you ever eaten a slice of pie in an English pub with the end of the egg in it?"

"I don't eat in English pubs if I can help it."

There is a scene in Jennifer's story, *Mixed Blessing* in which young Allen, a couple of weeks after he has left the seminary in which he is training to become a priest, is sitting in a pub drinking a pint of bitter. As I have said before, most of *Mixed Blessing* comes straight from Kilminster; when Jennifer was writing the story she kept pestering Kilminster for details of seminary life, Catholic ritual, his boyhood dreams and so on. The pub scene was modelled on his account of his first weeks of civilian life. Kilminster had told Jennifer that, as a novice in the seminary, he had never drunk anything stronger than coffee. Jennifer worked this into the story by describing Allen as sitting in the pub trying to decide if he likes the taste of beer or not. His only source of comparison is the one alcoholic drink he has previously tasted, altar wine. Allen, musing a trifle drunkenly on his fourth pint, decides that Double Diamond bitter has a slightly stronger nose than the blood of Christ, but is decidedly more flabby on the middle palate.

Jennifer showed her completed story to Kilminster who made a number of editorial suggestions and helped her tone down the blasphemy that was later to be resurrected (after a fashion) in my classroom in Oise.

"Do you think we can leave this blood of Christ stuff in?" Jennifer asked him, leaning on his shoulder and stabbing at the manuscript with her pencil.

"What did you say the editor's name was again?"

"Isaacs."

"Leave it in. We can't knacker the story too much."

The magazine's editor made a few more changes to the story, but didn't touch the altar wine bit. He was probably quite happy to annoy a small section of his readers in the interests of lively controversy. The lively controversy duly ensued with a number of letters to the magazine from people who didn't really appreciate the sacrament being used as a standard by which to judge booze. This didn't worry Jennifer at all; what did rankle were the two or three letters that pointed out that if the author wanted to mock other people's deeply held beliefs in order to raise a cheap laugh, she ought at least to get her facts right. Allen had left the seminary *before* ordination and, since only priests drink the wine in the Catholic ritual, he could never have tasted it.

"Bloody hell, Kilminster, you said this was all right."

"I didn't, I just said we couldn't knacker the story too much."

"You bastard."

Jennifer flung herself onto Kilminster (he was in bed reading the papers) and belaboured him around the ears with the magazine containing the hostile letters. Kilminster wrestled with her, subduing her, but not before she had bitten his wrist hard. *Mixed Blessing* was her first major story to be published and she was more sensitive to criticism in those days. Holding each other wearily at arms' length they sat on the bed.

"Truce?" Kilminster said.

"Truce."

Kilminster relaxed his grip, Jennifer cuffed him once more. He spun her to the bed, holding her wrists. Kilminster let go of one wrist in order to undo the belt of her dressing gown. She put her arm around his neck, kissing him aggressively. They made love amongst the crackling newspapers and hostile letters.

Afterwards (as they say when describing scenes like this) they lay beside each other. Jennifer said, "But, James, I really thought Christians did all drink the wine. I'm sure they pass it around in little thimbles."

"The Protestants, darling. They'll do any damn thing. Whole congregations going at it like pigs at a trough. Guzzle, guzzle, guzzle. Their churches are more like gin parlours than places of worship."

In those days Kilminster hadn't actually lost the faith, although the light was fading fast. Now, of course, he's a card-carrying atheist, and like a lot of converts to that position, very anti-church and very anti-Catholic. He will talk for hours about the stultifying effects of a religious upbringing, the evils of a belief in an after-life, the warping properties of the concept of sin ; one can say almost anything negative about God or religion or the Pope and he will agree. He's quite partial to the idea that monotheism went haywire in about thirty A.D. and that Judaism is the best of a bad bunch. But just try saying anything favourable about the Protestants, just try to tell him that the Church of England has a bit of an edge on the church of Rome and the poor man starts to rave like Cardinal Richelieu. Frankly the Saint Bartholomew's Day Massacre was a bit *soft* if the truth be known.

But all this is beside the extremely important point I am trying to make. Which is this: I'm not sure if Kilminster is being entirely honest with this continuous egg business. He might be inventing it, just to get it into my story. With that reservation I'll continue.

Kilminster sat in the bar of the Lord John Russell, a pint of bitter on the table before him. A slice of veal and ham pie on a leaf of lettuce on a plate with a dob of mustard near its rim lay next to the pint, a tinny fork was in his hand. Kilminster organised his copy of the Guardian next to the plate. He began to eat the pie slowly, reading the paper at the same time, occasionally taking a sip from the pint. He was sitting in a pub, eating and drinking food he had bought with his own money, wearing blue jeans and an immaculately ironed ex-army shirt, also purchased with his own funds—the wages of a biscuit van delivery driver. He had just completed enrolment procedures at the university. His grant would commence in a couple of months. Kilminster was very content; better in his soul than at any time since leaving the seminary. All he needed was a decent place to live; the boarding house in Bayswater just would not do—too many old soaks and Australians, too expensive, too seedy by far. Some reasonably bohemian pad in Bloomsbury was what he had in mind. He also needed a fuck.

Kilminster quite enjoyed the role he was playing, although aware of its well-worn and clichéd aspects. Many are called, few are chosen. There was nothing new in leaving the priest-hood, and he indeed had left long before ordination. Real, fully-ticketed priests were reneging on their vows all the time, flocking away from the bosom of the Church in droves. The Pope was worried. The College of Cardinals was worried. The Vatican Council was worried sick. Many had doubts these days. Doubting was entirely fashionable. It was at this point that young James departed from the set cliché. He had no doubts at all.

He had been thrown out. Well, he had been asked to leave. It had been put to him with some asperity by Father Aquinas that lust and celibacy were not the best of bedfellows. If James were to continue with his current practices there was no hope that he would one day become a serving priest. Perhaps he could best serve God in some lay capacity, a good Catholic wife by his side....

Kilminster glanced from the paper to the slice of pie. In the middle of the pie was a section of hard-boiled egg. He had been lucky, his slice contained the central section of the egg. His luck was holding quite well these days. He pitied the next customer whose slice would contain only the scrag end of the egg. He glanced back to the paper. Things were getting pretty nasty in Indo-China. A group of Yanks had landed on the Moon and were transmitting some of the most fatuous remarks in recorded history back to Earth. The war in Nigeria was grinding to a close; one of the paper's correspondents, some Frenchman called Jean-Claude Something had been captured by one side or the other and fears were held for his safety. These were stirring times. Kilminster regarded the egg, all that was left of his pie. The egg regarded Kilminster, baleful, malevolent. With a masterly stab Kilminster speared the egg and conveyed it to his mouth. The door of the pub opened and a woman and child entered.

Kilminster recognised them at once. The woman had also been completing some sort of admission procedure. Her daughter, a strikingly pretty child with long black hair and the beginnings of breasts just visible under her blouse, had been skulking about looking bored. There had been a small queue at the counter when Kilminster had entered the room. The woman had been ahead of him, talking to an African about the events in Nigeria. Passions were running high, at least on the African's part. He seemed to be pro-Ojukwu and anti-Gowan which didn't help Kilminster much, because the names meant nothing to him. At one stage the African said, "What you English don't understand...."

"I'm not English, I keep telling you," the woman said in an immaculate educated London accent, "I'm Jewish."

Someone in the queue behind Kilminster sniggered. The woman stepped slightly to one side, turning to identify the sniggerer. For a second Kilminster thought she would choose him, but she correctly picked an Asian in a dazzling white shirt.

"Look, we've got an Englishman living at home with us. I'll introduce you to him if you like. His name's Grearson, his feet smell."

The Asian sniggered again, someone else in the queue laughed, the woman turned back to her conversation with the African, the startlingly pretty girl yawned.

The woman now crossed the pub floor, saying to her daughter as she did so, "Anasuya, sit here," indicating the other end of the curved, padded bench on which Kilminster was sitting.

The child sat down and smiled at Kilminster who smiled back. Behind him Kilminster heard the woman say with exaggerated resignation, "I know you can't bring a child under fourteen into a pub; she is fourteen, she just looks a bit young, that's all."

The barmaid's reply was indistinct.

The woman said, "Oh for god's sake, I don't want to feed her neat gin, a lemonade will do."

Again the reply was indistinct, but the tone was harder. Kilminster exchanged glances with the girl. If she was at all embarrassed by her mother's performance, she didn't show it, she smiled unselfconsciously. Her mother reappeared.

"They won't serve us, darling. They're just being bloody minded. I think it's because we're wogs. Well, let's go."

The girl stood up, shrugged her shoulders at Kilminster in a gesture of resigned farewell, and started to walk to the door.

"And if you've got any self-respect, you'll stop smirking at my daughter and leave too, as a gesture of protest."

Kilminster looked up at the woman who regarded him intensely for a second, as if summing him up, judging him, and then turned and followed her daughter to the door. The pub was very quiet, but then there were only a few drinkers present anyway. Kilminster heard the barmaid say to someone, "They won't learn, they just won't learn. She'll go straight down the road and try to put it over at The Escape."

The woman's brief exchange with Kilminster had unsettled him. She was not as immediately arresting as the child, but her dark intensity made her very much the sort of woman Kilminster liked. Or imagined he liked; he didn't actually know any women apart from his mother and a few of her friends in Liverpool. And presumably this woman with the striking daughter was going to be one of his fellow students.

Slowly, so as to look as if he were leaving anyway, Kilminster finished his pint and folded his newspaper. He made his way to the door. For a moment he thought the woman and child had already disappeared and was surprised at the force of his disappointment. Then he saw them on the other side of the road, just about to turn a corner. When he caught up with them he didn't know what to say. He fell into step beside them.

"Hello," he said after a few seconds.

"Hello," the woman said.

"I walked out."

"So I can see."

"It's absurd, that law about children under fourteen. They don't have to drink alcohol…err, as you said to the barmaid.…"

"Did you walk out in protest?"

"Well I left a few seconds after.…"

"Did you up-end your glass on the table?"

"Well, no, not exactly."

The woman looked at him sadly. "Isn't that what you do when you walk out of a pub in protest, don't you up-end your glass spilling beer all over the place?"

"I don't know, I've never made a protest in a pub before."

"*Before?* I don't think you really made one just now. You're too good-mannered to protest properly. Do you know a café or somewhere that'll let her in?"

"Umm, not around here. What about that place over there?"

"It'll do. It'll have to do. I'm starving."

In the café Kilminster had another slice of veal and ham pie. Again he was lucky with the egg. Jennifer introduced herself and her daughter. The three of them spent an hour talking. Kilminster was very funny about the travails of life as a biscuit van driver and very vague about what he'd done prior to taking up this occupation. For some reason he was reticent about telling Jennifer that he had only just left a seminary, perhaps he feared she would inquire too closely into his reasons for quitting. Jennifer was equally funny about what it was like to be 'poor' and not at all reticent about the source of her previous (and future?) wealth.

"My husband's basically a crook. I mean he only goes in for the respectable white collar sorts of crime, none of the smash and grab stuff, he doesn't wear a striped T-shirt and carry a bag marked *swag* or anything. We're very respectable." She turned to the child, "Aren't we, darling?"

"Oh very," the girl said.

"At the moment, as I say, we are a bit sort of down-at-heel and genteel. Usually we have more flair and style. If Pieter can't pull off something big fairly soon we'll have to start taking in gentlemen lodgers."

"I thought perhaps Mr Grearson was a gentleman lodger."

Mother and daughter laughed. Jennifer said, "How do you know about Grearson?"

"When you were telling that Asian...."

"Oh. That. Then. No. Grearson doesn't exist, he's an illusion. Even if he did exist we wouldn't have him in the house, not with feet like his."

"Phew!" said the girl.

"Exactly," said the mother. "Where do you live?"

Kilminster described the boarding house in Bayswater.

"It sounds a bit grim."

"There's not much flair and style about the place."

"Perhaps you'd better come and be a gentleman lodger with us. You'd have to do a bit of babysitting though. What are you like at that?"

"Err, I don't know," Kilminster said truthfully. He'd never babysat in his life.

"Well, by *baby* I only mean her, she's quite civilised." Jennifer addressed the girl, "How would you like James as a babysitter?"

"Oh, all right I suppose," the girl said, a trifle off-hand.

"Only all right?" he asked.

"No. A lot."

"Excellent," Jennifer said, "When do you want to move in?"

After a bit more conversation, it was decided that Kilminster would come to dinner the following day, to see if he liked the cramped arrangement of odd-shaped rooms in our attic that a previous owner had converted into what is known as a bed-sit, and also, he told himself, to see if he liked the professional white collar crook.

There was, in fact, a small amount of confusion over Kilminster's appearance at dinner. Kilminster thought, quite reasonably, that van Niekerk would know of and, at least in principle, approve of, the plan for him to become a gentleman lodger. Perhaps Jennifer had meant to tell my father her plans for Kilminster, but had then decided to leave the suggestion until after dinner. Maybe she thought it would be easier for Kilminster to make a good impression if he were not being vetted for future tenancy, that the plan would have a greater appeal to van Niekerk if it were put to him after Kilminster had made this good impression. If so, she ought to have warned Kilminster first; but, for whatever reason, she didn't. And all van Niekerk knew was that Jennifer had asked one of her soon-to-be fellow students to dinner. As I say, my father wasn't very keen about Jennifer enrolling for a degree anyway, which would not have disposed him very favourably towards Kilminster in the first place. When Kilminster arrived, he was even less impressed. The normal run of guests in those days consisted of currency speculators, importers/exporters, wheelers/dealers—*crooks* in Jennifer's terms. For the most part they wore suits or sports jackets. If they came for Sunday lunch, they probably dressed informally, substituting a cravat for the normal tie. Their women only failed to wear stockings if they were wearing slacks. If they wore slacks they also wore jackets of the same material, an ensemble referred to as a slacks suit.

Ugg.

Kilminster arrived in his new blue jeans and his immaculately ironed ex-army shirt. His feet were encased in sneakers, the sole of one of which was coming away from the canvas upper. This, I have subsequently discovered is odd dress for refugees from seminaries. Most ex-priests, suddenly given free choice of clothing, dress like crooks, only more so. Everything is brand new, highly polished or dry-cleaned. The colours don't match; their watchbands, rings, and other jewellery are too chunky and too shiny. Ex-priests don't look as if they belong in their clothes and their clothes don't look as if they belong on human beings, but appear to have been specifically designed for store dummies. If the ex-priests are heterosexual they invariably have wives who are escapees from convents. They dress like crook's wives, only, again, more so. Anyway, Kilminster did not conform to type. He looked as if he well and truly belonged in his broken-down sneakers, jeans, and ex-army shirt. He had clearly decided to make a good impression too; he did not come without gifts. He carried a bunch of flowers in one hand and a half bottle of wine in the other. Not a *small* bottle of wine, not one of those bottles that is called a half bottle, but a full-sized bottle, half-full, with the cork rammed back in. The flowers he must have recently bought; their stalks were wrapped in crêpe paper which the water from the shopkeeper's bucket had soaked, giving the bottom end of the bunch a mushy papier-mâché effect.

"Hi" he said to Jennifer, handing her the flowers.

"Hi," said Jennifer.

"Hello, Anasuya," he said to me.

"Hello," I said.

Jennifer introduced him to van Niekerk. Kilminster changed the wine from his right to his left hand to effect the handshake. The liquid sloshed about in the bottle.

"Err, I've bought this. It seems a good year to me."

He looked at the bottle in his hand for a second and then passed it to van Niekerk. For a further second van Niekerk appeared not to know what to do with it, he too stood looking at the bottle as if it were some rare vintage, then he muttered, "Thank you," and turned to place it on the sideboard.

There followed a very stilted conversation. Van Niekerk was polite, but the opposite of expansive. Jennifer disappeared to the kitchen. Kilminster, stranded with van Niekerk and myself, asked bright questions like, "I believe you used to live in India?"

"Yes."

"Err, what was it like?"

"India is a big place."

"Yes, I know…but, umm, is there any hope for it?"

"Hope?"

"The green revolution. Is it working?"

"Yields have increased substantially due to the use of the new fertilisers, but there are some complications."

"Ahh," said Kilminster as if the solution to an enormously difficult problem had just been made clear. He glanced towards the kitchen; Jennifer could be heard humming as she cooked. After thirty seconds of silence, Kilminster turned to me and said, "And you, Anasuya, where would you rather live, India or England?"

"Oh, I don't know," I said.

After another half-minute of silence, van Niekerk said, "If you'll excuse me for a short while, I have a few urgent letters that I must finish this evening."

"Oh, yes, of course. By all means…," Kilminster said with obvious relief.

My father stood and I think Kilminster almost stood as well; he gripped the arms of his chair with both hands in a small convulsive gesture. Van Niekerk said, "Anasuya, you'll entertain Mr umm Kilminster for half an hour, won't you?"

"Yes," I said.

My father left the room. Kilminster and I looked at each other.

"In India there were snakes," I said.

"What sort of snakes?"

"Oh, I don't know. They came in baskets."

"You mean someone had trapped them and put them in baskets?"

"Maybe. Some snakes are born in baskets. The mother snake has her babies in the basket."

"Like kittens?"

"Yes, like kittens."

"Do you know the question, 'Do hamsters have kittens or do they lay eggs like rabbits?'"

"That's silly."

"I know it's silly. That's why I asked it. Would you like to show me the house?"

"Of course."

I showed him the kitchen and my room first. Jennifer said hello both times we passed through the kitchen. In my room I showed him some of my school books and my mogul picture of the dancing elephants. We spent five minutes observing a group of tottering, lurching, limbless inmates of the rehabilitation hospital who were out for an evening stroll of sorts. Kilminster developed a theory that people simplified by the loss of limbs would not require as much food as normal.

"I expect they serve rather small portions in there," he said, looking dubiously at the façade of St Mary's.

I next showed him my parents' bedroom and the room van Niekerk used as his 'office'. I pushed open the door saying, "This is where Daddy works."

Van Niekerk was sitting at his desk with his back to us. He had the telephone in one hand and a glass of whisky in the other. He was saying something about payment in Swiss francs, but broke off abruptly to say, "Hang on a minute, Carl," and clap his hand over the telephone's mouthpiece.

"Yes?" he said to Kilminster.

"Oh, nothing. Sorry to disturb you. Anasuya is just showing me the house."

My father didn't say anything, he just waited for us to go. We backed out of the door. He didn't start speaking into the telephone until we'd closed it.

"You'd better just show me the flat," Kilminster said.

I took him upstairs to the attic. The flat, if that isn't too grand a word, was small. There was a room just large enough for a single bed, a table, and a chair. The ceiling sloped down over the bed and an absurdly large gas fire took up almost one wall. Through a door there was a rudimentary kitchen with a shower recess in one corner. There was a lavatory in a converted box-room off the landing. Kilminster pulled the chain experimentally. The cistern emptied with a wild rush and then began to fill, the whistle of the incoming water rising slowly through the harmonics.

"Hell," Kilminster said, "Aren't we above your father's room?"

"I don't know."

"I think we are."

We returned to the bed-sitting room. Kilminster sat on the bed, testing the springs.

"Better than the last place," he said, "You could fit a dozen Indians in here with no trouble."

"In India the servants lived at the other end of the garden."

"Oh, yes, I suppose they would have."

Kilminster crossed to the table under the window, where my mother's typewriter lay beside some manuscript paper which had been weighted down by a half-full ashtray.

"What's this?"

"Mummy writes stories."

Kilminster removed the ashtray and read for a few minutes. "Hot stuff," he said, putting back the ashtray, "Oh, well, I suppose we'd better rejoin the company."

We returned to our original chairs in the living room. Jennifer appeared in the door from the kitchen.

"Where's Pieter?"

"He said he had some urgent letters."

"Jesus Christ, has he given you anything to drink?"

"No."

"The man's a pig. Anasuya, show James the drink cupboard. Pour me a whisky and soda, have whatever you like. I'll be with you in a second."

Jennifer disappeared. I showed Kilminster the cabinet in which the grog was kept. We both knelt in front of it.

There were a large number of bottles and glasses. We located a bottle marked Scotch Whisky with relative ease. Kilminster edged it past a few other bottles and stood it on the carpet. We both looked for the soda.

"It's a soft drink," Kilminster said, "It'll probably be in a smaller bottle."

To aid our search we removed a few more bottles and stood them on the carpet with the whisky bottle. We still couldn't locate the soda.

"Go and ask your mother where it is," Kilminster said.

In the kitchen I told Jennifer we couldn't find her any soda.

"It's the stuff you squirt out of the bottle with the wire cage around it. It must be in front of your noses."

I returned to Kilminster, picked the soda syphon from the cabinet, and handed it to him.

"Ah, yes, of course."

He selected a glass at random, half filled it with whisky and then blasted the contents all over me and the carpet with a single sustained burst from the syphon.

"Oh hell, I'm sorry."

"It doesn't matter."

Kilminster produced a not very clean handkerchief from the pocket of his jeans. "Here, use this. I hope you're not drenched."

When my father re-entered the room, I was kneeling on the floor, holding a half-full wine glass of whisky, down the side of which Kilminster was gently trickling soda in short, hesitant squirts. His whisky-soaked, not very clean handkerchief lay among the collection of bottles around us.

"Oh, err, hello," Kilminster said looking up, "Your wife wanted a drink, umm, perhaps you want one too?"

"No thanks, I already have one."

"Oh, yes, of course. That's right, you do. Sorry."

Van Niekerk continued through the room to talk to Jennifer in the kitchen. Half a minute later he retraced his steps, hardly glancing at Kilminster and me repacking the bottles into the cabinet, the completed whisky and soda triumphantly beside us on the carpet. We took it to Jennifer in the kitchen.

"Thanks," she said. "Do you normally drink whisky in wine glasses?"

"Always," Kilminster said.

"Where's your own?"

"I didn't feel like one."

"Rubbish."

Jennifer drank half the glass in one swallow and handed the remainder to Kilminster saying, "Here, finish this, I'll get some more. Watch that the sauce doesn't boil over." She left the kitchen, returning in half a minute with two normal whisky glasses.

Dinner, and I suppose the meal could be dignified with such a name, was a bit strained. Jennifer chatted to Kilminster most of the time, making little attempt to include my father in the conversation. Kilminster, I think, tried to rectify this by addressing a number of remarks to van Niekerk, remarks that were blatantly exercises in polite conversation.

"Have you seen the J. M. W. Turner retrospective?" Kilminster asked.

"No, I don't think so," my father replied.

"No, he *hasn't*," Jennifer explained.

There was a moment's silence, after which my father asked Kilminster, "What's it like?"

"I don't know. I haven't been yet."

"Oh, let's all go," Jennifer said. "Pieter can take time off from swindling people. When's a good day?"

"Jennifer, I do not swindle people."

At that time, if my memory is not at fault, my father was hyper-sensitive to Jennifer's insistence that he was a crook or that he swindled people. I cannot remember very clearly what he was then engaged in. I don't think he had yet become a gun-runner and sanctions-buster, but I could be wrong. Whatever he was up to, he didn't take his nine-year-old daughter into his confidence. I do know, however, that part of his business activities in those days had something to do with floating a series of companies that loaned money to people and organised overseas investment portfolios. In France, years later, Jennifer once described them as, "Funny companies; you know, they didn't make anything, there were never any factories or workshops, all they did was handle other people's money. Pieter set up a sort of whirlpool of money, all the companies lending and borrowing and investing in each other. A lot of the dough ended up in his Swiss bank account. It all went bust in seventy-seven or seventy-six, but by then Pieter had slid out from under, legally severed all his connections. The bugger had learnt a thing or two since Delhi."

That's Jennifer's view of things, but she knows no more about commerce and big business than I do. Whatever it was that he was doing, van Niekerk was highly touchy about Jennifer's continued, often public, insistence that he was a mastermind in the world of white-collar crime. Kilminster thinks van Niekerk was masterminding things all right, but he's dubious about the respectable white-collar aspect. He thinks van Niekerk was making excursions into the really seedy stuff, the fully illegal world of big-time heroin importing, standover rackets and call-girl agencies. Neither Jennifer nor I think this actually fits van Niekerk's character, he simply was too much of a Dutch Reformed holy rolling puritan to have gone in for that sort of crime. And the evidence for Kilminster's theories is a bit dicey; he bases all his insights on the obviously evil visages of a number of people he observed calling on van Niekerk after he'd become the gentleman lodger. Certainly, some of the men who came to visit van Niekerk at odd hours of the day or night were not the sort that normally called on him in his office in London. They were, to put the matter neatly, not the sort of crooks we entertained for Sunday lunch. And Kilminster's quite right when he says that some of them most assuredly *looked* as if they might have been gangsters, underworld heavies. I was to meet one of them again when I was nineteen, as I was to tell Inspector Michaels. I also used his name—quite without foundation—for the source of van Niekerk's information at the Newmarket races. I met him during a university vacation, part of which I was spending with van Niekerk and Bernadette in Kensington.

Van Niekerk had just returned from New York where he said he'd been working incredibly hard. It was easy to believe him; he looked thoroughly worn out, there were dark patches under his eyes, and his skin was pale and drawn tight across the bones of his face. I told him he ought to rest for a weekend, have an early night or two, but he insisted that both Bernadette and myself accompany him to a night-club. The night-club was awful. It had a floorshow in which a number of women took off all their clothes; some oaf swallowed a burning sword to a ten-minute drum roll of unbelievable monotony; Samiha Al Natar crooned soppy love songs in English, French, and Arabic. God knows what we were doing there. Bernadette and van Niekerk drank something called brandy crusters which must be the most revolting drink in the world. I drank soda water at one pound sterling per glass. Bernadette chirped and twittered and gushed and waved to people she presumably knew. I was about ready to throw up when our table was approached by a weasel in a dinner jacket. Weasel is probably the best word, he was lean and nosey.

"Hello, Pieter. Long time, no see."

"Oh...hello," my father said.

I've never heard him so unwelcoming in my life. I was intrigued. The sort of people van Niekerk associated with, just did not use expressions like "Long time, no see."

"How's tricks, then?"

"Fine," my father said after another pause, "And yourself?"

"Can't complain, can't complain. Hello, there. It can't be. Yes it is. I never forget a face. One thing I never forget, a face. Especially as pretty as yours. How are you then, Anna? that's it isn't it. No it's not. Don't tell me, don't tell me. I've got it, Anasuya! Never forget a name either. You've grown though, if you don't mind me saying so."

"It is a long time," van Niekerk said.

"Must be about ten years," the weasel man said, and then to me, "Suppose you don't remember, you was just a young slip of a thing in those days, but you and me, we were like this," he held his two index fingers side by side. "You and your old man here came for a ride in my Jag once, remember? Big old car, vintage like. Had trafficators, proper ones that stuck out the side, none of your flashing light nonsense. You worked them all the way home, remember. We went round a few extra corners just for the fun of it. Remember?"

"Vaguely," I said.

I did have a quite clear memory of twisting a lever on the dashboard of an old-fashioned car under the instruction of the driver and of watching the orange signal arms flicking out from the sides of the car. I remembered becoming acutely bored after the first half-dozen corners and wondering why the driver couldn't work his own levers. But I couldn't remember who the driver was or who else had been in the car.

"Well, they tell me, your old man's got a few good motors stashed away in his garage these days. Could afford a hundred vintage Jags now if he wanted them. Couldn't you, Pieter old son? Come up a bit in the world since we was knocking about together, has old Pieter."

There was some unspecified menace behind the weasel's bonhomie. Van Niekerk looked acutely uncomfortable. It might have been the strain of jet lag and hard work, but he seemed almost to twitch. I was fascinated; the man had obviously known van Niekerk well enough to be invited home in some capacity, to have met me and taken me for a ride in his car, and to remember my name ten years later. What on earth had my father been doing in this man's company?

"But he's a good one, your dad," the weasel said to me, "He doesn't forget his old mates. Always got the time of day for an old friend, has Pieter."

The man produced a thin gold cigarette case from an inside pocket of his dinner jacket and a matching gold lighter. He offered us each a cigarette in turn. Van Niekerk and Bernadette refused, although they both smoke quite heavily. If I had smoked, I would have accepted one. The man seemed not at all put out by the three refusals and slowly lit his own cigarette. When it was firmly alight and he had taken a slow draw he turned to van Niekerk and said, "Well, Pieter old son, can't stand around gossiping all night. Got to see a man about a dog as they say.

Been good to see you. Take care of yourself. Hooroo."

He made his way between the tables to the bar and disappeared around a corner.

"Pieter, who was *that?*" Bernadette said.

"Oh just someone I once knew."

"But Pieter darling, how on earth could you know anybody like that *man?* He really is quite *déclassé.* What in *heaven's* name does he *do?* How on earth did he know Anasuya?"

For once in my life I too wanted to know the answers to Bernadette's inane questions. But my father wasn't answering.

"I don't know. He was somebody I had some business dealings with years ago. He doesn't matter. I'm getting tired of this place. Let's go to the Sad Trumpet for a nightcap."

"What was his name?" I said.

"I don't know," my father said, very irritated.

"Can't you remember? He knew yours well enough. And mine."

"Oh, his name's Dino. Dino Torri."

"Oh, how too, too *sinister* for *words!*" Bernadette said, doing her little handclapping routine, "He must be a real live *gangster.* Oh is he Pieter, is he a real gangster? You *know,* the Mafia and all that sort of *thing,* is he?"

"No."

"Oh dear, I thought for a moment he might be a *mobster.*"

"We don't have mobsters in England."

"Oh dear."

By this time we had all stood up and were about to leave. Bernadette was fiddling with her handbag. A waiter arrived with two more brandy crusters and a soda water.

"Compliments of Mr Torri."

"We're leaving, I'm afraid."

"Very good, sir."

We made our way in the direction of the door, following the waiter with the tray of refused drinks. The door was in full view of that section of the bar that had been obscured from our table. As we left I saw that Dino Torri was drinking with two other men and a woman wearing a silk shawl with gold tassels. He bowed to me. I bowed back. Van Niekerk must have caught the gesture from the corner of his eye. Without turning his head he said, "Don't have anything to do with him, Anasuya. If you meet him again or he gets in contact with you, don't have anything to do with him. Let me know immediately. Is that clear?"

"If you say so, but who is he exactly?"

"It doesn't matter. He's just someone I once had dealings with when we lived in Putney. It would have been better if I hadn't, but I couldn't have known that at the time."

Six months later, I read in one of the Liverpool papers that a racehorse called Lone Pine had been mysteriously poisoned in its stable. Lone Pine's part owner, Mr Dino Torri, was quoted as saying that this sort of thing was becoming all too common in the racing world. He hoped the animal what did the deed would be brought to justice. Owning half a dead horse isn't quite the same thing as importing twenty kilos of heroin, but it has the same sort of feel about it. And my father knew Dino Torri in those Putney days, maybe even in the days when he was courting my mother. Enough; back to Kilminster's first dinner at our place.

"Well if you say you don't swindle people, maybe you don't," Jennifer conceded, "But why don't all of us go to the Turner exhibition?"

"Darling, I am very busy at the moment. And I don't much like Turner."

"You wouldn't, he's too free, too much of a messer. I'll just have to go with James then. James, when shall I meet you and where?"

Kilminster hummed and um-erred a bit. At that time—and he could only have been out of his seminary for three or four months—I think he was simply confused about the conventions of this sort of thing. He wouldn't have had a clue if it was normal practice or not for married women of Jennifer's class and age to arrange to meet young men with a view to attending exhibitions under the very noses of their husbands. And there was still the matter of his becoming a lodger, which hadn't been mentioned, let alone discussed. He blushed, not deeply or vividly, but with evident confusion.

"Oh, umm, anytime that suits you. Any time after I finish work."

The mention of work clearly interested my father more than the prospect of Kilminster escorting his wife around the Tate.

"What do you do?" he asked Kilminster. It was probably the first direct question he'd put to him all evening.

"I'm a driver. Biscuits. I deliver them."

Kilminster wasn't at all embarrassed by this. He spoke up like a man.

"You've been doing this long?"

"Three months."

"And before that? You've not just left school, I take it?"

My father was thawing a little. I think he really was interested in Kilminster's work history—in some ways he's a very good judge of people, how they make their money is one of the ways in which he judges them.

"Well, in a manner of speaking, I have. I was in a seminary."

"Training to become a priest?"

"Yes."

"Why did you leave?"

"I decided I wasn't cut out for the priesthood."

"Well, that was probably sensible. I don't think that the clergy have much of a role to play these days. They can be useful as social workers, of course, but then they might as well be trained as social workers."

"I wanted to be a theologian. A theorist, not a social worker."

"But you started to doubt that there was a god to theorise about." Van Niekerk said this more as a statement than a question.

"No," Kilminster said, "I'm sure there is a god."

"Really?" Jennifer said, half-incredulous.

"I have never doubted it."

"You still believe in Mary, mother of God, the immaculate

conception, the diet of worms, the thirty-nine steps, all that sort of thing?"

"Oh yes," Kilminster said, "And I believe Protestants all go to hell because they eat babies."

"He's quick, this lad, isn't he?" Jennifer said to van Niekerk.

"But it's true," Kilminster said very seriously, "Outside Protestant convents there is always this little pile of bones."

"And there are tins of pet food outside Chinese restaurants?" Jennifer said.

"Exactly."

"But why did you leave your seminary?"

"I just wasn't meant to be a priest, that's all."

"In what way?"

Again Kilminster blushed slightly. Van Niekerk said, "Leave the boy alone, Jennifer. Thousands of people decide they do not wish to be priests for all sorts of reasons."

"But I'm interested. I've never known a—what do you m' call it?—a seminarian before."

"I wanted to lead my own life, basically."

"Quite right too," my father said.

The meal proceeded to its conclusion without too much further strain. I think my father had typed Kilminster as a mixed-up boy, a likable lad who was slowly coming to see the error of his former beliefs and was doing something about it. I doubt that he thought Kilminster would ever amount to very much in the real world—he lacked drive and clear-sightedness—complete rehabilitation wasn't really on the cards, but the boy would find something useful to do with his life, that was the main thing. I suppose, in an off-hand, avuncular way, van Niekerk ended the meal quite liking Kilminster. He certainly didn't see him as a threat.

After dinner Kilminster offered to help with the washing up. I was sent to bed. I awoke to hear my parents arguing in the kitchen.

"But Jennifer, we don't need a boarder. We are simply not that poor. Very soon we will be much, much better off. Then we'll move from here to somewhere more pleasant."

"Well that will happen when it happens, but at the moment there is no reason why we shouldn't let the flat. Besides, we need a babysitter."

"We've managed quite well with Helen."

"Yes, but Helen has to be sent back to her mother and father by midnight. With someone living in the flat we can come home whenever we like."

This was a good point, actually. It was probably the one that did the trick. Van Niekerk does rather like to stay out until three or four in the morning if the spirit moves him. He put up a bit more resistance though, arguing that it was not quite, well, right to have a man as a babysitter and anyway I was now nine and quite capable of being by myself.

"Until four in the morning?"

"This isn't a student hostel, Jennifer."

"All I'm suggesting is that we give the poor boy the use of the flat for a reasonable rental."

I don't think I heard Jennifer refer to Kilminster as a *poor boy* or even *boy* ever again, but my distinct impression of that midnight discussion is that she reduced Kilminster almost to the status of waif. As I say, I don't think van Niekerk's objections had anything much to do with regarding Kilminster as a rival. By morning they had been overcome. Kilminster moved in a few days later.

* * * * * * *

Now to do the seduction of Kilminster scene. The education of young James at the hands of the skilled Mrs Jennifer van Niekerk. Tiddle *de pom*. I asked Kilminster about it yesterday. I told him he could confess everything to me without fear of embarrassment or censure, that my chosen role as the recorder of the *condition humaine* precluded any harsh judgemental attitudes.

"You're a creepy little voyeur, that's your trouble."

We were walking around the bay of Achilli. It is from here that Achilles set sail for Troy after Odysseus had run him to earth dressed as a woman in the local palace. He was one of the great drag-queens and draft-resisters of all time, Achilles. But it didn't do him any good in the end. There was a strong wind blowing and the waves were charging up the beach so that Kilminster and I had to jump sideways every now and then. We could have walked on the dry sand, of course, but it is softer and littered with plastic. There must be something odd about the tides in the bay, for all the plastic rubbish in the Aegean seems to end up on this beach. Otherwise the landscape is unspoilt, the mountains grey and green in the grey winter light. Yesterday there were half a dozen fires burning on the lower slopes where the shepherds had set a match to the shrubs and other ground cover—presumably as some sort of regeneration of pasture procedure—the flames from the fires were rushing before the wind, but still lagging behind the streams of smoke that flowed along the contours of the mountains in front of them. The flames themselves were a stunning bright orange in a landscape that was otherwise nothing but a hundred shades of grey and green. Inland from the plastic beach, people were harvesting olives, climbing into the trees and hitting the branches with sticks, or raking through the leaves with short plastic rakes. The olives fall to the ground to be picked up and loaded into sacks. In the evening a small procession of donkeys, weighed down under their loads of olives, passes the taverna. The pickers walk beside their beasts, belabouring them occasionally with sticks, much as they have spent the day belabouring the olive trees. But the beach, Achilles' last taste of home, is covered above the high-tide mark with tattered and broken plastic, like detritus from some long-forgotten Cristo work of art. So Kilminster and I took our chances on the hard sand, knocking each other occasionally, jostling for the favoured landward position.

"You're encouraging me to write this book or whatever it is. Tell me what I need to know."

"Jennifer and I took to screwing like rabbits."

"Yes, I know that. But the first time. What happened the first time?"

"You've read *The Crooked River.*"

"Yeah, but in real life, what happened? There's not much correspondence between you and that Spiros character."

"How do you know I'm not secretly a driving instructor, the whole academic thing may be a façade."

"Oh, come on James, talk sense."

We both increased our pace and held our breath until we were clear of the dead cow that has been rotting on the beach for the last month. It doesn't, in fact, smell very badly; it's now almost all bones and dried skin and it's half buried in the sand anyway.

By the time we'd walked along the goat track on the other side of the bay and reached the small promontory called, god help us, Achilles' Heel, I had more or less induced serious conversation. While Kilminster talked we sat in the lee of a rock, the collars of our jackets turned up around our ears, watching the waves break on the heel. In the *Odyssey*, Homer often talks about the 'grey surf'. It's a felicitous phrase, more so than the 'wine-dark sea'.

For the first few weeks after Kilminster moved into our house he continued to drive his delivery van. Once or twice, when he was making deliveries in the immediate area, he brought it home for lunch. On one occasion he off-loaded a tin of cream crackers. It was a large tin, one of those cubic foot ones. An extra tin had been inadvertently loaded at the depot. He kept some of the biscuits in his flat, but most of them he gave to us. Jennifer was delighted. Van Niekerk wasn't.

"But they are stolen, Jennifer."

"Pinching biscuits is honest, working-class crime—it's not like your sort."

I don't think van Niekerk liked the idea of petty crimes being committed from his house, it lowered the tone. But I also don't think he liked the idea of eating food that Kilminster had provided. He, van Niekerk, was the provider. I think he felt unmanned by eating Kilminster's cream crackers. In the light of his highly eccentric behaviour with food after Jennifer had divorced him, this seems almost certain. Anyway the cream crackers were eaten by Jennifer and myself, van Niekerk hardly touched them.

Quite often we didn't see Kilminster for days at a time. He had to pass through our part of the house to reach his flat, of course, but he came and went at such odd hours that we often missed him. The distant rumbling of his lavatory cistern was often the only sign we had that he was home. He ate with us occasionally, when Jennifer could catch him to issue an invitation. He and van Niekerk began to have real conversations of a sort. I don't think Kilminster had taken much interest in world politics in the seminary—perhaps he had not been allowed to take much interest. At our place he started reading the serious papers with considerable attention. Van Niekerk, of course, always had the world situation at his finger-tips, and anything that Kilminster had read that morning could easily provide a forum in which van Niekerk could instruct young James. Looking back to those scenes—van Niekerk explaining, Kilminster listening attentively—I have the strong impression that my father really enjoyed playing the teacher; it wasn't a role he had played before and Kilminster was a bright pupil. But all their discussions of world politics remained just that: discussions. There were never any arguments, the talk always remained safe, pragmatic. Van Niekerk had little time for ideology and was pleased to see that Kilminster didn't either. The trick to understanding the world in order to change it to one's advantage was to understand the power balances, the economic forces, the political structures, the real motives of real people. Kilminster seemed to grasp this very quickly. If he queried van Niekerk's interpretation of events, it was always in terms of the pragmatic considerations of the *realpolitik*. In these terms he challenged my father quite often, although in the end it was usually my father's superior wisdom and command of facts that carried the day. Once he'd seen the light, Kilminster always conceded the point gracefully. I suppose in a sense they became, or seemed to become, quite friendly. The qualification is more than necessary. Kilminster, devious little failed-jesuit that he was, thought van Niekerk a toad from the word go. He was interested in van Niekerk's politics only as far as they provided facts that could be radically re-interpreted in his own mind.

But the real question is obviously not about Kilminster's creepy little acts of diplomatic concealment, but about van Niekerk's. Did my father's measured, practical, no-nonsense approach really express what he felt? His views were not, it might be remarked, those of a professional gun-runner and swindler. For all his lack of ideology, there was a decent, conservative air to his pronouncements, and yet it was gun-running, swindling, and other activities of a similar ilk that were soon to be providing a good part of his bread and butter. His views were most certainly not those associated with heroin-importing and call-girl racketeering—activities which Kilminster readily ascribes to him. Nor, for that matter, was there much of the Dutch Reformed puritan hoarder to be discerned in his conversation—and yet that is the personality profile attributed to him by no finer student of human nature than Jennifer Saintenoy formerly Kilminster formerly van Niekerk *née* Goldstein. Who ought to know.

So was my father playing as elaborate a game of deception as Kilminster? I've thought about this a lot. I don't believe he was. I think my father works on different levels. Sitting at home, talking over the dinner table to this bright if somewhat naïve young man, passing the wine, van Niekerk *believed* what he was saying. The practical, conservative, civilised values that informed his talk were, at that moment, his real values. Half an hour later he might have been on the phone to god knows who—Dino Torri, Deitzinger, the gnomes of Zurich, the president of the Bank of Mexico,

Mac the Knife—and his values would have been those appropriate to whatever transaction was being mooted. And at that moment those values would have been just as much *his* as the dinner table ones of thirty minutes before.

Not long before my father's sudden disappearance, I was to experience in a very dramatic way the manner in which these levels (or compartments, if you like) of my father's personality, failed to clash with one another; how two utterly contradictory sets of actions could be performed without apparent conflict. It frightened me. It still frightens me. I don't really look forward to the time in the near future when I will have to describe in detail in my growing pile of blue exercise books just what happened.

All this theorising aside; relations between Kilminster and my father became cordial enough for van Niekerk to joke with Kilminster about their first meeting. After lunch one Sunday we all went for a walk in Richmond Park.

"So, James," van Niekerk said as we strolled past a herd of deer, "what are your feelings about India these days? Is there any 'hope' for that country?"

"Come off it, I was nervous at the time."

And things remained on this more or less amicable footing until, late one night, van Niekerk inadvertently sat on Kilminster. Things changed pretty rapidly after that, but they had been changing gradually before then as well, but mainly in relation to Jennifer, to whom we had better return.

About three weeks after Kilminster moved in, Jennifer discovered that the Turner exhibition had only two days left to go. She arranged to meet Kilminster at the Tate in time to see the paintings before lunch. They then ate in the gallery's restaurant, walked along the Embankment to Westminster, took a boat to Greenwich, jumped backwards and forwards across the zero meridian, looked over the maritime museum, took tea in a cafe and realised it was later than they thought. They came home in a taxi for which Kilminster insisted on paying half the fare.

I had arrived home from school to find the house deserted and so had gone to visit my friend Mandy, three streets away. Van Niekerk had arrived home not long after, but had not been unduly worried, thinking that Jennifer and I had gone somewhere together. When Jennifer and Kilminster arrived, slightly rushed, but in high spirits, my father was furious to find that I wasn't with them.

"The child's been kidnapped."

"Oh, don't be ridiculous, she's gone to play with one of her friends, probably Mandy."

"Where does Mandy live?"

"Somewhere quite near."

"But where, exactly?"

"I don't know, Pieter. Stop shouting at me. She lives over towards the council houses somewhere. Anasuya often plays with her, you know that."

"Yes, but she comes home first."

"She probably came home first today. None of us were here, that's all."

"What's Mandy's surname?"

"How should I know?"

"I can't look up her parents in the book if I don't know their name."

"That's right, Pieter darling, you can't. Now calm down. There is no cause for alarm."

"Jennifer, you are being extremely irresponsible. This is no laughing matter. There should always be someone here when she comes home from school. Always."

"Pieter, will you stop shouting."

"I'm not shouting. Now try to think. Have you ever been to Mandy's house? Do you know the street she lives in? Have you ever seen her surname written down? On her satchel or somewhere like that? Please *think*, Jennifer. This is very important."

"I will not be shouted at."

Jennifer marched from the room. Van Niekerk turned to Kilminster, "You don't happen to know where this Mandy lives do you?"

"More or less," Kilminster said.

"Well, good god, man, why didn't you say so? Where does she live? Speak up, man, speak up."

"About two or three streets away, towards the council houses."

"Oh my god, you are no better than Jennifer. We can't go

knocking on every house that is two or three streets away towards the housing estate."

"There is a whole group of kids who play in the street. Mandy and Anasuya often play with them."

"Well let's have a look. Come on, man, come on."

We were playing hopscotch on the pavement outside Mandy's place when my father's car came to a rapid halt in the street beside us. My father bounded from the driver's door and enfolded me in his arms.

"Oh my darling, thank god you're safe."

By craning my neck out of his embrace I could see Kilminster in the passenger seat, but not Jennifer.

"Where's Mummy?"

"She's at home, darling, I've been so worried."

Mandy and the other children were watching us in amazement. Mandy said, "What's the matter, Mr Kneejerk?"

"Is Mummy all right?" I said.

"Yes, she's all right, Anasuya. She's just very irresponsible, that's all."

"Why?"

"She left you all alone."

"I'm all right."

"But I didn't know where you were."

"I was here. I always come here after school."

"Well, never mind. You can come home with me now. I've been so worried."

"But it's not tea time yet. I want to play some more."

By now Kilminster had left the car and joined the group.

"Hello, James," I said.

"Hello, Anasuya."

"I think you should come home now," van Niekerk said.

"But why, daddy, I want to play some more."

"It's getting late."

"No it's not."

"Anasuya, it's time to go home."

"She never goes home till tea time, Mr Kneejerk," Mandy

informed him.

"Well, not today. Come along."

"I'm not going."

"Anasuya, please don't be obstinate."

"I'm not coming home till tea time."

"Anasuya, there have been enough worries without your being difficult. Now come along. Jump into the car and we will go home."

I refused point blank. The other children stood mute. My father picked me up and carried me to the car, dumping me bodily into the front seat. I sulked. As we turned the corner I looked back to where Kilminster stood talking to my friends.

"James isn't coming home, why should I?"

"Oh Christ, James." The car slowed momentarily. "No, he can walk, it was half his fault."

By the time Kilminster passed rapidly through our bit of the house on his way upstairs, Jennifer and van Niekerk were at it hammer and tongs. Jennifer probably did feel a little guilty about not being home when I returned from school, but she certainly wasn't going to allow van Niekerk the benefit of an admission. She accused him of not being able to accept that I was growing up, of being over-protective, of being paranoid. My father, further enraged by Jennifer's unrepentant aggression, redoubled his accusations of irresponsibility. My feeble attempts at insisting that I didn't mind that no one had been home, and anyway Daddy didn't really mean it when he said Mummy was irresponsible, only made matters worse. Worried, anxious, and upset, I made my way to Kilminster's flat. This was the first time I'd been there since he moved in. His door was closed. I knocked on it timidly and formally. He opened it, a piece of bread and jam in one hand, a mug of tea in the other. From downstairs the sound of my parents fighting came audibly to where we stood.

"Come in."

I entered.

"Do you mind if I shut the door?"

"No."

"Do you want some bread and jam?"

"No…yes."

"Well, I'll make you some, if you don't eat it, I will."

Kilminster shuffled around his kitchen for a minute while I sat on his bed in the other room. He'd furnished the room by sticky-taping a large Picasso print of a clown to one wall and nailing a crucifix to another. On the table under the window there was now an untidy pile of books. Kilminster returned and handed me a large slice of bread and jam on a saucer. He sat on his table, his head half an inch from the sloping ceiling.

"Do they often fight like this?"

"No…sometimes."

"It was half my fault really, I should have kept an eye on the time. Sorry about it all. Were you worried when you got home?"

"No, not very."

We finished our slices of bread and jam simultaneously. Kilminster licked his fingers one at a time, making popping noises as he pulled them from his mouth. I did the same.

"Want any more?"

"Yes."

From the kitchen he said, "Are they happy with each other, your parents? You know, most of the time?"

"Yes. I don't know."

"Sorry, I shouldn't have asked."

"It's all right."

Kilminster returned with more bread and jam. He said, "Jennifer told me she knocked your father out once."

"She threw an ashtray at him. That big one downstairs."

"Hell. Is that how he got that scar on his forehead?"

"Yes."

"I don't think they can be very happy with each other."

"Oh, maybe, I don't know."

"You don't know much. Can I offer you a glass of milk, or tea? Do you drink tea?"

"I don't know."

"Have you ever tried it?"

"No."

"Might as well try it now. I'll put lots of milk in."

Kilminster and I chatted for half an hour. The dim sounds of argument abated and then ceased. There was a knock on the door. Kilminster said, "Come in," and Jennifer entered. She turned and closed the door behind her.

"Sorry about all that. Did that bastard just leave you standing in the street?"

"It was only two-minutes' walk."

"But all the same. Did he just drive off and leave you?"

"Well, yes."

"He's a complete shit."

She crossed to the bed, sat down and put an arm around me. She peered into the mug I was holding.

"Tea? Is James leading you into decadent pastures?"

"He put lots of milk in."

"Watch it. It'll be gin next."

Kilminster said, "I've never even drunk gin myself."

"You can both become old soaks together."

"Would you like some?" he asked her.

"Gin?"

"Tea. It's that or milk."

We all had more tea and bread and jam. Nobody said very much. When we'd finished, Jennifer said, "Is this what you live on, bread and jam and tea?"

"It's good working-class food. Generations of my forebears survived on it. When they could afford it, mind you. Often it was just potatoes."

"I'd invite you down for dinner tonight, but the meal will be unbearable. Pieter and I have entered one of our glowering silence phases."

"I'm quite happy up here, thanks."

"We're none too happy down there. Still we ought to descend. Come on, Ansu."

She held out a hand to Kilminster so that he could help her

from the bed. This he did, pulling her to her feet without leaving the table he was sitting on.

"Thanks for the day," Jennifer said, still holding Kilminster's hand, "The middle was good, even if things did turn nasty at the end."

Jennifer and I descended to the promised gloomy meal. I'd rather have stayed with Kilminster.

* * * * * * *

There were a couple of weeks after Kilminster finished driving his biscuit van and before term started when he had nothing to do. He went to Liverpool to visit his parents for a few days. Jennifer and I both missed him more than we'd expected. He came back both happy and despondent.

"They can't understand. They just can't understand. They've lost face in the community. 'And is it true, Mrs Kilminster, that young James isn't going for the priesthood anymore?' 'Well, in a manner of speaking, Mrs O'Grady, yes, he's transferred his studies to the university.' 'Ah, well, Mrs Kilminster, never moind, there's many who find the life of the cloth not to their liking, and who's to think the worst of them for it?'"

"And you couldn't make your parents understand why you'd left?"

"No, no, they are utterly nonplussed. But it's good to be back in sunny Putney. I quite missed the place."

"We missed you."

"Yeah, well, by *place* I mean you two, of course."

Three days later Jennifer and Kilminster were alone in the house at lunchtime. They were both doing some 'pre-reading' for their university courses which were to start within a week. Kilminster sat at his table, occasionally looking up to watch the simplified people in the hospital grounds below his window. I'm quite sure his mind was on the matters raised by his reading. Jennifer sat at the table she had established for herself in a corner of her bedroom. My bet is she was doodling on a piece of paper, half a dozen books open at one unread page or another. She stood up, walked to the hall and shouted up the stairs.

"Hey, James!"

"What?"

"Do you know how to cook a soufflé?"

"What's that?"

"Come down and I'll show you."

After Kilminster had been educated in this art, he and Jennifer sat facing each other on stools in the kitchen, the remains of the soufflé on the table beside them.

"What did you actually tell your parents about leaving the seminary?"

"Just that I wanted to lead my own life. They couldn't understand. Being a priest would have been leading my own life, the best life possible. My mother kept asking me if I'd lost the faith. When I said no, she just stared at me in dumb incomprehension and then started the whole round of questions again. Round and round."

"What was it that actually forced you to leave the seminary, did you one day decide it wasn't for you—or did you have some sort of crisis?"

"I was advised to leave."

"By whom?"

"My confessor."

"And you were happy with his advice?"

"It seemed reasonable. I couldn't keep confessing the same old thing over and over again. They didn't make it easy either. I had to catch him, my confessor, any confessor, before he started saying mass. Confess, confess, confess. Catholics confess all the time as it is, but we used to have mass every morning at six o'clock."

"So?"

Kilminster blushed.

"Sorry, I'm embarrassing you."

"No, not really, I'd like to tell you. It's this confessing thing."

"Confess to me, then."

"As I say, we used to have mass every morning at six o'clock. You had to be in a state of grace in order to take the Host, you know, the wafer, the body of Christ."

"I might be Jewish, I'm not uneducated."

"Sorry—so one had to be in a state of grace before one went to bed at night and one had to stay that way until six the next morning...."

"And one got up to all these hijinks with the other novices in the dorm...."

"Hell, no. We had our separate cells, rooms...."

"So you masturbated?"

"...Yes."

Jennifer laughed. She stood up from her stool, embracing Kilminster.

"You poor thing. What did you do?"

"What do you mean, 'What did I do?'"

"In the morning, James. I know all about the other activity."

"It was necessary to confess and receive absolution before communion. So I had to find my confessor or one of the other fathers and confess and do penance before Mass. There usually wasn't all that much time, and it was embarrassing running around looking for someone too. And then the confession wasn't easy, although they got used to it in the end. 'Again, my son?' 'Again father.' 'The body is the temple of the soul, my son.' 'Yes father.' 'He who desecrates the temple denies Christ a dwelling in His house.' 'Yes father.' 'Are you truly penitent, my son?' 'Yes father.' 'I absolve you in the name of the Father, the Son and the Holy Ghost.' 'Thank you father.' 'Say five Our Fathers and ten rosaries.' 'Yes father.' 'Go in peace my son.'"

"And then you could scoff the wafer?"

"Yes."

"And you still believe all this stuff?"

"More or less. I haven't been to a Mass or confession since I left. But I believe."

"I went to a bar mitzvah the other day. A nephew of mine. Tamar's son. I cried, but I don't believe."

"Maybe I don't either. The ritual itself used to be comforting though, but it's become less and less so. I lit a candle in the cathedral last week, but it didn't mean very much. It was just a stick of wax I'd paid two bob for, burning away with various other sticks of wax. I don't think God could give a hoot how many damn two-bob candles he had lit for him. If I was God, if I was omnipresent, omnitemporal, omniscient, and omni just about everything else, I don't think I'd be worrying about candles or wafers or wine or prayers or anything—I wouldn't be that small-minded. I'm sure a god exists, but what's he got to do with us?"

"What are—were—your fantasies?"

"What?"

"When you masturbated?"

"I don't know."

"What do you mean, you don't know? You can't wank without fantasising."

"Making love."

"To whom?"

"A woman. Someone I'd invented."

"I masturbated the other night. Before my husband came to bed. I imagined I was screwing you. I haven't invented you. What are your present fantasies, when you're wanking away up there under the roof?"

"…err.…"

"Well you haven't stopped doing it just because they threw you out of a convent, have you? Don't blush. Jesus! What a scene, the pair of us wanking away, hard at it, you in your bed, me in mine, imagining each other and doing nothing about it. Let's go up to your flat and screw."

"But I'm a Catholic."

"Bugger that, Kilminster. Are you still a virgin?"

"Yes…but I've had lots of practice."

So that's how it all started, if Kilminster is to be believed, which he probably is—his account fits quite well with what Jennifer has already told me. I don't know about that last line of dialogue though; it looks too neat. It rounds off the scene too wittily. It's true that Jennifer has Spiros say it in *The Crooked River* under slightly different circumstances, and, of course, I once used it myself, but then I pinched it from the book. But maybe Kilminster invented the line; he's a bright lad and repartee under emotionally charged circumstances is not beyond him by any means.

* * * * * * *

Life proceeded fairly smoothly for slightly over a year. Jennifer and Kilminster conducted their affair discreetly but vigorously, which was quite easy since they attended the same university and lived under the same roof. They *did it*—played the two-backed beast—in the mornings or afternoons when I was at school and van Niekerk at work, putting Kilminster's narrow bed through its paces with gusto tempered with wit, passion, and tenderness. The cultural side of the affair, for this was no matter of simple lust, took place in the art galleries, cinemas, pubs, museums, and lecture theatres of Bloomsbury and environs. Regent's Park was no stranger to their wander-ings—arms entwined around each other's waists—or, if the day were warm and the grass dry, their languid conversations and gentle touchings while sprawled upon the green. They held hands in coffee shops, ate meals of dubious culinary delight, but hearty good cheer with other students in the utilitarian surrounds of the university cafeteria and attended the odd lunch-time meeting or concert. They also did some work. Kilminster, I'm afraid, a trifle more than Jennifer. The habits of the semi-nary still lingered with him. He arose at five-thirty and worked until Jennifer appeared in his doorway after van Niekerk and I had departed for office and school. That alone gave him a head start of four absorbed and uninterrupted hours. And often he would work until midnight. And Kilminster was very bright. But, as Jennifer explained to him, he was a scientist and hard slog was his appointed lot. For a humanist like my mother, one who's domain is the literature and wisdom of the ages, it was more a matter of allowing one's sensibilities to vibrate in harmony with the sonnets and plays that one, from time to time, read. Too much hard grind actually *dulled* the critical faculties, was indeed counter-productive. Jennifer, to put the matter bluntly, was only playing. The urgency that had informed her decision to become a student had vanished with the coming of her new lover. The necessity of earning a degree in order to give van Niekerk the slip faded in the glow of her present happiness. Her time of hard and sustained labour was to come, of course; the desk lamp that was to illuminate her clattering typewriter, her over-full ashtray, her growing piles of heavily corrected manuscript was to be overpowered repeatedly by the grey skies of dawn in the all-too-near future. But not yet. There was a light-hearted, floating feeling to that year that transfused every action, every mundane piece of living. Not that she and Kilminster didn't have the occasional lovers' tiff. This was the lad's first affair. He was learning. His mistress still slept every night, if not exactly in the arms of, at least by the side of, the gross beast van Niekerk; while more or less directly above the sleepers' heads true love burnt like a solitary candle through the dark watches of the night. And, of course, in the background, a black spot on the clear horizon, was the chance of discovery.

In Harrods' knitwear department Jennifer leant upon Kilminster's shoulder, looking critically at the piles of sweaters and jerseys displayed before her. Kilminster slid his hand under the waistband of the sweater she was, in fact, wearing, feeling the flesh warm over the bones of her hip. She leaned further towards him, turning her head to be kissed, oblivious of shop assistants and other purchasers. From behind hands descended on both their shoulders.

"Unwise, children. Very unwise."

"Jesus! Tamar."

"Jesus, Jennifer. Do you have to practically rape this young man in broad daylight? In Harrods? Your friends and relations do come here as well, you know."

But still, that sort of thing lent spice to the whole affair. The gods smiled. It was, after all, only Tamar they had sent. Tamar, whose loyalty to her oldest friend was no more in doubt than was her present disloyalty to her oldest friend's brother, Simon, her own lawful husband. The gentleman Tamar happened to be shopping with in Harrods grasped Kilminster by the hand, gave him a knowing wink, man to man. All four retired to the store's café for coffee and sticky cakes.

Ah, bliss it was to be thirty-one, the mother of a bright and pretty ten-year-old daughter and the mistress of a lean and hungry young student. But very heaven it was to be J. Kilminster Esq. escapee from a hard and celibate brotherhood, the lover of a brown-haired and passionate enchantress, held captive, but not possessed, by her swine of a husband.

So I write with a certain purpleness of prose, albeit tongue-in-cheek. Forgive me. The weather has turned warm again, I am sitting on my room's balcony. I can see Kilminster walking along the beach, silhouetted against the glitter of the Aegean. I am half asleep, drugged by the warmth, and the spirit of a hard, cold narrative style is not upon me. I have filled too many pages with it. I will fill more. For the time being flippancy rides my pen. Still, in my own defence, the style is not without its merits. It does fit the feel, the tenor of those days. I was happy then; we were all happy then. Even van Niekerk was happy after his fashion.

I was happy because my parents appeared to get along with each other. They did not fight. Well, they did not fight *often*. Jennifer sang and was radiant. Van Niekerk was busy at his dubious trade and talking with real confidence of his imminent re-election to the ranks of nature's millionaires. Our gentleman lodger, the mad student upstairs, became my new and close friend. Often when I arrived home from school I would climb to his flat, knock and enter. If he wasn't home I would feel a momentary pang of disappointment. If he was, I would sit on his bed and talk. I became mistress of his little kitchen—I became a dab hand at making tea and slices of bread and jam.

When autumn turned to winter and Kilminster began to use the hissing gas fire, Jennifer bought him a wire toasting fork. We added crumpets to the menu. In one of Elizabeth David's excellent cookery books there is a recipe for a dish called Sulaman's Pilaf. Relying as it does on left-over mutton and raisins, the meal can in no way be regarded as *haute cuisine*. Mrs David refers to it with her customary wit as 'a most comforting dish'. I would borrow that phrase to describe a plateful of crumpets and honey that have been toasted by an attic flat's gas fire while the evening descends outside the window. To induce the real womb-effect, add a few drops of rain to the other side of the glass.

* * * * * * *

So what happened? How did van Niekerk find out?

It's an old story: the guilty lovers surprised by the jealous husband, in delectable fragrance or whatever that Latin phrase is. As old as the poor old hills, part of the *condition humaine*, ho hum.

The husband goes away to fight a foreign foe, or for a weekend business trip, or, in our case, to take his daughter on an educational excursion to Bath.

The two lovers decide to spend a proper night together in a proper double bed. The marital bed itself. Why not?

For some reason the husband's trip is cut short.

He returns earlier than expected.

Ructions!

There are variations, of course. In the version of *Matty Groves* that Joan Baez sings, Lord Allan stands at the foot of the bed asking,

> How now, how now, little Matty Groves
> Its how do you like my sheets?
> And how do you like my fair young bride
> Who lies in your arms asleep?

And Matty, whose capacity for repartee under emotionally charged circumstances must have been phenomenal, replies,

> Oh it's good I like your feather bed
> And it's good I like your sheets
> But it's best I like your fair young bride
> Who lies in my arms asleep.

One of the great ripostes. Eat your heart out Oliver Mellors, eat your heart out Julien Sorel, eat your heart out James Kilminster. Kilminster was speechless, tongue-tied. Or maybe, to be charitable, he was winded. In our version of the story, the version that was to become common currency around the table of the *Après Fin de Siècle Dining Club*, that was later to pass into the folk-lore of the château, van Niekerk inadvertently sat on Kilminster.

My father and I had had a most successful visit to Bath, but on our last afternoon there it had rained steadily and van Niekerk had decided not to spend another night in the hotel, but to return to Putney. It can't have been very late when we arrived home, but all the lights were out. I woke from a doze in the passenger seat beside van Niekerk, allowed myself to be led sleepily to our front door, declined offers of a hot chocolate drink, accepted my father's observation that Jennifer was probably out visiting friends, and made my way to my bedroom and real sleep. My father apparently spent some time in the room he used as his office reading his mail and then took himself to the darkened matrimonial bedroom. Opening the door, he heard Jennifer's breathing and, wishing to be considerate, did not turn on the light, but made his way to the bed to alert her gently, without fully rousing her from the arms of Morpheus, to his return. He sat down beside her, perhaps to caress her neck or shoulder. Freak out!

Sod Morpheus and his chaste classical embrace. Jennifer slept in the all-too-carnal arms of James Kilminster, failed seminarian and student of physics. Jennifer was actually still asleep.

Kilminster had heard van Niekerk approaching the bedroom, had shot like a rabbit half out of the bed, seen the impossibility of even getting under the bed with all his scattered clothes, and shot back into his burrow, pulling the blankets over his head. 'Like an ostrich' as he would explain in the polished raconteur version. 'I thought if I buried my head he would cease to exist.' That sort of phenomenalism has brought more than ostriches to grief.

Sitting in the lee of the rock the other day, watching the waves break over Achilles' Heel, I tried to get an accurate version of what happened next.

"James, are you sure he actually sat on you?"

"Yes, of course."

"That's not just an embellishment for the sake of the story?"

"No, no. He actually sat on my face. I was lying flat on my back with the blankets over my head."

"Are you sure he didn't just sit down beside you, sort of nudge you a bit?"

"Who was in that bed, you or me?"

Take it or leave it. The bed, as I remember it, wasn't very high off the floor—about sixty centimetres, I'd say. It is just possible that my father sort of dumped himself halfway across it in order to be near the dark mass of Jennifer's hair on the pillow. But it seems more likely to me, the scene seems more plausible if we imagine, that van Niekerk merely sat on the edge of the bed, perhaps bumping Kilminster with his hip or discovering him when he leant across to touch Jennifer. But, as the man says, I wasn't in that bed, and he most decidedly was.

The scene then runs fairly true to form: exclamations of "What the dickens!", "Good god…!", "Who the devil…?"; the light being turned on; van Niekerk, cold, shocked, affronted; Jennifer blinking in sleepy, annoyed non-comprehension, suddenly sitting bolt upright, the sheet falling away from her breasts; Kilminster flat on his back, peering over the edge of the blankets as if from a burrow with ferrets below and terrier dogs above; van Niekerk commanding, "Out! Get out!"; Kilminster doing nothing, gripping the blankets at his chin tighter if anything; Jennifer saying, "For god's sake, Pieter, let him get dressed in peace"; van Niekerk slowly and contemptuously leaving the room; both Kilminster and Jennifer leaping from the bed, Kilminster to fumble his way wildly into his clothes, Jennifer to put on a dressing gown with slightly less haste; the two of them leaving the room—Kilminster to scuttle up to his flat, Jennifer to confront her husband in the living room. Old hat, the whole thing. At least Matty Groves and Lord Allan fought a duel with two fine beaten swords, Matty having the better of them and Lord Allan the worse.

I awoke to the sound of my parents fighting, really fighting. This was something that hadn't happened since the coming of Kilminster. All we'd had was the odd minor dust-up like the one I've described after Jennifer hadn't been home to meet me from school. This wasn't a minor dust-up. This was ashtray-hurling stuff. My father was saying things like, "In my own house!" Jennifer's replies started with phrases like "If you weren't so utterly cold and self-centred...." After about ten minutes I got out of bed and crept into the living room. Van Niekerk was still wearing his overcoat. Jennifer was clearly naked beneath her dressing gown. I stood in the doorway watching them. It was their faces that frightened me the most. They were both drained of colour, every muscle stretched tight, the lines etched into the flesh like a Dürer woodcut. Their voices were so cold and so charged with anger. It was worse than the time Jennifer had knocked my father out. I looked around for the glass ashtray. It was on its table exactly where it had been before. I edged my way around the side of the room towards it. Jennifer noticed my presence. "Anasuya, go back to bed," she said, but coldly, objectively.

I looked at my parents and I didn't want to run to either of them. I didn't want to be touched or embraced by either of them. I didn't *know* either of them. I wanted James, but first I had to remove the ashtray. I continued around the edge of the room. Neither Jennifer nor van Niekerk took any further notice of me, they remained locked in the depths of their controlled hate and fury. I secured the ashtray and reached the door to the hall.

I opened the door to Kilminster's flat without knocking. He jumped. He was fully dressed, standing in the middle of the little room.

"Oh, it's only you, Anasuya."

"Mummy and Daddy are fighting."

"Yeah, I know. What have you got there?"

I showed him the ashtray, he looked at it with non-comprehension. Then he smiled. I knew the smile, it was the same sad, rueful smile that Jennifer had given me when I'd told her I didn't think my father was very comfortable after she'd knocked him unconscious with the self-same ashtray. It was the resigned, hopeless smile that one human being may give another. It was in a totally different world from the ice and fire of confrontation below us.

"Smart thinking, Batman." Kilminster said.

I sat on his bed as I normally did. He took the ashtray from me, placing it on the table. He said, "It's a pity neither of us smoke."

"Mummy can use it next time we have tea."

"There won't be a next time we have tea, Ansu love. I will have to leave here."

It was like a blow to the face.

"No!"

"I'll have to, Anasuya."

"No you won't. Mummy and Daddy want you to stay."

"Well, I don't know about Jennifer, but your father wants me to go. That's sort of what they are fighting about."

"No it's not. They don't mean it."

Kilminster squatted on his heels in front of me. He took both my hands in his. Very quietly he said, "Listen, Anasuya, you can't keep telling yourself that your parents don't mean it when they quarrel. They do mean it, that's why they quarrel. In some ways they love each other, but in some ways they hate each other. At the moment they hate each other. They really do mean what they are saying to each other down there."

"Don't go, James."

"I'll have to."

From downstairs there came a loud crash.

"Jesus, Mary and Joseph," Kilminster said.

I shivered. Kilminster took his blue donkey jacket from its peg on the door. I put it on, the tips of my fingers just reached the cuffs. Kilminster squatted in front of me again, turning the cuffs back.

"Well we might as well have a traditional slice or two of bread and jam. A sort of last supper."

While he was in the kitchen I repeated my plea for him not to leave. He reappeared with tea and bread and jam. I rubbed my feet together.

"Put your feet under the eiderdown, there's no need to catch cold."

While I arranged myself, he put the room's one chair beside the bed with my mug of tea and plate of bread and jam upon it. He sat on his table and said, "Listen carefully, Anasuya; tomorrow, I will have to find somewhere else to live. I'd rather stay with you and Jennifer, but that's impossible. I'll tell Jennifer where I've gone and she'll be able to bring you to see me sometimes. But I don't think your father is going to like that idea at all. So you'll have to be very careful not to tell him you've seen me. Do you understand?"

"Yes," I mumbled. I was miserable.

I began to cry. I didn't sob. I made no noise at all. The tears just dripped from my eyes. Kilminster crossed to the bed, took the cup of milky tea from my hands and held me, saying nothing. I put my arms around him in their oversized, floppy sleeves. After a few moments Kilminster said, "Here, finish your tea before it gets cold. Then you'd better go downstairs. I think they've finished."

I didn't let go of him. I said, "I want to sleep here."

"No, love, you'd better go back to your own bed."

"You can sleep here too. You can sleep at one end of the bed and I can sleep at the other. Like I did with Samantha when we went to Cornwall."

"Jesus," Kilminster said, more or less to himself, "That really would make the bastard's day." Then he said, "No, I think you'd better go downstairs. Finish your tea first, though."

He disentangled my arms from around his neck and kissed me, saying, "I love you dearly, little Ansu."

When I entered the living room only my father was present. He was sitting in a chair, staring at nothing. The small table upon which the ashtray usually lay had been picked up and hurled at a bookcase. It lay on the floor, one of its legs broken, a few books scattered around it.

When I was almost through the room, my father said, "Anasuya."

"Yes."

"Come here."

I went over to him slowly. He held me in an embrace into which I did not yield.

"I'm sorry Mummy and I have been fighting," he said.

I said nothing.

"Where have you been?" he said, "You should be in bed, asleep."

"To the lavatory," I said.

* * * * * * *

There was a strained and stony silence during breakfast. It was all my parents could do to ask me to pass the butter. They said not a word to each other. My father drove me to school. I sat, small and worried, beside him.

"Anasuya," he said, "You know that I love you very much, don't you?"

"Why can't James stay?"

"Because he's filth!" my father shouted. Then after a few second's pause, he continued very quietly and gently, "Anasuya, James isn't what he seems to be. He fooled me, so there is no reason why he shouldn't have fooled you as well, but James is a very bad man. I know you thought he was your friend. I thought he was my friend too. But that man is incapable of real, decent friendship. We will just have to be thankful that we now know what he is like. I know it is hard for you to understand, but when you are older you will be able to look back and know what I'm telling you now is true. You will just have to forget about James, Anasuya. We all will. Don't cry, darling, I'll always be with you and love you. Tonight when I come home from work, we will all go to the cinema—you, me, and Mummy, just the three of us. And we will eat in a restaurant, that Chinese one, with the chop-sticks. That will be fun, won't it?"

"Mummy likes James," I said.

My father started, as though I'd slapped his face. He began to say something, but changed his mind. We were now parked outside the school; groups of children were entering the gate, the hubbub of yelling and running and game-playing that came from the playground was clearly audible in the closed car. I clutched my satchel to me with one hand and fumbled for the door handle with the other. Van Niekerk leant across, putting his hand on my knee.

"Mummy was fooled by James as well," he said, "She doesn't like him anymore. She doesn't want to see him again."

I cried. My father effected a rather clumsy embrace, saying, "There, there, darling. Don't cry. I love you and Mummy loves you, and some things are hard for a little girl to understand, but everything will be better soon, I promise."

He kissed me and wiped my face with his handkerchief. I clung to him, sobbing. He kissed me again. There was a tap on the window. Mandy and a number of other small friends were lined up on the pavement watching, waiting for me to join them.

"Hey, Anasuya," Mandy said. "Hello, Mr Kneejerk."

"Oh, err, hello Mandy."

I opened the door and climbed out.

"What's the matter?" Mandy said as we walked through the gate.

"James has got to go away."

"Why?"

"I don't know."

I spent a miserable day at school. I ran home, telling myself that James would still be there, that my father had suddenly discovered that Kilminster really was a good friend after all. Only Jennifer was at home. She made me a bowl of cereal. And then, as an afterthought, organised one for herself. We both sat at the kitchen table gloomily eating the stuff.

"James is your friend, isn't he, Mummy?"

"Yes, of course, that's the trouble."

"Daddy said he wasn't your friend anymore."

"That's what I told Daddy. I told him I'd never see James again. Your father hates the idea of me being friends with James."

"James said we could both go to see him at his new house. Only we mustn't tell Daddy."

"Good old James."

We both finished our cereal. Jennifer carried the bowls to the sink. As she was washing them, she said, "Would you like to live with him?"

"What?"

"Would you like it if you and I went to live with James?"

"What about Daddy?"

"That would be Daddy's problem."

"I want James to come back here."

"That's just not possible." Jennifer came over to me, stood holding me, she said, "Look, Anasuya, regardless of what Daddy says, or of what you might hear me say to Daddy, James and I are still good friends, and James is your friend too. I'll take you to see him as soon as possible. But it is best not to mention James's name when your father is around, it will only upset him. Do you see?"

"Yes," I said.

Jennifer bent and kissed me.

"You're my only Ansu and I love you," she said.

I clung to her, kissing her in return.

In those days I was spending quite a bit of time clinging to adults who made desperate confessions of love to me.

* * * * * * *

So life proceeded. My parents were cordial to each other in my presence. Not half as happy as they had been while James had been living with us, but pleasant to each other. They would joke about things in a relaxed way at times. When they remembered, they would tell each other the details of their day. We did a lot of things together, the three of us. We often visited Tamar and Simon, especially when Samantha and Randolph were home from their boarding schools. We went for drives in the country. Picnics. And Jennifer quietly took me to see Kilminster every now and then. He was living with some other students in Bloomsbury, in one of those flats that are below street level with a small area in front of the window. The area contained not only the dustbin from Kilminster's flat, but the dustbins from the three flats above as well. A small, neatly lettered card pinned to the door read: Garbage View Villa. But I liked James's flat; he had the room at the front, so it was possible to hang on the railings above the dustbins and look down into it. There was a clear plastic puzzle (one of those cubes you take to bits and then attempt to reassemble) on the windowsill. If the sun were shining, the puzzle refracted the light into the spectrum so that it sat in a puddle of fragmented rainbow. Jennifer took me there once or twice on Saturday mornings when we were allegedly shopping in town, and on a couple of occasions I was sent to school with a spurious note about a dental appointment which would prevent my attendance during the afternoon.

And Jennifer, of course, saw Kilminster whenever she felt like it. Somehow she managed to retain a nominal enrolment at the university, although she had, in fact, given up completely— she neither attended seminars or lectures or wrote essays. She went there only to see Kilminster; there or to Garbage View

Villa. But at home she moved her typewriter back into the upstairs flat and began, very seriously, to complete the novel with which she had been fiddling about for the previous year and a half. The novel, *Pig Fat and Chapatties,* was later to appear—to the mixed reception I have described—under her new name, Jennifer Kilminster. I suppose it must have been obvious to my father that Jennifer's literary activities were taking precedence over her academic pursuits. But strangely he did not appear to make the obvious deduction : that Jennifer's excursions to Bloomsbury had nothing to do with that section of the University of London found therein. Jennifer says she thinks van Niekerk really believed her when she told him she would see no more of Kilminster. And given my father's later behaviour it appears likely that this was so, since at this stage he obviously did *not* have a firm of private detectives detailed to follow Jennifer around. Perhaps he thought that her manic pounding of her typewriter at all hours was some sort of substitute for Kilminster. Or perhaps his own mood at the time prevented him thinking about Jennifer very much anyway, for he became quite manic himself. All his seedy vultures were coming home to roost in one dubious flock, Pieter van Niekerk was coming in from the cold wastes of Putney to where he really belonged— Kensington. The whirlpool of funny companies or the heroin importing racket or whatever it was that van Niekerk had been labouring to establish, began to pay off. Money flowed in and my father bought an elegant Georgian townhouse with a mews attached. The mews part of it, the old stables and coachman's quarters, had, of course, been converted into a separate and trendy dwelling place. My father reversed that smartly enough. The trendy tenants were given notice to quit, the downstairs part, which had once held horses and carriages, was gutted and made suitable for the numerous cars (very old or very new) that van Niekerk had a mind to invest in. The rooms above this commodious garage were prepared for the domestic staff that would soon be attending to our domestic comforts. The house proper was painted and papered, draped, and decorated. Jennifer and I were taken there with extreme frequency to hold bits of wall-paper in position, to consult with soft-spoken young men and women from interior design establishments and architects' offices. My father fussed. That's the only word for it, I'd never seen him fuss before and I was never to see him fuss again, but fuss he did, round and round in small circles, becoming quite hysterical at little details that the soft-spoken young men and women hadn't got quite right. Coming in out of the cold must have meant more to him than anything else he had ever done. I think he must have been simply too preoccupied with business, money, and Kensington to worry about Jennifer.

One day as I was leaving school, about a week before we were due to move to Kensington, I was met by Jennifer and Kilminster who were parked by the curb in a middle-sized van.

"Want a ride?"

"Hello James, is this yours?"

"For the afternoon. Jump in."

I climbed into the front of the van. I tried sitting next to Jennifer, but it was too squashed. I looked into the back, but it was full of furniture and kitchen stuff. Ours. I sat on Jennifer's knees. Kilminster drove off. They were both in extremely high spirits, we might have been going on a picnic.

"Where are we going?"

"To our new house."

"This is the wrong way. James, you should've turned right back by the statue."

"It's a different new house," my mother said.

"What do you mean, different?"

"We are going to live with James now."

"Oh, I see."

The move, the break with my father, had been planned with precision. Van Niekerk never forgave Jennifer for this, for the cold, calculated way in which she stood in the Kensington house holding lengths of wall-paper against the sides of rooms she had not the slightest intention of ever living in. I'm not sure I approve either. It has always seemed a point of honour with me that one does not leave one's lover (or husband) for somebody else. If a relationship becomes untenable you terminate it there and then. You do not keep up the pretence; you do not keep the relationship going for the time being, because nothing better is in the offing. Sometimes, of course, the arrival of the new person and the break with the old happen simultaneously. If they do, they do. But you should not engineer it to happen that way. I would never continue living with someone thinking "well, a bed with you in it is marginally preferable to a bed with nobody in it, but as soon as I find somebody else I'll give you the boot". I just wouldn't do it. I'd live alone. I'd sleep alone. I have little in the way of moral precepts, but that's one I do have. Here endeth today's lesson.

Jennifer, who says herself, she'd never live alone, jumped no guns. She slept with my father, fucked my father, played house in Kensington with my father, and found a flat in Clapham with James Kilminster. The flat had a large room that could be divided in two by closing a set of folding doors, a very small bedroom that would do for me, a kitchen of sorts with a shower recess in the corner—the same sort of arrangement as Kilminster's flat in Putney—and an outside lavatory. There was a bit of a garden, as they say, a long strip of permanently damp grass next to a long strip of asphalt that led to an incinerator, the whole enclosed by leaning paling fences. It is unlikely that the overall area of flat and garden was equal to that of the floor space in the garage beneath the staff quarters of van Niekerk's splendid Georgian townhouse.

"Home!" Jennifer said, when we arrived with the van full of furniture. In the large room with its folding doors, she kissed Kilminster and then me, picking me from the floor and whirling me round as if I were a six-year-old. I sulked. I was very confused. I was with two people I loved. It appeared I had deserted someone else I loved. I was in the smallest dwelling I'd ever been in. I smelt gas in the kitchen. I didn't like the way the linoleum in the kitchen turned up at the edges.

"Cheer up, Anasuya," Jennifer said, trying to pick me up

from the floor again.

I evaded her and made my way to the end of the narrow garden. I sulked next to the sulking incinerator—a blackened forty-four gallon oil drum with holes punched through it. It was full of half-burnt sodden newspapers. Through the kitchen window I could see Jennifer and Kilminster toasting bread on the leaking gas stove. I felt hungry. I always had something to eat when I came home from school, so I made my way inside and joined them.

* * * * * * *

It is very hard for me to separate the feelings I had for my father at the time of his divorce from Jennifer into the individual strands that composed the whole. I was definitely fond of him, and I suppose I loved him in the way in which children love the adults who have been most closely associated with them. And yet much of my affection for him was certainly bought. We all have our price, and, at eleven, mine was new and expensive clothes, tea in expensive hotels with fawning waiters, rides in his Rover or Bentley (I didn't much like the vintage cars, nasty, jolting, snorting machines), visits to matinée performances, gymkhanas, and the elaborate, catered children's parties that his fellow white-collar crooks sometimes threw. He had a chauffeur again—Brian, who didn't call him sir, and two live-in maids who did. Brian was employed as much to keep van Niekerk's cars running as to drive them. For all his love of Duesenberg Straight Eight Rattletraps, van Niekerk himself had never developed a penchant for oil and grease. Brian however only appeared truly happy when lying flat on his back with a spanner in his hand, whistling. He also whistled when turning out spare parts on his lathe. Otherwise he was almost entirely silent. The maids wore a sort of uniform and were always delighted to see me (perhaps they were, their boss and, later, his new wife, can't have been much fun). I had a room in the Kensington house that was four times as large as my room at home in Clapham and which had its own bathroom en suite. Under the terms of the divorce, van Niekerk only had legal right of access to me during the day. Jennifer could have insisted that I was not to stay the night at Kensington at all, but I liked staying there, the maids brought me breakfast in bed. It is a bizarre picture—a twenty-year-old maid bringing an eleven-year-old child break-fast in bed—but it happened. And I accepted it as my due. Had Jennifer tried to prevent my staying overnight, I would have objected strongly. I would have told van Niekerk next time I saw him that Jennifer was attempting to curtail my visits against my wishes. And this, I believe, would have been a satisfaction she would never have allowed him. Indifference became very much the name of that particular game. Yet there was a curious strand of honesty in it too. She could have attempted to turn me against van Niekerk in a dozen subtle and indirect ways, and yet I cannot remember a single instance of this. My relations with my father were to be my affair. She did not want to know about them, much less influence them. Which is more than can be said for van Niekerk's attitude to Jennifer and Kilminster. He was clearly obsessed; even at eleven I could see and under-stand that. He wanted to know what they did, where they went, who their friends were. He particularly wanted to know how they got on with each other. Jennifer is sure van Niekerk had a private detective follow them at this time. It is quite possible. My father was particularly pleased if I reported any sign of domestic tension, any argument or quarrel. I think he genuinely believed that Kilminster cut such a poor figure beside himself that Jennifer was simply bound to find him wanting in the reasonably near future. And for my part, little domestic spy that I was, I provided my father with what he wanted to hear and received my due rewards.

It was very easy to give him evidence of quarrels. Jennifer and Kilminster often shouted at each other. What I knew, and what my father totally failed to see, and what I didn't try to explain, was that these quarrels were warm-blooded, quite human, almost loving affairs. The cold, angry, indifferent silences, the ignorance-as-aggression tricks that had characterised Jennifer's life with van Niekerk had more or less disappeared. Jennifer had tried to play these games once or twice with Kilminster, but Kilminster wouldn't let her. I remember a scene at breakfast when Jennifer had repeatedly stalled Kilminster's attempts to air some sort of difference with her (I can't remember what it was, it isn't important). Kilminster very matter-of-factly said, "If you don't talk to me properly, Jennifer, I'll tickle you."

"What?"

"I'll come round the table and tickle you."

"Don't try to be funny."

"Oh, I'm not."

Jennifer made a show of reading her paper. Kilminster rose from his chair and walked around the table to where she sat. He embraced her, imprisoning her arms, infiltrating his fingers into her armpits, and tickled. Jennifer was wildly angry for a few seconds, struggled hard, kicked the table and tried to bite him, and then collapsed into a heap of laughter and shrieks for mercy.

"Hey, look at your mother, Ansu, isn't she pretty when she laughs?"

The moment he let her go, of course, she bit him on the wrist. Hard. But then they talked, seriously, amicably, and without histrionics. I became bored and went outside to play in the street with some friends.

That evening, Brian collected me in the Rover, spiriting me away to Kensington. Twenty-four hours after Jennifer and Kilminster had settled whatever difference it was they had been arguing about, I sat across the breakfast table from my father. The maid called Susan lifted the silver lid from a plate of scrambled eggs, the steam floating for a second in the air around her white-cuffed wrist. I told my father that Jennifer and Kilminster had been fighting-struggling with each other, biting—and then, when they'd got themselves under control, having long, long, serious discussions.

"It's what I expected, Anasuya, I knew it would come to this. It's not the atmosphere in which to bring up a child. It can't be very pleasant for you."

"Oh, I went outside."

"That was very wise. Very wise, indeed. You are becoming a very sensible girl, Anasuya. There is no reason why you should upset yourself or get involved when they start one of their fights. If you can, always go away when they start fighting; that's the best thing. If it gets really bad, you know the telephone number here and at the office. I sometimes become very worried for you darling."

"Yes, Daddy."

We spent the morning in Kensington Gardens. We had tea at eleven-thirty in Knightsbridge. My father was in a high good humour.

* * * * * * *

Among the other presents he bought me, van Niekerk took to giving me food. I would be sent back to Clapham loaded down with what were literally food parcels for the starving writer and her friend. Like some crazed parody of a Red Cross relief truck arriving at a famine-stricken village, Brian would bring the Bentley or Rover to a smooth halt outside the Clapham flat. He would leap from his door to help me stagger up the five-foot-long path laden with parcels and boxes of cheeses, hams, preserved goose livers in aspic, pâté de foie, glacé fruits, German sausages—virtually anything that a quick run through Fortnum and Mason's could provide.

"Shall we deliver it, sir?"

"Not necessary, not necessary. We shall take it ourselves."

It was intended, of course, that Jennifer and Kilminster should eat these things. I've no doubt at all that, had Jennifer taken the normal approach to divorce, that of trying to extract as much as possible from the estranged husband as a punishment for his crimes, van Niekerk would have resented every penny she legally obtained from him. But in the face of her determination to take nothing, and given the obviously straightened circumstances in which she and Kilminster lived, he automatically tried the opposite, to buy her, to humiliate her by forcing her to accept his patronage. And I think this applied to Kilminster as well, van Niekerk wished to reduce him to the status of semi-dependent, to make him eat humble pie—albeit one from Fortnum and Mason's.

There was little Jennifer could do. The food had been given officially to me, but it wasn't normal eleven-year-old's nosh and it came in quantities that would have taken me weeks to consume by myself. But Jennifer could hardly send it back (van Niekerk did actually once make the mistake of including a jar of walnuts preserved in rummy mother returned it by registered post. I was never sent home with anything alcoholic again). Initially there were one or two strange meals at which neither she nor Kilminster ate what I ate—but I felt silly and wouldn't eat. Suddenly their plates of fish fingers and frozen peas looked infinitely preferable to Scotch salmon or whatever it was that was on my plate. Some of the food Jennifer managed to give away to Tamar or one of her other friends. "You don't particularly like this stuff, do you?" she'd say, gesturing at some tin or jar. "No," I'd say, regardless of what it was. "Oh well, I'll see if Tamar can take it off our hands, she's got odd tastes." A lot of the food became automatically relegated to the status of left-overs, often before it had even been unpacked. The symbolism isn't hard to fathom; presumably by being down-graded in this fashion, it became something we were merely saving from going to waste; maybe we were down-grading van Niekerk as well. Kilminster's culinary skills were not great in those days, nor was his actual understanding of food itself. If his stories of the seminary are to be believed he had lived almost exclusively on shepherd's pie and slices of spam fried in batter. Under Jennifer's tutelage he learnt to fry omelettes, but he clearly regarded the filling of the thing as a matter of whatever there was in the fridge. If there was half a tomato and the scrag end of a piece of cheese, one had tomato and cheese omelette. If there was half a tin of sardines and a bowl of mashed potato in the fridge, one dined on sardine and mash omelette. By classifying van Niekerk's food on a par with scrag ends of cheese and half-tins of sardines, we managed to eat a surprising number of omelettes of a surprising number of varieties: caviar omelette, grouse omelette, roll-mop omelette, almost anything that could be chopped up and served between folds of egg was added to the list. Much the same went for bubble-and-squeak and mornay. There is very little that cannot be fried up with a mixture of boiled cabbage and egg, or doused in cheese sauce and baked for a while.

We didn't by any means starve. But we were poor. A student's grant doesn't go very far, especially in London. There's actually a London loading in recognition of this, but it's not much; a couple of quid a week extra at the most. Jennifer's writing paid little or nothing. She decided to get a job. Kilminster said he'd get one instead, that her writing was far more important than his studies. She told him not to be an idiot; the sooner he graduated, the sooner he could start earning real money. This was obviously true, but Kilminster, for all his disaffected nonchalance about bourgeois propriety, very much thought it was his job to support Jennifer, if not in the manner to which she had accustomed herself with van Niekerk, at least in some manner or other. And I suppose, for all Jennifer's reassurances to the contrary and the convictions of his own perceptions, Kilminster must have compared himself to van Niekerk, must have seen himself as competing with van Niekerk, and must have found himself wanting in some respects. He was, after all, from the Liverpool docks, with a tradition of Irish working-class, masculine pride behind him, and it was a pride that didn't really allow him to sponge on his wife. Or on his wife's ex-husband.

So Jennifer looked for a job. She had no qualifications of any kind. She answered advertisements for publisher's assistants (well, she was writing herself, wasn't she?), advertising copy-writers, librarian's assistants—the whole gamut of what she called the boltholes of the genteel spinsterhood. With no success. Sometimes she was shortlisted for interview, sometimes she was rejected sight unseen. It was a dispiriting process, but she never attempted to use what contacts she had (Simon, her ageing father, people in van Niekerk's circle of friends, uncles etc. etc.), she invented referees and wrote phoney references rather than use the perfectly genuine ones that any number of professional people of her acquaintance would have written. So she didn't find a job. So she found a job in a pub.

Kilminster and I were playing scrabble in front of the two-bar electric fire when Jennifer waltzed in, threw her coat over the back of a chair, and announced, "I've got a job, I'm employed, I'm a member of the proletariat. Arise ye starvelings from your slumbers, arise ye prisoners of want."

"What?"

"Want, dumbo, prisoners of *want*."

She was radiant (slightly manic as well, of course; Jennifer's radiance is always slightly manic) but I hadn't seen my mother so sparkling for months.

"What as?"

"Barmaid."

"Oh, yes," Kilminster said drily. He didn't believe her.

"Mummy!" I said. I believed her.

It embarrasses me now to recall just how shocked I was that my mother had taken up a perfectly normal job that is performed daily by thousands of women and men; a job, indeed, that some of the parents of my friends at school were engaged in. But, shocked I was. I who was driven about by chauffeurs in Bentleys, who took tea at Claridges, whose father had promised me a holiday in a flash hotel in the south of France—my mother was to work in a pub. Also, I just couldn't *see* Jennifer behind a bar serving drink. I might have been shocked, but I was also incredulous. Kilminster was simply incredulous.

Jennifer refused to be serious about it. Kilminster gave up all pretence of rational discussion and joined her in the construction of an elaborate fantasy about smuggling bottles of gin out of the pub. I usually joined in their fantasy construction. I can make up stories with the best of them, but this time I sulked. I didn't *want* Jennifer to be a barmaid.

Socially I was in a very odd position in those days. I was in my first year at the Comprehensive—a vast building, many gymnasia, an enormous Assembly Hall that could seat half the school's two thousand pupils at once, not much in the way of playgrounds. It was surrounded by a mixture of very submerged middle-class streets, proper working-class streets, housing estates. The tone of the school itself was most decidedly working class. I actually got on quite well at school. I had three or four close friends, I was effortlessly good at school work, I felt quite comfortable there. But I was obviously different; foreign in a school that boasted its fair share of foreigners. My friends tended to be quiet, not particularly bright, easily dominated girls. We sat together in class, played together at recess, ate together at lunchtime, but I rarely saw any of them outside school. In the whole time we lived in Clapham, I think I only ever visited two of my friends' homes, and only ever invited one friend back to my place. School was school and home was home and Kensington was Kensington. I operated effectively in all three areas, but only by keeping them as separate as possible. I was, for example, very vague at school about what I did when I visited my father. I would have been acutely embarrassed had any of my school friends seen me arriving home in the Bentley. I told them my father was rich, "Pots of money, like a bloody millionaire; big house, posh car, the lot." It was a good bit of imitation boasting; obviously he couldn't be *that* rich. I don't know how much van Niekerk was worth at the time, but there soon became nothing metaphorical about his millions. I suppose I chose my friends at school on the basis of ease of dominance; my friends would rarely challenge what I told them, could be kept at arm's distance when necessary, included in intense pre-adolescent intimacies when necessary. I liked them well enough, there was real friendship involved, but I suppose I also despised them a little, didn't really regard them as my equals. Perhaps they also despised me a little—they'd have been well within their rights.

Home was Jennifer and Kilminster, Kilminster's student

friends, Tamar, Simon, Samantha and Randolph, and a few of their friends. We often visited them, they visited us every now and then. My abiding image of the Clapham flat is that of a camp. There was nothing ordered or permanent about it. We ate strange meals at strange times. People worked at odd hours. Jennifer would sometimes write until three or four in the morning. I would wake sometimes in the still hours of the early morning to hear her typewriter chattering in the kitchen where she worked if Kilminster was asleep in that half of the big room that served as their bedroom. Kilminster would often get up in the small hours to join her, he said he studied best in the hours before dawn. Occasionally I would join them too and we would have a breakfast of sorts as the light from the kitchen's fluorescent tube began to lose its battle with the increasing daylight from the window. Jennifer would yawn and say to me, "Let's leave James to clear up all this. You need more sleep; come and keep me warm."

So I would sleep for a couple of hours in a curve in the big bed with Jennifer wrapped around me like a lover.

Quite often when I came home from school Jennifer and Kilminster would be in bed together. Kilminster says they did nearly all their screwing in the afternoons in those days. Given their nocturnal habits, it's easy to see why. I would make them tea, which I brought to them along with whatever else there was in the house that could be pressed into service as an afternoon snack. If there was no bread and jam, as there often wasn't, I might spread some of van Niekerk's caviar on a plateful of Weetabix split in half. I'd sit on their bed and we'd all eat the stuff and gossip. It was an incredibly productive household: Jennifer finished *Pig Fat* and wrote *Tides* in quick succession and then wrote her two love stories, *Tar Love* and *Bitter Love*— strange, light-hearted little pieces, quite unlike anything she's written since; Kilminster did brilliantly at his university work; and I waltzed through the minimal amount of formal learning we were offered at school and read half a dozen library books a week. Jennifer established her work-space on a small deal table in a corner of the big room; I had a desk in my bedroom, but Kilminster, true to the camp-like nature of the place, had no set area at all. For the most part, he worked on the kitchen table, keeping his books and papers at one end of it, but with various subsidiary piles of books and articles disposed around the flat on window-ledges, on the mantelpiece, on the floor. Sometimes, especially in winter when my room was cold, I'd join Kilminster at the kitchen table to do my homework. We'd sit opposite each other in pursuit of our several branches of knowledge, a communal jar of pens, ballpoints, pencils, and erasers between us.

"James, how do you spell *ruminant*?"

"Dunno. How do you unify force field theory?"

"Dunno."

"God, you're useless."

"So are you."

Jennifer lasted at the pub for eight months. They fired her in the end, but fairly amicably. Her skill with the cash register had never been great, but she became more, rather than less, erratic with the amounts she charged for a round of drinks. She became bored, not so much with the pub as with the process of ringing up the amounts charged. The machine looked a bit like a nineteenth-century typewriter, but produced less interesting results.

I never went into the pub, so I have to rely on what Kilminster and his friends told me. Our house had become a sort of centre for a group of Kilminster's fellow-students. At one stage, when van Niekerk's food parcels had begun to mount up, Jennifer had insisted that Kilminster gather a group of the thinnest, most desperate and interesting of his peers, and bring them home to dinner. She was employing the old Robin-Hood justification: ripping off the rich to feed the starving poor—banditry made honourable. Kilminster's friends arrived one Sunday evening and we all made short work of van Niekerk's food. The meal became a regular ritual and within a few weeks someone had coined the name *Après Fin de Siècle Dining Club*. There were, I suppose, about half a dozen hard-core members and as many again who came every now and then. The club would eat, drink, and talk, for the most part sitting in a circle on the floor. On occasions, the club talked and drank until well after the trains and buses had stopped running; it then either talked and drank some more or collapsed onto various sofas, cushions, and areas of floor. When Jennifer started work at the pub, the club began to meet there first, returning to our place after closing, which, I seem to remember, was earlier than usual on Sunday night, but even so the meal itself was rarely finished before midnight, especially if there had been any elaborate cooking to be done. I joined in these parties, of course. Whatever else Jennifer has done with her children and step-children, she has never insisted on anything so silly as a set bedtime. If I had wanted to remain awake almost all the night with the others and leave for school with little more than an hour's sleep, I'm sure I would have been allowed to.

The quality and quantity of the food at these parties varied. Sometimes van Niekerk sent me home from Kensington with no food parcel. Sometimes what was in the parcel provided a curious menu. At one point—I think it must have been about a year after the divorce was made final—it began to look as if van Niekerk was giving up supplying me with food parcels. For three weeks running I was sent back to Clapham empty-handed. Things got a bit tight. The board of the *Après Fin* became a little bare. On the fourth week I complained heartily to van Niekerk that, what with Jennifer working in the pub and Kilminster studying so hard, I was being forced onto a dreary diet of fish and chips from the corner shop.

"They're cold, Daddy. Cold and soggy."

The lie worked. Brian and I had to make a couple of trips from the car to the front door to ferry the booty home. I think, actually, that both Jennifer and Kilminster would have been glad if the food parcels had stopped flowing at that point. The *Après Fin* lot could have provided their own food without all that much strain, and, for all Jennifer's Robin-Hood ratiocinations, I don't think she ever really came to like accepting van

Niekerk's hand-outs. My reason for ensuring continuity of supply was simple: I liked the Sunday evening parties and since it was my food, after all, they were in some sense, my parties.

As for the pub, it was simply good for Jennifer, for like Kilminster when he'd first escaped from the seminary, she had never had the experience of earning money. There was something real and tangible about the modest barmaid's wages which no amount of hand-outs from van Niekerk or anybody else could have matched. But I think she was also proving something much more basic to herself. Working in a pub, serving other people, earning wages and accepting tips, was something no Delhi memsahib would ever have come within a hundred miles of doing. The pub episode was the practical side of the transformation effected spiritually in *Pig Fat* and *Tides*. Of course her more perceptive friends suspected as much.

"Jennifer, what are you trying to prove? Do you think sloshing out booze in a pub is some sort of penance?"

"Damn you, Tamar, I'm not proving anything. We need the money, that's all."

She still had all her pride and arrogance. She wasn't going to admit that she, Jennifer, could ever be in need of the cleansing effects of penance or repentance. Good for her, I'd never admit to that sort of thing myself.

But what was she like as a barmaid? As I say, I have to rely on impressions gained from Kilminster and his friends. Imagine them arriving at the back bar of the Queen's Arms on Sunday evening. They don't really match the other drinkers, middle-aged couples who have tottered down to the local for the regular Sunday-night tipple, but they are not unwelcome. They arrange themselves around a table; one of them, say Clax the student of biochemistry, makes his way to the bar and in exaggerated old soak tones says, "Err, the usual luv."

"Bitter luv?"

"Ta luv."

Jennifer arranges as many half-pint glasses as there are members of the group under the beer taps and squirts in the liquid. Clax says, conversational like, "Good weather for this time of year."

Jennifer looks up from the task in hand and mouths the words, "Piss off, Clax."

Clax grins and says in his normal voice, "Good to see you."

"Good to see you too."

Clax pays, carries the beer across to the group, and Jennifer moves down the bar to where a regular customer, call him Fred, is waiting to be served. Fred says, "How's the book, then?"

"Coming along," Jennifer replies.

The regulars all know about the book. They take an interest in the book, much as they would take an interest in a pregnancy, in some respects they regard it as *their* book. They await its publication as they would await a birth. Fred says, "Put any of us in it yet?"

"Come off it. I want it to sell."

Fred chuckles and says, "What's it about again?"

"The Indian Mutiny of 1857."

"Oh yes," says Fred, "We'll have one of them here soon. That or a Paki Mutiny, there's enough of them about."

Fred laughs quietly at his own joke. He has actually made it before and has only asked Jennifer the subject of her book in order to bring his wit into play for the third or fourth time. Jennifer smiles and moves away to serve another customer.

I don't like pubs. As I don't drink I have little cause to go into them and wouldn't at all if it weren't for the demands of my social life—a lot of my friends are never out of them. There is something about the subdued, jolly bonhomie of a quiet night in the snug of an English local that grates. I don't really know what it is—maybe it's the element of self-satisfaction, of complacency, in the chat at the bar that I can't stand. Maybe I'm just a prig. But I never feel that way about French bars or cafés. But then I can drink decent coffee in French bars, perhaps that's it. But one thing I do know, no proprietor of a French bar would ever be referred to in the pages of the local press as "Mine genial host" and I've read that phrase more than once in English papers. But, anyway, Jennifer learnt to operate quite effectively in the milieu of the Queen's Arms. She never served in the public bar and she only worked in the evenings. I don't know what the management and customers really thought of her, perhaps they believed she added a bit of class to the place; perhaps they saw her as an acceptable eccentric, a writer.

Van Niekerk was both horrified and confirmed in the rightness of his judgement. He was horrified to think that a wife of his, even an ex-wife, could accept such a menial position. In the circles in which he was now moving—the semi-legal fringes of capitalism, where houses, cars, yachts, and profits were owned by nominal companies in the Bahamas or the Channel Islands, where vast sums were made and lost by buying and selling and speculating in such nominal companies—the public knowledge that a previous wife had ditched him to marry a student and work in a pub would have done nothing for his reputation. And he was stung too, by the feeling that she had gone to work in the pub just to spite him, that it was the ultimate rejection of his money and of any claim he still might have been able to make upon her. But then, of course, he had known it would come to this.

"I am worried about your mother."

"Yes, Daddy."

"I know she has nothing but hatred for me, but I am still very concerned about her. Perhaps I see things more clearly, can take a more rational view of what has happened. Men are not as emotional as women, you know. Since she has married this student, she has been throwing her life away. Working in a pub. She will find that all the best years of her life have gone by and she will have done nothing but live in a cramped little flat and work in a suburban pub."

"She only works there in the evenings."

"And what does she do with the rest of her time?"

"Writes her book."

"Scribbling away in a substandard little flat is no way to live. Writers don't make money."

It's worth noting that van Niekerk was clearly relieved that Jennifer was proceeding with her Mutiny book and not writing one about him. Which is what she did, needless to say, the moment she'd finished *Pig Fat*.

* * * * * * *

We lived in Clapham for almost three years. In that time I grew from a skinny eleven-year-old to a slim fourteen-year-old, Kilminster graduated with first class honours, and Jennifer became a moderately successful writer. In Kensington, van Niekerk became richer and richer; once away and running he couldn't be stopped. And during this time Jennifer's marriage to Kilminster bloomed and faded. Maybe there's a better word than faded—say dissolved, changed, mutated, developed, evolved, devolved, I don't know. It would be certainly wrong to say that it failed. It would be wrong to say even that it broke up. Their friendship certainly didn't falter; even at the time Jennifer met Jean Claude and decided to move to France with him, things were amicable—amicable, but stormy in the manner in which they have always conducted their relationship. The contrast to the van Niekerk débâcle couldn't have been greater. Not that poor bloody van Niekerk could have guessed. All his gloomy prophecies had come true in grim Old Testament inevitability as far as he was concerned.

I can remember Jennifer saying to Kilminster once in the first Clapham year, "What you need, Kilminster, is an adolescence. You never had one in your monastery. What you need is the experience of getting the bra off in the back seat of the old man's car. The sticky finger in the cinema routine."

"You've been reading too many American novels. In Liverpool it was up against a wall by the docks."

"But you never did it."

"What did you do in Golders Green before you met Kneejerk?"

"Not much, but I had a delayed adolescence in Delhi."

"Maybe I should go on a package tour of India. See the Red

Fort and get a bit'."

"Maybe you should broaden your horizons in London."

"Really?"

I wasn't party to very much of this sort of conversation. Even in the libertarian atmosphere of the Clapham flat, there were some things that weren't discussed with me. Although subsequently both Jennifer and Kilminster have talked to me at length about it all, and I now have a pretty clear idea what happened. The point is, of course, that at roughly twenty-one Kilminster found himself knowing a great deal about love, sex, and the whole man-with-a-maid box of dice, but knowing about it from only one source, Jennifer, who knew about it from a plethora of experiences. And the irony is that Kilminster is, at heart, genuinely quite polygamous while Jennifer is monogamous— all her manic screwing around in Delhi and elsewhere notwithstanding. As far as I know—although I could be wrong, but not very wrong—since taking up happily with Jean Claude the only other man she's fucked is Kilminster. I hesitate to estimate what Kilminster's tally now stands at. Anyway, in Clapham it was decided that theirs was not to be an exclusively one-to-one arrangement; if only to allow Kilminster to grow up.

One member of the *Après Fin de Siècle Dining Club* was a funny, owlish girl of about Kilminster's age called Nara. I say "owlish" because she looked like an owl, she wore very wide, round glasses in wide tortoise-shell frames. There was, in fact, something wrong with her eyes and, at one point, she underwent surgery on one of them. For five or six weeks she would arrive on Sunday evenings wearing not only her glasses, but a pirate's eye-patch as well. She spoke in a quiet, hesitant, serious voice with a slight west country accent. She came from Bristol or Bath or somewhere like that. As I remember her, she had almost no sense of humour, which, given the company and the way Jennifer and Kilminster conducted the proceedings, should have made her slightly out of place, but didn't. She was, I suppose, the still centre of the group, as essential to the storm of drunken nonsense being bandied about as the eye of a cyclone is to the swirling wind and rain on its periphery. Certainly on the evenings that she did not turn up, things always seemed a little flat, a little empty. She was the only one, apart from myself, who didn't drink. Like Kilminster she was a Catholic and having doubts. (Kilminster was genuinely into Doubts by this time.) I can remember going for a walk with both of them on Clapham Common. Kilminster wasn't joking at all, he was being very serious; so was Nara, even more serious than usual. The talk was all about salvation and souls and limbo and the force of upbringing. Boring beyond belief. I began to wish I'd gone to Tamar's for the afternoon instead. I wandered off to watch the cricket while Kilminster and Nara sat on the grass and had their crises of conscience.

When I returned Nara was crying. Kilminster was comforting her, but obviously a little upset himself. I began to be worried for them, I wished Jennifer was with us.

"What's the matter?"

"Nothing, Anasuya," Nara said through her tears, "Just be thankful you're not Catholic, that you don't have to go through all this."

Kilminster said to Nara, "Do you want to go to St Mary's then?"

"Yes."

He said to me, "Nara and I want to visit a church, to light some candles. Do you mind?"

"No, of course not."

Even at that age, I can remember, I was perfectly aware that lighting candles would do neither of them any good. Their immortal souls were one thing, a birthday cake another. But the idea of visiting a church was novel and I was becoming increasingly bored with the Common. Also it was becoming cold. We left the Common and walked quickly down a number of suburban streets in a direction in which I'd never gone before. St Mary's was a pretty little church set behind some vast, dark trees, well back from the street. There was a small graveyard to one side and a couple of wrought-iron seats lining the path to the door.

Nara said, "If you just wait here, Anasuya, we won't be very long."

"Can't I come in?"

"Well...."

"Certainly. If you want to," Kilminster said, "But you better not suddenly see the damn light and get converted. Jennifer would kill me."

Nara looked slightly startled, but probably more at Kilminster's tone of voice than the words themselves; he had spoken with all his normal levity, a complete contrast to the serious way in which he had been conversing with her for the last hour-and-a-half. I think if anybody had asked me at that point which way I thought my two dithering friends were going to jump, I would have replied with complete certainty that Kilminster would lose the faith entirely and that Nara would return to the fold, her faith redoubled. I would have been right.

We all trooped into the church. The damn light, if that's what it was, came streaming through one of the sets of stained glass windows, splattering the columns and the floor at our feet with colours. It must have been about half an hour before sunset and the rays fell the entire length of the church. I was entranced.

"Pretty, eh?" Kilminster said.

The rest of the building was full of dully shining polished wood, brass fittings, and marble slabs. Both Kilminster and Nara went through a quick ritual involving dipping their fingers into a sort of bowl fixed to the wall, genuflecting and crossing themselves, but so quickly that I had hardly noticed they were at it before they had finished. It was like suddenly catching a glimpse of two rare birds performing a courtship dance. To one side there was a small shrine or altar which already had a single candle burning in front of it. Kilminster and Nara each selected a candle from a carton on a table that also held a rack of pamphlets, put some money in a box, and approached the shrine, bobbed, lit their candles and placed them in some sort of holding device. They backed off and then knelt. They appeared to be praying. I watched them for a minute, slightly amused, slightly embarrassed. Then I wandered round the church, reading the inscriptions, admiring the brass eagle with its vast bible on its wings. On the other side of the church from the shrine was a dark wooden box with two cubicles that could be curtained off. By this time I was aware of the reasons why Kilminster had had to leave his seminary; indeed I'd been present when he'd entertained the *Après Fin* lot to a rendition of the confession scene. (Jennifer later told me he'd improved it considerably since his first blushing account of it to her.) The phrase, "Not again, my son?" had passed into general currency around the flat. We all said it to one another; for example if Jennifer announced that she would be late for tea, I was quite likely to say to her in grave tones, "Not again, my son?" to which she would reply, "Again, Father." I realised now that this dark bicameral box was a confessional, the sort of cupboard in which Kilminster's original admissions had been so uncomfortably made. I entered one of the compartments and sat down on a padded stool; through the open curtains I could see Kilminster and Nara on the other side of the church, half obscured by the intervening pews, but obviously absorbed in prayer. I sat in the box, like a farmer in an outdoor privy on a quiet, sunny morning, watching my friends. Kilminster stood up, bobbed and crossed himself, and looked around. He saw me and began to stroll around the block of pews in my direction. I lost sight of him for a moment, but sat waiting for him to appear in the door of my box. With a click a panel next to my ear snapped open revealing a grille with Kilminster's half obscured face behind it. I brought the phrase smartly into play, "Again, my son?"

"Again Father."

"The body is the temple of the soul, my son."

"You don't say, Father."

"He who desecrates the temple denies Christ a dwelling."

"Christ should apply to the Fair Rent Tribunal."

I burst into a fit of eleven-year-old's giggles. These I tried to stifle. After thirty seconds of snorts and snuffles, I exploded into a quick burst of the real thing. Nara looked over her shoulder, she wasn't amused. I stumbled out of the box and ran out of the church and sat on a bench almost helpless with laughter. Now I wasn't laughing at Kilminster's only mildly funny remark, but at the situation, at my own reactions to Nara's shocked expression. I had a vision of me and Kilminster as she must have seen us in our separate compartments—two lunatics giggling and chortling like crazed figurines in a wet and dry barometer. My laughter reached that point where the origins no longer matter, where what is funny is the act of laughing itself. Kilminster emerged from the church and sat down beside me. When I recovered my breath, I said, "I think I've upset Nara."

"No, it's not you, it's me. She knows I made you laugh."

"Do you think she's very upset?"

"She's very upset anyway; we'd better be extra nice to her on the way home."

This was easier said than done. Nara was icy on the way home. Guardedly polite to me, but icy towards Kilminster. Kilminster tried to be jolly, to engage her in chit-chat. This was the wrong approach, even I could see that. At a street corner I managed to hold Kilminster back while Nara took advantage of a break in the traffic to cross.

"Be serious with her again. You know, James, talk to her about immortal souls and Catholic upbringing and stuff."

"You run on ahead, that's impossible with you around."

We joined Nara on the other side of the road and I set off at a smart pace in front of them. Running a stick along railings and fences, I managed a number of discreet backwards glances. At first Kilminster expounded something very earnestly to Nara who listened with evident mistrust. Then she took to arguing angrily with him. By the time we were a quarter of a mile from home they had their arms around each other's waists.

So Kilminster had his first extra-marital affair with Nara. I wasn't actually told that this was the case. I don't think even my precocious libertarianism would have taken that *completely* in its stride. I assume the fun and games took place at Nara's house, nothing out of the ordinary happened at Clapham that I'm aware of. Nara, of course, still came to the *Après Fin de Siècle* dinners, she and Jennifer were closer if anything. In a sense it was ideal for Jennifer, whatever else Nara was, she was no threat. The affair lasted, I've been told, about six months, during which a moderate amount of screwing got done and a vast amount of dogma and theology was discussed. It left Kilminster devoid of the one true faith and eager for further (and less spiritually taxing) sexual adventures, and Nara a confirmed believer looking for the good Catholic, intellectual husband she eventually found.

It would be wrong to think that Kilminster's departure from Catholicism was trivial or light-hearted compared to Nara's travails. In some ways it was probably more traumatic. Kilminster's apparent levity in holy places simply reflected the lack of importance to him of ritual or fetish. God, if he existed, could no doubt take a joke, and churches and sacred objects were collections of bricks, stones, bones, and other material, albeit sanctified. Much of Nara's anxiety came from the prospect of abandoning the services, confessions, prayers, rosary beads, scapulars, holy water, hymns, and the whole social and cultural life that being a believer entailed. Kilminster was only concerned with God, pure and simple; the budding high-energy physicist was turning all his attention to rarefied absolutes. I don't think for a minute that he would have suggested the whole candle-lighting episode unless he thought it would be comforting to Nara, and I'm sure that once in the church he only lit one as a companionable gesture.

* * * * * * *

And then it was Kilminster's turn to accept that Jennifer might sleep with others. He didn't accept it very easily. I asked him about the whole episode yesterday.

"I tried, Anasuya, I really tried. But that first time with Clax drove me to despair. It wasn't so much that I doubted Jennifer's reassurances that what she felt for Clax made no difference to the way she felt about me. It was bloody Clax himself. I kept thinking: that bastard is feeling smug at my expense, he's got all the joys of the seasoned adulterer and none of the risks, he doesn't even have to pretend to me that he's not sleeping with Jennifer. I kept seeing myself as being diminished in Clax's eyes. Who can respect the poor bloody cuckold, especially some poor weed who knows he's a cuckold and does nothing about it."

Kilminster finished the retsina he was drinking in one gulp and picked a sardine from the plate in front of him. He threw it to one of the taverna's cats and said, "The ould Oirish Liverpool background, Ansu, you can't make it disappear just by getting yourself a mad Jewish wife and a flat full of raving nutters for friends. And the point is, I knew all along that these fears were groundless, that Clax didn't think any the worse of me for letting him sleep with Jennifer, that he was decent and a good friend. I knew that because the evidence of my senses and all my intellect told me it was true. But I didn't *feel* it. And I suppose part of my trouble was that I remembered what I'd felt about van Niekerk when I was cuckolding him. A right smug little lout out of a seminary with a married woman for a mistress; I didn't think much of van Niekerk to begin with, but then I remember feeling: well if the nasty little Afrikaner toad can't keep his wife faithful, more fool him."

The cat started to rub itself energetically against Kilminster's leg. He tried to pick it up, but it twisted from his grasp, it wanted another sardine, not a cuddle. Greek cats are not used to being petted. I gave it a fish from my plate and said, "And yet Jennifer and Nara had got on very well together."

"Oh, I know, yes. And Clax and I should have emulated them. Clax did, he went out of his way to be friendly to me, but that only increased my paranoia. But, as I say, I tried. I tried hard to live in the way Jennifer and I had decided to live. Just as I once tried hard to be a priest. In the seminary I really wanted to become a good priest, I tried to live the life of the order as strictly as possible; you know, thinking the right things at the right times of the day, really meaning my prayers. There'd have been no point in the whole exercise otherwise. Well I tried like that while Jennifer was off screwing Clax. Only it didn't work. I'd look at the books and articles on the table in front of me and try to think about physics as I once thought about God, but all I'd see was the inside of that student commune Clax lived in with the shadowy figures of Clax and Jennifer; not actually doing it—my imagination baulked at that—but sitting around afterwards with the other members of the household, drinking coffee and laughing. Maybe if Clax had lived in some solitary bed-sit by himself, it wouldn't have hurt so much. I found I couldn't bring myself to call round at Clax's commune, although there were a couple of people in that house I liked very much. It had become Jennifer's private territory, or at least so it seemed to me. Are you getting all this down? Do you want your notebook?"

"No, I can remember it."

"Well, I discussed all this with Jennifer. I didn't say so directly, but I wanted her to give up her affair with Clax as a gesture.... I don't know, as a gesture of her love for me, a token of its genuineness. After all, I wasn't screwing anybody else at the time, so why should she?"

"To which she said...?"

"To which she said, 'Just because Nara's gone running back to the church and celibacy, you think the whole world should become monogamous on your account. What you really need is another affair. Try to pick an atheist this time.' So I did, I had an Affair with Tamar's au pair, a German-Swiss girl called Heidi. Do you remember her?"

"Of course."

"We all got the clap."

I burst out laughing.

"All of us. Me, Jennifer, Heidi, Clax, half of Clax's commune, various other people. We all went to the doctor's together—some friend of Tamar's who was guaranteed to be non-censorious. If we hadn't been such a middle-class group we'd have gone to the V.D. clinic, but we thought a nice, discreet doctor would be the better bet. He was non-censorious and discreet all right, but he was clearly amused by the whole parade. After he'd seen us individually he called the whole group into his surgery. God knows what the rest of the people in the waiting-room must have thought. We all sat around, perched on his chairs and his examination couch. He said provided we all took the medication we could continue screwing each other in whatever combinations we chose, but we were not to screw outside the group until he told us to. We all nodded. Maybe he thought we were running non-stop orgies rather than the odd bit of afternoon adultery. Then he said we must immediately tell anybody else who'd had contact with us. Was there anybody? A few people shuffled their feet and looked at the floor. 'Yeah,' he said, 'Well you tell them today. Send them to me if you like.' So we all trooped out of his surgery and went to a pub for lunch. We sat in this pub very subdued, very quiet, nobody saying very much, drinking slowly through half-pints of bitter. Just one half-pint per person for the whole lunch, partly because the penicillin or whatever it was didn't mix very well with alcohol, but mainly because the more one drank, the more one pissed. And pissing wasn't really where it was at. Ever had it?"

"No, but I've had other sorts of urinary tract infections."

"So you'll know what it's like. Anyway, we all sat there, as I say, very subdued. And then Jennifer started to laugh. First she smiled, then she giggled, then she laughed. Someone said, 'What's so funny?' and Jennifer just laughed harder. The rest of us just sat there a bit nonplussed, but it started to look funny to us too: this whole group of people united by a gloomy dose of the common clap. So I started laughing and soon everybody was laughing. Someone said, 'Let's have another half and bugger the consequences.' So we did. The thing was, though, that even given the doctor's permission to screw within the group, nobody felt like doing it at all. Certainly I didn't, and Jennifer didn't, and Heidi didn't. By the time we were all pronounced cured my relations with Heidi had faded back to the original friendly hello-nice-to-see-you state they'd been in before our brief affair. And Jennifer and Clax had more or less decided to call it off. So we were back to the old one-to-one monogamy. For a bit."

"I'd heard about you and Heidi, but Jennifer had never mentioned the clap episode."

"Ah, Ansu, there are some things on heaven and earth that even Jennifer's philosophy doesn't encourage her to talk about. Even to you."

We left the taverna and walked down to the port, Kilminster running through the remaining list of affairs, liaisons, freak-outs, and false alarms. Most of them I'd heard about from Jennifer anyway. I think I suspected a few of them at the time, but it's hard to separate real memory from the back-projection stuff (if that's the technical term—it'll do anyway). As he says, Kilminster tried, he tried hard. And he succeeded. The failed priest became a successful libertine. When Jennifer met Jean-Claude towards the end of Kilminster's final year at university, he was quite blasé about the two of them going off to Paris for a long weekend. Besides, as I was going to Cornwall with Tamar and Co., it left him the flat free for the entertainment of one Ms Lucinda Symmonds from the biochemistry department of the university.

In Cornwall Samantha, Randolph, and I drank a number of bottles of cider. I became drunk and then hung over for the first and last time in my life.

Kilminster says he cannot remember who first suggested that Jennifer should live with Jean-Claude while continuing to spend a considerable amount of time with him, rather than remain living with Kilminster while spending a considerable amount of time with Jean-Claude, which is what had been happening. The idea suited them both. Kilminster was finding marriage as a way of life a bit boring, Jennifer had decided that much as she loved Kilminster he wasn't really the man she wished to spend the rest of her days with. The Clapham phase of our lives was played out. It was time to strike camp. We did so very smoothly, to a plan we'd worked out well in advance, a plan that allowed for Kilminster and I to finish our academic years, Jennifer to finish a novel, Jean-Claude to finalise his divorce in France and for the legal battles over my removal to the other side of the channel to be fought out with van Niekerk. It would bore me to write a detailed account of all this. What I will do, however, is reconstruct at length a weekend Kilminster and Jennifer spent alone in the château a couple of years later. This happened about a year after the birth of my half-brother, Bernard. With me playing nurse-maid to Bernard, Jean-Claude, Philippe, Silvie, and I had gone to Normandy for a couple of days, giving Jennifer her first time by herself for eighteen months.

* * * * * * *

At the end of the eleventh game Jennifer owed Kilminster two hundred and twenty francs.

"You'll have to wait," she said, "We're skint at the moment. I'll send you a cheque sometime after Christmas."

"Forget it," Kilminster said, "Playing Go for money is vulgar anyway. It's not like poker."

"Very Christian of you."

Kilminster slid the red and white ivory counters into their lacquered box and stood up. He kissed Jennifer and together they walked through the darkening passages of the empty château to the kitchen. Standing beside each other, leaning lightly against the kitchen table, they finished the bottle of wine left over from lunch. Beneath the window the hens could be heard scratching; the trees in the orchard were turning yellow and brown, the late afternoon sun shattered in the leaves like glass.

"How long are you going to be in America this time?" Jennifer asked.

"A year. Are you going to come and see me?"

"I might, if we can afford it. Or if *I* can afford it, rather. I don't like using Jean-Claude's money to flit around seeing you. He's got all that alimony to pay as it is."

"Get yourself onto the lecture circuit. The Yanks love

listening to visiting writers reading their stuff aloud, it saves them the trouble of reading it themselves. Afterwards they ask you bright questions like, 'Who are your favourite authors?' and 'Do you write in the mornings or the afternoons?' Then they give you a cheque."

"But if I spent all my time doing that, I wouldn't be able to see you."

"That's a point."

"Finish your thesis. Get a highly paid job, then you can fly me around the world in a manner to which I will rapidly accustom myself."

They stood in silence for a while watching the light. Jennifer leant her head against Kilminster's shoulder.

"When I've finished this book, I'll write a novel about you. *Mixed Blessing* doesn't really count; I'll do the adult bit this time."

"The self-indulgent lure of autobiography."

"You're biography, not autobiography."

"You couldn't write about me now without putting yourself in."

"That's true," she said, "Let's go for a walk before it gets too dark."

They walked in the beech forest behind the château. At times, when the path allowed, they held hands, otherwise they walked in file. Jennifer's hair hung, brown and slightly tangled, below the level of her shoulder blades. She was wearing one of her step-son's leather jackets. The words *À bas le fascisme* had been stencilled onto the back, but were beginning to wear off. Walking behind her, he watched the fabric of her jeans hugging the curves of her bottom. He would love her like that tonight— riding up over her bum, the skin of her back and shoulders white in the candlelight and her hair dark and glistening. He would cradle her head and she might, as she came, bite his arms and he would carry the twin purple horseshoes for a week or so until they faded. By then he would be half the world away.

They left the little forest and for a while walked along a cart track. Jennifer said, "Help me gather some grass."

She and Kilminster picked a couple of bunches of long grass from the verges of the track and then climbed the fence into the neighbouring field. Jennifer called: a high trilling sound that lost itself without echo in the twilight.

"He usually comes," she said, "They've pensioned him off, which is extraordinary for the French; normally anything too old to work gets eaten."

Across the fields the black bulk of the château rose from its surrounding orchard, while beyond the stream the willows presented an unbroken, rolling mass as dark as storm-clouds, against which they could just see the shape of the cart-horse turning, listening. Jennifer called again and the animal lumbered across the grass, a shape without colour or markings, its hoof-beats thudding like drums.

"It's quite sprightly for a pensioner."

"It's lonely, there are no other animals on this farm except for the geese."

As they fed the grass to the horse, Jennifer talked to it in French, petting it. Then they left the field and walked towards the château, Jennifer sliding an arm around Kilminster's waist.

"I really ought to pay you those two hundred and twenty francs," she said, "It's terribly, terribly bad form not to pay gambling debts. Honour demands it."

"How very English," Kilminster said.

"You're English too."

"Liverpool Irish isn't English."

"Neither is Golders Green Jewish."

"God it would be awful to actually *be* English. Some people are, you know."

"Poor bastards."

They walked in silence for a few moments and then Kilminster said, "If you really want to repay your debt, why don't you write that novel about me, that would do more for my ego than a lousy couple of hundred francs."

"It would be a lot bloody harder than paying a lousy couple

of hundred francs."

"Yeah, but I'm interesting, fascinating, the stuff of romance and passion."

"You're dead bloody boring, the stuff of papers in clinical psychology."

"Jennifer," he said, more hurt than he wished to betray.

She stopped walking and turned to face him. In the gloom her earrings shone like bones; he could not distinguish the features of her face.

"To make you interesting as fiction," she said, "Now that you've given away religion and all that guff, to make you into a novel, I'd have to have you crack up or go mad. You're too bland, Kilminster. Nice but bland."

"I wouldn't have described our marriage as *bland*."

"No, sure, we fought a bit. You had your little trauma over me and Clax. But you never really admitted the possibility that there was anything really wrong, ever, ever at all. Between us you never admitted the possibility of real pain. And hence you denied the possibility of real ecstasy. Do you see what I mean?"

"No."

She was silent for a few moments and then continued, "Look, you've created a certain image of yourself and the way you relate to other people. The key words are 'pleasant', 'well', 'fine'. In your letters to me things are always fine; you're always well; your bloody research is always going well; your women are always happy, your relations with them pleasant. Sometimes I could scream reading your letters; I sit there thinking 'who does he think I am, his favourite aunt?' When you write to your mother do you say anything different from what you've written to me?"

Kilminster was silent. Jennifer said, "Do you?"

"Maybe not often, but then my life is fairly pleasant. I'm not complaining."

"Jesus, Kilminster, it can't be like that. Not all the bloody time. Your idea of yourself coincides with reality sometimes, certainly, but what happens when it doesn't? I'll tell you what happens: you create fictions, lies, you force reality into your pleasant little mould. Even though it won't fit."

"Yes, well," Kilminster said, "That's a theory. It's also a closed system. If I disagree with you it shows that I'm resistant to the truth as revealed by your amazing insights; as good a proof of your position as you could possibly get."

"James, you're beyond hope. Let's go in, it's getting cold."

He cooked in the brightly lit kitchen, making up the recipe as he went along: duck stuffed with pâté and oranges. While he worked, he drank from a glass of local cider, rough cloudy stuff of uncertain alcohol content. Through three open doors and a passage the sound of Jennifer playing the piano came to where he cried silently over the onions. The playing stopped abruptly and Jennifer said, "Fuck!". She started the piece again, building up to the part in which she had become unstuck. Again the music stopped suddenly, restarted, and built up to the difficult passage. He sat on a kitchen stool, listening. He understood little about music; Jennifer's playing sounded all right to him—a pleasant tinkling sort of noise. This time the cessation of playing was followed by the bang of the piano's lid being slammed shut. Jennifer appeared in the kitchen.

"I'll never be able to play that bloody piece. I should never have tried to learn it."

"It sounded fine to me."

"You'd know as much about music as I know about physics."

She picked up the glass of cider and drained it. Taking a handkerchief from her pocket she dabbed at Kilminster's eyes.

"Darling," she said, "I never knew you cared so much, please don't take it so hard."

He clapped an onion-scented hand over her nose. She jumped backwards and then turned to the fridge and took out another bottle of cider. She filled the glass and then sat across the table watching him work. She said, "You're right about any novel about you being autobiography; I couldn't write about you without putting myself in the book."

"All your novels are about yourself."

"Rubbish. Do you ever actually *read* my novels?"

"Sure. These days I'm always in need of light stuff to fill in plane trips. I buy them in transit lounges."

"I send you lovingly autographed copies."

"I prefer paperbacks," Kilminster said as he placed the duck in the oven, "They're easier to carry around and discard when finished."

Jennifer left the kitchen. Moments later, the speakers on the wall began to relay music from the record player. She reappeared.

"That's mediaeval court music."

"Bluegrass is better, it has more of that distilled misery."

"You can just wait till California."

While the duck cooked Jennifer talked about her neighbours—the farmers and villagers of the immediate area.

"What happened during the war?" Kilminster asked.

"Some collaborated, some joined the resistance, some died, most did nothing, some got their heads shaved after it was all over."

"They'll talk about this?"

"No. Only one old man—Dupoint. He's lonely like that carthorse. He lost his sons in the resistance. He thinks I'm sexy. I buy poisoned wheat from him."

"What?"

"For the rats."

"Oh."

"I go round to his place and argue about the price of the wheat while he feeds me cognac and tells me stories about everyone in the district. God knows what he tells everyone about me."

"Do you feel accepted here?"

"A bit more accepted than I suppose I was in Delhi, not as much as I am in London. I don't think people like you and me belong anywhere in particular. My real world is made up of ignorant philistines who read my novels in transit lounges."

"I re-read your novels in transit lounges. You're the only modern writer I ever do re-read."

They ate at the kitchen table, wiping their fingers on the roll of toilet paper Jennifer placed beside the baking dish. Jennifer talked about her children, Jean-Claude, and Jean-Claude's children. Kilminster watched her leaning her elbows on the table, taking a half-eaten duck leg from her mouth to gesticulate with. Her face was still brown from summer, her forearms where her black roll-neck sweater had been pushed up at the sleeves also showed brown. A collection of cheap African bangles clicked when she flexed her left wrist. On the table between them the single glass now showed greasy lip marks on both sides of the rim.

"Are you missing your children?"

"It's very odd not having Bernard about. Yeah, I'm missing him a bit. As for the others—not at all. I'm glad to be on holiday. I suppose if it went on for a week I would start to want them around me again."

"And Jean-Claude?"

"Not when I'm with you."

Kilminster was conscious of the dark, semi-decrepit bulk of the château enclosing the brightness of the kitchen. He watched Jennifer talking and laughing across the table. He was entirely at home and entirely a stranger. He said, "What about the dead weight of property?"

Jennifer shrugged. "Of course," she said, "when Jean-Claude suggested we move into this place rather than sell it, I thought he was mad. I insisted the kitchen be totally done up and the roof fixed and some sort of central heating installed. So we had that done and we've been more or less broke ever since. All we seem to do is pay off the interest on loans. I've actually gone against my principles and borrowed money from Anasuya."

"That is to say, van Niekerk."

"That is rather where she gets her money from."

"Does van Niekerk know?"

"Bound to. Anasuya hardly spends anything. Ninety per cent of her clothes she steals. Her sudden request for two thousand quid could have only meant one thing."

"Nasty."

"And Philippe and Silvie have started to demand money for weekends in Paris and skiing holidays. They are all little bourgeois delinquents, Anasuya not the least. Soon it will be drugs and abortions. Ansu can pay for all that though, it's got nothing to do with me."

"So your chances of slipping off to California are slim?"

"Fuck, I don't know. It's only money."

They put the remains of the duck in the fridge, washed the dish and their greasy hands and kissed over the shared dish-cloth.

"Go and run us a bath," Jennifer said, "I'll make coffee."

Kilminster walked through the passages and climbed the stairs of the château, intoning the opening lines from Marienbad: *Once again I walk on, once again, down these corridors, through these halls, these galleries....* He did not turn on any of the lights. An almost-full moon had risen and the cold light fell through the windows, patterning the floor and walls with rectangles of phosphorescence. In the bathroom he ran the taps and then made his way to the bedroom, returning with a candle. The candle and moon combined to light the steam which rose from the bath like ectoplasm. Jennifer arrived with two mugs of coffee. They drank in silence, sitting on the edge of the bath, watching themselves in the mirror, their dim reflections outshone by the candle's single flame. Jennifer stirred the water behind them with her hand. She stood up, turned off the taps and emptied a sachet of salts into the water.

She undressed beside the candle, knowing she was being watched. Naked from the waist up she took a step towards Kilminster, putting one riding-booted foot on his knee. He held the boot while she leaned backwards, withdrawing her foot. After repeating the manoeuvre he placed the boots on the floor by the bath. They smelt slightly of leaf-mould from the forest. Quite naked, she stood a few feet from him, the shadows from the candle giving her breasts and face a sub-aquatic delicacy. She shrugged, blew him a kiss and said, "C'est moi," and then stepped into the bath. Kilminster undressed, experiencing some difficulty with his underpants. Jennifer laughed.

"You shouldn't watch ladies undressing. It sends you blind and they have to cut your underpants off with bolt-cutters."

They lay in the water with their feet under each other's bums, once or twice standing up to soap each other. Kilminster talked about California and his research. The facility in which he was working was actually on the San Andreas fault. One end of the linear accelerator was on the North American tectonic plate, the other on the Pacific.

"What happens if the whole shooting match falls apart while you are doing an experiment?"

"Nothing. Anyway, we measure our experiments in microseconds."

"I wish you'd get an honest job."

"I would if I could think of one."

"The Americans are great ones for oral sex."

"I didn't know you'd been there."

"I had a couple of American lovers in Delhi."

"It's a hard life."

The water cooled. She stepped out of the bath. Kilminster followed and they dried themselves without ceremony. Still only using the candle for illumination they walked hand-in-hand along the corridor to the bedroom.

"Why don't you get an en suite bathroom?"

"This is a falling down château, lad, not a bloody Hilton."

In the bedroom he found two more candles which he lit from the stub of the first one; he located the brandy and poured two glasses. Jennifer sat on a stool brushing her hair, having trouble at first with the knots; then, as the brush ran freely and the dampness dried, starting to emit audible sparks. Occasionally she stopped to take a sip of brandy. Kilminster sat on the bed; across the worn Persian rug the doors of a large wardrobe stood open. Jean-Claude's suits and ties hung in a neat row. Kilminster crossed the rug and closed the doors.

"Can't we sleep in some other room?" he asked.

"What on earth for?"

"I feel it's not proper; screwing you in the marital bed."

"Have a nasty incident in one during your formative years?"

"Don't be silly."

"What the hell's the matter with this one. It's never seemed inappropriate to you before. Why the sudden attack of sensibility? You're in Jean-Claude's château aren't you, drinking his brandy, eating his food, burning his candles?"

"I'd feel more at home in another bed."

"Poor old Kilminster. The only other beds made up are the children's, and they're all single."

"Oh, all right," he said, "It was only a thought."

"Tell me about this research assistant," Jennifer said.

"Eh?"

"This what's her name...Diana."

"What about her?"

"You tell me. I'm interested, I'm not jealous. What's she like?"

"Nice."

"Nice! There must be a bit more to her than that. How long have you been sleeping with her?"

"A bit over a year."

"So she's quite important to you?"

"Yes."

"Well, what's she like then."

Kilminster said nothing for about thirty seconds. Jennifer sat on her stool looking directly at him. He avoided her gaze.

"Well?" she said quietly, "What is Diana really like?"

"She's about your height. Fair hair, cut short...."

"I don't bloody care what she looks like. What is she like, what sort of person is she?"

"She has a sense of humour."

"And...."

"Well, I don't know. She's nice. I enjoy being with her."

"Do you, dearest James, have a thoroughly nice time with her?"

"Of course."

"Oh good, I'm so happy for both of you."

"Sarcasm doesn't suit you, Jennifer."

"Well tell me what this bloody Diana woman is like then… just bloody talk to me for Christ's sake."

"I can't seriously discuss anyone with you in an atmosphere of hostility and jealousy."

Jennifer threw the hair-brush in his direction. It went wide, hitting an unframed painting on the wall, denting the canvas. She said slowly, giving each word as much weight as possible, "I'm not jealous of Diana. I have nothing but goodwill towards her. I don't really care what she is like. What I do care about is that you are incapable of talking about her to me."

Kilminster said nothing.

Jennifer said, "Your trouble is that your vision of reality fits so perfectly with what you allow yourself to see that you never experience anything that calls this image of yourself into question. You are always so well in control. But the cost of maintaining this vision is a deadening of your more delicate perceptions and responses."

Kilminster said, "I'm sorry to be so inadequate. I'm glad you've found someone better."

"Jesus, Kilminster," Jennifer exploded, "I'm trying to get through to you. I'm trying to talk to you. I'm your wife, your ex-wife. I'd like to think I'm your closest friend. Look, some of your actions are so weird as to be positively bizarre. And you just won't see this.…"

"Like what, for instance?"

"What's the use?" she said slowly, "If I started listing them you'd have a perfectly rational explanation for all of them. We'd just bicker for hours about bits of behaviour. Why can't you just accept what I say for once. I do know you fairly well, James. I probably know you a lot better than this Diana lady."

Kilminster started to mimic her, "Dear James, I desperately want to talk to you, but you'll have to accept that our discussion must be without content and on my terms, because otherwise you might win the argument.… For god's sake, Jennifer, what sort of talk is that?"

After a silence Jennifer said, "Look, I'll make one more attempt. Why do you think you're so sexually inhibited?"

"What!"

"Why do you have such a limited range of sexual expression, it's as limited as your facial expressions: gentle, tender, loving, kind, *nice*…but as for a passionate awareness of the other person's persona.… You don't really know what I'm talking about, do you?"

"No. And all this is getting a bit wearing. I think I'll go to bed."

Kilminster left the bedroom and groped his way down the passage to one of the children's rooms. Within five minutes he was asleep, his feet sticking from the bottom of the undersized bed. In her bed Jennifer lay watching the moonlight die from the walls. Kilminster dreamed an old dream.

He was thirteen again. He was on his summer holidays in county Tyrone, staying on a small farm belonging to a distant relative, a man called Sean. He dreamed now of the cold heavy metal of the shotgun Sean placed in his hands, explaining the manner of its loading and firing. The weight and the coldness of the barrels shocked him. He walked away from the farm, over small fields surrounded by stone walls. The air was still with the stillness of early morning. Once or twice a rabbit crossed his path, but either out of range or too quickly to be aimed at. He climbed a wall, first breaking open the breech of the gun, and then, when safely on the other side, swinging the barrels upward to click the mechanism shut. Suddenly he wanted, needed, to look into the twin barrels of the gun with the cartridges in the breech, the safety catch off, and his fingers resting lightly—ever so lightly—on the triggers. He wished for one long instant to look at his own death, to know that it was only by a consummate act of will that he prevented the two black depthless holes from being the last sense data his mind would ever register. The gun in his hands began—seemingly of its own accord—to describe the arc required to bring the barrels in line with his face. And then stopped. Violently trembling, he laid the gun on the ground and sat with his head between his knees, sick, giddy, dry-retching. When he lifted his head, the landscape in which he sat had become insubstantial—the fields and hills formed a washed-out water-colour, powerless to hold his vision against the stare of the close-set gun barrels. He struggled to replace the picture of death with that of the gun lying harmless on the ground. He started to pray, stuttering and babbling the words, mixing Latin and English and schoolboy cries to the deity in one desperate stream.

The moonlight vanished. Jennifer muttered, "Bugger him," and jumped from her bed. She strode down the passage, throwing switches. In her step-son's bedroom, Kilminster jerked awake as the electric light hit his face. Jennifer tugged the blankets from the bed, throwing herself on top of him.

"Fuck me, you bastard."

At one stage they hung half-on, half-off, the small bed; one of Kilminster's arms around Jennifer's shoulders, the other braced against the floor to prevent both of them from collapse. Jennifer turned her head, biting him hard on the forearm. He allowed himself to slide further over her, taking advantage of her exposed neck. They fell onto the floor and finished at a hard missionary gallop, Jennifer pressing against a leg of the bed with the palms of both hands.

"Can we go back to bed please?"

"Why not?"

In the dark warmth of her own bed Jennifer said, "You weren't nice, gentle or tender. You're lucky you didn't sever my jugular."

"I'd been dreaming."

"What about?"

"When I was thirteen. On that farm in Ireland. I tried to look down a loaded shotgun, keeping my fingers on the triggers."

"You actually did this?"

"I don't really know. I don't know how much of the dream

is true, is memory. Even in the dream it's not clear if I actually look down the barrels or not…. As I remember it, as I like to remember it when I'm fully awake, I just had this idea that it would be interesting, a sort of Russian roulette I suppose, and I sort of lifted the gun slightly as if I were going to do it, but then good sense and self-control took over. But I also have this vision, this image, of actually looking down the thing, the barrels gazing back at me. Maybe I did do it."

Jennifer shivered, "You've never told me this before. Do you have this dream often?"

"Not these days. Only when I'm upset."

"Poor love."

"I remember after I'd done it, or tried to, I sat on the ground, shaking and praying. I picked up the gun as if it were a snake, unloaded it, put the cartridges in my pocket, and walked back to the farmhouse. I put the gun back in the cupboard where it was normally kept. I went back there—to Sean's farm—a couple of times when I was in the junior bit of the seminary. I didn't touch the gun. Then there was that time just after I'd moved into the Putney house. I took Anasuya to the circus on Wandsworth Common. You remember that mug she came back with, a thick toby-jug sort of thing?"

"Not really, but go on."

"Well, I won it for her in a shooting-gallery. You had to shoot at these ducks that kept popping up. If you hit four of them you got a prize. Anasuya wanted me to have a go, she wanted the mug. I refused at first, but then I thought: this is absurd, why not? So I had half a dozen shots and they gave me the mug. Then last year I came back through Ireland from America—the charter flight landed at Shannon—so I called in to see Sean and his family and stayed a couple of days. As a sort of exorcism, to see if I felt anything, I took the gun out one morning, loaded it, and walked to the place where I'd tried to look down it. I felt nothing. Or rather I felt like a melodramatic idiot. It all seemed so silly and unreal, forgettable. If it wasn't for the dream, I think I'd forget the whole incident all together."

"Then be thankful that you dream."

"What would you know," he said, folding her in his arms, "You have a vested interest in all this murky psychodrama stuff; you need it for your writing. You can use the shotgun incident in your novel about me."

"I will," she murmured, "I will."

They awoke in the morning and made love as they had often done—gently exploring each other with their fingertips. She came once, kneeling over him, and kissed his closed eyes as he came in her, her nipples grazing his chest.

After lunch she drove him to Charles de Gaulle, switching lanes on the autoroute with random aplomb. She was wearing her one expensive blue suit, stockings, jewellery, and a silk scarf knotted around her neck—after the airport she was going to see her French publishers with a view to extracting an advance on an as-yet-unwritten novel about a demonic high-energy physicist.

"I like the scarf."

"Get fucked, Kilminster."

Outside the terminal they kissed. "I love you," he said.

"And I you," she replied.

In the airport bookshop he could find only a French edition of her collection of short stories, *Dubious Thesis*, but he knew two or three of them backwards in their original version. By the time he'd worked his way through *Tar Love*, the plane was crossing the Breton coast and beginning its long fall over the horizon towards the big sub-atomic guns of California. He laid the book aside and wondered about the possibility of a drink, pushing his sleeve up ten centimetres further than was actually necessary for the consultation of his watch. The bruise was good for a fortnight at least.

* * * * * * *

Torrid stuff. But I think it redresses the balance a bit. When I re-read my account of our Clapham years, especially the bit towards the end where I describe the dissolution of Jennifer and Kilminster's marriage, it struck me that I'd made it all too easy, too civilised. I was being at such pains to stress the difference between that breakup and the one between my parents that I left out all the clashes, all the fairly futile attempts on Jennifer's part to explain to Kilminster the nature of his own unconscious mind, all the unproductive, circular arguments that ensued. Well now I've got them in.

I suppose I should also declare my sources. The weekend in question, of course, conformed to the essentials I've just described. But I wrote the account using my recollection of Jennifer's description to me of what went on. Jennifer is not the most accurate of witnesses and anyway she didn't tell me about it all until three years after the events, so a lot of it was pure invention. I didn't ask Kilminster about his version of the events until I'd finished writing. I gave him the exercise book to read last night. We'd both been working late, Kilminster in his room, me in mine. He came in, bringing two shot glasses of coffee—the strong local stuff, full of grounds, but without the sugar. I went on writing while Kilminster sat on the bed and re-read the letters we'd received yesterday morning. When I'd finished, I gave him the story and lay down beside him. He read in silence, occasionally resting a hand on my shoulder. When he had finished, he put the exercise book down saying, "Kinky."

"It's not kinky at all. There's only that biting sequence, and...."

"No, no. Not the story itself (a mundane little tale); your writing of it. Most twenty-two-year-olds I know don't spend their time writing descriptions of their mothers fucking."

"Most twenty-two-year-olds don't talk to their mothers."

"True. Are you glad Jennifer is so open with you?"

"Of course. Why not?"

"I don't know. I think sometimes that she hasn't really grown up. She shares confidences with you like she shared them with Tamar when they were kids. She's a sort of superannuated teenager in some ways."

"She admits it. Says so herself."

"Yeah, I know. I just get uneasy about it sometimes."

"Why?"

"It's hard to say. It doesn't matter. I'll tell you one thing, though; it wouldn't have happened in my family."

"That is true, James."

Kilminster lay down beside me. The wind was getting up and the sound of the waves on the beach was louder than normal.

"I suppose I'd better close the shutters," he said, "We don't want the damn windows blown in half-way through the night."

When he had finished securing the shutters, I said, "Well, did I get it right? Does the whole story ring true?"

"You've romanticised it a bit; all that steam rising like ecto-plasm and candlelight and empty château stuff. You've laid it on a bit thick."

"Well it can be a bit like that. God knows there are enough drawbacks to living in that place without not being able to enjoy the Gothic side. But what about the dialogue between you and Jennifer?"

"You've got all her theorising about the state of my poor crip-pled soul down pat. I can't fault that."

"So I should hope. I've spent hours and hours listening to Jennifer psychoanalysing you. I could do that sort of stuff from now to Christmas."

"She can be a bit obsessive, your mum."

"But is she right?"

"What do you think?"

"I'm too close to you."

"Diplomatic, aren't you? But how is one meant to read all that stuff about Jennifer not being jealous of Diana? You haven't put any adverbs in. If I'd been writing it, I'd have said things like, 'I'm not jealous of this Diana lady,' Jennifer said jealously."

"Do you really think she's jealous of your other women, even now?"

"She's not jealous of the ones she knows she can dominate, like Nara the first time, and like you now, but she's as jealous as a cat of those she's never met. She's scared I'll take up with one who'll stop me sleeping with her. And that, of course, as you've no doubt guessed, is the main reason I can't talk freely to her about any of them. If I'd really talked to her about Diana she'd have been as bitchy about her as possible, especially as Diana was quite a formidable woman herself. She wants me to talk about my other attachments, but she wants to be told that no one else quite measures up."

"What do you think I think about your other women?"

"You? On this island you don't have to think. I might not be monogamous by nature, but I don't fancy a shallow grave in the hills."

* * * * * * *

In my last year at school I had the uncommon experience of finding both of my parents in agreement about a matter concerning my life. They both thought I ought not to attend university in France. They were, however, at loggerheads about which one I should attend. Van Niekerk thought I should follow in his footsteps and go to Leiden.

"Leiden! I can't even speak Dutch."

"You could learn. It is not a difficult language and you are very good at languages. Besides everyone at the university speaks English and French and the other civilised languages. The Dutch are not insular like the French. Or the English for that matter."

Jennifer was more liberal. She thought it mattered not at all whether I chose Oxford or Cambridge.

"They are both very good, Anasuya. A lot of the men's colleges are now taking women undergraduates."

"Undergraduates. Under-bloody-graduates. Come to my place, Ansu. Be a proper student." And then, as an afterthought, Kilminster added, "And you won't have to live in a college, we won't throw you out for screwing and you won't have to eat institutionalised food."

That did it. I'd sampled English institutionalised cooking in Putney, Clapham and Bury-St-Edmunds. Muck.

In the year after Kilminster took up his appointment at Liverpool University I enrolled as a student of psychology. For a few weeks I stayed with Kilminster and then moved into a large flat in Huskisson Street with half a dozen other students. Two of them, Clara and Sam, had found it, signed the lease, and then moved in with a couple of their friends. The other two of us, myself and Magpie, had been recruited via the students' union notice board. It was an odd house and had been subdivided like one of those puzzle cubes that had sat in Kilminster's window at Garbage View Villas. The first two storeys had been divided into four flats, the third storey and the attic were one large flat, ours. However, our bathroom and lavatory were on the second storey. In order to integrate these rooms with our part, the stairs had been divided down the middle. It was possible to ascend what had once been a quite generously proportioned staircase, enter our flat by one door, leave it by another and descend to the bathroom on the same staircase only on the other side of the plywood partition. For obvious reasons we referred to our ablution enclave on the second storey as Berlin. The flat proper held one large room complete with bay windows and marble fireplace which obviously still retained the proportions, if not exactly the bourgeois elegance, of its original design. In this room we ate, drank, smoked, listened to music, played darts, and generally lay about. The rest of the rooms had once conformed to the architect's spatial generosity, but in them the sub-divider's genius had been at work again. Ingenious use of L-shapes and T-shapes had insured that each misbegotten segment had access of sorts to a window of sorts. The top floor, where my room was, had obviously once been the servants' quarters. No further diminution in size of rooms had been possible. The whole house was run-down, seedy, and falling to bits. The other tenants were Indian, Irish, and Scouse. An odd mixture of cooking smells wafted up to us. The front door of the building held traces of the original lead-light windows which had cast their variegated colours into the hall. Three panels, however, had been replaced—two with frosted bathroom glass and one with plywood. I loved the place, it was almost as decayed as the château had been when we moved in. My room under the roof had space for my bed, a small table, a straight-backed chair, and a few cushions. I organised a wooden rail across one corner from which to hang my clothes.

The household worked fairly well after the fashion of such *ménages de raison*. Clara and Sam were very much a couple; the rest of us became quite friendly although no really close intimacies developed. The flat was really just the place we all ate and slept in, our real interests and close friends we found elsewhere. But we had large convivial meals at which our numbers were swelled by various friends and waifs and strays. Kilminster came occasionally and enjoyed himself. He said to me privately, of course, that students these days weren't a patch on what they had been in his time. Now take the brilliance of the *Après Fin*....

"Yes, James. I know. I was part of your student days if you'll remember. You know, all that time ago in the early seventies when the world was young. I provided the smoked goose liver in aspic that we all subsisted on, not to mention half the repartee across the table."

"They smoke too much pot, Ansu."

"I know, James. There's nothing wrong with a joint or two *per se*, but the stuff inhibits conversation. Now if my friends would only take a leaf from the *Après Fin* book and switch to booze...."

"Mock me if you like. It's true."

Bloody reactionary. And in those days the lad was still under thirty.

* * * * * * *

Towards the end of my first term at Liverpool I took the train to London. I stayed at Tamar's, but one Saturday had lunch, and then dinner, with my father. Over dinner I must have said something about the train. My father wanted to know why I hadn't driven down to London. I explained I'd left the Mercedes in France. Not to upset him, I didn't try to explain why. I had, in fact, left the thing there because I wished to live like a normal student. I didn't want my social relations constantly queered by the ownership of an absurdly expensive car. Those last six months as a schoolgirl in Oise had taught me all I wished to learn about the effects of conspicuous consumption. But I had to say something to van Niekerk; so I explained that in Liverpool I lived within walking distance of the university and anywhere else that mattered. He didn't look impressed. I'm sure he thought that nowhere in Liverpool mattered, that the further one was from its so-called university (a place whose standards were so degraded as to allow the appointment of that boy Kilminster) the better. So I went on to say that perhaps I'd bring the car back after my next visit to France, but that I was dubious about the safety of driving a left-hand drive car in England. This last was actually true; on the one occasion I had brought the Merc to England I'd been traumatised by the necessity of bringing half of it onto the wrong side of the road in order to see past the car ahead of me. And my reactions to the English traffic were all wrong. The motorways were manageable, but as soon as I tried to drive on ordinary streets I had a constant tendency to turn onto the wrong side of the road. My father seemed to see the merit of this. He was nothing if not concerned for my comfort and safety. So he bought me another Merc. A right-hand drive Merc. I was furious. I was furious with my father, but also with myself. I should have foreseen this outcome. I should have told him the truth about my disinclinations.

He had it delivered in much the same way as the first one. A representative of the dealer turned up at Huskisson street with it one afternoon. But unlike good old Henri Boufflet, this sour-faced servant of the motor trade clearly regarded the whole exercise as a joke in bad taste. I don't think he normally delivered his cars to places like ours, I don't think the recipients normally cursed and swore at the inconvenience involved in signing for them. The rest of my household was stunned. I was stunned. The delivery man was stunned. If I'd had my wits about me I would have sent it back there and then, but I wasn't thinking too clearly. At that time we had no telephone in the flat, so I drove the new Merc to Kilminster's place in order to use his.

"I don't want it, Daddy."

"What?"

"I don't want another car, you've already given me one."

"But that one is in France. It's left-hand drive."

"All the same, I don't want another car. I've got nowhere to put it. We've got no garage."

"Hire a garage. Move to another flat, one with a garage."

"Daddy, it's the *affluence* I don't want."

"What do you mean?"

"It's a ruling-class car."

My father laughed affably at this. "Of course it's a ruling-class car, as you put it. You don't see shift-workers driving them, do you? Even in England there are some things left for the enjoyment of those who have brains and determination."

"I'm embarrassed in front of my friends...the car's an embarrassment."

"Oh come on. If your friends are as small-minded as that, you had better find some new friends. Many people are jealous of those who succeed; one does not have to have them as friends."

"Daddy, I want you to take the car back."

"We'll see, Anasuya, we'll see."

"There's nothing to see about."

"Anasuya, you feel this way now, but in a few days...."

"In a few days be buggered. I don't want it, Daddy."

Kilminster was silently laughing his head off on the other side of the room. It was the funniest scene he'd witnessed for months. The girl who'd been with him when I arrived sat on her chair smiling with dopey non-comprehension. Kilminster made encouraging sock-it-to-him gestures with his fist.

My father said, "Now, Anasuya, you *need* a car...."

"I do not *need* a car. I certainly do not need another Mercedes-Benz. "

"Go, Anasuya!" Kilminster said.

"Shut up, James."

"What's that?" my father said.

"Nothing, just Kilminster."

"Is he there?"

"I'm in his flat."

"So he put you up to this! That man is evil, Anasuya, he's an evil influence."

"He is not evil, for Christ's sake. He's got nothing to do with it. *I* don't want the car...."

The word *evil* was too much for Kilminster. He came bounding across the room, caught me in a one-armed embrace and tried to get his ear next to the phone. I pushed him away. He struggled his way back.

"Fuck off, James."

"Anasuya, are you all right? What is that man doing to you?"

"Why am I evil?" Kilminster said.

"Kilminster? Can you hear me?"

"No, he can't hear you," I said.

"Yes I can."

"Kilminster, if you touch one hair on my daughter's head...."

Kilminster ran his fingers through my hair.

"Daddy, Kilminster's just mucking around, I don't want that car, understand?"

"Anasuya, are you all right?"

"Yes I'm perfectly all right. Stop worrying. James is one of my oldest and closest friends, as well you know. He's only mucking about. But I'm not. I don't want that fucking car."

"We will see, Anasuya, we will see."

"We will not see...."

"Anasuya, I can't discuss this with you now. Not when you are in that man's flat...."

"He's got nothing to do with it."

"...but next time you are in London we can talk privately and rationally."

"Oh Jesus," I said. "All right, Daddy, all right. If that's the way you want it. Privately and rationally it will be."

I put the phone down. There was no point in going on.

"And you needn't laugh," I yelled at Kilminster. He was collapsed in his chair, parodying the three monkeys: putting his hands behind his ears the better to hear evil, shading his eyes and cupping his hands around his mouth the better to see and speak it. The girl giggled nervously.

"And you can shut up too," I snapped at her.

I marched out of the flat. Kilminster came to the door and yelled down the stairs, "Hey, Ansu, come back. I'm sorry...."

But I was in no mood to stay. I flung myself into the Merc and switched on the engine. I almost drove off, but thought better of it. I was damned if I was going to drive the thing back to Huskisson Street. I stepped out and walked away, leaving the door open and the engine running.

I made my way home by a circuitous route. I was furious with everybody and everything. After a while I absolved Kilminster and his drippy girlfriend. As I'd told van Niekerk, James was only mucking about. The idea of him as an evil influence was really quite funny. Then I forced myself to absolve van Niekerk: he'd only been acting according to his lights—I had completely concealed from him my true feelings about my first car. Which left only me to blame.

I had coffee and cheesecake in a café near the ferry wharf. The Mersey surged and swirled. Too many fucking sports cars. It's a hard, hard life.

"What so funny then?" the waitress said.

"Do you want a sports car? New, nothing the matter with it. Free."

"I don't drive, do I?"

Hard all right. You can't even give the things away. But, of course, you can. And being able to drive has nothing to do with it.

I arrived home to find that Sergeant O'Flaggon of the

Merseyside Traffic Section had called, leaving his card and a message to the effect that my car had been in collision with a lorry. The sergeant craved my earliest attendance at the station. I did nothing. The next day he came round again, but I was out. The next time I was in. He wasn't amused. Didn't I care about my car? No, I couldn't give a button about the thing. The sergeant looked around our living room, at the posters that showed students at the barricades, Ché, Angela Davis, *Todays Pigs are Tomorrow's Bacon*, *Give me Liberty or give me Freedom*. He looked at me and he summed me up very neatly. Rich bitch heiress slumming it during her student years; owner of a car that cost twice his annual salary and couldn't even be bothered to find out what happened to it when it was stolen. I had been about to apologise for the inconvenience I'd caused him, but I was suddenly, violently angry. That look of contempt was the last straw.

"Look, Sergeant, I don't care about that fucking car. I don't care what you do with it. Throw it in the river if you want to, but don't bother me."

I walked out of the room and he walked out of our flat. The next cop to call wasn't Sergeant O'Flaggon or whatever his name was, the next cop was Constable Pierce and he carried no visiting cards, he carried a clip-board with a neatly filled in blue summons sheet. I, Anasuya Tamar van Niekerk was hereby duly charged under section this and clause that of the Traffic Offences Act of 1947 amended 1972 with the crime of abandoning a motor car in a public thoroughfare in a manner likely to cause small boys with time on their hands and the devil whispering in their grubby little ears to take said motor car for a bit of a spin or jaunt or joy-ride upon the highways and byways of Liverpool to the considerable danger of the citizens of the aforementioned city not to mention the little lads themselves. And, furthermore, and pursuant to the Act of 1934, I was further charged with having failed to heed the lawful and legal request of an officer of the law to remove said motor car—now a trifle battered to be sure—from the police compound to which it had been towed after being further abandoned by the aforementioned small boys who had scarpered, as well they might, after causing said motor car to come into smart contact with a large lorry, truck or juggernaut....

I invited Constable Pierce inside while I signed for the summons. He was a nice boy, bright and helpful.

"There's nothing much the matter with it," he informed me, "They didn't hit the lorry very hard. You could still drive it in daylight."

"What's the damage, then?"

"They just smashed the headlight."

I smiled, then I giggled, then I laughed.

"Which headlight?"

"The nearside."

"Which side is that?"

"The left."

"The first one of those cars I ever owned I smashed the left-hand headlight half an hour after I got it."

"Did you now?"

Constable Pierce was practising his nothing-you-say-can-amaze-me tone of voice. He'd been around a bit, he'd seen it all before, had young Pierce. He would go a long way in the force, no doubt about it. I accepted a lift in his Panda car and drove the damaged Merc back to Huskisson Street where it sat outside our flat—abandoned, smashed, out of place.

I appeared before the Justices of the Peace on the same day as the three fourteen-year-olds who hadn't scarpered quite fast enough from the crashed car. Two of them were Pakistanis, the other was Liverpool Irish like Kilminster. Nice kids. The chief Justice of the Peace had a thing or two to say about my attitude towards the whole affair. I was utterly irresponsible, completely selfish and a disgrace to my university. It wasn't his job to comment on the sort of birthday presents my father chose to give me, but when he was a lad he'd had to earn the money for his first bicycle, every penny of it, fined fifty quid. One of the Pakistanis had no previous record, the other two boys were dab hands at stealing cars; although in the present case it could be said there were mitigating circumstances since never in all his years on the bench had the chief Justice of the Peace come across a case of temptation being put so blatantly in the way of impressionable and foolish people of tender years; in many ways the previous defendant could be said to be responsible for the sorry state of affairs in which the lads now found themselves, fifty quid for the first defendant, one hundred and fifty for the other two and it would be borstal if they ever showed their faces in here again next case. The clerk at the window wouldn't accept one cheque for the sum total, so I had to make out four separate cheques, one for each of us. I had another Bottomless Pit to draw on by then: some equally anonymous bank in London.

I kept the car. I left it sitting outside the flat for ten days gathering rust and soot. Somebody wrote, *please wash me* in the dirt on the back window. Somebody else wrote *National Front Rules. O.K.*, but I rubbed that out. The radio aerial was removed. Then one morning Clara and I were in a hurry to go somewhere. It was raining.

"Can't we use your car?"

"Oh, I suppose so."

So I started driving it. After I'd been stopped by the fuzz for only having one headlight, I took it to the dealers and had it fixed. While they were at it they replaced the aerial and a complete side panel. I hadn't noticed anything wrong with the panel and the aerial was ripped off again within a week. I really don't know why they bothered.

I found a lock-up garage in a row of similar lock-up garages at the back of some council flats about a quarter of an hour's walk from Huskisson Street. I paid the old woman whose garage it nominally was almost as much rent as I was paying for my own room at home. Mainly the Merc stayed in its garage. I found the social effects of owning it not so bad as they had been in France. But they weren't good. Everyone knew I owned it. When they talked to me they were conscious of talking to the owner of a Mercedes-Benz sports car.

* * * * * * *

Halfway through second term Philippe came to visit us. It was planned that he should stay at Kilminster's place and he arrived there one evening, done up in full *blouson noir* outfit: crash helmet, leather jacket, high flying boots, wrap-around dark glasses. He had just graduated from *mobylette* to real, one-hundred-and-twenty-five-cubic-centimetre-capacity motor bike. The trip was his first celebration of the adult status thus obtained and he'd ridden the entire distance in one go—virtually the only time he'd been out of the saddle was on the cross-channel ferry.

"Jesus, Philippe," Kilminster said, "You haven't been wearing those glasses in the middle of the night?"

Philippe grinned, took off the glasses and snapped the clear plastic visor up and down a couple of times.

"Poseur!" I yelled at him, "Fraud!"

He picked me off the floor, spun me around a few times, and kissed me. I kissed him back.

"Why don't you do something about your pimples?" I said, "They have this stuff, you know, Clearapimp, I'll buy you some."

"I'm hungry."

In the kitchen Philippe ate a quantity of bread and cheese. He gangled over to Kilminster's fridge and extracted a couple of tins of beer.

"Jim?" (Philippe is the only person I know who calls Kilminster Jim.)

"If you are."

Philippe ripped the tops from the tins, handed one to Kilminster and tipped his head back to drink straight from his, his Adam's apple joggling up and down, his pimples and sparse adolescent bristles riding the muscles of his jaw.

"Lout," I said, "Beast."

Kilminster leaned from his chair towards the draining-board, plucked up a glass, decanted his tin into it and began to drink. Philippe finished his tin, crushed it with one hand, threw it into the swing-top rubbish bin and extracted another from the fridge. This he drank more slowly, sitting down.

"Do you know how long they give me?"

"Who?"

"The immigration."

"Twenty-four hours."

"Two weeks. Have you anything to declare? *Non*! No drugs? *Non*! No marijuana? *Non*! No hashish? *Mais non, monsieur*! Who is this Dr Kilminster?" Philippe scrutinised a phantom disembarkation card. "He is my father's wife's husband." Philippe looked suspiciously at his phantom self. "You will be staying at this address all the time you are in England? Certainly. How much money do you have? Two hundred and thirty francs. Show me." Philippe mimed the slow counting of a small pile of money. "There is only one hundred and eighty-two francs here. I spent some on the boat. You have not enough, I cannot let you into Britain. Do not worry, *monsieur*, Dr Kilminster is very rich. Ha! Two weeks!"

For half an hour or so we sat in the kitchen talking. Then we left for an Indian restaurant Kilminster and I frequent. Philippe insisted on riding his motorbike there. He followed close behind us and, on one long straight piece of road, overtook us, gunning his engine as he roared past. The headlights of the Merc picked out the faded *À bas le fascisme* sign on the back of his leather jacket.

"Rebel with a non-specific cause," Kilminster said.

"It's good to see him."

"He's an engaging yobbo."

At the traffic lights he drew to one side, waving us magnanimously past.

In the restaurant we lingered over the meal, gossiping about the château and all therein. Kilminster and Philippe washed down the curry with beer. I drank water. I mentioned that I'd been invited to a party by some theatrical people from the university. I didn't particularly want to go—I had had nothing to do with the production and the party wouldn't start until the play had finished—but Philippe and Kilminster were all for going. We lingered and gossiped and drank some more. When it was time to go, I suggested we went via Kilminster's flat so that Philippe could leave his bike there.

"No, no. I will ride to this theatre. You lead."

"No, it's late, it is getting later. You've come all the way from France without stopping. You've been drinking. You will drink some more. I don't drink. It's best you come with me."

"Anasuya the big sister, I love you but I will ride. It is not late, there is an hour difference between here and France."

"The wrong way. It's an hour *later* in France."

"Of course it is an hour later there. I have gained an hour by coming here."

"That's not how it works. You've *lost* an hour."

"Rubbish."

There was to be no persuading him. Kilminster was being useless, sitting on the bonnet of my car waiting for us to finish, although as Philippe was retreating into a fast *pied-noir* argot that he had picked up from television, there was probably not much being said that Kilminster could understand. I compromised: "Promise you won't drink any more then?"

"Certainly. I am not like the English. Always drunk."

"Don't bet on it."

The party was one of those last-night, set-striking affairs. It was in full swing in the dressing-rooms and on the stage of the theatre itself. At the time we arrived all but a few of the flats and other paraphernalia had been loaded into a truck. Only a handful of stalwarts were still staggering around with armloads of property, most people were partying, some in nineteenth century bourgeois dress—I think the play had been one of Ibsen's. There was loud rock coming from the theatre's sound system and someone played around with the lighting until a loathsome purple effect was achieved on stage. The three of us wandered around as a group for a while until dancing began on the stage and Kilminster was drawn into a discussion of something fairly tedious with one of his students, a rather dim girl called May Sullivan. I danced with Philippe, his great boots clattering wildly. Kilminster and May appeared out of the purple gloom, also dancing. We swapped partners—although with the sort of dancing going on it was hard to say if anybody really had a partner or not. Anyway, I ended up in a mushy waltz with Kilminster through the throng and into one of the dressing rooms where the hard-drinking and dope-smoking was proceeding. As we left the stage I looked backwards to where Philippe and May were cavorting, she had a slightly moonstruck expression on her dim, purple face. I had gathered the impression that she was in love with her lean, handsome lecturer, James Kilminster. It seemed quite likely that this love could be transferred without strain onto Kilminster's lean, gangling, spotty-faced, French pseudo-stepson.

"Do you think Philippe's found himself *une petite ama*?" I said.

"May? I doubt that he'd encounter much difficulty."

In the dressing-room we talked for an hour while Kilminster drank a bottle or two of beer. I sat in front of one of those mirrors with half a dozen naked light bulbs around it. There was a box of grease paints on the bench top, so I painted a small green and red flower on my cheek. Kilminster stood up from where he'd been sitting on the floor.

"A piss and then home," he said.

He disappeared in the direction of the lavatories while I went back on stage to look for Philippe. I spotted him and May sitting in the gloom of the front row of seats. Kissing.

"Hey, lover-boy, she's got the clap," I yelled at him in French. "Time to go home."

"*Un moment, chéri,*" Philippe said to May in a parody of Hollywood's parody of French lovers. He stood up, took two steps towards the stage and in one mad leap flew up to where I was standing, leather jacket billowing out behind him, great boots thumping the boards, arms outstretched. I have this picture in my mind of Philippe coming up at me out of the gloom of the pit into the lurid purple of the stage: great irrepressible, lunatic, adolescent superhero leaping tall buildings with one bound. It was the second last time I ever saw him leap anywhere.

He wouldn't come home of course. He said he hadn't drunk anything all the time we'd been at the theatre which was probably almost true. But it was one o'clock in the morning. Two o'clock in the morning in France. I argued. It was pointless. I took five pounds from my handbag and shoved it into one of the pockets of his jacket.

"If you want to take her home, take her home in a taxi. If you want to come home alone, come home in a taxi. Leave the fucking bike here, understand?"

"Sister of mine, I love you," he said embracing and kissing me for an instant before throwing his arms wide and jumping backwards into the gloom of the pit in an exact reversal of his initial leap. That was the last time I saw Philippe jump.

The phone call came early the next afternoon. I'd dropped Kilminster at his flat and driven straight to my place. Kilminster hadn't waited up, of course, and had assumed in the morning that Philippe's absence merely indicated his presence in May Sullivan's bed, wherever that was.

Philippe was conscious, but in deep shock and could speak only French. His back was broken. May had broken both her legs and suffered slight concussion, but was otherwise all right. The police car that Philippe had ridden straight into was slightly damaged, but the two constables who had been inside it were unscathed.

I drove to the hospital. They wouldn't let me see him, but required permission to operate. As he was under eighteen he couldn't give this himself. After an enormous amount of red tape and fast talking they accepted that I was kin and allowed me to sign the consent form. Where it said relationship, I wrote half-brother's half-brother. I drove to Kilminster's and together we rang France.

The next couple of weeks were one blur of misery and shock. Jean-Claude flew over, as did Philippe's mother, Marie. Jean-Claude could only stay a few days, but Marie settled into the spare room at Kilminster's place, planning to stay until Philippe was well enough to be transferred to the spinal injuries hospital at Stoke Mandeville. She spent her days sitting beside her son in the hospital, caring for him, stroking his brow, reading to him. I took half the French novels on my shelves round to Kilminster's place for this purpose. Marie was calm, loving, and gentle with Philippe in a manner I can only describe as wonderful. She talked and read to him endlessly, attempting to raise his spirits, being non-censorious about his idiot actions on the bike, listening patiently to him as he told her in utter despair that he wished he'd died in the accident rather than cripple himself and break that poor girl's legs. I had never really liked Marie, but watching her with Philippe I was awe-struck at her calm, her reserves, her strength. Sometimes, if I arrived at the hospital in a bitter depression myself, an hour spent listening to Marie read to Philippe in her clear, modulated Parisian accent would lift my spirits, send me away from the hospital far calmer than I had been when I arrived.

Outside the hospital, away from Philippe's bed, Marie collapsed entirely. She cried, she needed massive doses of pills to enable her to sleep, she railed at motorbikes in general and English traffic laws in particular (entering a narrow street, Philippe had swerved to avoid the oncoming police car, after the French manner, to the right; the cops had swerved to the left, of course). She berated me for having left him alone at the theatre. I tried to tell her about the five quid, but I doubt that she heard. I tried to reassure her as best I could, I talked about how brave Philippe was being, how there were chances of recovery. I accompanied her to the great concrete tent of the Catholic cathedral and found a priest who spoke a modicum of French. I suppose I discovered within myself hidden reserves of calm and compassion. I don't know.

Away from Marie, I collapsed on Kilminster. I'd go to his room at the university and quite literally cry on his shoulder while he patted my back and said the same sorts of things that I said to Marie. I assumed the chain of support stopped there, on Kilminster's bony shoulder. It was only when I was next in France that Jennifer told me about the long, midnight, cross-channel telephone conversations. And Jennifer had Jean-Claude to console as well.

One morning about a fortnight after the accident I drove Marie at a snail's pace behind the ambulance and fire-engine to the nearest secondary modern. The cavalcade came to a slow halt on the asphalt surface of a basketball court. Across the football pitch the long, low, glass and concrete faces of the classrooms shone weakly in the greyness. The cloud cover was almost at ground level, there was almost a mist. A dozen or so sea gulls strutted and quarrelled around one of the goalposts. The firemen leaned against their truck—it wasn't immediately obvious what they were there for, but whatever it was, they'd clearly done it before. They looked at the sky and muttered among themselves about the chances of cancellation. I walked across to the ambulance and the driver opened the passenger door for me. I leant over into the back compartment. Philippe, another ambulance man, and the doctor were smiling at some-thing.

"Hi, Anasuya," Philippe said almost cheerfully.

"Hi," I said.

"They pull my prick off, almost."

"Who did?"

"My friends here," he indicated the other occupants of the car. "When they lift me off the bed onto this thing, the rubber bag is still hooked to the bed, but the tube, ha, the tube is hooked to me. *Merde*! I shout, *vous* have castrated me. And you know the matron, the big one. Very *féroce*. She says now, now young man, watch your French. No need for language." He almost giggled.

I almost cried. He couldn't feel a thing below his waist, he had no control over urination at all. But Philippe almost giggled, the other three men smiled. The driver said, "They're tricky, them catheters. They hide the bag under the sheets. Not like a drip. You can see a drip, you know it's there."

I stayed in the ambulance for a couple of minutes. The radio squawked a few times, the driver turned down the volume. I leant over the back of the seat, touched Philippe's shoulder and said, "See you this afternoon."

"See you."

I walked to where the firemen were still leaning against the bright red side of their truck. Marie sat in my car, sad, alone. I was about to go to her when one of the firemen said, "This is it, now."

Everyone looked up at the greyness. The helicopter appeared from the one direction in which no one was looking. It came in slowly, the rotors thudding. It was big, bright yellow, with RAF RESCUE in large black letters along its side. The seagulls scattered like litter in a gale. The machine's doors were open and the crew could be seen peering downwards as if they suspected hidden boulders on the smooth surface of the football pitch. It touched down and for a few minutes sat in the centre of the field, its rotors gradually slowing to a halt. The windows of the school became lined with faces. In one classroom the figure of an adult could be seen vainly trying to manhandle the children away from the glass. The world is riddled with oafs and killjoys. In all the other rooms the figure of the teacher rose placidly, head and shoulders above the line of younger watchers. The ambulance drove slowly up to the helicopter, the ubiquitous fire-engine following. Marie and I watched from the basketball court as the doors of the ambulance opened and Philippe was lifted slowly into the helicopter. As the doors closed, we could see one of the crew placing earmuffs on his head. He looked very small, very far away, the child of a cold mechanical womb.

We watched the machine take off, sway gently above the flattened grass, steady itself and disappear into the greyness, a yellow light under its belly blinking. I drove slowly down the motorways to Stoke Mandeville. We arrived in time to have tea and biscuits with Philippe.

When someone breaks their back, blood and other gunk flows through the cracked vertebra into the spinal column itself.

This unwanted matter prevents the neural impulses passing along the column, an effect something like a short circuit in an electrical system. The degree of resulting paralysis is determined by the position of the break. Very low down the column, a break results in little more than a numb bum; high up in the neck a break causes total paralysis, all control over limbs, bowel and bladder functions, and even the ability to turn one's head, ceases. Sensation does not cease; the ends of the foreshortened nerves still supply the odd impulse or two to the brain, the victim still "feels" that he has arms and legs, but the "feeling" is the product of habituation and fantasy. The leg that feels as if it is snug in bed may well be on fire. The smell of burning flesh is often the first indication a paraplegic has that he ought to move his foot away from the electric radiator. The vertebrae are numbered: starting from the head there are seven cervical, twelve thoracic, five lumbar, five fused sacral, and between three and five fused caudal bones. In the world of the spinally injured, one's general state of being can be designated by a number and a letter. Philippe was L4, Lumbar Four. Above his electrically tiltable bed was his name and number, "Philippe Saintenoy L4". Next to him was "Joseph Manning C3". Philippe had perfect control over his arms and torso; Joseph had a very small amount of control over his neck, but nothing else.

If the entry of foreign matter into the spinal column is the only result of the broken vertebra, almost total recovery is inevitable. The broken bone heals, the foreign matter is carried away by the body's normal regenerative processes and the nerves slowly come back into play. All the patient has to do is exercise his limbs, regain his former strength, and he is completely back to normal. This happens in quite a few cases of spinal injury. If the break in the spine has been accompanied by a break in the nerves themselves—if the electric circuit has not only been shorted, but cut as well—no healing is possible. The nerves will not reconnect themselves. However, the break in the bundle of nerves may not be complete, some nerves may be still unbroken. In this sort of case, obviously, partial recovery of sensation and motor control will result.

This rudimentary physiology is learnt very quickly by all spinal injury patients. It is the framework on which the whole folk wisdom of a ward operates, the basis for much of the bizarre gallows humour with which many patients come to terms with their injuries. It informs the hours and hours of ineffectual and obsessive thought that the victims and their relatives devote to the prospect of a life of paralysis.

It takes about six weeks for the bones to heal and the short circuit effect to begin to wear off. During this time all a patient can do is lie on his side and wait. If he can't feed himself, he is fed. If he has no control over his bowels and bladder, nurses and orderlies change his nappies and attend to his catheter. Then, as the magic six weeks approaches a sometimes sad, sometimes ecstatic, scene begins to be played out around the patient's bed. The patient's friends, relatives, or other patients in a more advanced state of recovery, fold back the sheets from the end of the bed, exposing the toes. These the patient tries to wriggle while the onlookers attempt to detect signs of movement.

"Man, I can feel them moving. I can feel them, man!" Joseph said with more desperation than conviction the first time I ever watched this scene.

"No, man, you cannot," one of the orderlies said, "They's rock still."

"Have another go, Joe," a patient called Ronnie said, leaning forward in his wheelchair to scrutinise Joseph's toes, "Give 'em the works, old son."

But the only muscles working in Joseph's body were those of his face. His expression was that of a weightlifter at the very limits of his capacity.

"Not today, old son," Ronnie said, "not today. Have another go tomorrer." And he leant sideways over the big bicycle wheel of his chair and solemnly covered Joseph's toes as if drawing the sheet over a dead man's face.

Actually, it was a muscle in Joseph's forearm that came into play first. I arrived at the ward after an absence of a week, kissed

Philippe, and sat down next to his bed.

"Show her, Joseph," he called over my shoulder.

"Jus' watch this, Anasuya, jus' watch my arm."

Joseph's thin black arm lay along the sheet at his side. As I watched, it twitched. Once, twice, three times.

"See that?"

"I did, I did."

I crossed the four feet between their beds, kissed Joseph, held his face between my hands—the only part of him I could embrace and be felt.

"Show me with the mirror, Anasuya. Show me with that mirror."

I picked up the mirror from his bedside trolley and held it so he could watch his own arm. Again it twitched.

"Hey, sweet Jesus, jus' watch those muscles. Man, I'm going to dance out of this hospital. I am going to dance!"

Ronnie scorched into the bay on the other side of Joseph's bed, spinning his chair through 180 degrees on its back wheels alone.

"Watch out for Tarzan here. At night he gets up and goes swinging around the rafters. He's a bloody menace, I'm telling you."

After a couple of minutes I returned to the chair beside Philippe.

"And you?"

Philippe shrugged slightly, but said nothing. This was Joseph's day, but it was now over seven weeks since Philippe's accident. If he were to have his day, it would be soon or not at all.

* * * * * *

I spent that winter on a restless triangle. I would leave Liverpool before dawn, hurtling under the Mersey with the early morning lorries, roaring down through the Wirral to Chester and then, more slowly, down through the Welsh border towns to Hereford. At Gloucester I'd turn east for a straight traverse across England, narrowly missing Oxford and on to Stoke Mandeville for lunch. I'd spend the afternoon with Philippe and the lads in Ward 2X and, in the evening, leave the hospital for London. I'd stay the night at my father's place or with Tamar and Simon, spend the morning sleeping or shopping, and leave for Liverpool after lunch, filling in the triangle's hypotenuse with a straight run to the north-west up the M1 and M6. Sometimes, when Marie, or one or other of the French lot were in the country, I'd give the whole trip a miss, but usually I visited the hospital on Friday afternoon. I drove the Merc thousands and thousands of miles in those months. I once told my father how glad I was that he'd given it to me.

Stoke Mandeville was an odd place. It didn't really look like a hospital, it looked more like a permanent army camp, painted white. Long, weather-board wards ran off wide corridors, and everything—wards, canteen, swimming pool, therapy rooms, operating theatres—was on the same level. If there were any two-storey buildings in the whole complex, I can't remember them. There were no steps anywhere, just gently sloping ramps. The whole place was liberally surrounded with trees and grass. To walk in civilian clothes through the hospital's endless corridors was to declare oneself an outsider, for this was wheel-chair country. They came in flocks. The wide, empty reaches of a corridor would stretch in front of one, a peaceful expanse of gleaming linoleum. Suddenly half a dozen chairs in tight formation would scorch around a corner, their occupants shovelling at the wheels like cross-country skiers. Pedestrians would stand aside, duck into doorways. Sometimes a slower group of chairs would be overtaken by a faster.

"Damn high cervicals," a lumbar lad would mutter as he roared past, his perfectly functioning arms going like pistons.

There were in the hospital some old and middle-aged victims of one sort of accident or another. There was a small minority of women. But mostly there were adolescent boys, Philippe's age or a few years older. Anybody can break their back, of course, but primarily Stoke Mandeville is a monument to the motor-cycle and the idiots who ride it. Or rather, who fail to ride it. And Philippe and Ronnie and Joseph were the archetypes, the quintessential Stoke Mandeville men.

That first evening when Marie and I were having tea and biscuits with Philippe, there was some sort of discussion taking place at one of the tables in the centre of the ward. I heard Ronnie say, "Hang on a bit, I'll ask him again."

He reversed away from the table, spun his chair to face us, for no apparent reason tipped its front wheels off the ground and zoomed up to Philippe's bed.

"Hello there," he said to Marie and me, and then, without waiting for a reply, said to Philippe, "What was it you come off again, Phil?"

"Suzuki."

"I told 'em it was. It was Joe that come off the Norton. That's right, isn't it, Joe?"

"That's right, man," Joseph said from where he lay, unable to move a limb.

"I told em," Ronnie muttered, spinning his chair to rejoin the others.

Sometimes, especially after Philippe had become mobile himself, I would spend my afternoons at the hospital sitting at one of the tables in the centre of the ward, either on an ordinary chair, or sometimes, by invitation, on a spare wheel-chair—an honorary paraplegic. I would gossip, play chess or cards, or watch television with the boys. One of the ways they filled in their time was sketching. Their sketchbooks littered the tables. Sometimes they sketched absurdly powerful bikes, at other times they drew pictures of wheel-chairs modified by the addition of huge tyres and motor bike engines.

"Hey, Joe, do you reckon we'd get a Trumpy-Bonniville 650 donk under this chair or d'you think we'd havter raise the suspension a bit?" Ronnie was only half joking.

The contempt for the little blue three-wheeler invalid cars that the government would eventually supply some of the boys with was enormous.

"When I get my noddy car," Ronnie would tell me, "First thing I'm going to do is rip the guts out of it. Put a proper donk in it, get a set of Norton handlebars and rip that fuckin' stick thing outer it. The boys will give me a hand."

Ronnie's boys were his motor-bike club or gang, "The Avengers". The two halves of Ronnie's leather jacket, emblazoned with the gang's insignia, hung at his bedhead.

"They cut me colours in half, Anasooya, the bastards."

"You were unconscious with a broken back."

"But me colours! They've got no respect, some of these doctors."

Sometimes the Avengers came to see Ronnie, their combined motor-bike engines sounding weirdly like the thudding of the helicopters that came every now and then. If it wasn't actually raining or snowing, Ronnie and some of the others would pull overcoats and rugs over their dressing-gowns and wheel themselves out to inspect the machines in the car park. One evening the Avengers gave me an escort into London, two chevrons of bikes in front, one behind. I'm sure they rather liked having an expensive bird in an expensive car as a sort of mascot. I drove as slowly as I decently could. I kept envisaging some monumental pile-up that would send us all back to the hospital in ambulances. I wished they wouldn't ride two abreast. They were nice lads—"Just working class yobbos like me, you know, Anasooya, right layabouts". I doubt if any of them were over nineteen. I was only nineteen myself. On the entrance ramp to the A41(M) I flashed my lights at the bikes in front and pulled over for a hitch-hiker. The bikes came to an untidy stop all over the ramp, the ones behind revved their engines, their wheels inches from the back of the Merc. The hitch-hiker got in, startled. He was wearing a college scarf and spoke with the accent of the decrepit university I by-passed on the eastward leg of the triangle.

"Who are they?" he said as the whole convoy roared out onto the black empty spaces of the motorway.

"Me mates, sweetheart," I said from the corner of my mouth.

Joseph was one of the older victims of the motor-bike. He was twenty-three or four. He was really the victim of economic circumstances. He'd owned a car, but the upkeep had proved too expensive when he'd been made redundant at the plastics factory.

"So I sold it and bought the fucking bike, man. Two weeks later I was in this place."

He didn't say so in front of Ronnie and the rest, but he loathed motor-bikes, loathed and detested them.

As for Philippe, I'm not sure, but I think he was quite ambiguous about the machines. He could join Ronnie in his absurd and obsessive worship of the false god that had brought them to the odd limbo of ward 2X, or he could talk quietly to Joseph about the idiocy of having believed for so much as a second that anything but destruction and mutilation attended its followers. Both attitudes were a way of coming to terms with one's predicament; Philippe milked them both for all they were worth.

Limbo is a good word for Stoke Mandeville. It was a place apart from the real world. Inside its halls and corridors and wards there were no seasons; it was always just slightly too hot, after the manner of hospitals everywhere. But more than that, it provided a type of clearing house, a way-station between the trauma of accident and the eventual life of para- or quadriplegia, or recovery and normality that in one form or another awaited all its inmates. Driving into London with Kilminster after one of the visits on which he'd accompanied me, he said, "It's like the bloody seminary, that place. In reverse, in a sort of mirror image. Many are called to paraplegia, some are chosen. The chosen enter the priesthood of crippledom, the others are thrown out to become bus conductors or postmen."

"I think Philippe is going to become a priest."

"It's still early."

"It is not still early, James. It's nine and a half weeks. Joseph has got bits and pieces of movement in all his limbs. He gets better every week. Philippe stays the same. He stays the bloody same, James. Nothing is happening. Nothing is going to happen. He is going to be a cripple for the rest of his life. He will never walk. He will have to wear nappies for the rest of his life. He'll have to have a kipper strapped to his leg. He will never have another fuck. He is going to be a cripple until he dies."

"Pull over, Anasuya, you'll crash."

I stopped on the verge. I could hardly see. Kilminster held me. He said nothing. There was now nothing to say. All the consoling phrases had been said a hundred times. They'd been said when there was still a vague chance of recovery to give them weight. Now there was nothing. Philippe's break was in the nerve fibre as well as the bone. And the break was total, his paraplegia was total and assured.

"I'll drive," Kilminster said after a while. He opened his door and got out. I bumped myself into the passenger seat. We drove towards London in silence. At one point

Kilminster said, "Find something on the radio, Anasuya."

But I chose a cassette of Mahler that Jennifer had recently sent me. The music was warm and sad, loving and grieving at once. There was solace somewhere within it, and I searched for and found it after some fashion or other. Kilminster, of course, understood nothing. He drummed his fingers on the wheel "in time"—as if it were a march or a ballad. Normally this grates on my nerves like fingers on a blackboard, but that evening it seemed appropriate, fitting. In the depths of my misery I loved him for his tuneless, musical incompetence. The black wastes of Buckinghamshire gave way to the suburbs, and the suburbs to the city. By the time we reached Tamar's, I was resigned and sad, but in need of conversation and food. So, Philippe was a paraplegic. He wasn't dead. He wasn't a quadriplegic. He'd suffered no brain damage. Jesus, he was hardly scratched by comparison to some victims of road accidents.

But on my next visit I'd never seen him so depressed. That morning he had had what was known around the hospital as "the talk". "The talk" occurred at the point when the doctors were satisfied in the depths of their professional wisdom that recovery was impossible (or at least highly unlikely—they appeared incapable of committing themselves to anything with real conviction). The doctor had sat on the other side of the examination room from Philippe and talked about adjusting to a life in which he would never walk again, in which he would always be in a wheel-chair. It was a strange thing, the doctor said, but some people emerge from the trauma of paraplegia as better, stronger individuals than they had been before the accident. It was a matter of attitude, of not giving in.

"Monsieur," Philippe had said, "I do not wish to be a better individual, or a stronger individual. I wish to walk and to fuck."

Then he had burst into tears and wheeled himself from the room.

We rolled along the corridor to the canteen. I had a slice of Kilminster's staple, veal and ham pie with a dead egg in the middle. Philippe sipped listlessly at a cup of tea.

"Two nights ago I dreamt I was a cripple," he said. "I was in this thing," he banged the armrest of his chair. "It was the first time. In all my other dreams I have been able to walk. Other people have been in wheel-chairs, but not me. But now, even asleep I am a paraplegic."

Joseph and a couple of visitors that I had not seen before came into the canteen. Joseph was still far from being able to operate his own wheel-chair although he could now almost manage to feed himself simple things like slices of apple. The visitor pushing the chair was a tall, taciturn West Indian to whom I later gave a lift back to London. I forget his name. All the way to Notting Hill Gate he sat in the passenger seat of my car saying almost nothing, the contrast with Joseph's normal ebullience couldn't have been greater. Joseph's other visitor that afternoon was his sister, Mary. As the three of them crossed the canteen floor I waved to Joseph who managed a quite respectable wave in return.

"Hi, Anasuya," he called.

"Hi, Joseph," I called back. But the group did not join us. The tall man pushed Joseph's chair to an empty table and the three settled to an intense, hushed conversation.

Philippe said nothing; he had barely glanced at Joseph. I had noticed a cooling of the friendship between them. Joseph had failed to enter the inverse priesthood, he would be thrown out to become a postman or bus conductor, to walk and to fuck and maybe even to dance. Philippe was already trying on the vestments, entering the celibate brotherhood. While both of them had been in the uncertain phase, waiting for the signs of possible recovery, they'd been able to support each other with endless stories of what they had done before their accidents and what they planned to do afterwards. Philippe had learnt more English lying in a bed for a month than I, Jennifer, and his school had been able to teach him in years, and most of it he'd learnt from Joseph. I am sure Philippe had taken his friend's initial signs of returning movement as an omen of his own eventual recovery. Sitting in the canteen I remembered Philippe's ecstatic "Show her, Joseph," that first time anything happened. Now he sat, listless, self-engrossed, self-pitying, almost silent, while across the canteen Joseph talked earnestly and animatedly about whatever it was his sister and friend were discussing. And Joseph, I had noticed, now preferred to talk to me alone, when Philippe was out of the ward, or playing cards or talking to someone else. Then Joseph would light up, demonstrate his new movements, tell anecdotes about his first clumsy attempts to pick up things, to drink from a beaker of water. In his friend's presence he tried not to talk about his own recovery. He had natural tact, Joseph. I suppose if the roles had been reversed Philippe would have shown equal tact. Perhaps Joseph would have retreated into the same self-pity that Philippe was now displaying. I doubted it, but who was I to say? I was only nineteen and I could walk.

I was utterly inadequate. I knew that consoling words would be useless, vague prophecies of a future happiness would be seen as mockery. What Philippe needed were a few hard, even brutal remarks about his own inadequacy, his gutless wallowing in self-regard. But it was beyond me to deliver them. I couldn't fake the brutality, and I knew any attempt to deliver a brisk, buck-up-young-man speech would sound as empty and pretentious as the doctor's remarks about better and stronger individuals. We sat at the Formica table, trading occasional, polite, hopeless sentences.

We were joined by a woman in her early twenties who sat down next to Philippe and addressed a flood of remarks to him in a strong Swiss accent. To me she said in English, "How do you do?"

"It's all right," Philippe said gloomily, "She speaks French, she's my sister."

The woman, relieved, introduced herself. She was Sophie, a physiotherapist, just arrived from Geneva. She chatted brightly for a while, taking no notice of Philippe's gloom. There was something professional and polished in her jollity. Perhaps she had even been taught to carry on in this fashion in physiotherapy school: *Bright chatter, depressed patients for the cheering up of.* But I thought I detected real warmth under all the smile-and-the-world-smiles-with-you bonhomie. Either way, it worked. Philippe did appear to rouse himself out of his despondency, and I felt better as well. Sophie was pretty in her animated way. I felt that if she ever stopped talking and smiling she would appear plain, dowdy almost. But she never did, so I couldn't tell. After ten minutes she left us. I suddenly felt that I should leave too, that there was no point in staying in order to slip back into the mutual gloom and silence. I said, "Philippe, do you mind if I go early today. I've things to do in London."

"No, no," Philippe said, "Please go." And then, after a pause, "If you have to, that is." The feeling must have been mutual.

I pushed him back to the ward. Joseph and his sister and friend had arrived just ahead of us. Mary kissed both me and Philippe. I shook hands with the tall man. Joseph, learning that I was about to leave, suggested I give the tall man a lift, as Mary was staying for a while and the tall man was about to take the train. I didn't really want the company, I wanted to be alone in my car, but as the request had been made, I said I'd be delighted and we left together. To all intents and purposes

I suppose I might just as well have been alone. I doubt if the man said more than a couple of dozen words the whole time he was my passenger. Perhaps he sensed my depression, perhaps he was shy with strangers. After I'd dropped him at Notting Hill Gate I drove to van Niekerk's place in Kensington. The way I was feeling, I would rather have gone to Tamar's, but I'd arranged to spend the night at my father's house and it was too late to cancel. I arrived depressed, had a dreary evening with van Niekerk during which we bickered about the most trivial things in a gratuitously bitter fashion, went to bed early, and left for Liverpool in the morning, my depression worse than ever.

THE BOTHY NOTEBOOKS

I've changed my writing habits. Instead of working in my room or on one of the taverna's tables, I've come up here to this shepherd's bothy on the side of the mountain that overlooks the bay of Achilli. The bothy is old and part of the roof has fallen in. It now clearly affords shelter only to the goats themselves. From where I am sitting, on a flat rock just inside the entrance, I can look over the bay to the hamlet; the taverna itself is clearly visible. I can just make out my towel, which I washed this morning, hanging over the balcony railing. The water of the bay is very clear, the surface quite unrippled by the wind, patches of seaweed cover the sand of the bottom—dark splotches against the fawn. Kilminster and I have investigated the bothy with some care; we have discovered a loose stone low down on the back wall, the stone can be removed to reveal a cavity large enough to secrete one of these blue children's exercise books that I work in. I bought a new book yesterday, found a small sheet of hardboard that I can rest on my knees as a makeshift table and a plastic bag that can contain the exercise book and save it from the damp that must certainly run between the stones of the wall when it rains. Kilminster is lying on his back on a smooth patch of ground a couple of hundred metres away, looking at the sky, and I suppose, occasionally, at the view. It would be impossible for anyone to approach the bothy without us seeing them miles off. Not that there is much chance of anyone coming up here at this time of year. The only people to cross the mountains are the shepherds. Kilminster and

I meet them occasionally on our own wanderings. They appear over a skyline, their crooks laid across their shoulders, their arms draped over the crooks in restful crucifixion—wandering Christs, scarecrows, cormorants drying their wings. They unfold their arms from the crooks, which they then lean on like bishops after a hard day at the altar. They look at the sky and talk about the weather, ask us where we are going and tell us how long it will take to walk there, ask us if we've visited Brooke's grave yet. Poor old Rupert, poetaster, war hero, golden boy laid to rest, turned to dust. There is a little corner of this island that is forever Grantchester. The locals are convinced that the body of a wordsmith second only to Homer lies within it. Kilminster can remember some lines,

> And is summer still a golden sea
> From Haslingfield to Madingley?

Who knows? At the moment the Aegean lies still and grey and the heather is beginning to give the grey and green land a purple tinge. Kilminster lies on his back like Auden's wall soldier,

> And when I am old with only one eye
> I shall do nothing but look at the sky.

He says he is not to be disturbed, that he is working. I suppose he might be. He says his job consists of thinking and that he can think just as well lying on his back as he can sitting at a table. It's true that when he appears to be day-dreaming or simply asleep he will often leap up, start scribbling formulae or tapping at his calculator. Something must have been going on in his brain to produce this activity. So he lies there and I sit here with my new exercise book on my knees, digressing like mad. To work.

There is a reason for all this seclusion. I find I can no longer keep writing in quite the way I have been—with the knowledge that what I write may fairly soon be read by others, whether I wish it or not. I said in an earlier exercise book that one of my reasons for writing was to examine my relations with my parents, especially my father, and to come to terms with the possibility that he might be dead or living somewhere else under an assumed name, that either way I might never see him again. Well that's true enough. There are, however, certain facts about my father and others that I cannot afford to write down in exercise books that I leave lying around in my room or on the taverna tables, that I often abandon to go for a walk along the beach. Kilminster agrees. He simply would not let me write what I now wish to write under conditions other than these. When I started writing I intended not to consider these facts at all. I thought I could examine my feelings for van Niekerk *et al.* without reference to them, but that has proved impossible. Put bluntly, I have Jennifer's disease: the compulsion to write down what happens is too strong to be simply denied. And the slight element of deceit, of deliberate and consistent lying, in what I have written so far is beginning to make the whole process fraudulent. I find I am writing slower and slower, the words have less and less power. For while the need for exploration, analysis, and therapy that I spoke of is entirely genuine and the main reason for writing, there is also a separate and ulterior motive for telling this whole story; that of establishing an alibi. If any gentlemen from Scotland Yard or the Athen's police or Interpol or whatever turn up on this island, it might help if any manuscript material they impounded confirmed the plausibility of the story we would tell them. But the need to work within these constraints, and the need to tell the truth have started to pull in opposite directions, half paralysing me. Hence this note-book.

For the past four days I have been writing in the taverna about Philippe's accident. Late yesterday afternoon I reached the point where I met Albert. I said I couldn't remember his name, that he was tall, a West Indian like Joseph, that he hardly said a word in my car. I said I spent the night at my father's bickering about nothing in particular.

I have no difficulty remembering Albert's name: Albert John Mbumbira.

He is not particularly tall.

He is not West Indian, he is from southern Africa.

He didn't say all that much in my car, but what he did say affected me more than any other small collection of remarks ever has.

I fought bitterly and violently with my father about apartheid.

I left for Liverpool at midnight in a tearing rage, not having slept at all.

* * * * * * *

I walked from Ward 2X to my car with Albert. He was quiet, thin, and serious. He asked one or two polite questions about Philippe and Joseph. It appeared that he didn't know Joseph very well, that he was Mary's friend. When we reached my car, he said, "Is this yours?"

"Yes."

"You own it?"

"Technically it belongs to my father, but it's mine."

I was used to people being interested in my bloody car and whether or not it actually was mine, but Albert's interest was of a different sort. He wasn't impressed by the Merc itself, he seemed to see it as a specimen, some cultural artefact to be labelled and recorded. He gave a shrug as though to say, "never mind, it doesn't matter", almost as though I'd just admitted to not having a licence to drive it. I opened the driver's door, got in, and leant across to unlock his. He settled himself in the passenger's seat; on the floor at his feet was a clip-board with some lecture notes. As I drove out of the car park, he picked up the clip-board and ran his eyes over the notes.

"First year psychology," he said.

"Yes."

"An inexact science."

"So I'm finding out."

"Is that your name?" He pointed to the ballpoint lettering that I'd etched into the board itself during a number of tedious lectures.

"Yes," I said, "It's Hindi."

"Van Niekerk?"

"No, that's not."

"Dutch?"

"No. I mean yes. Sort of."

"Looks Afrikaans to me."

"It's my father's name, I just inherited it."

"That's the custom in this culture."

Albert turned around, placing the board on the back seat. After about ten minutes of silence, he said, "What's your relationship to Pieter van Niekerk?"

It was a startling question. My father might have been very rich, but he wasn't well known. At least he wasn't well known in the circles I moved in. I suppose in the boardrooms of certain types of companies, among the readers of the *Financial Times*, his name might have been familiar, certain gnomes in Zurich might mention him one to the other as a household word, but I had no contacts in these realms. No one I knew at all well had such contacts; I couldn't imagine that Albert did either.

"He's my father," I said, "Do you know him?"

Albert laughed, a short, almost amused laugh. "I know about him."

"What do you know?"

"I know where his money comes from. And where it goes."

"He's a crook," I said, using one of Jennifer's phrases, "Respectable, white-collar crime, the more or less legal sort."

If I thought this disarming directness and candour would cut any ice with Albert, I was wrong.

"So that's what it is," he said, abandoning the conversation.

I drove in silence for a while, my anger mounting. On the surface I was angry with Albert. He was so self-contained, so dismissive. I simply did not count. At a deeper level, I was angry with myself. I don't think I guessed exactly what sorts of things Albert knew or thought about my father. At that point, if my memory is not playing tricks, I think I still believed that van Niekerk, although a crook, although part of the whole capitalist machine that deprives a large number of people of their wealth in order that a few might live in absurd luxury, was still basically decent. I didn't know, or didn't want to know, how deeply he was involved with the South African régime. He hadn't lived in South Africa for thirty years, although he visited the place from time to time. But then he visited Rio de Janeiro, New York, Tel Aviv, Zurich, Rome, Mexico City, and dozens of other places from time to time. He was often abroad. My ignorance was genuine, but I'm not offering it as an excuse. My ignorance was of the same order as the ignorance of those perfectly amicable peasants and farmers around our part of France who didn't know what had happened to the Jews, communists, and Gypsies whom the Germans sent to the east. They genuinely didn't know, but they genuinely didn't want to know either. They could have found out, or guessed. And I could have found out, or guessed, about van Niekerk's involvement with Pretoria. And I wasn't a peasant; I was a young, very privileged intellectual with a thoroughly knowledgeable international journalist for a step-father, access to any number of books, newspapers, and films; I'd even served my time with Amnesty International—in Paul's warm, untidy flat on those winter evenings after school, I'd written some of those polite, impotent letters to South African ministers of justice with ugly Afrikaner surnames not very unlike to my own. *Your Excellency, I am writing to you out of a deep concern for....* So, as I say, whatever the real state of my knowledge, it was covered with a thin skin of ignorance. Perhaps, unconsciously, I wanted to lance the boil. To see and smell the pus. And to be rid of it. But consciously, on the surface, I was angry with Albert's curt dismissal. In his world I was a child with an expensive toy, and a child of the tyrant to boot.

And then, of course, I was upset and depressed about Philippe. I didn't want this silent, indifferent stranger sitting next to me. I wanted Kilminster or Jennifer or Tamar. I wanted someone who shared my feelings. I looked sideways at Albert. His head was slightly too small for his body. His hair was cropped very close to his skull, quite unlike the afro styles that most of the blacks at university were then sporting, that Joseph had me comb from time to time. By now it was almost dark and the lights from an oncoming car gleamed on Albert's black, shiny forehead. Like the light on the third rail of the London Underground.

"Tell me about my father," I said angrily.

"What do you want to know?"

"Whatever it is you know."

"How much do you think this car is worth?"

"How would I know? What does it matter? Five thousand pounds, ten thousand pounds. I've no idea."

I hadn't actually. I had no notion at all. And anyway, whatever the figure, you could double it, I had two of the bloody things. Albert said, "How much do you think it's worth in human terms? In terms of the lives of the miners who dug the gold and diamonds to pay for it? How many men do you think died to pay for this car?"

"You don't know what you're talking about."

"Pieter van Niekerk is a member of the board of directors of the Kotzenberg and Potgieter Minerals Company of the Transvaal. It is not known how many shares in that company he owns, but their value is believed to exceed half a million rand. Van Niekerk is also a major shareholder in Kotzenberg and Potgieter's wholly owned subsidiary, De Volks Consolidated (South Africa), and he holds a portfolio of shares in other diamond and gold mining companies, the total value of which cannot be less than four million rand. It is known that at least two Johannesburg merchant banks in which van Niekerk has considerable interests contributed to the pro-apartheid Nationalist Party at a time when opposition-sponsored legislation was being prepared to permit African miners to live with their families in the compounds in a greater number than the three per cent legal limit. It is known that....."

The list went on and on. Albert detailed all my father's South African dealings and then started on the companies in other parts of the world in which he had an interest, companies that worked through subsidiaries and dummy companies to break sanctions and trade bans. He mentioned companies that had contributed to the payment of mercenaries in Angola and Mozambique. He did not really tell me all this. Once started he did not seem to be talking to me at all. He recited the list in a flat monotone, like a clerk reading from a stack of filing cards into a Dictaphone. When he had finished he was silent, switched off.

"How do you know all this?" I asked.

"It's my field, my area of specialisation."

"I didn't know any of it."

"You know now, Miss van Niekerk."

After a few seconds I said, "Anasuya."

"You know now, Anasuya." And there was a slight human touch to his voice, but it was the touch of irony. The ultimate rip-off: a third-world name to which I had no right.

Apart from a few polite and formal words of thanks when I dropped him at Notting Hill Gate that was all the conversation I have ever had with Albert John Mbumbira.

I drove the couple of blocks to van Niekerk's house and parked my car in the commodious garage under the mews flat occupied by the chauffeur, Brian, and the live-in maids. Bernadette's car was in, as were a couple of old crocks and my father's current Rover. The Bentley was out. How many men died in the gold mines for this lot?

Bernadette, dear Bernadette, met me as I entered the main house. At that time she'd been married to my father for five years, she was twenty-six, seven years older than me, twenty-four years younger than van Niekerk himself. It was taken as gospel around the château and in Liverpool that she'd only married my father for his money, although as the sole source of everyone's information was me, this consensus hardly amounts to a confirmation of my own views. She was also a colonial like van Niekerk; she'd grown up in Southern Rhodesia where her parents had owned a farm of some kind. Maybe that provided some sort of shared culture for her and her husband; it was beyond my powers to see what else they had in common. Bernadette always wore elaborate and expensive clothes. Bernadette's hair was styled in the very best salons London could provide. Bernadette was an expert in the art of make-up, as befitted one whose dressing-room table groaned under half a ton of bottles, jars, creams, crèmes, unguents, pungents, gunk, and goo. Bernadette had pale grey eyes and skin like the proverbial alabaster statue, although if one had scrubbed the make-up off her anything might have been revealed—scurvy, leprosy, tertiary pox. She greeted me with a dazzling smile. If it were possible to freeze water by smiling at it, Bernadette would have been able to perform that trick to perfection. I permitted her to kiss my cheek. Followed by Bernadette's charming chatter I made my way to my room which—along with the rest of the house—had been redecorated three or four times since I'd taken possession of it at the age of eleven, but which still looked like a child's room. There were even a couple of books with titles like *She Wanted a Pony* and *Gymkhana Gillie* on the shelf above the bed.

I wanted peace. I wanted to be by myself. I wanted to lie on my bed and think. I wanted to lie on my bed and not think. Bernadette leant elegantly against the door frame.

"Anasuya, dear, it's such a *bore* you don't drink. You could join me in my evening tipple. Are you sure I couldn't *tempt* you? What about a bloody Mary—that's vodka and tomato juice—one really can't *taste* the vodka at all! I'm sure it will do you *good*. Dearest you look absolutely *done in*, do please let me make you a drink. Doctor's orders." She giggled a delightful naughty schoolgirl giggle, the tinkling notes descending the scale like Cinderella on the ballroom stairs. "For medicinal *purposes* only."

That's not a caricature of her speech. That is how she speaks. I wished she'd go away, but she was too good a hostess for that. I was to be made welcome, and welcome I was to bloody well become.

"Just the tomato juice," I said.

"Not just a teensy-weensy smidgen of vodka?"

"No please, Bernadette, just the fucking tomato juice. I'll join you in a minute."

She waltzed away to the living room. I lay on my bed for as long as I decently could. I stood up, looked at myself in the mirror; she was right about one thing, I was done in, I was utterly wrecked, there were blue shadows under my eyes like bruises. I went into my bathroom and splashed cold water on my face. Then I joined Bernadette in the living room and had an argument about South Africa. It was an idiot, stupid argument. Bernadette is an idiot, stupid woman. But I was a fool to even start the argument with her in the first place. Well it wasn't an argument exactly. Bernadette would never do anything so unnecessary as to argue. It was a discussion, really, wasn't it? You see, what I didn't understand was that the tribal migrations took place at the *same time* that the Boer Trekkers were arriving in their waggons. You see, it's not that the Afs were *dispossessed* of their *land*, both parties just happened to turn up looking for a new home in this utterly deserted country simultaneously. And that's what the Tribal Homelands are *all about*, a place, the places in fact, where the Afs initially settled. And the South African government has given them complete *autonomy* in their own areas hasn't it? Not, of course, that Bernadette agreed with everything the South African government was doing, far from it. Both she and Pieter were quite *critical* of many of the more silly aspects of apartheid. Had I heard the phrase petty apartheid? You know, the park benches and things like that? Well, that was just *silly* and it gave the South Africans a bad image overseas. But the government in Pretoria was in a very difficult *situation* and it would help if people overseas, people like me, in fact, tried to *realise* just what the problems were. Bernadette knew, of course, she'd grown up next door in Rhodesia. You see, my trouble, if I didn't mind Bernadette saying so, was that I'd grown up in India. And the Indians are so much more advanced than the Afs. Of course they are, they've got hundreds and hundreds, probably even *thousands*, of years of Ancient Civilisation behind them. I should really try to see things in *perspective*.

And so it went on. I should have stopped it. It was pointless. And my replies weren't particularly brilliant either. My real political education had only started a couple of hours previously in my car. I kept wishing for Albert's cold command of facts. I wanted to regard Bernadette with the dismissive indifference with which Albert had regarded me. But we were still arguing, discussing, when van Niekerk arrived.

My father entered in his well-cut suit, shrugging off his well-cut overcoat for the maid to hang in the hall cupboard. He embraced me, then Bernadette, then kissed me, then Bernadette. I didn't want to be embraced, I didn't want to be kissed. At least, not by van Niekerk. He was very hearty, after the fashion of successful businessmen who have had a good day at the office. The discussion of apartheid stopped. Van Niekerk made himself a drink, which he drank with us, and then announced his plans for the evening.

"Bernadette has to visit some sick girl friend or other, don't you dear? So if you and I just slip out to Henry's, we needn't bother the staff, they can have the night off."

When I visited my father in those days, he normally managed to separate the two of us from Bernadette at some point. I don't think this was just tact on his part, a realisation that I could not stand the woman, I think it had a lot to do with *his* feelings about his wife. Whatever else van Niekerk might have been, he was no fool. He had a hard, quick brain. He was tough and he liked to match himself against tough people. In some ways, intellectually primarily, I simply outclassed Bernadette to an extent that was embarrassing. But even if Bernadette's company was retained, we almost always ate out, giving the staff another night off. My father liked being seen with me in public. And I suppose we cut a fairly impressive tableau entering a restaurant. His hair was that grey colour that is usually called steely and his face was still lean and well defined with the same long straight nose that I have. His jaw and his neck were separate entities, which is a lot more than can be said for most businessmen past fifty. All the fat and flab of excessive eating and drinking was around his belly, but under evening clothes, this showed more as substance than ballast. And people tend to look at me whatever I'm wearing, but tarted up in expensive clothes on van Niekerk's distinguished arm, they probably look even more.

That evening, the idea of parading off to one of those restaurants appalled. I wasn't hungry, I needed sleep. Sleep and solitude. I said, "No let's eat here. I'll cook something simple. The staff can still watch telly."

My father smiled understandingly. He said, "The best cure for not feeling like a night on the town, Anasuya, is a night on the town. Once we're there, you'll wonder why you ever thought of staying at home."

"I haven't anything to wear."

This was obviously untrue. I had a whole cupboard full of the sorts of clothes necessary for a night out with my father. I kept them all in Kensington, having no call to wear them anywhere else. But the cry of "Oh, but I've got nothing to wear" made by women with sufficient clothes to outfit an orphanage is often heard in van Niekerk's circles. He said, "Never mind, borrow something of Bernadette's; she's about your size."

"Oh, yes, do!"

I swear Bernadette clapped her hands with delight at the prospect. It was just the scene she'd adore: me and her with all her damn clothes all over the dressing-room, primping and preening in front of the mirror. Taking them off, putting them on, her dragging more of the bloody things out of the cupboards by the armload, squealing with joy at a particularly fetching little number, frowning with critical appraisal at something that wasn't really quite me. And me, half the time, half naked under her attentions. It would beat uncomfortable conversations about South Africa by a mile.

I would rather have worn a hair shirt than anything of

Bernadette's.

"It's not that, Daddy. I just don't want to go out. I'm very tired. I'd like a quiet night here. And an early bed."

But my father failed to see the merit of my position. I was too tired to argue. I compromised for a promise that we would come home as soon as we'd eaten. Van Niekerk left us to have a bath. Bernadette had a last go at trying to convince me to wear some of her clothes and then left to visit her sick friend, if indeed that is where she really was going. I was about to go to my bedroom when van Niekerk called to me from his bathroom to bring him a drink. Just the whisky bottle and a glass, forget about the ice.

I have few inhibitions about nakedness. At the château everybody wanders about in whatever state of dress or undress they happen to be in—even the au pairs after they've become acclimatised to the place. Much the same happens in Liverpool, although, given the weather in that place, most people are rugged up most of the time. But I did not wish to see van Niekerk naked. As far as I can remember, this feeling had been building up over the previous year or so. There was nothing very specific about it, I probably only really became conscious of it that evening, a result, I suppose, of my general state of hypersensitivity. Perhaps I half suspected him of deliberate exhibitionism. Looking back now—informed by the hindsight that subsequent events have given me—I strongly believe there was a major element of the exhibitionist in my father's makeup. Still, whatever my feelings, it was a normal and reasonable request—a lot of people I know drink in the bath occasionally; Jennifer, Kilminster, and Jean-Claude to name but a few. So I took the bottle and a glass into my father's bathroom. He wasn't lying in the bath, he was standing up, soaping himself. I plonked the whisky on a plate-glass and wrought-iron table near the basin and walked out.

"Stay and talk to me, Anasuya," he called after me.

"I've got to have a bath myself."

"Well, can you pour me a drink first. I'm covered in soap."

I walked back into the bathroom, half-filled the glass, splashed some water into it from the basin tap, handed it to my father, and walked out—all more or less without looking at him.

"Thank you," he said, quite cheerfully.

I retreated to my own room, selected the clothes I was to wear more or less at random and ran myself a bath. I lay in the bath with the water up to my chin. For the first time that day the tension began to recede rather than increase. I began to relax. I closed my eyes. I was half asleep when my father appeared in my room. From where I was lying I could see through the open door into my bedroom; one half of my bed was visible, my father in his evening clothes was sitting on the bed, his glass in his hand.

"I thought you were asleep," he said.

"I almost was."

"The sooner we go, the sooner we return."

"Yes," I said.

The point is, there was nothing really very unusual about my father being where he was. In my family—in my families—people often talk to each other under these conditions. For example, if I were talking to Jean-Claude in his bedroom, I'd regard it as decidedly odd if he asked me to leave while he changed his clothes. But my father's presence was suddenly a monstrous invasion of privacy. I wished to Christ he'd go away. But he didn't, of course. He started to chat about some absurd interview with the exiled Idi Amin that the idiot programmers from the BBC had been billing as a dramatic scoop. So I stood up, dried myself, walked into the bedroom, took my clothes from the other end of the bed and dressed. My father had now gone back a couple of years to the Israelis' raid on Entebbe. My getting dressed a few feet from him hadn't halted his flow of comments for a second.

"The only regret, Anasuya, is that the Israelis didn't finish the job when they had the chance. They should have shot Amin, there and then. It would have saved a vast amount of time and expense and lives. But now the man is still alive in Libya, talking a lot of tommy rot to the BBC. He is a monster."

"I know."

"The first black Hitler."

"Which pleases you, I suppose."

I was sitting in front of my mirror by this time, putting on my earrings. I watched his face, he took the comment completely in his stride.

"I don't understand what you mean."

"It is useful to have a black leader who was so vile he could have been legitimately assassinated, like Hitler could have been legitimately assassinated."

"What do you mean 'useful'? The man is a monster, Anasuya, he has murdered thousands of his countrymen. Uganda's economy is in ruins. Almost all the elephants have been killed for ivory...."

"Yes, but it's useful to you. Emotionally useful...."

"How?"

I knew what I was saying was correct. I knew I was speaking the truth. But I couldn't put what I felt into words. The formulation escaped me. I was too tired, too strung out. I just repeated myself, "It's useful. It helps you do what you do."

"I'm sorry, darling, I still don't understand...."

"Oh, it doesn't matter. It doesn't matter...."

Nothing in my father's manner had changed. He was having a friendly conversation with his almost adult daughter about world affairs, he was genuinely puzzled about her talk about Amin's vileness being useful. I knew I was a million miles from provoking him. Jennifer could have done it; I remembered the ease with which she had been able to bring van Niekerk to the boil. But Jennifer had hardly spoken to him for almost a decade. We had all changed in those years, van Niekerk included. Between the ages of forty and fifty he had become more urbane, less subject to emotion, more controlled, the arrogance of his vast wealth and power isolated him from the petty human barbs of envy and jealousy. Perhaps even Jennifer would have found herself bouncing her words off his suave and distinguished evening clothes. I looked at him in the mirror, he looked back, smiled warmly. "Come," he said, "If you are ready, let's go."

I loathed him. I loathed myself. I was angry because I had not been able to put into words what I thought about his attitude to Amin, and I was angry because I hadn't been able to provoke him to a display of temper. And as we left the room I became angry with myself for *wanting* to provoke such a display. Albert would have had better things to do with his time. But he would also have had better arguments at his fingertips, if—for some odd reason—he had wanted to pronounce on the psycho-pathology of Pieter van Niekerk.

I can't remember much about the meal. I know I hardly ate anything, I know my father did most of the talking. I know that at one stage I mentioned Philippe and van Niekerk said, "Oh yes, the poor boy who fell off his bicycle, how is he?"

It didn't matter to my father that at that time Philippe mattered more to me than anyone else in the world. Philippe was Jennifer's husband's son, and a polite enquiry as to his health was all I was to be granted.

As we left the restaurant my father suggested we visit a gambling casino of which he was a member. Casino is prob-ably the wrong word—I'd been there once before—it was a very exclusive, private club with elaborate security measures at the doors, bright lights hanging very low over the green beige tables and wheels, a gloom of cigar smoke, and low-cut dresses every-where else. In between the tables the silent waiters brought drinks that no one paid for, pocketing the occasional plastic chip by way of a tip. It was a revolting place. I'd been interested the first time—I was glad I'd come, just to see the joint, to look at the hard, preoccupied faces of the gamblers, to feel and smell the stink and fever of money being made and lost by pure and capricious chance. I had allowed Jennifer to pump me for every last detail I could remember for a story she eventually aban-doned; but there was nothing to be gained by revisiting the club, and that evening the thought of going anywhere but straight to bed was pure hell.

"No, Daddy, take me home. I'm going to sleep on my feet. You can go out again if you wish, but I'm going to bed."

"All right, darling."

The real fight started in the car on the way home. Van Niekerk said, "I still don't understand what you meant by Amin being 'useful'."

"It doesn't matter, Daddy."

"Do you know what you really mean? You said it was useful to what I am doing."

"I believe you are a director of the Potgarter and Kotzenberg Mining Company of the Transvaal and that your shares in that company are valued at something in excess of half a million rand."

My father laughed easily. "Have you taken to reading the *Financial Times*, Anasuya, we'll make a capitalist out of you yet. It's Kotzenberg and Pot*gieter....*"

"I believe you contributed heavily to the Nationalist Party at a time when it was opposing legislation which would permit more than three per cent of African miners to live with their families in the compounds...."

"Who have you been talking to?"

"A friend."

"Your friend is misinformed. I have never contributed to any political party, anywhere."

"Not you personally, perhaps, but your companies...."

Van Niekerk was enjoying himself considerably, it was all a jolly tiff as far as he was concerned.

"Which companies in particular? How much and to whom?"

"Oh, I don't know, you're mixed up with so many companies...."

"That really won't do, Anasuya. Tell me their names."

"I can't remember them. I've heard the list."

"From your friend?"

"Yes."

"Who is he?"

"A specialist in his field."

"And what's his field?"

"He's.... Oh, I don't know. Mercenaries...."

"He's a mercenary? I doubt it, mercenaries know nothing about corporate finance. They only know who pays them. They take their pay and are dead."

"*He's* not a fucking mercenary. He *knows* about mercenaries. He knows about the mercenaries you finance."

"He's a liar! Who is he? What's his name?" Van Niekerk wasn't amused anymore, but he'd got his voice under control for the next statement. "You shouldn't believe everything you are told by political hot-heads, Anasuya. Of course I've never financed mercenaries. The idea is absurd as I'm sure you'll realise when you think about things. Anyway, mercenaries aren't hired by individuals. A mercenary army costs millions of pounds to run. They are hired by governments. The Russians for instance. Or the Cubans...."

"Or the bloody great multinationals that run the governments."

"Russia and Cuba aren't run by multinationals. The world would be a better place if they were, of course, but unfortunately they are run by communist parties."

My father laughed easily. The ideas of his impulsive, lovable, teenage daughter were delightful. He was a man hugely enjoying himself. The tone was perfect. He was well in control now. Nothing, absolutely nothing I could say would dent the armour. But it *had* cracked. For one instant the mask had dropped. I'd provoked him. I knew I was right; that Albert's cold, detailed list was right. I raged at van Niekerk. I shouted across the three feet of car. I tried to remember as much as I could of Albert's list, but he dodged it, sidestepped it, denied it, blandly admitted it, filled in some of the points I was unsure of. Yes he had interests in a whole network of companies; no, the companies were not agents of repression. Once or twice he said, "But who has been telling you this, who is this 'friend' who distorts the activities of honest businessmen to make them appear gangsters?" I almost said Albert's name, but even in the height of my rage I had the wit to keep silent on that point. Van Niekerk didn't press me. I tried to hurl the facts of apartheid at him, but found

I only really knew about the petty stuff, the park benches of which Bernadette had assured me she and Pieter were so *critical*. When I tried to talk about pass laws and money spent per capita on education and the conditions in the mines, about elections, about torture, about the secret police, I had no facts, no figures. I just knew the whole place was loathsome. And in my rage I suddenly realised I'd known this all along, that Albert had told me bugger all about South Africa itself, all he'd done was list my father's dealings and interests. But I couldn't name the laws that enforced the vileness, could instance no specific acts of torture, could only recall Nelson Mandela as a specific political prisoner. Van Niekerk now came into his own; with a jovial display of candour *he* told *me* the figures per capita for the education of blacks and whites. And then, when I said, "Well?", told me the figures for other countries in Africa like Botswana and Tanzania, He told me the difference in post-natal deaths per thousand for whites and blacks. And then he compared the black South African figure with the figure for Julius Nyrere's socialist paradise. He was now loving the argument. It wasn't a set-piece affair either; these weren't the tired arguments of a hack apologist—in the circles van Niekerk moved in no apology for Pretoria was ever necessary. He was a loving father with a beautiful hot-headed nineteen-year-old daughter, cutting her intellectual teeth on the burning issues of the day—getting it all wrong like idealistic youth everywhere. I wanted to smash his fucking head in.

We arrived back at his house. I was actually shaking with rage. The doors of the mews garage open automatically when van Niekerk presses a switch on the dashboard. They can be closed either by pressing the switch again, or by pressing another switch on the wall by the door that leads through to the main house. As we waited for a few seconds in the cobbled mews itself, watching the steel slatted doors rolling upwards like blinds, he said, "Anasuya, let's not discuss this any more tonight. We are both too tired. Tomorrow we can talk as much as you like. Meet me for lunch and then come back to the office and I'll show you all the figures. You'll see that the blacks in South Africa enjoy a higher standard of living than their brothers anywhere else in the whole continent."

"I don't want to see your fucking figures."

As we rolled the few feet into the garage my father said sagely, "Then your judgements will always remain irrational."

He placed a fatherly hand on my thigh. I shivered, opened my door and stepped out of the car, knocking his hand away as I did so. I was standing next to the Merc. For once I loved it. It was mine, my little world, my nest. Van Niekerk emerged from his side of the Bentley and came around the bonnet towards me saying, "Darling, I'm sorry. I've upset you. I shouldn't have argued with you when you were so tired. And then there's this boy in hospital…it must be very upsetting."

He held his arms out towards me, moved forward between the two cars to embrace me.

"Don't touch me!" I screamed at him.

He faltered for a moment, but continued the gesture. His arms enclosed me, pulling me gently to his chest. I flung myself backwards, striking out with both arms. I was free of him. The cold low body of the Merc was behind my back.

"Anasuya! Calm down," he commanded—the verbal equivalent of the sharp slap across the face that is recommended for hysterical women.

"Don't bloody well touch me," I hissed at him.

I felt the Merc behind me. My escape. But it wasn't enough. Nothing could be gained by throwing myself into the security of its cabin. My father took a step towards me, half closing the Bentley's open door as he did so. My handbag still lay on the passenger seat. The key! The door was closing on the key. I threw myself forward and sideways, flinging the Bentley's door open and my father backwards at the same time. The top of the door hit his lip. I grabbed my handbag from the Bentley's seat and stepped back. Searching blindly with my hands in the bag, I watched my father. He stood about six feet from me between the bonnets of the cars. He put his hand to his lip and then held it in front of him, looking at the small splotch of blood.

This whole tableau is fixed, quite silently and quite still, in my mind. I can examine it at will. The handsome, greying man in the immaculate black and white of his evening dress confronts the expensively dressed, desperate, but determined young woman between the gleam of two very expensive cars. Other cars, both vintage and new, gleam behind the man's back. The harsh, fluorescent light and the naked brickwork of the garage both expose and trap the figures. There is blood on the man's lip and on the hand that he holds towards the woman in a half-threatening, half-conciliatory gesture. The scene is missing two elements. It needs a gun. Perhaps the man should hold a slim pistol in his other hand. Perhaps the woman should be holding him at bay with a pistol. The other element is the title and the author's name. In the black space above the fluorescent light should be a tough, hard-bitten title, *The Dying Breed*, say, and, below the woman's high-heeled shoes, a terse, thriller writer's pseudonym, *by Hardy Cliff*. At one point in the long discussion of this incident that took place when I was next in France, Jennifer threatened to write the book. I think she would like to be the author of a cheap detective novel, to have some alter ego to play games with, a crude macho nom de plume to hide behind. I know a lot of what I told her went into her commonplace book, including the cheap-thriller-dust-jacket quality of my memories. Jennifer was delighted with the scene for other reasons, of course. She saw it—quite rightly—as the beginning of my break with van Niekerk. At the age of nineteen I was seeing the light she had seen nine years previously. I had even bloodied his face, although not as spectacularly or permanently as she had done with the ashtray. She loved my story; she muttered, "the pig, the pig" during my descriptions of the argument in the car; she described my roaring get away in the Merc as brilliant. Jean-Claude was more worried. The thriller-dust-jacket atmosphere of the scene I described probably affected him more than it did Jennifer. Perhaps he saw the phantom gun in the steely-haired man's hand.

He's never actually met van Niekerk.

"But what if van Niekerk had managed to close the door? What if he had trapped her?"

"Oh, Pieter wouldn't actually do anything violent. He hit me a couple of times, but only with his hand. He never did anything as dramatic as throw a heavy glass ashtray. I'm more violent than he is. Anasuya would have had to spend the night there, that's all, and then left as soon as she could in the morning. But scraping that silly car out at the last second, that was superb."

In a way I think Jean-Claude had a better idea of the tensions in the scene than Jennifer had. Jennifer was projecting herself into her daughter's high-heeled shoes. In her version of the dust jacket, she sees me as being more contemptuous, more disdainful, more in control of my disgust than I actually was. Jean-Claude, I believe, understood better my very real terror, my feeling of being trapped. And even though he has never met van Niekerk, he probably has a better appreciation of what he had become. That decade of change had also left him more brutal, colder, and harsher, for all the urbanity and reserve with which he greeted the world.

I wrenched open the Merc's door and threw myself into the driver's seat. I slammed the door shut. My father appeared beside the window, his hand found the door handle. I jerked the locking mechanism to—I actually felt the resistance of his thumb pressure on the door's internal workings. He swore— something he rarely does. I fumbled with the key in the ignition. His face appeared at the window, inches from mine, isolated by glass.

"Anasuya, don't be stupid. This is madness. It's the middle of the night. Where will you go?"

"To Tamar's," I yelled at him. I don't really know why, perhaps I was more talking to myself, saying the name of my nearest friend, evoking her flat and my welcome in it.

I couldn't get the key into the ignition. My hands were shaking very badly. My father stood up; I saw his figure pass in front of the Merc's bonnet. I reached wildly for the passenger-door lock. But van Niekerk went straight towards the door that leads to the house. The instant relief of knowing he was leaving me was instantly replaced by the knowledge that he wasn't. He had his hand on the switch that controlled the garage doors. He was locking me in. The key in my hand suddenly turned and the car jumped forward a couple of feet under the impulse of the starter motor alone. The old crock in front of me wobbled under the impact. I slammed my foot onto the clutch and yanked the gear lever into reverse. The motor came smoothly alive and I roared out of the garage through the closing gap of the roller door. There was a harsh screech of metal as the bottom edge of the door ripped along the roof of the car.

I can't remember much of the first few minutes of my escape. I know I was halfway down the Bayswater Road before the flashing headlights of oncoming cars brought me to a realisation that mine were off. I remember feeling utterly free, like a bird in the night sky, the lights of London blinking around me like stars. I know it wasn't until I was accelerating away from the entrance ramp to the M1 that I realised I was not on my way to Tamar's.

"Jesus," I said to myself. "I'm on the triangle. The fucking triangle."

I was too tired to face the drive back through the streets of London to Chelsea. I drove to Liverpool instead.

It was an idiot thing to do. I could have killed myself. I could have killed half a dozen other people. I knew perfectly well that it was lack of sleep that had broken Philippe's back. But I was too tired to think clearly. I was also too tired to sleep; I'd reached that high, empty plateau of sleeplessness in which everything is very clear and very distant, in which one is aware of every square inch of one's body, but where the body itself feels insubstantial, weightless. So I lost myself in the black empty reaches of the motorways—the nearest experience to interstellar travel possible on earth. The Merc purred through the night, Grieg keening in his pine forests from the speakers, the cabin warm against the black wind outside. I stopped in one of the service areas for petrol and coffee, I can't remember which, they all have the seedy anonymity of forgotten space stations, those places. At one point, I gave Albert Mbumbira a lift. My memory of this is so strong that if I didn't know it to be impossible, I would swear in court that he was with me for part of the drive. I think I explained my fight with my father to him. He shrugged sardonically, the black night rushing past his black face. *Well you know now, Miss van Niekerk.*

I came into Liverpool at dawn. Both of our ridiculous cathedrals were lost in a low, grey, ecumenical mist. I parked outside my house and went inside. Everyone else was still asleep. Without haste, very methodically, I combed the living room, the kitchen, and my room in the attic for every vaguely left-wing periodical I could find: the *New Statesman*, *New Society*, *Time Out*, *Liberation*, *Red Mole*, *Green Terror*, *Intervention*, etc. etc. etc. I knew there were still a few choice addresses to be had in the sorts of angry, jargon-filled off-set publications that Clara read, so I slowly opened her door, tip-toed into her room and found what I wanted on her shelves. Then I sat down at the kitchen table and worked my way through every black liberation, anti-apartheid, third-world, revolutionary group I could find. There must have been about twenty cheques in my current cheque book. I filled in the lot. I varied the amounts at random, but I insulted no organisation by offering them less than a thousand pounds. And then, with my last cheque, I sent Amnesty International twenty-five thousand pounds. Without haste I signed my name twenty times above the printed words *Pieter G. van Niekerk and Anasuya Tamar van Niekerk.* My signature looked too long. I decided that in future I'd drop the *van Niekerk* bit. I put the cheques in envelopes, addressed them, took the jar into which the household threw its spare 1p and 2p pieces and walked, still in my evening dress and high heels, the three blocks to the post office. I extracted a couple of yards of 2p stamps, found that my mouth was incredibly dry, but managed to lick them all.

I walked dreamily back to Huskisson Street through the

awakening, battle-pocked, urban decay of Liverpool 8, the taste of postage-stamp glue in my mouth. A milkman crossed my path, looked at me for a couple of seconds and said, "Had a good night out, love?"

"Yeah," I said.

*   *   *   *   *   *   *

As I told Michaels, it didn't work. There are a dozen different ways in which I could have intelligently and systematically over a long period of time syphoned off a steady flow of van Niekerk's money. It simply needed "laundering" as they say in the world of crooked money. I could have opened another account at another bank in my own name, made cash withdrawals from the Bottomless Pit, rebanked the money, and sent cheques to whomever I bloody well pleased. As it was, van Niekerk's toady little bank manager must have rung him the moment the cheques started to be presented. And my father stopped the lot. Well, not quite the lot. I gained the strong impression next time I saw van Niekerk that some of the cheques had been honoured before the bank manager woke up. After that interview with Michaels in which the policeman said he could not remember a cheque for Amnesty being among the collection found in van Niekerk's desk, I rang that worthy cause. I identified myself and said I was terribly worried that a cheque I'd sent them some time previously might have bounced; my own accounts were in a terrible mess and I just couldn't be sure what had happened, could they please check for me? Indeed they could; after a certain amount of rustling of papers and requests to hold the line I was told cheerfully that the thing had been honoured. Very pleased to receive it they were too, but I hadn't given them a return address for the receipt.

"Donations are tax-deductible, you know."

"Don't worry about it, comrade. I never pay tax."

[End of entry: Bothy notebooks.]

THE TAVERNA
NOTEBOOKS

And then Philippe began to get better. Ecstasy! Freak out!
He rang me late one evening.

"I've got my prick back."

"What?"

"It works. I can feel if I need a piss. I can piss when I want to.
All day I haven't had the kipper on."

"Is that really true?"

"*Merde alors!* She asks me is it true. Do you think I'd joke
about my own penis?"

"And what about the rest of you?"

"It will come. It will come."

"Are you sure?"

"Of course I'm sure.… Well, the doctors won't say. They
never say anything. Maybe I'll walk with a limp. Who knows?"

I was laughing and crying so much I could hardly speak. On
the other end of the phone Philippe started a garbled lecture in
a mixture of French, English, and Latin.

"What are you talking about, Philippe? Speak sense."

"Hyperflection.…"

"What's that?"

"You get flected, only hyperly. Like a broken spring."

* * * * * * *

Elementary physiology for the pig-ignorant, Part Two. In a

very small percentage of spinal injuries, the break in the bundle of nerves occurs not inside the spinal column, but outside it. Small ropes of nerves leave the spine at various points through holes in individual vertebrae and travel through the body, continually branching out into smaller and smaller ropes until each individual nerve fibre reaches the muscle or area of skin that it helps to control or from which it receives sensations. Once outside the spine, the nerves are encased in flexible tubes. Mierlynn tubes, they're called although that may not be the correct spelling. Perhaps they are made of mierlynn, perhaps Dr Mierlynn discovered them. I never did find out and I don't really care. Now although, just as inside the spine, the two ends of a severed nerve will not connect themselves again, it is possible for the section of nerve that is still attached to the brain to grow down the tube until it eventually reaches its original terminal point. I don't know what happens to the spare bit, maybe it just fades away, maybe it is shouldered aside by the growing bit. Hallelujah! Neural regeneration is the name of the game.

If neural regeneration takes place, it does so at about one millimetre per day; say thirty-five centimetres a year. So a nerve growing down the mierlynn tubes from a point just outside the L4 vertebra to the end of a normal adult-sized person's toes takes about three-and-a-half years. The nearer bits of the body come into play sooner, of course.

So, when Philippe had gone twisting and somersaulting over the roof of the police car and cracked his L4 vertebra, the real strain on the nerves had been external to the spine. It was a hyperflection break, neural regeneration was occurring.

* * * * * * *

"It's like the metro, Anasuya. They're down there, in their little tunnels, creeping along."

Joseph came on the line. "Hey, Anasuya."

"Hey, Joseph."

"Tell him to calm down. The orderly has gone for the straitjacket."

Joseph and I raved on to each other for a while and then I got Philippe back on the line. He had already rung both his parents. He would ring Kilminster in a minute. He hung up and I rang the château. Jean-Claude and Jennifer were half way through their second bottle of Champagne. Then I rang Kilminster who'd just finished speaking to Philippe. He was laughing, but he was also the rational subatomic physicist who claimed to understand things.

"It's not yet in the bag, Anasuya."

"What?"

"So far, he's only got partial recovery of the sphincters that control micturition and a very slight return of sensation in the subcutaneous nerve endings of his prick itself. That's a start, but there's a lot more to go. He still has to wear nappies. His arse is still totally out of action."

"But neural regeneration...?"

"Neural regeneration may still only be partial. *Will* only be partial; it's quite impossible that he'll get everything back. He's never going to jump."

"Jump. Who wants to jump? When did you last jump?"

"Anasuya darling, the chances are good, they're very good, but be cautious, be just a little bit cautious, in your optimism. Okay?"

"You're wet and cold and heartless, Kilminster, but I love you."

"I love you too. And your idiot half-brother."

Philippe got his arse back into gear (as Joseph put it) about a month later. He and Joseph started to leave the hospital at weekends. Once I took them both to Tamar's. Once Philippe stayed with Joseph's family in Kilburn. There were no real medical reasons for them to remain in Stoke Mandeville any longer— it was all now a matter of physiotherapy, learning to walk on crutches, learning to make the most of whichever muscles they had control over. Indeed, spinal injury isn't really a medical problem at all. There are no spectacular cures, no stunning exercises in micro-surgery, no brilliant operations possible. The doctors and surgeons perform a few standard manoeuvres such as bracing broken vertebrae with silver plates and carrying out an operation known to the patients as a dick job, and, for the rest, sit back and wait for time and the body itself to effect whatever degree of recovery is on the cards. Among the patients the doctors were regarded with what I thought was an unreasonable degree of contempt, if not outright hostility. It was understandable, I suppose; the quacks were patently not the high-powered angels of mercy that they were often shown as being on television, they were not miracle workers, for there were no miracles to be worked, and they were very guarded about anyone's chances of recovery; as well they might be, they'd waited for weeks before having "the talk" with Philippe, and then got it wrong. But the patients didn't see it this way.

"If you can kick the bastards in the eye, Anasooya. You know, if you can really put the old boot in, have a spot of bovver, a bit of real agro, well then they'll say yeah, maybe, just maybe, you've got a bit of movement in the old foot. Otherwise you might as well not try. They're a right tight-lipped pack of cunts, begging your pardon, but they are."

But much as Ronnie hated the doctors, he loved the physiotherapists.

"She's good, that one," he told me one day when Philippe's friend, Sophie, came into the ward. "She's a fuckin' miracle. You ought to see her with Joseph. She has him doing this knees-up-mother-Brown routine all over the bloody therapy room. And the poor sod's only got about half a dozen muscles." He called across to her, "Hey, Sophie, come and have a bit of a parlay voo with your mates."

Sophie came over to us, Ronnie said to me, "She fair nearly drowned me the other day. There we was up the deep end, getting on real well, having a bit of slap and tickle, and along comes your brother. Well, it was abandon ship for old Ronnie boy, wasn't it? Sink or bloody swim. Every man for himself like. She's sweet on your brother, this one. Aren't you love?"

"Are you greedy, Ronnie?" Sophie said.

"Greedy? That's a good one. I'll say."

"*Comment dit jaloux?*"

"Jealous," I said.

"Are you jealous?"

"Yeah, greedy and jealous, that's old Ronnie. Trouble is I don't speak the lingo, not too good with the *old plume de mon tante* bit. So what chance have I got with old lover-boy over there carrying on like a two-bob watch all day long, yabber, yabber, yabber, can't stop him."

"Tomorrow, Ronnie, we will start with the bicycle machine."

"Oh Christ, the bloody treadmill."

* * * * * * *

Towards the end of my university term, both Joseph and Philippe were declared fit to be discharged. From now on they were to be outpatients, Joseph at a clinic in London, Philippe at one in Compiègne. Joseph could walk short distances using his crutches, his legs stiffened by steel and leather devices. Philippe had some movement in his hips, but his legs were still useless and he had yet to graduate from his wheel-chair to crutches. A downstairs room in the château had been prepared for him, and various steps around the place were reported to have been covered with wooden ramps. I was to take him over the channel, stay a week at the château, and return to Liverpool. Philippe invited Joseph to stay for the week.

I lent Kilminster the Merc and took his station-wagon. The three of us, the two wheel-chairs, one set of crutches, and all our luggage filled the car completely. Those ward 2X patients who were mobile wheeled or swung themselves out to the car park to see us off. It was a fine spring day. The sun was warm for almost the first time that year. Someone had bought a number of tins of beer. A couple of the physiotherapists, including Sophie, joined the group. The beer exploded from the tins every time anyone pulled a top off. Everyone cheered. Toasts were proposed. I was given a tin of beer from which I pretended to drink. The memory of absent friends, including Ronnie who had been discharged a month previously, was celebrated with jokes and beer. A camera was produced and group photographs taken. We all shook hands, a few restrained English kisses were exchanged, and we drove away. As we swung out of the gates I looked back; the group was shambling and rolling across the grass towards the canteen, dressing-gowns flapping.

"I feel I should have been given a diploma," Philippe said.

"Ah, man, but it's good to be out. Sweet Jesus it is good to be out."

The sound of a helicopter came faintly over the noise of the car. The machine's shadow slid across a field to our right, slithered over the hedge and crossed the road a hundred yards in front of us.

"Poor bastard, he can have my bed if he likes."

After a bit of discussion with the crew of the ferry, Philippe and I were allowed to stay in the hold or whatever the car and lorry compartment is called. One of the crew did offer to carry Philippe up the narrow companion way, but Philippe said he'd be happier staying in the car. Joseph said he'd stay as well, but Philippe told him not to be an idiot, it was all right for the likes of me, I'd crossed the channel so many times I couldn't count them, Joseph hadn't been on a boat since he left Trinidad at the age of three. Without much further prompting he left for the sights and bars of the upper decks, picking his way carefully on his crutches to the companion way and then pulling himself upwards with both hands on the rails, his aluminium crutches dangling from his forearms by their metal clips.

It must have been a smooth crossing, the movement of the ship was barely perceptible in the dim, silent hold. There was a vast lorry in front of us and a caravan to our left. Philippe lay down on the front seat and slept. I tried to read a newspaper, but the light was too bad, so I slept for a while across the back seat. We both awoke at the same time and chatted about the imminent prospect of French food. And then, when we'd exhausted that topic, Philippe said, "Can I suggest something to you?"

It was a strange question. I'd never known Philippe to ask anyone's permission to make a suggestion in his life—if he thought you needed a suggestion, he jumped in and made it, boots and all.

"Of course."

"It's a serious suggestion."

"Yes, all right, what is it?"

"If you felt like it, I think you ought to sleep with Joseph."

The thought had crossed my mind, but even with

Philippe's new-found tact I didn't like the project being suggested to me.

"If I feel like it, I'll do whatever I bloody well want to."

"Don't be angry."

"Have you discussed this with him?"

"No, of course not. *Merde*, Anasuya, you are my sister after a fashion. I'm hardly likely to go around…to go around pimping."

Now *he* was upset. (It was a good performance. I discovered later that he and Joseph had discussed it.) I said, "Oh all right, it doesn't matter. Just don't try to organise my sex life for me."

"Sorry."

"Forget about it."

We sat in silence for a while. And then Philippe said, "What do you think was the main topic of conversation, the main preoccupation, in the hospital?"

"Motor-bikes."

"No. First it was walking, then it was sex. The whole place is designed to teach you to walk. Sex is not on the agenda. Nothing is done about it officially. The doctors think that paraplegics don't have any sexual feelings. But in the ward, most of the jokes, most of the talk is of sex. It was only in the afternoons when the visitors were there that people talked about motor-bikes. In the mornings and at night we talked about sex."

And of course, in those first weeks, when I had thought about Philippe lying on his bed in the ward, feeling nothing below his waist, half *my* thoughts had been about sex. I had thought about it, but I had not wanted it. The guilt of the survivor. For over a month after his crash I had neither screwed nor masturbated. I didn't say anything to Philippe, though. After a pause he went on. "Do you know what a dick job is?"

"No."

"Sometimes one of the results of a broken back is a permanent erection. It just stays up, twenty-four hours a day. It's useless of course. The victim can't feel anything. It's just there, sticking out in front of him. So they disconnect it. They cut the nerves or the veins or something. That's a dick job. When they do one of these operations, it's a bit like being in a prison when someone is guillotined. You know how in a prison—well in the films anyway—when they take someone to the guillotine, all the other prisoners stand very silently in their cells. Even if they can't hear anything, everyone is very conscious that it is happening. Everyone knows it is happening. It's like that with a dick job. We were all quieter, more subdued, the jokes were made more softly, but more bitterly. In the occupational therapy room sometimes we used to spend hours cutting holes in the little nipples on the ends of condoms and gluing the catheter tubes onto them with rubber solution. Can you imagine, a whole table of sexual cripples with an enormous pile of condoms in front of them. That was the sickest joke of all."

"What happens to women? How do they attach the catheter?"

"It's even worse. They have to stick it straight up the...whatever it's called, the urethra. Even a limp prick has its uses." He laughed and then changed his tone of voice. "But this is all too morbid. I am getting better every day, Joseph is getting better every day. We are going home to where they speak a civilised language and eat proper food. Sister of mine, you have been good to me over these months...."

"Jesus, Philippe, I don't need a formal vote of thanks."

"Without you and Sophie, I'd have cut my throat."

He ran his finger across his windpipe, letting his head fall to one side, eyes rolling. I was intrigued by Sophie's inclusion.

"I would have thought Sophie was more help to Joseph, she

taught him to walk, you are still....”

“Ah yes, walking. Well she teaches everybody to walk. Walking is walking.”

“Philippe! You didn’t.”

He was grinning his old, idiot adolescent grin. As smug as a cat with cream.

“Where? Philippe? In a broom cupboard? Where in that hospital could you find....”

“In her bed, of course. Where else? In the nurses’ quarters. She has a very nice room. Very comfortable. Very comfortable bed as well. A little machine that makes tea in the mornings and turns on the BBC. ‘This is the BBC. The time is oh eight hundred hours Greenwich mean time. Here is the news. In Cairo today President Sadat announced that....’”

Philippe yawned and stretched his arms, the parody of a man waking from sleep to face the rigours of the day.

“You great lout,” I said, falling forward to embrace him. “You smug, self-satisfied, pimply-faced yahoo.”

He held me around the shoulders, kissing my head. I buried my face in the crook of his arm. His biceps were like small cannon balls from pushing the wheels of his chair. I loved him, and I loved that fast-talking, frizzy-haired Swiss physiotherapist as well.

[End of entry: Taverna notebooks.]

THE BOTHY NOTEBOOKS

One night towards the end of that visit to France with Philippe and Joseph, I woke to find the full moon blazing straight through the window onto my face. "You awake?" Joseph murmured.

"Yeah, it's the moon, shall we draw the curtains?"

"It will go away in a few minutes, stay in the warm."

We both lay for a while, not talking, watching the disc of light drift towards the edge of the window-frame.

"Joseph, who's Albert John Mbumbira?"

"You met him, Anasuya. He's that weird friend of Mary's you gave the ride to London to."

"Yes, but who is he?"

"He's a hard man, that one, Anasuya. His brain is like ice. It is filled with cold, cold figures. He don't forget nothing. When the revolution come in South Africa, he's going to be the brains, the cold man behind all the shouting and gunfire."

"Do you see much of him?"

"Hell no. I'm not serious enough for Albert. Even Mary's not serious enough for Albert. A twenty-four-hour-a-day revolutionary ain't serious enough for that man. You got to be a revolutionary twenty-five hours a day minimum. He only come out to the hospital because he wanted to talk to Mary before he left. He was going the next day."

"Where?"

"For training was all he said. For training. Your guess is as good as mine. Havana, Moscow, Peking. He don't send no get-well cards. Not to me he don't."

* * * * * * *

I received a letter from van Niekerk. He was conciliatory. He said he shouldn't have argued with me when I was so tired and upset over that poor boy in hospital. He was sorry he had tried to close the garage door. He had not behaved very well. We both of us had been a bit impetuous. He had rung Tamar's later that night to make amends, but I had not arrived there. He had been worried. Tamar and Simon had probably been worried too. But he understood I must have stayed somewhere else that night and that I was now back in Liverpool. He hoped my studies were proceeding satisfactorily. He looked forward to seeing me when I was next in London and to making amends and clearing the air. It would be a tragedy if our differences of opinion came between us. We meant so much to each other. He hoped that we would be able to laugh about the whole scene at a later date. There were actually some funny sides to our contretemps: my departure in the Mercedes had been quite spectacular. What had I done about the car's roof? The bill had not come through yet.

I vacillated. I vacillated for weeks, months. More letters arrived. There were times when I felt so antagonistic towards my father that I could barely sit still, when I would walk from home to the university in a blind rage and find I could not remember by which route I had come, when I would sit in lectures or the library, unable to absorb a word. And at other times I was overcome by guilt. All my father had done was disagree with me, to argue in a quite civilised fashion with me. And I had smashed him in the face with the door of his car and driven off in mine in an hysterical rage. There was a lack of dignity, of maturity in my exit. I saw myself as petulant, wilful, a perfect spoilt, rich adolescent. There almost seemed, at times, something fraudulent in my being the recipient of van Niekerk's letters. They were serious, civilised, urbane letters from one adult to another. There was nothing recriminatory, nothing petulant, nothing angry about it. He did not belittle the importance of our disagreement, but he was not so melodramatic as to see it as an irreparable break.

One grey afternoon in the university library, I selected a fresh sheet of writing paper and wrote a short, adult-to-adult note to van Niekerk. I said I too regretted our disagreement, that I wasn't happy with my own behaviour, that I looked forward to our next meeting when we would be able to discuss things rationally. I pondered over the final salutation, settling for the one I normally used when writing to him: *much love, Anasuya.* I left the library and posted the letter forthwith. But then I started to read seriously about South Africa. I read about apartheid. I memorised the statistics: there are 700,000 convictions under the pass laws p.a. 10% of the population (i.e. the whites) receives 58% of the National Income. The average monthly pay for Africans is 230 Rand, for whites it is 950 Rand. 80% of the industry and 80% of the workforce are situated in 28% of the country's area, none of this area is in the so-called Bantustans. That statistic that Albert quoted at me about the maximum percentage of the African workforce that is allowed to live *en famille* in the compounds attached to the mines is quite correct. The mining companies are not allowed by law to have more than 3% of their miners accompanied by their families. And so on and so on and so sickeningly on.... And that's just the economic and formal legal muck. It's when one reads the accounts of the torture, the arbitrary suppression, the electric shocks, the beatings and murders that the useless impotent rage takes over. The place stinks, stinks to the fucking heavens. I memorised an incident, memorised the author, publisher, date of publication, and page number. The secretary of the Black People's Convention, Moke Cekisane was detained by the police at the same time and in the same offices as the murdered leader Steve Biko. With other detainees, Moke Cekisane was handcuffed to a cement wall with his forehead only a few inches from the surface. Electrodes were attached to the backs of the prisoners' necks. When the current was switched on and off rapidly the prisoners' heads jerked forward against the wall. As a result of this treatment Moke Cekisane is now a chronic epileptic. When he tried to sue the Minister of Justice for damages, he and his black lawyer were imprisoned. The action did not proceed. A drop in the ocean.

And I spent hours in front of microfilm readers and at the desks of the library's periodicals room, slowly putting together a rough approximation of Albert's list. There was a very pleasant young man in the Companies Office who delighted in spending his time helping me with my research. Actually a great deal of information about my father's commercial connections was freely available in publications like *Who's Who*.

I don't know what I thought I was doing. On one level I wished to be able to confront van Niekerk with a greater degree of assurance. I wished, in our next argument, to put up a better performance. I wished to improve my image of myself. I wished to be more like Albert. But I think also I was goading myself, that I knew there could only be one real result of my self-education: rejection of my father and all my father's wealth.

I had lunch with my father in a restaurant overlooking the Serpentine. He was affable, he made no mention of our previous encounter. The real argument did not start until we were back at his house and were relaxing after dinner. The real argument was not about apartheid at all.

We had that one in the afternoon, walking through Hyde Park. We were at loggerheads the whole time, but restrained and civilised about it. I recited all the information I had swotted up like a good schoolgirl. My father countered with various articulate but spurious arguments. Ten minutes into the discussion I'd mentally withdrawn from it entirely. It was a set piece. We were acting out a reconciliation. It was insulting to Moke Cekisane and everyone else. Apartheid is so obscene it cannot be argued over rationally. There can be no common ground on which an argument can take place. Its supporters should be ignored or shot. But the man I was talking to was my father, and he was offering friendship, reconciliation, maybe even love. So I said my piece and walked beside him through the grass and trees of

Hyde Park, as I had walked beside him as a child when we lived in Putney and he had taken me on excursions to Richmond Park to look at the deer. He was my father, and I was his daughter. And I knew, as assuredly as it is possible to know anything, that the time had come to follow in my mother's footsteps. Knowing that, there was no need to rail at him, no need to shout, no need for anger, no need for argument.

But later, that evening, we did argue. Or rather we fought. But not about politics or human rights. We fought about Kilminster. At the moment I do not wish to write about it. I suppose I ought. Indeed I will have to soon. But not now, not today. It is getting late, I should hide this notebook in its place in the bothy's wall and return to the taverna. Kilminster and I have been invited to dinner this evening by a woman who took us goat-shit gathering the other day (Manure, the grape vines for the nurturing of) and I'd like to be reasonably sane when we sit down to eat, which I wouldn't be if I had spent the intervening hours writing about that other evening in Kensington. Let's just say that by the time I got back to Liverpool it had become clear to me that I would have to effect a total break with my father. Total.

[End of entry: Bothy notebooks.]

THE TAVERNA
NOTEBOOKS

After that argument over South Africa which I mentioned to Michaels during our interview, I decided that, for my own good, in order to grow up properly, I would have to cut myself off from my father. It was quite easy. I wrote letters to the bank managers in charge of the Bottomless Pits informing them that I no longer wished to be a signatory to the accounts and that I was ceding my ownership of the funds to van Niekerk alone. I included cheques made out thus "Pay Pieter van Niekerk the entire amount currently in this account". I don't know if this is accepted banking procedure or not, but I received letters indicating that this had been done. I wrote to Henri Boufflet telling him I no longer wanted the French Merc and would he please arrange to take it away. I drove the English Merc to London and parked it in a fifteen-minute parking spot outside the offices of the hire company who were its nominal owners (even ordinary companies in England don't own cars, they hire them because it's a tax loss or something). I gave the keys to the girl at the desk and told her to keep the machine for her personal use if she'd a mind to.

Then I discovered I was foreign. I'd thought I'd just live on a student grant like the rest of my friends. But I had not been resident in England for two years previous to my becoming a student. I didn't qualify. Furthermore, I would have to continue paying fees at the rate in force for foreign students which is four times higher than the nominal fees paid by Britons, or rather by one British government department to another British government department.

"But look, mister, I'm English," I said to the man behind the desk, slapping my passport. "See here, *The holder has the right of abode in the United Kingdom.* I might have been born in New Delhi, but I'm English. I've a right to an education."

"You entered Liverpool University on your results in the French *baccalauréat* and your previous address was this château place."

"That's my mother's address. My father lives in London, has done for years."

"Can you produce a statement to this effect from him?"

"No."

"Why not?"

"I don't speak to him."

"Not much we can do for you, then."

The Liverpool Local Education Authority office is full of creeps and bureaucrats. Actually, as far as fees went I was all right for the remainder of that year, but I needed money to live on. So, like Jennifer before me, I got a job in a pub. Only, unlike Jennifer, I had no idea about the consumption of alcohol. But I learned fast enough. There wasn't much variety in the drinks demanded in the Lord Nelson—three or four types of beer and stout, the occasional whisky. Kilminster came in for a drink with a couple of his students on the second evening I worked there.

"Three pints love," he yelled at me above the noise.

"Bitter, love?"

"Ta, love."

I served the grog up professionally enough, slopping it about, sideswiping the towel on the bar with the glasses' bottoms.

"This is a proper pub," Kilminster said when I handed him the change. "A right stand-up, farting, and pissing pub."

"I know."

As I say, I loathe English pubs, but I didn't really mind the Lord Nelson. No one was ever referred to as "mine genial host" in that little ale-house. The only thing I resented about working for my living was the demands the job made on my time. I only worked there in the evenings, but I was a full-time student as well, I did have the odd essay to write, the occasional dinner or film I would have liked to have attended. Also I didn't quite make enough to live on. As the academic year drew to a close, I cut down on the amount of time I worked in the pub and obtained three, then five, hours' work coaching 0 level French. My pupils were not very bright middle-class kids whose parents were desperate to buy them middle-class exam results. I was a poor teacher; I had no patience with them at all. I'd tell them something, they'd look as if they'd understood the point, but two minutes later would betray total ignorance. I simply could not comprehend this phenomenon; I still can't. The psychology of the dunderhead is a very sadly neglected field. I became a trifle overbearing and sarcastic at times, and then hated myself for being so. I'd apologise to my pupils and then make an effort to bear with their slow, plodding, thick-headed efforts to master their own total linguistic incompetence. They were all nice kids in a way, just dim. They didn't really deserve me. Two of them passed the exam, not very well.

At the end of term, I gave up the pub job, borrowed some money from Kilminster, fought unsuccessfully with the LEA about next year's grant, passed my own exams with my routine brilliance and suspended my degree course for a year. I needed a year to earn some money, but

I also needed a break from the university, from the student life. My ratty little soul *demanded* a year off.

As for my new-found poverty, it worried me not at all. The whole trauma that Jennifer had worked her way through before and after cutting herself off from van Niekerk's money had no sequel for me. I lived among people who survived on their grants, the dole, National Assistance, the wages of short-term unskilled labour, the profits of small-time hash peddling. Despite the ownership of two absurd cars and a wardrobe of expensive clothes in Kensington, I had never used the Bottomless Pits for expensive living. And, of course, I am a skilled shoplifter. Which helps, which helps no end. And, of course, I could always borrow money if I had to. Kilminster had his academic salary and no dependants. Simon was treating sheikhs in Harley Street and had more money than he and Tamar knew what to do with. If you are bourgeois you can slum it, but you cannot look real, unavoidable poverty and starvation in the face. The children of my social class often eschew respectable clothes for multi-coloured rags, they sometimes live for a month in Goa on the proceeds of a pint of blood they sold in Kuwait, but when the going gets really rough and they need a good lawyer in a hurry, or the air fare home because of hepatitis, the money is only a telephone call away, and they know it. And I know it.

* * * * * * *

I went to France and lounged about the château for a while. Philippe was now lurching around like Long John Silver, his knees and ankles supported by devices of steel and leather. I met up with a couple of my old friends from school and we hitch-hiked to Provence and picked grapes for three weeks. When I got back to the château it was to learn that Tamar had left Simon to live with Ivan Pavlavic, an exhibition designer. The news was unexpected, but not surprising. She and Simon had both been leading fairly independent lives, keeping on the Chelsea flat "for the children's sake". The children, now both at university, were judged to be of an age when the trauma of their parents' separation and divorce would not affect them unduly. My own feeling is that Samantha and Randolph could have taken the "trauma" of this event in their stride at a far younger age. I think the Chelsea flat was a pleasant base for both Simon and Tamar to operate from. They could have gone on indefinitely, living with each other in Chelsea, having their affairs elsewhere. If it now suited Simon to move into a flat in Harley Street itself, and Tamar into Ivan Pavlavic's Hampstead house, it was more because both Ivan and Simon's mistress,

Deirdre, were becoming insistent about changing their positions in the scheme of things, than out of any regard for the children's sensibilities. Anyway it was lucky for me that all this happened since Ivan tendered for, and was given, a commission by the Liverpool city fathers to design and mount an exhibition showing the potential of the Liverpool docks and ship-building industry. In a way it was a sad joke—they have no potential and everybody knows this—but as it would obviously be great fun to do, I rang Ivan and offered my services as an assistant, citing my intimate knowledge of the area, willingness to learn, intelligence, and so forth. I was hired forthwith. I arrived in Liverpool a couple of weeks later to find that Ivan and Tamar had rented a solid middle-class basement flat in a solid middle-class suburb whose very existence I had previously been unaware of. The exhibition was to be extensive and they had taken the flat for a full six months. Although the exhibition was to be staged in the town hall, we had been given the use of two small rooms in the museum for our preliminary work. Later we would expand our operations, be given the use of workshops, take on extra workers, and start assembling the whole show on site, but initially there was just me, Ivan, and Tamar in these two small rooms in the basement of the museum.

I loved the work. It wasn't really work at all. I spent a lot of time in the library, at the offices of newspapers, talking to shipbuilders, unionists, local historians, gathering pictures and other material. In spite of our being commissioned to show the potential of the docks and industry, we were quite unashamedly concentrating on the past. Our exhibition should really have been called "The Glory that was the Mersey". I love Liverpool, present-day, run-to-seed Liverpool, but I would give anything to be able to go back to the great maritime days of Empire, when all the docks were full of ships and the electric tramway ran high overhead down the whole length of the waterfront.

I spent a lot of time at Tamar and Ivan's flat. I had them round to dinner at Huskisson Street a couple of times. I began to save money. Jennifer came over from France after we had been working on the exhibition for a couple of months. She stayed for a fortnight, one week with Tamar, the other with Kilminster. It was during this time that my father suddenly turned up, unannounced. He must have known that Jennifer was in Liverpool, but how isn't quite certain. Perhaps a firm of private detectives had a watching brief on me. Perhaps that is being unduly paranoid.

On the day in question, Jennifer had called at the museum at lunch-time and the four of us and an architect whom Ivan was pumping for details of early warehouse construction had gone to lunch in one of the small cafes nearby. After lunch the architect took us all for a walk by the river to show us examples of what he had been talking about. By the time we got back to the museum the afternoon was well advanced. The passage outside our offices was not very wide, we walked down it in file, Tamar first, then Ivan, then Jennifer, with me last. The door to the offices was open and as Tamar turned into it, I heard her say, "Hell, hello. Pieter. I haven't seen you for ages."

My father's voice answered, "Tamar, how nice, I hoped you'd be here."

By this time both Ivan and Jennifer had reached the door.

"Jennifer."

"Pieter. What are you doing here?"

I turned around and walked away. From behind my back I heard van Niekerk say something about being in Liverpool on business and hearing that Jennifer was in town. I walked the remaining twenty or thirty feet of corridor as quickly as I could without actually running. As I was turning the corner at the end, my father's voice called loudly, "Anasuya, Anasuya, come back."

I ran down the next corridor. Once outside the museum I walked rapidly and at random. I simply did not wish to meet my father. I had cut myself off from him, and I was going to stay that way. I eventually made my way home. Magpie and Clara were there. I told them that if my father arrived they were to say I'd left home for a few days. Then I lay on my bed in the attic and tried to read. At about six o'clock Kilminster rang to see if I was at home. He and Jennifer arrived about ten minutes later.

The scene had gone like this. After my father had said his piece about being in Liverpool on business, there was a pause during which nobody said anything. My retreating footsteps could easily be heard. Van Niekerk took a couple of steps into the corridor, squeezing between Jennifer and Ivan to do so, and called to me to come back. When I'd turned the corner, van Niekerk said to the others, "I wish I knew what has turned her against me. It is the most upsetting thing in my life."

Jennifer said, "Why are you here?"

"I wished to see you, and Anasuya also."

Ivan and Tamar exchanged glances. Ivan started to arrange things on his desk. Tamar said, "Oh, Pieter, this is Ivan Pavlavic. Ivan, Pieter van Niekerk."

The two men shook hands and exchanged a few pleasantries. Jennifer said, "Well, if you've come here to see me, I suppose we'd better go somewhere and leave these two in peace."

As they were leaving the museum Jennifer said, "I can't say I'm all that pleased to see you, Pieter. I do think it would have been slightly more decent of you to have warned us of your arrival."

"Oh Jennifer, let us be civilised. We were once married, after all."

"Fairly disastrously, Pieter. Fairly disastrously."

They reached van Niekerk's car. He unlocked the passenger door.

"Where have you a mind to go?" Jennifer asked him.

"I thought back to my hotel. We can have a drink and talk in peace."

"We can't have a drink. It's past three o'clock."

"There is a small bar in the back of this car. We can take whatever we like to my suite."

"Pieter, I don't want a drink, and I don't want to go to your hotel. If you've got anything to say, you can say it to me here."

"Jennifer, please. We can't talk just standing in the street."

"Well, let's walk in the street, let's go for a walk."

My father hates walking anywhere but in a neat, ordered park, where strolling is *de rigueur*. I think he feels that to walk in an industrial, urban setting is to proclaim one's lack of a car. It's almost undignified. Jennifer began to walk away from the parked Rover. Van Niekerk could do nothing but hasten after her. He fell into step beside her.

"Well?" Jennifer asked.

"I am worried about Anasuya."

"Why are you worried about Anasuya?"

"I think she is throwing her life away."

"You mean to say you are narked because she's living her own life, rather than the one you chose for her?"

"She has given up the university."

"She can't afford the damn university. The English won't pay for her."

"Which is absurd. She has all the money she needs."

"She is earning enough to live on and saving some. Perhaps she will go back next year."

"Which is ridiculous...."

"Look, it might be ridiculous to you, but it's not to her. Or me either...but I'm not going to argue with you about money, Pieter, it's too sordid and quite pointless. Besides it's anally retentive."

"What?"

"It's shit. Money is shit. That's why you make so much of it, that's why you want to make more. You were never potty-trained properly."

Jennifer's brush with psychiatry probably did her no harm, although it obviously did her no good either. It's main legacy is a hotchpotch of dubious theory that she can produce at will in order to annoy people. It's possible that she still half believes some of it. But that's not why she uses it.

"Jennifer, please. I haven't come all this way to talk nonsense with you."

"You've come all this way on matters of business, remember? You are here to make money, shit."

"All right. I admit I came here especially to talk to you and Anasuya. Can we talk about our daughter, please?"

"What have you got to say, apart from admissions of not being able to accept that she wishes to be financially independent?"

"She has cut herself off from me completely."

"Well, I can understand that. What do you think I've done?"

"You I can understand. I wish you hadn't, but I can understand why you have. But Anasuya is different. She and I had a warm and deep friendship, which for some reason she suddenly destroyed."

"My heart bleeds."

"Jennifer, it is not easy for me to talk to you like this. I wish you would try to be a bit more understanding."

"What do you want me to do?"

"I would like you to talk to Anasuya, to suggest she at least gets in contact with me."

"She obviously doesn't want to get in contact with you, can't you see that? That's why she walked out of the museum just now."

At this point Jennifer caught sight of me. I was walking along the opposite footpath towards her and my father. Jennifer says I had my head down and was muttering to myself. She also says I was a couple of hundred yards away. I doubt that she could have seen whether I was muttering or not. A few doors away from her and van Niekerk was one of those small corner tea-shops. I've since been there myself. It's called the Three Star Café, it serves tea in enormous quantities and plates of eggs and chips, sausages and chips, or just chips. Bottles of Worcestershire sauce stand on every table. The windows are permanently fogged up. There is a pinball machine in one corner.

"Tea" Jennifer declared.

"What?"

"Tea. I need a cup of tea. I don't know about you, but I need a cup of tea. In here."

My father started to say something, but Jennifer had already entered the shop. He had no choice but to follow her. At lunchtime the Three Star is a loud, crowded, steamy place, patronised by the workers from the factories along the other side of the street. One could have a shouted conversation with one's neighbour without fear of being overheard. In the dog hours of the afternoon, it is usually almost deserted. On that particular afternoon there were four other customers: two old-age pensioner women drinking tea and two teenage boys playing the pinball machine. The girl behind the counter was reading a true confessions magazine. Jennifer flung herself onto a tubular-steel chair. She was wearing jeans and a paint-stained jersey, she felt quite at home. Van Niekerk sat opposite her; he was wearing a three-piece suit of expensive cloth and conservative cut. He did not feel at home.

"What'll it be, then?" the girl behind the counter said, looking up from her magazine.

"Tea for me," Jennifer said, watching through the steamy glass the blurred figure of her daughter pass on the other side of the street.

"Oh, err, a pot of tea as well," van Niekerk said.

"A pot of tea for two, then," the girl said rhetorically, not expecting an answer.

"Yes, that's right," van Niekerk said, "One pot will do for both of us."

The girl arrested her gesture of reaching for the teapot to stare at van Niekerk for a second. Jennifer said, "If Anasuya doesn't want to talk to you, there's nothing I can do about it."

Van Niekerk leant forward on the Formica table, speaking softly. "Well, perhaps you can help me in another way."

There was a hiss of steam from the café's urn as the girl filled the teapot. The pinball machine emitted a series of "dings" and fell silent. "Fuck it!" said the boy who, with his hands on the machine's flanks had been jerking his hips as if that was, in fact, precisely what he had been doing.

"How?" Jennifer said.

"Oh, err, I'll tell you later. When we've had our tea."

The girl came round the counter and placed two aluminium teapots and two cups and saucers in front of my parents.

"Oh, and err milk," van Niekerk said.

"In the pot."

"Oh."

My father picked up one of the teapots and poured from it experimentally into his cup.

"Why can't you tell me now?" Jennifer asked.

A stream of hot water came from the teapot's spout. Van Niekerk replaced it on the table and lifted the lid of the other pot, checking its contents. He then poured a stream of milky grey tea into the cup.

"Jennifer?" he said, holding the teapot over her cup.

"Of course," she said, "But why can't you tell me now?"

Van Niekerk filled her cup and leant forward again. "Really, Jennifer. This is hardly the place *pour une tête à tête à deux.*"

"*Un tête à tête. Une tête, mais un tête à tête.* The head is feminine, but two of them are masculine."

"Give us a go," one of the boys said. He changed places with his friend, inserted a coin and began jerking the machine. On the backboard his score increased by hundreds and thousands.

"Can we just drink our tea? We can talk again outside."

"Surely," Jennifer said, shrugging.

For a while they drank in silence. Van Niekerk hurriedly, Jennifer slowly. Van Niekerk finished his and placed the cup resolutely on the saucer. Jennifer studied the calendars on the walls. One showed three kittens in a basket, one a naked woman sitting under a palm tree, and another a biplane with German markings on its wings. She returned her attention to van Niekerk.

"Can we chat?" she said brightly over the rim of her cup.

"Yes, of course."

"How are you these days? How's your wife?"

"Well. We are both well."

"Oh good."

After a moment's silence during which Jennifer sipped and

the machine emitted its end-of-game dings, she said, "Well, don't you want to ask me how I am?"

"How are you?"

"I too am well. So is my husband and our various children."

The girl behind the counter was now leaning on her true confessions magazine with her elbows, watching my parents. Van Niekerk looked at her. She looked away, exchanging glances with the two pensioner women. The boys remained absorbed in the pinball machine. Jennifer put down her cup. Van Niekerk half stood. Jennifer slowly poured herself a second cup. Van Niekerk sat down.

"How's your car collection?"

My father said nothing. He said nothing until Jennifer had slowly finished her second cup. They both stood. Van Niekerk made straight for the door. He stood on the pavement, while inside the café Jennifer paid for the tea and exchanged a few pleasantries with the true confessions girl.

My parents began walking back towards the museum.

"Well?" Jennifer said.

"You're impossible to talk to."

"Bit of a waste of a trip then, wasn't it? Next time announce your arrival beforehand."

"If that's the only crime I've committed, I think you've punished me enough. Can we have a serious conversation now?"

"Surely."

"You don't sound as if you mean it."

"I do, I assure you."

My parents walked in silence for a few minutes. Then van Niekerk, talking slowly and softly, said, "I do not understand why Anasuya has destroyed the friendship and love that existed between us. Jennifer, I simply do not understand it. I know all about her not wanting to be dependent upon my money. She can earn her own money if she wants to. She doesn't have to accept anything from me. I know that we have differences of political opinion, what father and daughter don't? We had a couple of arguments over South Africa, but they were not irreconcilable, our differences should not have prevented any further contact between us. And that is what she has done. She has severed all contact. She won't answer my letters. If I can manage to get her on the phone in that madhouse she lives in, she puts the receiver down the moment she realises it's me. She won't come to see me when she's in London. And I don't know why."

"Perhaps she feels that she cannot do things by halves; that if she is to reject your money, she must reject you as well."

"She is not that cruel. Anasuya is not naturally cruel, Jennifer. She knows how much I love her."

"Do you really love her, or do you just want to own her?"

"Look, Jennifer, try to put yourself in my shoes. Imagine how you would feel if Anasuya suddenly severed all contact with you. Never came to France, never wrote, avoided all your attempts to contact her. Just imagine how you would feel and then try to put yourself in my place. I am a parent just as much as you."

Jennifer says that at this point my father was almost crying. He stopped walking along the street they were in, stood alternately looking down at his feet and at Jennifer, blinking.

"She's touched you, hasn't she?" Jennifer said. "You've suffered, are suffering. You're experiencing a real human emotion."

"For Christ's sake. I am human. I always have been human, regardless of what you might have believed. I love Anasuya more than anyone else in the world. More than Bernadette. More even than you; and once I loved you to distraction."

For a while my parents just stood in the street, facing each other. Then Jennifer said, "Come on."

She took my father's arm in hers and walked in silence for a couple of minutes. Then, gravely, she said, "Look, Pieter, I'm sorry I was teasing you in the café just now. I believe you to be genuinely very upset by Anasuya's actions. I'll tell her how upset you are. I'll suggest to her that she gets in contact with you again. I can't do more than that. I'd advise you to go back to London now, nothing would come of your staying around

Liverpool or trying to see Anasuya against her will."

"Thank you."

When they reached the car Jennifer disengaged her arm. Van Niekerk said, "But there's nothing you can tell me about why she's rejected me, she hasn't said anything to you about her feelings?"

"No. And I wouldn't betray her confidence if she had. You must speak to her yourself."

My father kissed Jennifer for the first time in ten years. My mother allowed herself to be kissed. Van Niekerk said, "Can I give you a lift?"

"No, it's all right."

"Are you going home? It's on my way."

"Where's on your way?"

"Tamar's flat."

"Pieter dearest, I'd get a new firm of private eyes if I were you. That was last week's address. This week I'm staying with Kilminster."

My mother turned and walked away.

She walked to the university. She found Kilminster in his room, marking a pile of his students' work. He was sitting at a small table by the window. Jennifer sat in the swivel chair in front of his normal desk. She put her feet on the desk, leaning back against the springs of the chair.

"Guess who I just met?"

"Dunno. Give me ten minutes to finish these things."

For ten minutes Jennifer played with Kilminster's calculator, tapping the buttons at random, watching the random numbers flicker and change on the liquid crystal display.

"Who?"

"Guess."

"The ghost of Roger Casement."

"Pieter."

"Shit. Where?"

"He turned up at the museum."

Kilminster stood up, knocking over his chair.

"Jennifer, are you joking?"

"No, I've just had a cup or two of tea with him. In the Three Star Café."

"Where's Anasuya?"

"She left when he arrived. He was very upset."

"Who was?"

"Pieter."

"That arsehole. Where is he now?"

"James, calm down."

"Where is he, Jennifer?"

"He's gone back to London. I think he's gone back to London."

"And Anasuya? Where's she?"

"James, for God's sake. There's nothing the matter. Pieter's all right; you might not like him, but he's genuinely upset about the way Anasuya's rejected him. She is his daughter after all...."

"That fucking bastard...."

"James. What is it?"

"Have you any idea why Ansu broke with him?"

"She wanted to be independent."

"Independent, independent. He half killed her. She had a fight with him. I'm not meant to tell you this. She had a violent fight with him over me and various other things. When she got back to Liverpool one eye was so swollen she could hardly see out of it. Her face was bruised. She had bruises on her arms and legs...."

"She never told me."

"The only person who knows the full story is me. I'm not meant to tell anyone, even you. She told everybody around here that she'd been attacked by some hoods on Euston Station."

"But why?"

"I don't know. Her pride. Her privacy. She just didn't want people to know."

"But I'm not *people*. She told me she'd broken with him over South Africa. She didn't say anything about a fight."

"I know she didn't."

"But why, James? I can't understand why she didn't tell me."

"Because she didn't."

"How weird."

"It's not weird at all."

"Anyone would think she was trying to cut herself off from me as well as Pieter."

"Jennifer, you ought to stop regarding other people's privacy as a personal affront."

"She's my daughter, James."

"And she didn't choose to tell you."

"So you say, so you say. What actually happened in this fight?"

"Look…I don't know, I don't actually know the details. Even to me she hasn't talked at length. You'll have to ask her yourself."

"But Pieter seemed so genuine just now."

"Genuine?"

"He said he didn't know why Anasuya had broken with him. He really seemed not to know. He was very upset. He said they'd had a couple of arguments about politics, but he didn't mention a fight."

"Perhaps he can't remember."

"How could he not remember?"

"Anasuya says he was drunk."

"He'd have had to have been very drunk."

"Maybe he was mad as well. Insane. Off the air."

"Just how badly was Anasuya hurt?"

"She was bashed about. He didn't break any bones or knock her teeth out. But almost; her lip was all cut."

"Jesus."

"Look, have you any idea where she is?"

"I saw her pass the café I was in with Pieter. I think she was going home."

"I'll ring."

* * * * * * *

Kilminster had exaggerated a bit when he told Jennifer that I'd been half killed. I had a spectacular black eye, a small cut on my lip and a few minor bruises on my limbs. The bruises freaked out Kilminster entirely. They would have done so under any conditions, but with van Niekerk as their cause I'm sure they took on the awesomeness of broken bones and mangled flesh. Kilminster had raved around his flat threatening to hire some Irish thugs that his uncle has contacts with. At first he said we ought to put a contract out on van Niekerk's life, but later amended the plan to putting a contract out on his arms and legs. Apparently professional hit-men don't have to be lethal, one can specify the required injury. I convinced Kilminster to do nothing. I insisted that he refrain from spreading the story around. I wanted to be allowed to effect the break with my father in peace, as it were, without the complications of everyone in the château knowing the details. I wished to avoid the long cross-channel telephone conversations, the endless discussions next time I was in France. So I wrote to Jennifer, just saying that I had had enough of my father and his money and the way he made his money, and that, as a consequence I was severing ties with him.

But now she knew about the fight. Kilminster had told her. The three of us sat on my bed in the attic in our traditional three monkeys position. Me in the middle, hearing no evil.

I did, however, hear a certain amount of pique in Jennifer's voice. She seemed a bit put out, one might say peeved, that I hadn't told her about the dust-up with van Niekerk. It was, I suppose, the second major incident in my life over which I'd deliberately misled her. But she had a point: not knowing the facts had put her in a totally false position with van Niekerk. But perhaps not knowing the facts had put *van Niekerk* in a totally false position with Jennifer.

"Are you sure he was genuine?" Kilminster said. "Do you really think he couldn't understand Anasuya's actions?"

"As far as I can tell," Jennifer said, "he thought he'd only had an argument with her, a not particularly acrimonious verbal argument."

"Maybe he's suppressed it. Had a memory blackout. Drink can do that after all, not to mention the subconscious."

"The man's criminally insane," Jennifer said.

"Quite possibly."

"He *is*," I said.

I rooted around in the drawer of my desk in which I keep letters, photographs, and the like. Most of the letters van Niekerk had sent me since the break I'd thrown away, usually in their envelopes, but I found one I'd retained. Jennifer read it, Kilminster looking over her shoulder. It was one of those adult-to-adult letters. It talked about what we meant to each other and the necessity of not allowing differences of political opinion to come between us. He wrote in a restrained way about my silence. The letter was fundamentally *decent*.

"Jesus," Jennifer said, "this is crazy."

"Well, what do we do?" Kilminster said, "If van Niekerk is going to come snooping around Liverpool, Ansu's not safe."

For a while we talked about the possibility of bringing charges against my father, or of having a court order made which would prevent him trying to contact me—actions that would have required proof in a court of law of van Niekerk's behaviour. Impossible. It was a frustrating and disturbing conversation. It went nowhere. In the end Kilminster returned to his hire-a-hit-man scheme.

"Oh talk sense, James," Jennifer said, "It would be pointless to just have some toughs rough him up. And none of us are going to have him murdered."

"Why not?"

"Because we're not. And anyway they might catch the hit-man, and the hit-man might say who'd paid him. Then we'd all be in clink ourselves."

Clara called up the stairs, wanting to know if we were in the market for pea and ham soup. So we all went down to the living room and slurped soup and toasted bread in front of the fire and talked of other things.

And then dear Bernadette cast herself in the role of concili-ator. She sent me a letter written in her own dead-elegant hand on pale mauve notepaper almost as thick as cardboard with the Kensington address embossed (printed isn't the word) across the top half of the top sheet. Bernadette was most distressed. Bernadette was quite upset. Bernadette was sure, however, that the love between the two people she loved most was stronger than any disagreement or misunderstanding that may have arisen between them. Bernadette wished me to know how deeply Pieter had taken my estrangement. He was not an emotional man, he was not easily moved to a demonstration of his real feelings, but she, Bernadette, knew how profoundly he was hurt. She had not told him she was writing to me; this little note was just a private communication, woman to woman. She was sure I understood, that I wouldn't take her interest amiss. She was, after all, my father's wife and we were both very dear to him, were both very close to him, even if I had, well, not been able to find the time to see him for the last six months. And Bernadette had a little plan! It was this: she and Pieter had been invited to a house party by a very close friend of hers, down in Sussex. A mere tinkle on the phone would secure an invitation for me too—there was no question about this! It would provide, as they say, neutral territory on which to see my father again. And then, as she, Bernadette, would be staying with her friend for a few extra days, I would be able to drive up to London with my father on Sunday night, if I wished to, of course, which would give me time to be alone with him!

Bernadette's letter was full of exclamation marks. It is a poor substitute for the hand-clapping gesture: just a stroke of ink with a dot under it. But Bernadette did her best with the limited tools of the written language; the exclamation marks were at least half an inch high.

It seemed churlish to remain completely silent. So I sent a quick reply. Thanks for the invite, but I wouldn't be free that weekend.

It was a reply, even if curt. She should have got the message.

She didn't. Three weeks later I was the recipient of another packet of mauve notepaper covered with some rambling suggestion that I should accompany her and my father to Ireland for some damn horse race. Again she held out the tantalising possibility that I could be alone with my father who would be taking the car across on the ferry while she, Bernadette, who hated long journeys, would fly over! And Dublin had such interesting architecture! Pieter and I would be able to indulge ourselves in retracing Bloom's walks while looking at the buildings. Just like we had done once in Bath with Jane Austen's *Northanger Abbey*. Pieter often talked about that weekend, even though it was now so long ago…and so on and so on.

Apart from the preposterous hint that Bernadette was somehow acquainted with Joyce's *Ulysses* (I'd read the relevant Sunday paper colour supplement myself a couple of months previously—*Doomsday for Bloomsday* or some crap) the letter was nothing but a collection of the woman's empty-headed ravings. This time I did nothing. She didn't give up. She came to see me.

I was about to leave for the museum one evening (the pressure was mounting by this time—on occasions we worked all night) when Clara looked out of the window and said, "Jesus, who's this?"

My father's Bentley, or something very like it, was backing into a parking space immediately below the window.

"It's my father. If he knocks on the door, don't answer it."

We both stood back from the window as much as possible, just managing to look down over the sill to the roof of the car below. It came to rest beside the kerb. After a few seconds the front passenger door opened and Bernadette stepped out. She stood on the pavement, looking dubiously up at our house. I withdrew further into the room, but as we had not yet turned on the lights and the window carried its normal complement of dirt, I was fairly sure she couldn't see me. She was wearing a long fur-trimmed coat and a pillbox hat which concealed her hair. Her elegant white neck just showed above the fur collar of the coat. I waited for the other occupant of the car to emerge. Since Bernadette had alighted from the passenger seat, she obviously had not been alone in the car. Since it was the front seat and not the back, it was obvious that the driver was not Brian the chauffeur, unless, of course, there were at least two and probably three people occupying the rear of the car. Since the car was my father's Bentley and not Bernadette's own Volvo, there was only one solution: the driver was van Niekerk. The toad.

Bernadette was going to come tripping up to the flat, claiming to be alone, to have come off her own bat, just as she'd written those letters off her own bat, while all the time van Niekerk would be sitting in the car outside.

Bernadette walked warily up to the front door of our house. Clara and I lost her from sight. I could imagine her—I knew quite well what was happening. She had arrived at the door with its frosted-glass and plywood panels and had pushed the old-fashioned bell that is still affixed to the wall, a relic of the time when the building had been, in fact, one single dwelling. She stood there for some time, pressing the bell, waiting in vain for its ring. There was a muffled shout from the outside; I looked down at the roof of the car again. The driver's door opened and a figure emerged. It wasn't my father. It was Brian. He stood beside the car, only his shoulders and head visible, and shouted across the roof to the hidden figure of Bernadette.

"Just go inside, knock on their door."

Poor Bernadette. She'd never entered a building that contained more than one dwelling and neither doorman nor intercom. The idea that in our house anyone could enter the hallway and climb the stairs hadn't occurred to her. Brian retreated into the car. Clara and I waited for Bernadette to find her way up the divided stairs to our place. I couldn't imagine who else was in the car. Who was in the back? Obviously not my father alone. Perhaps only Bernadette and Brian had made the trip to Liverpool, perhaps the degenerate, democratic spirit of the times was even getting to dear Bernadette. Could it be that on long trips she might allow herself to sit next to the driver, rather than languish in the splendid isolation of the rear seat? I couldn't quite picture it myself, but then I find it hard to imagine Bernadette doing anything vaguely human and civilised. There came a tentative knock on our door.

"What now?" Clara asked.

"I suppose I ought to let her in."

Bernadette was relieved to see me.

"Oh, Anasuya, how are you? I'm glad I've found the right place. I was so worried that I'd got the *address* wrong. I've never, ever been to Liverpool before."

"Bernadette, I'm just leaving for work."

"Oh dear, what a pity, when do you finish?"

"Half an hour before closing."

"Closing?"

"…Time. I'm meeting Kilminster in a pub. The one I used to work in, the Lord Nelson."

"Oh, yes. Of course. Pieter did *mention* it. He said you were doing the same thing as your poor mother."

Bernadette was quite agitated. She took off one grey kid glove and twisted it in her hands. She looked unhappily past my shoulder into the flat.

"Oh dear," she said, "I do so want to talk to you, Anasuya. I've come all this *way!*"

"Come to the pub. I'll give you directions.…"

"Oh, Anasuya, *I couldn't*. Dr Kilminster will be there and I do so want to talk to you *seriously*."

"Various other friends of mine will be there. Kilminster can talk to them. You and I can natter in a corner. You can even have a drink, which is more than I'll be doing."

"Oh dear, Anasuya. I really don't think your pub would be *quite* the place. I do so want to *talk* to you really *privately*."

The poor woman was in considerable distress, I let her off the hook.

"Well let's talk tomorrow morning. Are you staying the night?"

I'm not sure if Bernadette took this as an invitation to stay the night in our flat or not. All I'd meant initially was to ask if she were staying the night in Liverpool, but her confusion, her evident, tongue-tied embarrassment gave me the idea she thought I'd issued an invitation. For the fun of it, I did.

"You can stay here, Bernadette. You're most welcome. I'd love a chance to repay all your hospitality in Kensington. We've a full-length sofa and there are plenty of spare sleeping bags around. Have you come by yourself?"

"Yes. No. I mean, Brian drove."

"Fine, there'll be plenty of room for him too."

"Oh dear. Oh, Anasuya dear. We couldn't. I couldn't. It would be too much to ask. I'll find a hotel...."

The glove in her hand was assuming a twisted likeness to a strand of rope. But, for all her confusion, she wasn't blushing. I'll say this for Bernadette, she doesn't blush. Her alabaster skin, her dove-grey eyes, the few locks of her expensively coiffured hair that had been permitted to stray from beneath her pillbox hat, remained as composed as a photograph in *Vogue*. But she said, "Oh, Anasuya darling, I mustn't keep you *waiting* now. I'll come round tomorrow. Or, or would you like to come to my hotel? I could ring and let you know where it is?" She ended on a hopeful rising inflection.

"No. No," I said affably, "Come and visit me for a change. For once you must be my guest."

"Oh. Yes. Well, of course I must. I'll come round at half past ten tomorrow if I may. That's not too early, is it, dearest?"

"Come for breakfast. Come at half past seven."

"Oh, Anasuya, you know I never get up till nine."

"Sorry, I forgot. Come any time in the morning. Half past ten will be fine. I have to be at the museum by lunch-time, but the morning will be fine."

We both descended the stairs, Bernadette repeating her assertions of absolutely overwhelming *desire* for a really long, serious, private chat with me. When we reached the front door, I said, "There is only Brian out there, isn't there? My father isn't in the car as well?"

"Oh no, of course not. Pieter is in *Turin* at the moment. He has no *idea* I'm not in London. I've come to see you off my own bat!"

This repeated "off my own bat" nonsense was beginning to make her sound like a cricket ball. I opened the door. She was right. Only the faithful Brian was in the car. I made my way to the driver's door to exchange the few pleasantries that common courtesy demanded. I've never really had much rapport with Brian, although we have always been friendly enough towards each other, and I've known him since I was ten. While I was talking to Brian, Bernadette got into the car. Into the back seat—her newfound democratic tendencies couldn't have been all that strong. She retracted the window nearest to me, asked me if I wanted a lift, extended a grey-gloved, fur-wristed arm, squeezed my hand, withdrew her arm, and said something to Brian who drove smoothly away after saying, "So long, then, Anasuya."

I walked as quickly as possible to the museum. I didn't really welcome Bernadette's visit one bit. After the initial fun of teasing the woman had worn off, I was annoyed with myself for allowing her to arrange the next day's meeting. I knew perfectly well what she was going to say. I knew perfectly well what my answers would be. I should have given her the brush-off, sent her back to London there and then. She had a bloody cheek, arriving unannounced. I couldn't live my own life in peace without some damn van Niekerk or other popping up at every turn like an insurance salesman. Bernadette could have rung, she's not without the wit necessary for efficient use of the telephone.

But had she rung, of course, I would have stalled her visit there and then. She must have known her chances were better if she suddenly appeared, having come all the way from London especially to see me. She was a twit, all right, but not so much of a twit she couldn't use a few insurance-salesman tricks when she needed to.

When I arrived at the Lord Nelson, the whole pub was awash

with drunken, riff-raff including Kilminster, Clara, Magpie, and a couple Kilminster's brighter students. Clara had already informed everyone of Bernadette's visit. I contented myself with observing that the silly woman had obviously come on an errand of reconciliation and I wished to Christ she hadn't bothered. Clara described Bernadette's reactions to my offers of hospitality brilliantly. She's a fine mimic. Our group was joined by a couple of Magpie's friends whom I hadn't met before. I moved away for ten minutes to talk to my previous employer who was playing darts for drink with his own customers and winning. When I returned to my friends they had already formulated the next day's reception of Bernadette. They were enjoying themselves immensely. Kilminster (whom Bernadette had never actually met) was almost falling off his stool with laughter.

* * * * * * *

Here's a short intermission. I include it because (a) Jennifer once told me that the secret of good story-telling was the establishment of tension, by which, if I understood her correctly, she meant the constant interruption of the plot with bits of old rubbish dragged in from here, there, and everywhere; the reader must under no circumstances be told everything too quickly. And (b) this bit of dialogue occurred this morning and I think it's significant.

Kilminster and I were lying in bed listening to the rain on the taverna's flat roof. I had been thinking about the scene I recounted a couple of days ago, the one where Jennifer becomes really narked because I hadn't told her about my fight with van Niekerk. I said, "James, do you think Jennifer is god?"

"Eh?"

"When you gave up the faith, was it because of Jennifer?"

"We hardly ever discussed theology as such; she was much more interested in the ritual, the social relations in the seminary, Catholic attitudes to sex, that sort of stuff."

"Yes, but do you think it was because she became your sort of Mother Confessor that you didn't need a Father Confessor and so there was no need...."

"Ansu, your amazing psychological insights would reduce...."

"Reduce what?"

"God knows...reduce *Hamlet* to the problem of the existence of ghosts."

"You're being defensive. You know what I mean. Jennifer likes being omniscient in everybody else's lives. There's a real pressure to tell her things. She likes to know. And if there is an answering need to tell her...then...."

"Then what?"

"Then you set up a little closed system in which there is no need for anybody else, including god."

Kilminster said nothing for a while. He just lay there, maybe thinking. He said, "What about you? Is Jennifer your god?"

"She was once. I used to tell her everything. I used to feel I had to tell her everything."

"For a short while," Kilminster said, "For a year or thereabouts. I used to feel the same way. And you're right, of course, it was during that time that I stopped believing in god. And you're right too about confession; talking to Jennifer was often very much a search for absolution. Go in peace my son."

"But there's a sort of blackmail involved in it all as well, isn't there? If she finds out that you've been in possession of some bit of information, gossip, something that happened to you or to somebody else, and you haven't told her, she can get really aggressive. She sees your withholding the information as an aggressive act on your part, so she gets nasty back."

"True. True. The lady thy god is a jealous god, avenging the sins of non-communication upon her children, yea, and upon her husbands also, with a tongue of iron...or something...."

Snappy eh? Now for more of dear Bernadette.

* * * * * * *

The Bentley found a parking space about fifty yards down the street from our house. Bernadette emerged from the front passenger seat and Brian from the driver's side. The two of them stood on the pavement talking for a few minutes before Brian turned to walk away—presumably to sit in the café on the corner, warming his hands with a mug of tea while his boss's wife held her urgently desired private chat with his boss's daughter. It was typical of the woman that she hadn't thought to invite him inside as well, this was a student flat after all, *my* student flat, not some society bitch's palace. But off Brian strode. Perhaps Bernadette would have been ashamed, or at least embarrassed, had she been present while Brian took a good look at the sort of place I was living in.

I opened the door to Bernadette's knock and showed her into the living room.

"Do sit down while I make us both a cup of coffee," I said. "We can go up to my room in a minute."

I cleared a couple of the empty gin bottles from the sofa so that she could sit down. She did this very gingerly, holding her coat around her. One of the junkies in the sleeping bags—the apparently naked one—groaned.

"Actually it's a good thing you didn't stay the night here," I said. "We had a bit of a party and a dozen people ended up sleeping here. Those two haven't woken up yet." I waved at the junkies. "Of course, we'd have found room for you. You wouldn't have been unwelcome, it would have just been a bit squashed."

A shambling wreck entered from the direction of the kitchen, fixing the flies of his torn and baggy trousers with a safety pin.

"Hello then," the wreck said to Bernadette, "How's tricks?"

"Oh, James," I said, "You've never met Bernadette, have you?"

"Naw."

"Mrs Bernadette van Niekerk, Dr James Kilminster."

"How nice to meet you. I've heard so much," Kilminster said, finally managing to fix the safety pin and extend a hand to

Bernadette.

Bernadette shook Kilminster's hand briefly with her dove-grey, kid-gloved one. I said, "James, can you engage Bernadette in conversation for a minute while I make coffee?"

"Delighted, my dear," Kilminster said, "I always get on very well with van Niekerk's women. I have," he assured Bernadette, "what you might call a *penchant* for them."

Kilminster sat on the sofa about six inches from Bernadette. One of the junkies groaned, the other farted. As I left the room, Kilminster was telling Bernadette that, "There is no truth in the rumour that Anasuya has joined the Church of the Blood of the Lamb. I can say this with some authority, there is no truth in it! I was once myself an aspirant to the life of the cloth, mam. I was called, but I was not chosen. The weakness of the flesh, I'm afraid. Do you have any spiritual leanings yourself?"

I returned with three cups of coffee, cleared away a few of the pornographic magazines and copies of *Das Kapital* that littered the table in front of the sofa, swept a collection of cigarette butts and used hypodermics to the floor, and placed the coffee before my guest. I almost offered her the cup with the chipped rim and no handle, but, ace hostess that I was, arrested the gesture and gave her a handle-equipped cup. Kilminster said to Bernadette, "I believe the world to be in a parlous condition, mam. Parlous. There is a surfeit of licentiousness and greed abroad in the streets of our cities. Yea, and in the bawdy houses and places of ill repute also. Have you noticed this, mam?"

Kilminster looked intensely at Bernadette from a distance of half a foot. Bernadette said, "Oh, Dr Kilminster, I never ever go to places like that. I just wouldn't *know*."

Bernadette sat very prim and proper, the untouched coffee on the table in front of her. Once again she had taken off a glove and was twisting it into rope. She looked at me and said, "Anasuya dear, I would just love to discuss…the problems of the world. Dr Kilminster has been so *fascinating!* But I'm sure you do not have very much time before you must be at the museum. And I do so *want* to have a long discussion with you."

The groaning junkie groaned. The farting junkie farted.

Bernadette's smooth, immaculate face appealed silently to me. If grooming and poise actually constituted composure and reserve, Bernadette would be a woman of icy imperturbability. They don't, of course, the poor woman was almost having kittens for all the fashion plate chic of her complexion and haute couture. I said, "James, if you'll excuse us, I think I'll take Bernadette up to my room."

"Of course, of course."

I don't know if Bernadette suspected the contrived nature of her reception. The laughter that floated up the stairs and through the closed door of my room could have been taken as merely the manic cackling endemic to a house full of depraved students, drug fiends and religious maniacs. Whatever Bernadette's true feelings, she made no comment on what she had seen or heard. She came straight to the point in her over-emphasised, half-wit way. The point was, of course, my reconciliation with my father. I can't be bothered writing a description of the whole scene. It simply consisted of an hour of oral analogue of her written communications with me. This time she had some crazy scheme for me to meet my father in London and drive with him to Cornwall. She seemed to think that if she could once get my father and me alone in the same car, all would be forgotten and forgiven. God knows why, perhaps the intimacy of a long drive somewhere is the only real intimacy that she, Bernadette has ever experienced with my father. Although, I suppose, some degree of togetherness must be generated between them in bed. The only point of interest for me in the whole rambling, pleading, fuckwit monologue was the reiterated assertion that van Niekerk himself had no idea why I had severed relations with him.

"Anasuya dear, Pieter is so *upset*. He just doesn't understand it! He loves you so much. We *both* do."

Finally, to get rid of the woman, I told her I would think about her offer of the Cornwall weekend. I'd let her know. With constant assertions of how much my reconciliation meant to both Pieter and herself, I showed her down the stairs, through the living room, where the shambling wreck, the two junkies, and a few other people were praying before an icon which bore a marked resemblance to the present Queen, down the main staircase and out to the car, where Brian was already re-ensconced behind the wheel. Bernadette got into the back and the two of them drove away.

The woman is a fool.

[Taverna notebooks: end of entry.]

THE BOTHY NOTEBOOKS

This is what happened.

This is what happened on that evening in Kensington when I had the "argument" or "fight" as I've called it, with my father.

For once we ate in. Bernadette was in Paris or somewhere. "The staff" served us, i.e. the cook cooked the meal, and Brian, poor bastard, brought it to the table. Van Niekerk himself organised the wine. I have never seen van Niekerk drunk in the way that my other drinking friends and relations can get drunk, in the way that Jennifer and Jean-Claude sometimes get drunk: celebrationally drunk, falling about and laughing drunk. My father is always in control. But drink he does. He drank a number of glasses of whisky before dinner. A bottle and a half of wine with dinner and some sort of cognac after dinner. There was a programme on television that I wished to watch; part of the reason for our staying at home was my desire to see it. We retired to an odd sort of room in which my father has a billiard table, a record player, a television, and a booze cabinet. I switched on the telly, but kept the sound off, the programme not yet having started. I took a cushion from one of the chairs and placed it on the floor in front of the sofa. I sat on the cushion, my back against the sofa, a mug of drinking chocolate beside me. My father sat on the sofa, behind and to one side of me. A glass of cognac rested on the sofa's broad arm. The programme started. I turned on the sound with the remote control device. My father placed his hand on my shoulder. We watched in silence for a while. I sensed that he wanted me to lean against his knee. If I can remember rightly, I felt vaguely annoyed. I wanted to watch the programme undistracted, but the day had been one of tacit reconciliation, even if I had decided that his South African interests precluded my ever really respecting him again. So, thinking that if the gesture would please him, I would demonstrate my fondness for him as my father, I leant against him. To prove the point I put one arm on his knee, leaning my head on my arm. More or less in this position we watched to the end of the programme. My father refilled his glass a couple of times, but as the bottle was to hand, he could do this without leaving the sofa. I would have preferred to have been sitting by myself, but our contact didn't really bother me. After a few minutes I don't think I was really aware of it. The programme was about teaching chimpanzees deaf and dumb language, I was simply absorbed.

Touching. I touch the people I like all the time. I always have. I did it when I was little and I've never grown out of the habit and I have no wish to. In the château I'll hug, kiss, walk around with my arms about, pretty well anyone in the place. If I meet any of my friends in the street, around the university, in a shop, at a party, I'll always kiss or hug them unless their inhibitions are strong enough to make my gestures obviously unwelcome. A great deal of this touching is sexual, all of it is sensual, and I neither know nor care what the difference is. Occasionally people tell me to grow up, that all this touching is immature, or evidence of insecurity, or soppy, or that it debases real touching—that explosion of sensation that comes when the hard, reserved Lawrentian barriers are suddenly swept aside in an ecstasy of passion. I don't know what they are talking about, and I'm sure they don't either. Certainly D. H. Lawrence hadn't a clue, as the most elementary reading of his tedious, over-rated books will demonstrate. When I was young, I always cuddled, and was always cuddled by, both my parents. And in those Clapham days, whenever I visited van Niekerk I would expect to be picked up, kissed. I would lean into his embrace in the back of his car if Brian were driving. It is true, I suppose, that in those days I was sometimes anxious, often nervous—I still am—and that much of my touching was a seeking for reassurance. But even had I been rock steady in my security, I think I would still have touched those I loved and felt fond of. These days I would like to be a little less highly strung than I sometimes am, but I would not like to stop touching. So there was nothing out of the ordinary in my leaning against van Niekerk or in his placing his hand on my shoulder as he did. Given our state of implicit reconciliation, some sort of physical intimacy was almost demanded of the situation.

The programme finished and I switched off the set. I made a move to stand up, but my father gently pressed on my shoulder.

"Stay here, Anasuya. Talk to me."

I settled back. After a moment's silence my father said, "Tell me about your life in Liverpool. You don't often talk about it."

"Well, it's just a normal sort of student life. I live in a house full of students. A lot of my time is spent in the library. I go to films and to parties. I was on the staff of the student paper last term. I don't take much notice of the political situation. Quite a few of my friends are actors, but I don't have all that much to do with the theatre myself. My life gets filled up. I don't suppose it bears much resemblance to your student days, but Liverpool isn't Leiden and times have changed."

"Do you have a boyfriend?"

"What?"

"Anyone special?"

"Jesus, I don't know."

I resented this question. It really was an invasion of privacy. And yet it was the sort of question that anyone in the château would quite naturally ask. Philippe would probably say, "So who are you screwing these days?"

Jennifer: "How's your love life?"

"You must know."

"No, I don't. No one special."

My annoyance must have communicated itself. Van Niekerk started to describe his own student days in Holland, as if by offering me an intimate glimpse or two of his early life, he were evening things up—making a fair exchange. Sitting there with his hand on my shoulder I really didn't wish to know about his student days. I hadn't asked him.

"Of course," he said at one point, "even with all the silly restrictions, there was something about college life that young people like you probably miss. There was a thrill to having a girl stay illegally in one's room all night, the danger of discovery added something. I don't think for a minute that those sorts of restrictions should be brought back, but in a way we *earned* our sexual initiation."

He went on to describe his first affair. He had entered into it not long after he'd arrived in Holland from South Africa. The girl had been a farmer's daughter, or milkmaid, or some such. Her name had been Erica and she had had red hair, was not quite as tall as I was, and they had fucked in the traditional haystack or Dutch barn.

"It is not as romantic as it seems, the hay is not at all soft."

There followed a period of silence, during which my father stroked my hair. To break the silence I said, "Perhaps it was straw."

"What?"

"Perhaps the hay was really straw."

"Oh…yes, perhaps it was." He had clearly needed to drag his thoughts back to the previous anecdote. I was feeling very uncomfortable. My father moved slightly and I heard another glass of cognac being poured. I shifted and stood up.

"I'll make myself some more drinking chocolate," I said. "Do you want any?"

"No. No, I'm content with this."

I dawdled around the kitchen, taking as long as I could.

When I returned to the billiard room my father was still sitting where I had left him. There was a large, leather armchair on the other side of the room, but when I sat in it the billiard table came between us.

"Come over here, Anasuya."

I sat on the sofa with about eighteen inches between me and my father.

"Sometimes I worry about you, Anasuya."

"Really? Why?"

"It seems to me sometimes that you are wasting your time. That you are not fulfilling your potential."

"What?"

"This house you live in in Liverpool, the friends that you have there...." Van Niekerk's voice trailed off into silence. Then he said very sharply, "That boy!"

"Eh? What boy?"

"Kilminster."

"Oh, for god's sake, Daddy. You might not like James. I can understand that. But he is one of *my* oldest and closest friends. He is my oldest and closest friend."

"So I understand."

"What?"

"First your mother and now you."

"What do you mean?"

"Anasuya, you know what I mean. I am not completely blind. That boy is a pernicious and evil influence. I believe he drives your car whenever he can get his hands on it."

This was madness. It was also infuriating and puzzling. I had no idea how my father knew that I sometimes slept with Kilminster, or, for that matter, how he knew about Kilminster driving the Merc—although that was, by the nature of things, a somewhat more public act. Neither Kilminster or I had ever really tried to hide the truth about our friendship, although we hadn't gone about flaunting it. To some people he was a sort of step-father to me, so a de facto incest taboo might be seen to be broken. He was also on the staff of the university at which I was a student, although as I was in no danger of ever becoming one of his students it was unlikely that anybody would have so much as raised an eyebrow. Still, all my household and most of my friends knew, everyone in the château knew of course; but I had no idea how my father knew. I certainly had never told him, and he had no contact with any of my friends. The remark about poor old Kilminster using my car was absurd. Totally absurd. I used Kilminster's nondescript station-wagon whenever I could get my hands on it. I often needed it: for transporting my friends in numbers greater than one or two, for picking up tables and chairs bought at auctions, for taking Joseph and Philippe and their wheel-chairs on outings. Kilminster didn't mind lending me his car, of course, but he profoundly disliked driving mine instead. When I swopped with him, he usually managed to leave mine sitting in its expensive garage behind the council flats for the duration. He said parking it outside his place lowered the respectable working-class tone of the street, although he was a bit happier now there were two thick streaks of rust along the roof, the legacy of my brush with van Niekerk's electric door. It suddenly occurred to me that my father regarded Kilminster's use of my car as an even worse crime than sleeping with me. That's probably an exaggeration, but my father is odd about cars. Or maybe he is perhaps normal about them.

"How do you know what I do in Liverpool?"

"I know, Anasuya. I have my informants."

Informants? I remembered that both Jennifer and Kilminster were convinced that van Niekerk had had them followed by a private detective after Jennifer had moved in with Kilminster. They had been very angry, there had been no need as far as evidence for divorce proceedings was concerned; that they could supply themselves in quantity. "The bastard must be just snooping for the sake of snooping," Jennifer had said. One afternoon, she and Kilminster had been walking on Clapham Common. They were followed at a distance of about a hundred feet by a man in a traditional private eye's raincoat.

"He was really seedy, wasn't he, James?" Jennifer said during one of the *Après Fin de Siècle Dining Club*'s drunken evenings.

"The quintessence of seed," Kilminster said.

The man had followed them while they walked in a deliberately circuitous route. For a while they sat on a bench watching the man wander about aimlessly in the vicinity.

"If he'd had a dog, he wouldn't have looked so suspicious. As it was he was just wearing down the grass, going nowhere."

Jennifer and Kilminster started to leave the park, but suddenly turned and walked back the way they had come, forcing the man to pass them in the opposite direction. As they drew level Kilminster stepped in front of him and hissed, "If you show your ugly mug around here again, mate, it'll be the old concrete boots in the canal trick. Get it?"

Without a word the man had side-stepped Kilminster and continued walking. Jennifer and Kilminster then followed him back to a parked car—both of them parodying the bloodhound-like demeanour of the born sleuth. As the man drove away, Kilminster made a great show of writing down the car's number. They had not seen him again, although for a while both of them suspected anybody who happened to walk behind them for more than a couple of hundred yards. Kilminster had once started his concrete boots speech to a man loitering on the corner of the street we lived in, but he had been so evidently startled and annoyed that Kilminster had ground to an embarrassed halt and uttered a hurried apology before walking away. After a while both he and Jennifer had more or less come to the conclusion that the first man on Clapham Common had just been a nut or pervert or other private citizen, his behaviour really had been too blatant for a professional. But now *I* wasn't so sure.

"What the hell do you mean, *informants*?"

"It doesn't matter, Anasuya. Just sometimes I get worried at the way you are living."

"Daddy, what do you mean by informants?"

"Anasuya, let's not fight again. We have been getting on so well today."

"Tell me who these damn informants are."

"Look, I meet a lot of people. I have friends in Liverpool."

"Not among my friends you don't. What you have in Liverpool are hired detectives."

There was a momentary pause before van Niekerk began to deny this nonsensical suggestion. If he had been sober it is possible that even I, who know him so well, wouldn't have apprehended it. But for a split second the defences were down.

"Like you have hired mercenaries in Africa."

That got him too.

"Oh really, Anasuya, I thought we had cleared up that notion long ago. Or has your friend Joseph Manning been inventing things again?"

Well his detectives couldn't be all that efficient. Joseph was eloquent enough about the West Indies—which he had left at the age of three—or about being black in Britain, but he knew less than I now did about Africa. Before his accident his political involvement had amounted to little more than attending Rock Against Racism concerts. Albert was his sister's friend, and not a very close one at that.

"You leave Joseph out of it."

"Anasuya, it's not that I mind you having black friends...."

"Who the fuck asked what you mind at all?"

"...it is just that there are some political hot-heads around and it would be a great pity...."

I stood up. I had to pass between my father and the billiard table in order to reach the door. He leaned forward and grabbed me. He held me by a handful of dress.

"Let go!"

"Anasuya...."

"Fucking bastard. Let go!"

I hit him across the face with my open hand. He swore, and, as he had done at Jennifer when I was a child watching their confrontation in Putney, he swore in Afrikaans. I jerked wildly backwards, ripping my dress, but freeing myself. Van Niekerk lurched to his feet, knocking over the cognac bottle. I tried to dodge him, but he managed to grab me again. This time by my right wrist. I swung at him with my left hand, but he clumsily caught that as well. I screamed, pushed, pulled, and kicked out with my right foot. My shoe flew off. My father pulled me towards him. His face was only inches from mine. He smelt of cognac and his face was very pale, the lines etched like a Dürer woodcut. I couldn't recognise him. I brought my teeth down to the hand that was holding my right wrist and bit. Wildly. Desperately. Van Niekerk released my wrist. The back of his hand smashed against my face.

"Filth," he said in English. Then some more words in Afrikaans.

I tried wildly to jerk my other wrist free, but he closed on me, putting his arm around me, imprisoning my free arm between our bodies.

"You are filth, Jennifer," he screamed at me from three inches in front of my face. "Worse than filth."

We swayed, struggling. I brought the foot that was still in its shoe down on his toes and then tried to kick his legs. I lost balance. Van Niekerk swayed against me and we both went down in a heap. We rolled struggling on the floor. Again van Niekerk swore in Afrikaans, again he called me by my mother's name.

I cannot really remember how long we fought on the carpet between the sofa and the billiard table. I know that at one stage I almost wrenched myself free, that I saw the door to the room in front of me, promising haven and safety, that as I lurched towards it, my father caught me by my ankle and pulled me back. I have in my mind only those frozen, lurid, still pictures like the covers of cheap novels. They are not worth describing. But I remember, as a physical sensation as real and vivid as the sensation of being thrown into a lake of ice, the realisation that my father was about to rape me. He was kneeling on top of me, pinning me. "We will see, Jennifer. We will see," he was hissing between clenched teeth. His face was utterly distorted. It was not human. Those horses. The horse in Picasso's *Guernica*. And the lake of ice engulfed me in a wave that spread upwards from my waist where van Niekerk was sitting to my face and hands, and downwards to my feet. I was made of ice. He had freed both my wrists in order to tear at his flies. I twisted madly under him, almost throwing him off. And the ice turned to fire. I burnt. I twisted again, and again almost dislodged him. He cursed and hit my face. He hit my face again. He hit my face for the third time. For the third time I twisted convulsively under him. The cognac bottle lay on the carpet. Amber and green. Glass. Like the glass of ashtrays. I reached for it. Held it. Van Niekerk moved backwards to sit on my knees, ripping at my underwear. His head was bowed so that I could not see his face. Only the steel grey hair. I hit him as hard as I could. The blow glanced sideways off his head. The bottle left my grasp to bounce off a leg of the billiard table. Van Niekerk swayed. His face turned towards mine. For a moment the muscles relaxed. Picasso's horse became my father. He was bewildered, kindly.

"Daddy," I sobbed.

He shook his head as though trying to clear away the fog of non-comprehension.

"Daddy, Daddy."

I tried to pull my legs from under him. The muscles in his face snapped back into the hard etched lines. With every ounce of strength I possessed I jerked myself into a sitting position, trying to pull my knees to my chest to free them. My father hit me on the side of my face. The room clouded over. He hit me again, but the light was already gone.

I vaguely regained consciousness during the actual rape.

Again I have only a tawdry fixed image: a photo taken from somewhere above the edge of the billiard table. The semi-conscious, battered girl lies unprotesting beneath the heaving man. The couple's clothes are in disarray. A brandy bottle lies by the leg of the table.

The pain, the shock, the coldness and desolation were all to come. The anger, the cold, cold anger, that too was to come. I was never to feel the degradation, the shame that many raped women talk about when they can no longer stand their own silence. I am a child of my generation. I am Jennifer's child. But I was to feel cold, oh so very, very cold. In that lake of ice something, some sliver of the ice, ripped through every layer of myself and entered my soul. It ripped through my laughter, it ripped through my tears, it ripped through my boredom, it ripped through my loving and my hating. Through the child stamping on the gardener's flowers, through the schoolgirl on her mobylette frozen by nothing more than wind and snow, through the student sobbing over her brother's broken back, laughing and embracing Philippe in the hold of the ferry, through the daughter arguing with her father about the burning issues of the day, through every experience, remembered and unremembered, through every human feeling that made me what I was, the sliver of ice passed like a dart.

Six months later in the quarry, when Kilminster was shouting at me, "Don't do it, Anasuya. Don't do it!" trying (as he thought, and probably still believes) to shout reason into the face of blind, unreasoning, white-hot passion, I was nowhere to be found. For there was no white-hot passion in that quarry, there was no unreason; there was nothing, nothing save that cold, cold lake of ice and me in it, looking with reason and precision at the dim figure beyond the short steel instrument in my hands.

The wound has healed all right, but the scar tissue remains. And the coldness is locked inside me.

* * * * * * *

I wrote the account of the rape yesterday. I left Kilminster in the taverna, waiting for some fishermen he'd met the night before who were to take him out in their boat. I came up here and wrote what I had been avoiding writing about ever since I started scribbling in these exercise books. Re-reading what I wrote yesterday, the words seem inadequate, banal. Perhaps they ought to be banal. Hannah Arendt's phrase, "the banality of evil", might apply. I don't know. Writing about the rape was at first hard. The day before yesterday I came up to the bothy with Kilminster, who was in an intense self-absorbed mood. He thought he'd discovered something important about his subatomic particles. It was windy but not very cold. Kilminster sat outside, his knees drawn up to his chest, his padded jacket around his shoulders, writing in one of those little spring-backed pads and tapping at his calculator, sometimes just staring into space and occasionally muttering, "It works, the bloody thing works." I sat in the doorframe of the bothy, on my rock, the exercise book open on its piece of hardboard on my knees. I could remember all the details of the scene, could examine the lurid book jackets at will, could see my father's face and hear his voice, but could not write anything down. For the first time since I started this account the words would not come. I left the bothy and walked out along the small promontory that runs away from the bothy between the bay of Achilli and the next nameless little cove. Two black, shaggy goats jumped away from me as I rounded a rocky outcrop on the ridge. In the nameless cove three seabirds were swimming, riding the swell, occasionally diving into the water beneath them. On still days one can see the bottom of the cove, can watch the birds swimming under water, but on the day before yesterday the surface of the sea was too ruffled. The birds disappeared completely for half a minute at a time. I was tense and irritable. Kilminster irritated me; I resented his obvious absorption, his joy in his manic tapping and scribbling. I returned to the bothy. He was still there, still practising his arcane science. I sat down beside him and extracted the feta and bread and olives we had brought with us. I handed him a thick slice of bread and feta. He munched it without interrupting his scribbling and tapping. I ate a few olives. I wasn't hungry. When I'd fed Kilminster another slice of bread and cheese, I said, "James, do you mind going away. I can't write with you here at the moment."

"Why not?"

"I just can't. I'm blocked."

"What are you trying to write about?"

"Rape."

"Yeah, that would be hard. I'll go."

He stood up, looked at his watch, complained that eleven o'clock wasn't lunch-time and that I shouldn't have fed him—it was news to me that he even knew he'd eaten—and started to descend the goat track to the beach. After he'd gone about a hundred metres he stopped and came back to me.

"If you still can't write anything with me gone, work backwards."

"What?"

"Start writing about what happened in Liverpool afterwards, and then work backwards to what happened in London. I always work backwards from the conclusion I want to its proof. I never start at the beginning."

"Thanks."

"Think nothing of it."

He squatted quickly in front of me, kissed me, and left. I remained sitting with my back to the stone wall of the bothy, my arms around my knees. Kilminster more or less skipped down the goat track. I watched his stick figure on the beach; halfway along the plastic-strewn sand he stopped, stood still. I could just make out his posture: head bent over the calculator in his left hand, right hand madly tapping.

I didn't work backwards. I didn't write anything that day. I spent the afternoon where I was, looking at the view and remembering what happened. In my mind I ran through everything, minute by minute, that happened both before and after van Niekerk raped me. That done I knew I'd be able to write about it the next day. I returned to the taverna to find Kilminster lying flat on his back in the little room he works in.

"It's no good, Ansu. It won't go. There's a flaw a mile wide."

"That'll teach you to work backwards."

"Let's walk to the port and eat fish. We'll get one of the taxis back."

In the café at the port we started talking to the fishermen who offered to take us out if the next day were calm enough. Our Greek is becoming pretty good, although Kilminster will keep slugging the locals with words and pronunciations that went out of fashion when Achilles was still in residence. That bloody seminary has quite a bit to answer for. Anyway, I cried off the fishing trip and Kilminster accepted, brightening up considerably at the prospect. So the next morning I came up here and wrote the rape scene. Now for what happened afterwards.

* * * * * *

I remember lying on the carpet by myself. My father must have left me there, but I cannot recall his departure. I remember the cold. I wished to be warm, so I got groggily to my feet and made my way to my own bedroom. I pulled the eiderdown back and lay curled up into a foetal ball. I shivered but did not sob. I moaned quietly to myself. For a little while I moaned in a crooning, consoling way. My face started to sting. I touched my cheeks, first one and then the other. They both hurt. My lip was swollen and felt cut inside. I ran my tongue over my teeth. They were all there and intact. I crooned and moaned a little more and then left my bed for my bathroom. I looked at my battered face in the mirror. By morning I would have a black eye. My legs and wrists would sport black bruises. My cunt was sore, but not much more than an ordinary night of hard screwing can make it. I looked at my face again.

"I will not be traumatised," I muttered, "I will not be traumatised."

I put on jeans, boots, a shirt and two jerseys, pulled on a blue duffle coat, made sure I had enough money for the fare to Liverpool, and left the house. When I opened the front door a loud bell began to ring, a burglar-alarm type of bell. I walked away from the house, leaving the door open and the bell ringing. I knew vaguely that I ought to go to Tamar's or Joseph's, or any of the other dozen places in London where I would be welcome. Instead, as before, I returned to Liverpool. I had not brought my car this time, so there was to be no midnight drive up the black motorways. In the Bayswater Road I caught a taxi to Euston. I bought a ticket to Liverpool and walked up to the barrier just as the train was leaving. It was the last train.

From eleven forty-five to four-thirty I sat on Euston Station. I didn't sleep. I just sat on a seat. I might have muttered to myself. Occasionally I put my hand up to my face to test my bruises.

Porters and other night workers passed, they looked at me, and looked again. No one hassled me. At one point a cop asked me if I had a ticket. I showed it to him.

"Miss your train?"

"Yes."

The cop strolled off to put the same question to a German couple who had arranged themselves and their bright red rucksacks on another seat. They too had valid tickets: the passports to legitimate vagrancy on the facilities of British Rail. The hours clanked by. A mail-train was loaded with sacks of letters and bundles of newspapers three platforms away. I spoke my phrase to myself a few times. *I will not be traumatised.* I had a feeling that I was "in shock", that it was necessary for me to reach Liverpool before the shock wore off. I clung to my shocked state as if it were a lifebelt, monitoring my feelings. The cop reappeared, put some coins in a coffee machine, and received a white plastic cup from which the steam rose over his face as he drank. I walked to the machine and bought myself a cup. I stood beside the cop, sipping. The coffee hurt my lip.

"You live in Liverpool?"

"Yes."

"You a student or something?"

"Yes."

"Had a fight with your boyfriend?"

"Father."

"Leave in a hurry?"

"Yes."

"Thought you must of. Not many travel as far as Liverpool with no luggage. Even if they live there." The cop looked sideways at my face. "It's going to be a beauty, that eye. He bash you up much then?"

"No, not much."

"You could take him to court. Any witnesses?"

"No."

"Be hard to prove. Probably wouldn't be worth it."

The cop's radio squawked. He pressed a button and said

something into the microphone. The radio gibbered in return. The cop said to me, "It's all action in this job. Some drunk's falling about in the street outside." He left in the direction of Euston Road. I returned to my seat.

I slept most of the way to Liverpool. From Lyme Street I went straight to Kilminster's flat. He wasn't home. He couldn't have been home all night. I let myself in with my key. I was cold. The whole world was cold. I lit the gas fire, made myself some tea and sat for a while watching the strata in the coloured columns of flame. Then I pulled off my boots and slept in Kilminster's bed. He arrived sometime in the middle of the afternoon. I heard him clatter through the door.

"James."

He came into the bedroom. "Ansu. What the hell's the matter?"

Kilminster came across to the bed. I half sat up. I held him. He held me for a while. I felt the shock diminishing, I began to tremble. Then he pulled away a little, looking at my face.

"For Christ's sake, what's happened?"

"I had a fight with Daddy."

"The bastard. How badly are you hurt?"

Kilminster clucked around me, muttering obscenities about van Niekerk. In reply to his questions I told him that the fight had been about him and Joseph. I didn't tell him I'd been raped. Kilminster made a cold compress using a tea towel and chunks of ice that he chipped from the inside of his refrigerator.

"Good job I never defrost this thing. He's a bastard, Ansu, an utter bastard. Do you want to take him to court?"

"There were no witnesses. It's very hard to prove that sort of thing."

"We ought to just shoot him. Or put a contract out. My uncle knows people in the crim scene who'd do it. Probably only cost three or four hundred quid."

I held the compress over my eye for a while. Cold water ran down my wrists and under my clothes, some dripped onto the bed. It was pointless. I'm sure cold compresses have to be applied immediately one is injured for them to do any good. Kilminster rattled on with one fantasy after another about doing harm to my father. I got out from under the bedclothes and took the sodden tea-towel to the kitchen. Kilminster came out after me. We ate bread and jam and drank tea in front of the gas fire.

"Take me to bed, James."

"Eh?"

"Please James, I want to fuck with you."

"Ansu?"

It was only the situation he was reacting to, the total lack of sexual charge. Kilminster and I often fuck in the afternoons. Often after bread and jam and tea in front of the fire.

"Please, James."

"Come to bed then."

We undressed. One on each side of the bed. Kilminster pulled back the covers and we got in. We held each other, stroked, kissed very gently. Even so my lip hurt. I didn't mind. I trembled. The cold receded a little.

"Ansu, Ansu, what else happened with your father?"

"It doesn't matter...I'll tell you later."

"You're trembling like a leaf, little Ansu. And I'm impotent."

"I don't want to be traumatised."

"You won't be. You won't be. What happened?"

I said nothing. I clung to Kilminster. I started to cry. Kilminster said nothing, he held me while I cried and cried. When I had finished he said, "Did he try to rape you?"

"Yes."

"Try?"

"No."

"Jesus."

We lay for a long time, doing nothing, just holding each other. I slept for a while. When I awoke, Kilminster lay around me in a shallow curve. After a few minutes all his muscles tensed suddenly, a spasm like a paraplegic's passed over him.

"What are you thinking, James?"

"Nothing. Of castrating him."

For a while neither of us said anything. I asked Kilminster the time.

"I don't know. It's dark outside."

"Are you hungry?"

"More or less."

"Let's go to Veejay's," I said, "eat, then come home and make love."

"Why not?"

In the restaurant we talked about nothing in particular. Kilminster made an effort to be witty and normal. He just about succeeded. Back in his bed we talked some more; about the château, about Jennifer's new novel which had come out a week previously, about the members of my household.

Then we did not make love. We slept, like children, tangled around each other.

For almost a month I slept every night in Kilminster's bed; his hard, bony shoulder the only pillow I needed. The only anything I needed. We talked a lot, talking in fragments, with fragments of silence and sleep and our intertwined fingers for punctuation. And then one morning I knelt over him and kissed his face and ran my tongue over his eyelids and sat up and rode him slowly to his climax with my breasts cupped in his hands. I didn't come. But I knew I would that night, or the next day, or sometime in the next week.

There is, of course, no mystery about the sudden disappearance of the merchant banker, swindler, and arms dealer, Pieter van Niekerk. No mystery at all. I kidnapped him.

Me and Kilminster together, we kidnapped van Niekerk. There was nothing personal about it. Our motives were wholly political. But you must realise that we were rank amateurs at the game. We bungled it somewhat.

* * * * * * *

I was in a shouting and drinking club in a basement somewhere near the Everyman when Joseph materialised out of the gloom. We kissed. His hair clinked—it was done up like one of those dainty little covers for milk jugs, weighted around the periphery with beads.

"What are you doing here?"

"Looking for you."

"What for?"

"Haven't seen you for years."

"It must be all of a fortnight."

"I can't hear you."

I shouted louder. Joseph shouted back. It seemed he'd been offered a lift to Liverpool and had taken it on the spur of the moment. I was introduced to the driver. He was even more stoned than Joseph; it was a wonder that they'd managed to find Liverpool itself, let alone track me down to that obscure basement. We raved at each other. Given the noise, the state of Joseph's metabolism and my own unwitting susceptibility to the clouds of exhaled smoke in the room, *raved* is probably as good a word as any. The hard datum embedded in Joseph's words only made itself slowly apparent. I wasn't thinking too clearly. I yelled at him to say it again. He said it again.

Friends of his sister Mary whose habit it was to monitor the South African press had arrived with the news that a guerrilla, one Albert John Mbumbira, had been captured deep within that stinking republic. *And those perfectly amicable peasants around our part of France hadn't known what happened to the Jews and communists and Gypsies whom the Germans shipped to the east, they genuinely hadn't known, but they hadn't wanted to know either.* But I knew. And I knew about South Africa. I was well educated, very well educated; the place, in a modest way, had become my area of specialisation, my field. I could quote chapter and verse, author and publisher. I could quote specific examples. With other detainees, *Moke Cekisane was handcuffed to a cement wall with his forehead only a few inches from the surface. Electrodes were attached to the backs of the prisoners' necks....* Oh, I could tell you a thing or two about South Africa. If I wanted to I could cut a very impressive figure in any ego-enhancing, liberal, pinko fabian denunciatory conversation about the régime.

Back at Huskisson Street in the early hours of the morning I managed to extract the details from Joseph, as far as he knew them, which wasn't very far. I realised I'd have to do a bit of research myself. Luckily Joseph remembered the name of the newspaper that had provided the information. We slept until midday, had lunch in the Lord Nelson, and then Joseph and his friend left for London. I went round to Kilminster's place, borrowed his station-wagon and left for Wales.

I found the place I was looking for with surprising ease. I had been there four years previously with Kilminster when he and I and Jennifer and Jean-Claude et al had been holidaying in a rented farmhouse on Anglesey. Kilminster and I had gone for a day's drive, just following our, or rather Kilminster's inclinations. At one stage we had parked the car by a small lake just off the Bala to Llan Ffestiniog road and walked over the bare, rocky mountainside to a larger, more desolate lake. We had eaten our sandwiches watching the mirror images of clouds moving deep under the surface of the water, and then returned to the car by a different route which took us through some abandoned quarry workings. Kilminster has a penchant for bare, ruined choirs, castles, factories, and any sort of deserted wreck. So we had spent half an hour trying to work out from the remains what the buildings had once been used for, where the narrow gauge railway had run and so forth. We had also discovered the drive into the mountain and explored it to the point at which it ended in a cavern in the centre of which was a vertical shaft. We'd stood in the gloomy half-light and thrown rocks down the shaft. It must have been fifty feet deep.

"You wouldn't want to get stuck down there," Kilminster had said, "You wouldn't get out in a million years."

Quite so.

We had returned to Anglesey and talked vaguely of where we had been and what we had seen, but not so that anyone could—even if they wanted to—identify the particular location. And that had been four years ago. There was now nothing to connect me with the quarry except Kilminster's recollections of that distant summer's day. And it was Kilminster I was going to recruit.

I arrived back at Kilminster's flat very tired. I'd driven almost non-stop from Liverpool to Wales and back. It was late evening; Kilminster was just about to go out to dinner somewhere with a woman who looked slightly like Jennifer, ten years younger. I usually get on quite well with Kilminster's women. This one, I forget her name, looked at me a bit suspiciously. Kilminster introduced me as, "Anasuya, my step-daughter." He only does this in situations that he feels need defusing. The formula works every time; god knows why.

"Can I stay the night, James?"

"Of course."

His friend said, "Don't you want to come to the restaurant with us?" as if she meant it. Maybe she did.

"No. No. Thank you all the same. I'm very tired. All I want to do is sleep."

I managed to get Kilminster by himself in the kitchen for ten seconds.

"James, I've got to talk to you urgently and at length. Can you come back alone?"

He looked at me for a moment, puzzled. I don't normally make this sort of request.

"I'll try."

"Good. I'll be asleep, but wake me."

The pair of them left. I drank two glasses of milk and ate a couple of biscuits, wandered into James' bedroom, noted that the bed was unmade and had been recently fucked on. A good sign, the poor girl could be escorted to her own home not entirely unsatisfied. In the spare bedroom I kicked off my boots, which were covered in Welsh mud, pulled a blanket over myself, and was asleep instantly.

Kilminster woke me gently at some time of the night or early morning. He was slightly drunk and looked as if he could do with some sleep himself.

"Do you really want to talk, Ansu? Can't it wait till morning?"

I was awake in half a second, I'd been dreaming of endless tunnels.

"No, I want to talk now. James, we've got to act quickly and effectively."

My words sounded unbearably pretentious, even to my ears. Kilminster obviously wasn't impressed.

"Not tonight, little one," he said tiredly.

I decided to come straight to the point. "I'm going to kidnap van Niekerk."

"What?"

"I'm going to kidnap my father. I need your help."

"Oh sure, anything else?"

"I'm serious, James."

"Look, Anasuya, I'm going to bed. You can stay here or come and sleep with me, but I'm not going to kidnap van Niekerk tonight."

"We've got to talk about it tonight."

"Anasuya, have you gone quite nuts?"

"James, I am very, very serious."

He stood looking down wearily for a few seconds, then said, "Yeah, you are, aren't you? Well we had better talk about it, I suppose. Come and make some coffee."

We spent the rest of the night facing each other across three feet of Formica table in his kitchen. At one point, in despair of winning his co-operation, I said, "If you do anything to bugger up my plan, like tip off Daddy or tell the police, I'll never speak to you again, or sleep with you, or want to know anything about you. If you don't want to come in on the deal, don't. But don't you dare do anything to muck up my plans."

"You can't do it by yourself. If I don't help you, who will?"

"I've got friends."

"I know. French *marginaux*, hot-headed black power adolescents, idiot baby Maoists...."

"That's why I need you. With you the chances of success are

twenty times higher. And you hate Daddy as much as I do."

"That's a very bad motive for a political kidnap."

"You hate the way he makes his money. You've got a better idea than I have how hot it is in those mines. How deep they are. If all those 'rich, gold-bearing deposits' were in any other country they wouldn't be worked. They're not rich at all, they're very poor. And they're a million miles underground. It's only economic to mine them because they've got all this slave labour. When the miners are allowed out of the diamond mines, they get strip-searched and fingers stuck up their arses to make sure they haven't stolen the stuff they've dug up. And Jesus, Kilminster, the miners are the bloody aristocrats, the fortunate ones. Kilminster, you *know* what happens under apartheid.... You've read the reports, seen the films, talked to people who've been there. And I've been living off that sort of money all my life. Those cars, my clothes, holidays, books, the money Jennifer allowed herself to accept from me. Blood. All of it's blood."

I dried my eyes. I went on, "And all the other companies and banks. You read that stuff about breaking sanctions against Rhodesia. He was up to his fucking ears in it. All over the bloody world. Ripping everybody off. Albert asked me how many people died to pay for my Merc. He'll die now. They'll kill him. They'll hang him or put him on Robben Island for the rest of his life. Look, *we're* not going to kill anyone, we're not going to kill Daddy. We'll just dump *him* down a mine for once in his life. And the bastard won't even have to dig for anything. We'll give him all the food he needs, a sleeping bag, the lot. Just think, fucking Daddy cooling his heels down a fucking mine for a week."

"And it's safe, this quarry?"

Ecstasy! Once Kilminster started asking practical questions like that he was half way to agreeing.

"Safe. Dry even. You remember. He couldn't get out in a million years. You said that. Just think, James, just think. Bloody van Niekerk waking up in a mine shaft. 'What? Where am I? Get me Scotland Yard. I've been kidnapped!' Poor bastard, he'll go bananas without a secretary and six telephones."

"We can't do it, Anasuya," he said without real conviction. And *you* had become *we*.

"Of course we can. And we get Albert out of jail. Otherwise they'll hang him. Otherwise he'll be dead. It's all right for us. We will be still able to go jaunting around England and France, slipping out to restaurants with our lovers, flying to conferences here and there, staging exhibitions, cluttering up universities. We will still be able to go on leading our soft, academic, useless lives—you can still worry about subatomic particles and have a dozen girlfriends. But just once, just for a few days, we take time off, we do something real. We strike a proper blow. We'll never be full-time revolutionaries, not you or me, we're too weak, too soft. But just this once, surreptitiously...."

I harangued Kilminster for hours. I doubt that I became any more coherent, but the rudiments of my plan were simple enough. The thing about Kilminster is that he still worries about his immortal soul. Not in any literal sense—he's given up the one true faith all right—but there's a void in the place where his immortal soul once was. The failed priest still needs a clear-cut series of actions that will lead to some sort of secular, humanist salvation. And he knows that being a middle-class academic doesn't provide it. But the need isn't great enough to send him straight out into the revolutionary jungle, or even to the head-quarters of the local Labour Party. Hence the appeal of my plan. I drove the point home.

"At some stage, James, we've got to do something good, moral, useful. If only for a weekend."

"How can we be sure that the South Africans will crack under this pressure?"

"We can't. But the whole place is riddled with corruption. The boards of directors of van Niekerk's companies are cluttered up with members of parliament, generals, ministers, the lot. And they are all in the Broderbund. It's like the Freemasons only a hundred times worse. I can't prove it, but I'm sure van Niekerk is in the Broderbund. They could easily let one captured guerrilla go. But before the trial, before he's formally charged. The sooner we put the screws on the better. Albert isn't famous, hardly anybody knows he's been captured, it hasn't been in any of the western papers. They can let him go quietly without being seen to crack. But we've got to act fast, James. And if they don't release Albert, if we fail completely, then obviously we don't carry out the death threats. That'll be just show. If the worst comes to the worst and we get no results, then we just tip off the cops to Daddy's whereabouts and leave it at that."

By morning Kilminster was to all intents convinced. He still claimed he wasn't, but he was asking a lot of questions and they were all practical: how would we effect the capture, contact the South Africans, arrange for tape-recordings of van Niekerk's voice, make sure we weren't seen, avoid recognition by van Niekerk himself? He said he'd have to think about it, that he wanted to revisit the mine shaft. We decided that he would drive to Wales that afternoon, immediately after a lecture he was due to give, that he wouldn't park the car anywhere near the quarry, but would approach from a point five miles away, looking like an ordinary hiker in boots and an anorak, carrying a rucksack and map-case.

We had breakfast and then slept for three or four hours. Kilminster left for the university, I rang the museum and pleaded urgent and unspecified business in London. I took the train to Euston and spent twenty-four hours checking and researching the fine details of my plan. The beauty of it was simply that, as I had had so little contact with African liberation groups, any number of informers could be bribed or pumped to no avail. Once my father had been kidnapped, no amount of detective work among the urban terrorist fraternities would throw up any leads at all. Even Joseph, the actual source of my knowledge, had no idea that I intended, or was in a position, to do anything about Albert's capture. No one except Kilminster and myself would be involved in the scheme. No one except Kilminster and myself had any real measure of my revulsion for both my father and the way he made his money. And this was even true of van

Niekerk himself: if he had no idea why I'd severed my connections with him, he'd have no idea that I might contemplate his entombment in a Welsh quarry with equanimity. The quarry itself was perfect, the impossibility of van Niekerk climbing out of the shaft would allow Kilminster and me to carry on our normal lives while awaiting the release of Albert, gravity would be van Niekerk's only gaoler. The really tricky bit was going to be the actual kidnap and transportation of van Niekerk to the quarry. The main difficulty we would face was obviously van Niekerk's intimate acquaintance with both of us. There could be no fool-proof disguise effected by our merely pulling balaclavas over our heads. Still, I had a plan and Kilminster hadn't been able to fault it, although he had been trying hard enough.

* * * * * * *

I really ought to try to get inside Kilminster's head at this point. I've become aware that one of the drawbacks to writing this account with Kilminster looking over my shoulder, as it were, is that I'm much more circumspect about what I say about him than I would otherwise be. He only reads the bits I show him, there's no rational reason for not writing about him as fully as I write about myself or Jennifer, but because he is *here*, because he is sharing my daily life, I don't have the distance from him that I really need. His mere presence inhibits me. But since my story now becomes very much Kilminster's story, I had better force myself to see it through his eyes.

Kilminster finished his lecture. He loitered around the lecturer's podium as he normally did for the benefit of any of his students who might wish for further enlightenment. One did; May Sullivan, a girl whose natural lack of ability had not helped her overcome the disruption of her studies caused by her involvement in Philippe's motorbike crash. Kilminster felt absurdly guilty about May, almost as though he, and not his immature pseudo-stepson, had ridden straight into the police car. He led the girl to the blackboard and began to explain the subtleties of vector analysis in a non-unified force field (or whatever the Christ it is that Kilminster teaches his little charges).

"I had some difficulties with vector analysis when I was your age," he said to May as they left the lecture theatre and began to walk to the cafeteria.

"Really?" the girl said, disbelieving.

"Oh, yes, I had difficulties all right. I had quite a traumatic life as a student."

"Oh well," May said, "I suppose there's still hope for me."

Kilminster did not remark that most of the difficulties he had encountered had revolved around his mistress's highly jealous husband, the feasibility of whose kidnapping he was just about to investigate. He drank a cup of coffee with May in the cafeteria and then made his way to the car park. In his car he already had his walking clothes, boots, and two hundred feet of nylon climbing rope he'd bought that morning. He took the road under the Mersey and set course for Wales.

Anasuya was mad, of course, quite mad. The scheme was absurd. And yet she was so intense, so overriding in her advocacy. The trick would be to walk around the quarry, find some obvious fault, and hope the damn girl was in a more sober and receptive frame of mind when it was pointed out to her. The simple fact of the matter was that neither he nor she was an urban terrorist or a Red Brigader or anything else of the sort. Besides they were English. Well, English after a fashion. Still, there was this African. Albert. *They'll hang him, James.* He was alive, Anasuya had met him. But he might not be alive much longer. Even now he might be undergoing torture. In a remote cell, in a remote jail, in a remote country. Van Niekerk's country. Far, far from the brown waters of the Mersey. A long way from Liverpool, a long, long way from the groves of academe. And it might work. Oh, Anasuya was mad, quite mad, but it might work. And, Jesus, he loathed and detested, hated and reviled, wished harm and hurt on van Niekerk. Ansu's battered face. And who was worth more in balance? Albert John and his African surname with its impossible syllables or van Niekerk?

Or James Kilminster PhD (passed) SJ (failed)? It began to rain. Kilminster realised he was talking to himself. The knot in his stomach was intensely familiar. The taste of his own saliva. The tingling that came and went in his finger tips. Christ, I'm losing the bloody faith again. The physical concomitants of indecision. The *déjà vu* of crisis. I have lost my faith, but never myself. The conceit pleased him. If loss of self meant suppression of ego, Kilminster had never lost a thing. From somewhere he watched the man at the wheel of the car, monitored his wildly swinging moods, noted the comparisons with the earlier crisis when the man had contemplated giving up God, knew that within twenty-four hours he would have committed himself one way or the other, and from that point onwards would function with the efficient calm that attended his usual engagement with the world.

He changed into his hill-walking clothes in a layby just before the Welsh border. By the time he'd reached Betws-y-Coed the rain had increased to a steady downpour. For half the remaining drive to Blaenau Ffestiniog he was in cloud. In a nondescript back street he parked the station-wagon and then walked out of town, taking the road that would lead to the point at which he could start the cross-country approach to the quarry itself. The rain drifted in long striations across the landscape; high on the mountain to his left the piles of slate from a still-functioning quarry gleamed dully in the dull light. Kilminster strode on, his head sunk deep into his anorak's sopping hood: a typical English nutter out proving the sterling qualities of the breed by climbing mountains in the rain. A sight as common as sheep. He left the road and began the approach. The spongy tussocks of grass squelched under his boots. He jumped a couple of streams, scaled a stone wall, small common Welsh sheep with long tails scattered slowly at his approach. He reached the incline to the quarry and began climbing. The surface was overgrown with grass and reeds, but still obviously navigable by Landrover. The incline continued at an unvarying rate of ascent to a knoll from which a level track ran to the ruins of the quarry buildings: a gothic folly of tumbled-down winding houses, machine shops and other constructions, all roofless, all built from the rough slate slabs that also formed the piles of discarded tailings that rose around him, the grey and green of the slate and lichen blending into the sodden greys and greens of the mountains themselves. He climbed a low mound of tailings and walked along the bed of the old tram-tracks on its ridge to the entrance of the tunnel. He stood just inside the tunnel looking across the valley to the workings on the opposite mountain, and down to the grey roofs of the township just visible through the rain at the valley's mouth. The incline approach wouldn't do. It would be possible to see the Landrover's lights from the township, not to mention any one of a dozen farmhouses. They'd have to bring van Niekerk in on foot, carrying him like a sack of potatoes. The distance to the little lake on the Bala Road must be about half a mile. How much did van Niekerk weigh? God knows, but he wasn't weedy. Half a mile over rough ground (possibly wet) at night. It could be done, but it wouldn't be easy.

The tunnel ran back into the mountain, a drive about fifteen feet wide and twenty high, the ground was dry and covered with sheep droppings. A hundred yards into the mountain a dry stone wall barred further access to sheep.

Kilminster climbed the wall, dug in his rucksack for his torch and proceeded further in. The tunnel narrowed and continued for another fifty feet or so, where it opened out into a cavern the size of a small meeting hall. In the centre of the cavern another low wall completely enclosed the mouth of the vertical shaft, like the surrounds of a village well. Kilminster peered over the wall, shining his torch straight down. The beam played on sheer walls, descending almost fifty feet to a smooth dry floor. Whatever else, Anasuya was right about the impossibility of van Niekerk climbing out. In the corner of the cavern was a rock of a couple of tons weight which appeared to have fallen from the roof. Kilminster secured his nylon rope around the rock, threw both ends over the wall and down the shaft, removed a few rocks from the top of the wall which looked as if they could be dislodged by a sudden jerk, secured the torch around his neck by its lanyard and climbed into the shaft. He abseiled smoothly to the floor of the shaft, hoping that his rudimentary rock-climbing abilities would allow him to climb back up the rope without too much difficulty. A further tunnel ran back into the mountain for fifty or sixty feet before ending in a solid fall of rock. Kilminster walked back towards the shaft, noticing the imprint of his own boots in a drift of loose dust. He would have to get rid of his boots. In fact when the time came, he and Anasuya would need to abandon all their outer clothing. Burn them, bury them. They had better buy a set of dark overalls each. And gloves. He ought really to have worn gloves for this exploration—when the police came to rescue van Niekerk, they'd go over the place with every gadget they'd got. Kilminster sat on the floor of the tunnel with his back to the wall and the fifty feet of vertical shaft above his head. He switched off his torch. No light penetrated. The air was not particularly cold, the tunnel was quite dry. But it was very dark. It was simply black. It would be necessary to leave van Niekerk with a sufficient supply of light—batteries, maybe a gas lamp, he'd need gas for a cooker anyway. Without light, the sensory deprivation would drive him insane, he'd start imagining things. Should something to read be left for him? What? *The Bible, Das Kapital, The Collected Works of Mao, Cry the Beloved Country*? What should he be left to eat? A collection of tinned meat and fish and half a dozen packets of rolled oats, a few plastic drums of water, tea, sugar, condensed milk. That would have to do, this wasn't a bloody four-star hotel after all. All the tins and packets etc. would have to be gone over very carefully for finger-prints before being dumped down here. How long could van Niekerk be decently left in a place like this? Kilminster sat silently for a minute. Van Niekerk was sure to be wearing a watch; he could keep track of the days. Still, time would drag. Anxiety and despair would be very real. What if he killed himself? If van Niekerk knew that he would eventually be released unharmed, if he could be reassured that his entombment was only temporary, he'd have little but boredom to contend with. There would be no harm in letting van Niekerk know that he was in no personal danger, once, that is, that the tape recordings had been made. A note could be left for him down here, explaining the real parameters of his kidnap.

Kilminster looked at the blackness over his head, there was a pale grey disc just visible where the mouth of the shaft was. Presumably on a brighter day it would be far more clearly defined. Van Niekerk would be quite snug. There was no need to get sentimental. *How long could van Niekerk be decently left in a place like this?* Decently? Van Niekerk? Let him rot. The question to consider at the moment was that of lowering the drugged van Niekerk down the shaft. Some sort of tripod would be needed, say three lengths of four by four, and a block and tackle with a mechanical advantage of at least three. But that sort of stuff could all be brought in with the food and sleeping bag on the preliminary run.

So my mind is made up, he thought, I've decided to go ahead. Seduced by the practicalities of the thing—another problem needing solution. James Kilminster, urban terrorist.

He switched on his torch, climbed the doubled rope without too much difficulty, replaced the stones he had previously removed from the well-like wall and left the tunnel.

* * * * * * *

The light is fading over the bay. Kilminster suggests walking to the village to eat squid if any of the cafés are serving it. I've asked him what his day's work has produced. He says he feels closer to the centre of things. I feel that way myself. I don't know if I'll come up to the bothy tomorrow. Kilminster says we ought to actually visit poor old Rupert's grave. The locals would never forgive us for staying on the island this long and not paying tribute. He's buried somewhere down in the uninhabited southern part of the place. According to Kilminster Rupert cut himself while shaving and contracted blood poisoning en route for the Dardanelles. His fellow officers and poets stopped the ship and buried him. And he never got a crack at Johnnie Turk.

* * * * * * *

Rupert's grave is quite pretty. Marble and wrought iron, wild olive trees and goats. You could paint a picture of it, except that Kilminster's ragbag memory has thrown this up:

> There is an evil which that Race attaints
> Who represent God's World with oily paints,
> Who mock the Universe, so rare and sweet,
> With spots of colour on a canvas sheet.

No friend of the dauber, young Rupert. More into words. Pretty immortal some of them. I had better return to my own all-too-mortal prose. We are due to leave the island in a few weeks and I ought really to have my story finished by then.

The actual kidnap of my father was planned with precision. Kilminster hired a one-ton truck—the sort you don't need a special licence to drive. In Kilminster's garage we built a large wooden crate, seven foot long, three foot wide and three foot high. We used Oregon boards, one and a half inches thick, which we bolted together rather than nailed. We lined it completely with four-inch-thick foam rubber, except for a six-inch-square patch on the lid where we drilled a few holes for ventilation and the insertion of the microphone. We also built two simple and practical benches for Kilminster's kitchen, using the same materials. We weren't fools. We knew all about the impossibility of removing all the sawdust and specks of foam rubber, we realised that a few people would remember that they had heard us sawing and hammering away through half a night. We tried out the crate, it was quite comfortable in a dark, soft, womb-like sort of way. We put Kilminster's transistor radio in it, tuned it to a rock program and bolted down the lid. From outside the garage we could hardly hear anything.

We put the crate in the back of the truck and drove to London. We parked in a street of factories and warehouses in Fulham and then took the tube to Kensington. It was early evening. We walked to the mews behind van Niekerk's house. There were lights on in both the staff quarters over the garage and in the house itself. The dozen or so lighted windows in the houses opposite the garage's roller doors showed no faces. I walked straight up to the doors, inserted the key I had forgotten to give back to van Niekerk when I broke with him, and heard the automatic motors whirr into life. Kilminster and I had not been able to decide whether to open the doors to a sufficient height to allow us to saunter nonchalantly in like honest citizens, or simply to raise them a foot in order to allow us to roll under them. I had not been able to recall if the sound of the doors opening was audible in the staff quarters immediately above them or not. As it was, it sounded as if the noise of the doors' mechanism could be heard all the way to the Albert Memorial.

"Under," Kilminster said.

I stopped the motors, removed the key, and dropped to the cobble-stones at my feet. By this time Kilminster was already inside the garage. The whole manoeuvre hardly took a second. We did it very professionally, just as we'd practised it in Kilminster's flat. We didn't try to crawl under the doors, one at a time with our arses sticking up in the air. Kilminster took one door, I took the other. We dropped to the ground parallel with the doors and rolled smartly sideways. We were in. I crossed to the switch on the wall and closed the doors. The mechanism sounded even louder. It was pitch black in the garage. Kilminster shone his little torch around the place; all the cars were there except the Rover and Bernadette's Volvo. The first parking space to be filled would be the one next to the Issoto Franchini (or whatever the old crock was called). Kilminster climbed into the front seat, I into the back, and Kilminster switched off the torch. In the dark we both pulled first a stocking and then a bala-clava over our heads. I heard Kilminster fumbling with the soda syphon, fitting the little bomb of compressed carbon dioxide to its mechanism.

Then we waited.

"It will be the waiting that will be the worst of all," Kilminster had said. He was right. We waited in complete silence for an hour and twenty-eight minutes. I hadn't seen van Niekerk for slightly over six months. The last time I'd seen him had been on the carpet between the billiard table and the sofa. Meeting him again under any circumstances would have been traumatic, but these circumstances were highly charged to begin with. All the physical attributes of stress made themselves felt: heart like a jack-hammer, hands cold with sweat, muscles stretched tight. In the staff quarters above us someone turned on a radio, its noise coming dully to where we crouched. "We'll both want to piss," Kilminster had also said. He was right again. I was about to whisper to him that I would have to squat beside the Issoto in order to piss into the grate in the concrete floor, and mentally cursing the impossibility of doing so without half removing the overalls I was wearing, when the garage lights flickered on and the doors whirred into life. We both jumped like shot rabbits, but we went into the routine quickly enough. Kilminster crouched on the floor of the front compartment, his head well below the level of the side door. I slumped on the back seat, my head twisted to look out of the small, oval, rear window. My vision of the car turning into the garage was obscured until the last moment by the old crock immediately behind the Issoto. As the car turned, its headlights hit me between the eyes, dazzling me, but not before I'd recognised it as the Volvo.

"Bernadette," I whispered, sliding off the seat onto the floor.

The headlights went out. A door opened and closed. High heels tapped across the concrete. A key entered the lock of the door to the house with a slight snick. The motors above the doors started and the lights went out. We both stayed crouching where we were for ten seconds. My heart pumped wildly. My hands shook. I wanted to piss more than ever. Kilminster eased himself slowly back onto the seat.

"Fucking hell," he murmured.

Had I been by myself, I would have abandoned the plan at that moment. Kilminster later told me he would have done the same thing.

"We'd better get into the other car."

"I need a piss."

"Jesus, Ansu, not now."

"He might not come for hours."

"Well, be quick."

Kilminster made his way to the front seat of the crock behind the Issoto. I located the grate on the floor between the Issoto and the wall. I'd got my arms out of the overall's sleeves when the doors began to retract and the lights came on. As my father's Rover swung into the garage I was crouched on the floor behind the Issoto, struggling wildly back into my overalls. The car came to a halt and its headlights blacked out. There followed about ten seconds of heart-stopping inactivity while my father pressed the button on the Rover's dashboard that closed the doors and extinguished the overhead lights. I watched him from my position between the two old crocks' bumper-bars. The only illumination was provided by the Rover's internal light. It showed van Niekerk collecting his briefcase and some papers from the seat beside him. As we'd feared the evening had been too cold for him to have had the windows down, we would need to wait for him to open the Rover's door. I can remember the feel, the sensation, of those few seconds with utter clarity. I have never felt quite that way before or since. Although the feeling, or sensation if you will, was clear, unified and unconfused, it's hard to describe in words. The words don't exist. Unified, though it was, I think it was an equal mix of loathing and love. The handsome, fine-featured face of the man in the car was that of the father whom I had loved, and who had loved me. His actions, as he opened and shut the briefcase, as he trans-ferred something from his overcoat pocket to an inner pocket of the briefcase, placed papers inside it, were the homely, human actions of my father returning to his family. He was ready for his whisky, the evening papers, the embrace of his wife, the embrace of his daughter had his daughter been at home to greet him. The face of the man in the car was not the face that had screamed my mother's name at me, raped me.

Van Niekerk opened the Rover's door and stepped out. The blast of ether from the driver's section of the old crock hit him straight in the face. He gagged, lurched sideways, brought an arm up to shield his eyes, choked, and began to slide towards the floor. The hissing ether followed him. The briefcase clattered on the concrete. Kilminster's hooded figure leapt from the crock, catching the subsiding figure under the armpits.

"Ansu."

Action. I darted between the cars. We did everything as planned, as we had rehearsed it a dozen times in Kilminster's flat. Only that first sharp use of my name had been against our policy of zero speech, a break with protocol. I picked up the soda-syphon from the crock's front seat and knelt beside my father on the concrete, placing one hand over his eyes—both to prevent him seeing anything should he regain consciousness and to protect him from the further blast of ether I would fire at him. Van Niekerk lay under my hand, breathing evenly, inert. The whole fucking garage stank with the stench of a thousand hospitals. In my stomach I felt again the empty desolation of those first few days after Philippe's crash. The corridors, trolleys, trays of instruments on green linen. Detached, maybe a little stoned from the ether myself, I watched Kilminster slide the hypodermic into my father's vein, watched the little red flower blossom and wither as he tested the needle's position, saw the plunger slide gently to the bottom of the cylinder. Kilminster stood and placed the hypodermic into its box and the box into the grab bag. I handed him the syphon and stood to open the rear door of the Rover while he located the travelling rug in the boot of the Issoto. There wasn't much room, but we managed to roll van Niekerk onto the rug, wrap it around him, and feed the whole sausage into the Rover's back seat.

Kilminster and I jumped into the front seats, ripped the stockings and balaclavas from our heads and dragged the false beard and long blond wig from the grab-bag. They were absurdly inadequate disguises—we had bought them in a novelty shop—but they were not intended to stand close inspection, just to give anybody who might remember seeing us the wrong memories. I grasped the syphon between my knees and leaned over to press the switch that operated the garage doors. Kilminster started the car and then suddenly re-opened his door and almost crawled out of the car. He came upright again in a second, the retrieved briefcase in his right hand. He shoved it onto the floor at my feet and reversed the car out of the now fully open doors.

We drove soberly through the London traffic. We said nothing to each other in accordance with our arranged procedure, although we could probably have chanted our names in unison for all the consciousness my father had at the time. I watched his rug-shrouded form as casually as I could, sitting half-twisted in my seat, my head against the window. Kilminster opened his window; we didn't expect to use the syphon in the car, but we wanted a supply of fresh air for ourselves if it did become necessary. Van Niekerk in his rug did not look much like a human being.

Buses were the most unnerving of the other road-users. At times we were stopped at traffic lights next to one. The interior of the car lay naked and exposed to the dull gaze of the passengers. But no homebound commuter suddenly jerked into a surprised examination of the strange parcel on the rear seat of the adjacent car. We reached Fulham without incident. The street was deserted. We transferred my father into the truck in about ten seconds. We climbed in after him and pulled down the roller doors.

For the first time we had leisure. We were unobserved. Nothing suspicious was happening. We sat on the crate and looked at the sausage of rug at our feet. Kilminster turned to me. He smiled, a tight, optimistic smile. His beard was coming unstuck behind one ear and I pushed it back into place. He touched the back of my gloved hand with his lips in a sort of kiss. I realised we'd left the bag containing the balaclavas in the Rover. I made a rolling gesture over my face. Kilminster nodded. I forced up the door a foot, peered out from a kneeling position, couldn't see anybody, forced it up another foot and jumped down. Two men were walking towards us from the direction in which I had not been able to look. They were about two hundred yards away. I pulled the roller door shut, opened the driver's door of the Rover and got in. The men approached, talking softly to each other. They both wore dark felt jackets with shiny PVC shoulders. I sat in the car; my father's briefcase was on the floor where Kilminster had dumped it. I quickly picked it up and began to rifle through the contents, bending my head, trying to cause the thick nylon hair of the wig to fall forward. The footsteps approached. I consulted the papers before me, absorbed. They would look at me. That much was certain. Unaccompanied blondes parked in expensive cars in deserted industrial streets at night get looked at by passing men. My hands touched a solid metal object. Some papers slid out of the briefcase. A gun. A pistol. I held it, looked at it. It was sleek, short, black; there was a dull gleam of copper from the rims of the bullets in the magazine. The footsteps approached. I slammed my hand into the bib pocket of my overalls. Blondes in Rovers might get looked at, blondes in Rovers with guns in their hands get positively stared at. There are certain universal truths. I felt the men pass, heard the slowing of their feet as they caught sight of me, heard the footsteps recede. I waited. I waited until I could hear them no longer. I was profoundly uncomfortable. I still needed a piss. My knickers were, in fact, damp. I climbed out of the car, found that I had forgotten the grab-bag and had to re-open the door and reach inside to accomplish my original purpose. I pushed up the roller door of the truck a foot, shoved the bag through and, in the space between the back of the truck and the Rover, struggled out of the top half of my overalls, pulled my jeans and knickers down and squatted. As I was pissing the gun fell out of the dangling pocket of my overalls and clattered on the tarmac. I left it there for a few seconds, then picked it up and looked at it. There was a catch under the butt marked "safe". I pushed it forward with my finger and the word disappeared. I pulled the catch back. For a few more seconds I squatted, allowing my bladder to deflate completely. I stood up, rearranged my clothes, stuffed the gun into a side pocket of my overalls and climbed back into the truck. Kilminster looked anxious, but not puzzled: he must have heard the footsteps and me pissing and guessed the reason for the delay. Silently we pulled on the balaclavas and stockings and unrolled my father from the rug. Van Niekerk lay on the truck's floor, breathing easily, like a baby. He looked peaceful and harmless—just a sleeper, neither loving father nor drunken rapist. I took his feet and Kilminster his shoulders and together we lifted him into the yawning coffin of the open crate. We closed the lid and tightened the bolts. We gathered the syphon and other paraphernalia, put the lot in the grab-bag along with the balaclavas and the wig and beard and left the back of the truck.

The relief. Just to be sitting normally in a truck cabin, driving through the night-time streets of London. Just a bloke and his bird in a hired truck like.

I almost sang. Kilminster did hum a little. I turned on the radio and selected a pop station of the sort that Kilminster and I never listen to. I moved across the seat until my shoulder touched his.

"We've got him," I said. It was the first time either of us had spoken since Kilminster had inadvertently used my name after blasting van Niekerk with the ether.

"So far, so good," Kilminster said.

* * * * * *

We almost forgot to post the letter to the diamond company.

[End of entry: Bothy notebooks.]

THE TAVERNA
NOTEBOOKS

My father knew a great deal about architecture. At Leiden he had studied fine arts.

"They never took me seriously," he once said, "I was too much the colonial, too brash. I wasn't pansy enough."

Whatever the truth of this statement, he had a deep feeling for buildings, for their form, design, style. He was competent with a sketch book, although he had had little cause to exercise this journeyman talent since leaving university. Then, on one occasion when I was about nine, he was driving with me through the area behind Printing House Square—I forget where we had been—when he suddenly said, "There is something you should see near here; I'll show you."

We diverged sharply and after a few short streets my father brought the car to a halt in a nondescript bit of roadway.

"We'll walk, it is best to come upon it by foot."

We walked to the end of the street and emerged into Lloyd Square. As we walked slowly around it my father pointed to various houses, noting details of construction and design. I don't know how much of what he said registered with me on that first walk—we were to visit the square three or four times in the future—but my abiding memory is of him saying, "Anasuya, imagine there were no cars here, just horses and carriages; and that this road isn't made of tar, but cobblestones."

"What are cobblestones?" I said.

"Have you never seen cobbles? You must have. Well maybe

you haven't. They're oblong stones like little loaves of bread. They made the roads with them; like stone walls only lying down. There are still some roads left in London like that, we must find one for you."

My father was quite perturbed that I did not know what cobblestones looked like. After we left Lloyd Square we went in search of an example, but before we did we sat on a bench, looking at the houses in the terrace before us.

"The thing about Georgian architecture," my father said, "is that it relies on proportion more than any other style. It is very simple, but if you change the proportions even slightly all the harmony and elegance disappears. Do you see?"

"Yes," I said.

"Do you really see?"

"Well, sort of."

"Look, I'll show you."

He searched in the pockets of his coat and produced an envelope and a fountain pen. Quickly he sketched the outlines of one of the houses opposite us. I watched, fascinated. My father kept looking up from the envelope and then down again. I did the same.

"Now look, Anasuya, do you see how the two windows on either side of the door balance each other and the door as well? Do you see how they are slightly bigger than the three windows above them, and yet they all have the same proportion, height to width?"

"Yes."

"You don't really, but you will in a minute."

He drew the same house again on the back of another envelope, but this time got all the proportions wrong. It was the same house, but plain, ugly, and deformed. I can remember very clearly the feeling I had then as I looked from one sketch to the other. I felt I was being inducted into some mystery, was being shown, if not the secret of the universe, at least a significant minor secret. Van Niekerk started to explain again the nature of balance and proportion.

"No, it's all right, Daddy. I can see now. I can see what you mean."

My father smiled. After a few seconds silence, he said, "The only real way to learn about architectural style is to make sketches of buildings. You have to re-create the building on paper in order to understand it."

He split the envelope he was holding along its edges, folded it inside out and handed it to me with the pen.

"You try."

It was hard trying to hold the envelope in one hand while drawing on it with the other, and I found that even though I tried to arrange the windows and door in the right proportions, my initial outline of the house left me not enough room for the upper windows once the lower ones had been sketched in. I looked at my poor, misshapen child's drawing. It was such a travesty of what I wanted to put on paper, it was so unlike the magic repro-duction of the house that my father had managed with just a few effortless lines. In a burst of frustration I screwed up the paper and flung it to the ground. My father picked up the ball of paper and put it in his pocket.

"Never mind, we'll get you a proper sketch-book and pencils. Let's see if we can find a cobbled street somewhere."

And so started my education into architectural styles and Georgian London in particular. We obtained sketching blocks and all the necessary pencils and pens and often on Sunday afternoons would drive to some building we had selected from the pages of Pevsner or Summerson. If the building were open to the public we walked through its rooms and grounds. My father had a strong feeling for the way the buildings had been lived in or used, although, as I came to realise later, his Afrikaner-Dutch education had left him with only a rudimentary idea of English history. But he would people the buildings and streets we visited with ghosts from the appropriate period.

"Imagine, Anasuya, that a messenger has just brought news of...I don't know...the Treaty of Amiens or Napoleon's abdica-tion. He arrives on a panting horse, but because the news is important, he does not ride around there, through that arch, to the stables. He dismounts before the steps here. He is met by the head footman in knee-breeches and a boy who leads the horse away. He goes up the steps two at a time, with the footman lagging behind slightly. Let us say that the Duke is in the orangery over there with a party...."

After we had thoroughly inspected a building, we would retire to a bench or simply sit on the grass, our sketchbooks on our knees. My father would continue to talk about the building, sometimes stopping drawing to read to me from the guide book or Pevsner. I still have some of my early attempts at sketching. They are not particularly talented, run-of-the-mill, child's drawings. They are fussy in many respects. I often redrew them when I returned home and had a table to work on and could use a ruler to draw straight lines. I believed in straight lines and proper right angles. Even when I had learned about perspective and vanishing points and knew that right angles were almost invariably represented on the single plane of paper by something more acute, I would often use a protractor to establish the angle I wanted. My father's sketches were more freehand, but not very much more. At home he would often add details to his sketches: people in period costume, carriages in driveways, and so forth. Sometimes he would add ink-wash colouring. A few of his better pictures he had framed and hung on the walls of the Putney house. He offered to have any of mine framed that I might choose, but, although I often stuck my drawings to the wall above my bed with sticky tape, I did not wish for the permanence, the public declaration, that a frame seemed to imply.

It was all very amateur, but as my father had originally said, the only way to really learn about architectural styles is to recreate them on paper. I have a feeling for buildings, for the way in which a builder has achieved what he has achieved, that is both intuitive and informed. And this feeling, this way of seeing, is something my father gave me. I have it now and will always have it. It is part of me. Van Niekerk even managed to teach me to look at ugly modern blocks of flats in a new light.

Once we were walking on Putney Heath at a point where the skyline was dominated by three huge blocks of council flats.

"What do you think of those?" my father said.

"What do you mean?"

"How do they strike you? Are they ugly, impressive, pretty, what?"

"Daddy, they're horrible."

"They mass well."

"What?"

"Look."

As on the previous occasion in Lloyd Square, van Niekerk produced envelope and pen. This time he simply sketched the solid blocks of space that were occupied by the flats, shading them to appear as if made of blank, undetailed concrete.

"See how the three blocks stand in relation to each other, this one rising up above the other two like a rectangular mountain behind square foothills? And see how the angle in this one echoes the angle made by the other two? The buildings themselves are ugly because they have no coherence, they are just messes of windows and doors and concrete balconies, all piled up on top of each other, layer upon layer of thoughtless modern mass production, but the three of them, seen as shapes from this angle are impressive. They belong to each other. That's just an accident, of course, from another perspective they would probably be three undistinguished lumps."

To prove his point we walked towards the flats. We left the heath and continued through several suburban streets, losing sight for a while of the flats. When they reappeared again—one entirely visible, the other two rising separately from the roofs of a line of houses—they were unimpressive, just racks of dwellings. From where we were standing, though, we could see children playing in the area around their base. We began to walk towards them. The children were playing with a bicycle among the columns that supported the first floor of flats; they were riding through some complicated slalom course, towing one of their number on roller-skates. Three girls were playing with a skipping rope. As we walked past the building I became foreign. I didn't belong here, it wasn't my territory. Or rather, it wasn't van Niekerk's territory, and I was with van Niekerk. From an interesting problem in aesthetics, from things that "massed well", the flats had suddenly become places where people lived and rode bicycles and towed their friends on roller-skates. For once a building that interested my father was peopled not by Dukes who received news of the Treaty of Amiens, but by living adults and children, some of whom I actually knew in another context.

"Hey, Anna!" the boy on the bicycle shouted. He was called Reggie. He went to my school, although he wasn't in my class. I didn't know him very well. He was short with a snub nose and red hair.

"How you going, Anna?"

"Fine," I managed to mumble.

"That your dad then?"

"Yes."

"Hello, Mr Kneejerk," Reggie called.

"Hello," my father said.

The whole group had come to a standstill. The boy on the roller-skates now detached himself from the stationary bicycle to stand, his arms dangling at his sides like a rag-doll, staring at us. The girls with the skipping rope had stopped their chant. Reggie was the only one I knew by name, although two of the girls I also recognised from school. All the other children were strangers. I suddenly wished my father were not with me. I was only foreign because he was foreign. I was conscious of him standing a few feet from me, wearing the sort of light overcoat that was not worn by the people who lived in these flats.

"You going visiting?" Reggie asked.

"No," I said.

"Anasuya and I are just out for a walk," my father said.

I wished he hadn't. I didn't know if Reggie and his friends ever went for walks with their fathers or not. I suspected not. They'd probably go fishing in a reservoir. There was an awkward silence while we stood on the footpath looking at the group under the concrete bulk of the flats. The group stood looking at us. I could think of nothing to say. Van Niekerk broke the silence by saying, "Well, come along Anasuya."

"Hooroo then," Reggie said.

The group came to life rather like the inhabitants of the castle, once the prince has kissed the sleeping princess, but instead of the cook boxing the page boy's ears, Reggie rose slightly from the bicycle's seat, pushing down on the pedals; the boy on roller-skates drifted across the intervening space to regain his grip on the bicycle; the skipping rope began to twirl, rhythmically slapping the concrete. My father and I walked away. I was determined that all our architectural investigations would remain Georgian or earlier.

I liked having my father to myself. Much as I loved Kilminster, I did not wish him to come on these expeditions. I would show him my completed drawings, but only, I think, because I liked his praise, not because I wished to include him in the mysteries of perspective, proportion, fan-light, architrave, lintel or cornice. But as well as sharing the mysteries exclusively with my father, I also wished to have the pleasure of his company in whatever tea-room or coffee-shop we refreshed ourselves, and I wished the pleasure to be mine alone. From the age of ten onwards, almost all the serious conversations I had with my father were in restaurants or cafés. He liked eating out, and I liked eating out with him. After Jennifer left him, the main event in any visit of mine to Kensington was an expedition to eat somewhere. The type of restaurant gradually changed as I grew older, but in those Putney days, when we had completed our architectural investigation, we would track down some small, genteel tea-shop. In these places, with me sitting opposite him, I think my father was more relaxed than he ever was anywhere else, including home. We would put our sketchbooks on the table and talk about what we had drawn or anything else that came into our heads.

One Sunday afternoon after we had done Somerset House,

we were sitting in a café in The Strand when my father said, "We should really go to Bath to see Regency building at its best. We should make a weekend of it. But first we should read that Jane Austen novel your mother talks about, *Pride and Prejudice* I think it is called. It's set in Bath at the period when all the main public buildings were being erected. It will be good for both of us, I've read very little English literature myself."

Indeed he had. As Jennifer quickly pointed out when he started to read *Pride and Prejudice* to me. We started again with *Northanger Abbey*, which actually is set in Bath. By that age I had more or less grown out of being read to, and previously it had always been Jennifer who read me bedtime stories, but my father embarked on our joint reading of *Northanger Abbey* with dedication. He would read a chapter a night to me, either with me sitting beside him on the sofa or, if I were in bed, sitting where the pillow normally was with my head resting against his thigh. He read well. The stilted, formal manner in which he normally spoke, with its well-constructed, colourless sentences, took on life and subtlety when the words were Jane Austen's. He would stroke my hair as he read, often pausing to explain the story to me or to comment on its development. I was not meant to read the book by myself—this was a joint reading— but of course I did. By the time my father's nightly readings had reached chapter five, I'd privately finished the book. But I missed nothing by having it read to me a second time—my literary tastes were precocious, but Miss Austen required a degree of effort, even from me. We planned our expedition well in advance. The reading would end just before a long weekend. Fully primed by Jane Austen we would motor to Bath, spend two nights there, return via Bristol and Windmill Hill, arriving home late on Monday night.

This expedition was the high point of my architectural education. I continued sketching with my father for a few more years—until I went to France, in fact, and even after the sketching activities had been abandoned I often visited build- ings with him, but we never again captured the innocence, the simple pleasures of that Jane Austen weekend. We stayed in a hotel near Queen's Square and did nothing out of the ordinary—just trucked around like proper tourists, listening to guides, consulting our books, *Northanger Abbey* included. We visited the Pump Room, the upper Assembly Room, the Circus, the Crescent, the lot. We ate sticky buns in the Red House cakeshop. My happiness, my feeling of security, was never higher than on that weekend. It rained heavily late on Sunday afternoon and we decided to abandon Monday's excursion to Bristol and Windmill Hill, but I don't think either of us felt disappointed by this; we had already seen and done so much. I fell asleep contentedly in the car on the way home.

And then, as I've already described, my whole world collapsed, disintegrated. But before it did, on that last evening of innocence in the Eden of our hotel's dining room, my father said to me, "Very soon we will be able to move to another house. Now that you know so much about architecture you should help me look for one. What sort of house do you think we should have?"

This was confusing information. The whole idea of choosing a house with my parents was, of course, very appealing. But I had also grown very fond of the Putney house. Or rather, I had grown fond of Kilminster's funny little flat, with its hissing gas fire and its mad occupant.

"Can James come to our new house?"

My father's expression changed momentarily. I don't think he was really annoyed by the suggestion *per se* that James might come with us, more at its irrelevance.

"Oh, I don't know. I haven't thought about it. But what sort of house do you think we should have?"

"If we got one with a flat upstairs, then James could live there."

"Well, maybe. But would you like us to have a Regency house like the ones around here?"

"Any sort of Georgian," I said.

We settled down to a discussion of Regency architecture. I

wasn't happy with the conversation. I wasn't happy with the prospect of leaving Putney and possibly Kilminster as well. I interrupted my father as he was suggesting that some Victorian architecture was not entirely worthless by saying, "If James doesn't come to our new house, who will babysit?"

"Anasuya, you are almost eleven, you could very well stay at home occasionally by yourself. But, anyway, in our new house I think we might have a live-in maid, possibly a couple."

I returned to a gloomy dissection of the Dover sole I was eating. Van Niekerk said, "You have grown very fond of James, haven't you?"

"Yes," I said.

"Well, there is nothing wrong with that; but sometimes it is not always wise to grow too close to people. Life changes, things happen, one cannot expect to stay in close contact with everybody we come to like."

Looking back on this scene I see myself as being very aware of the feelings involved. Perhaps I was, but it is probably more likely that I simply knew intuitively that on this occasion, away for a weekend with my father, I should not talk too much about Kilminster. I am sure that van Niekerk did not know how much time I actually spent with Kilminster. On the evenings when he "babysat" I spent all my time in his flat, often leaving it at least two or three hours later than my appointed bedtime. Once when my parents arrived home earlier than expected I had had to scramble down the stairs and hurl myself fully clothed into bed. I'd pulled the blankets around my chin and feigned sleep. An adult opened my door, looked in, and quietly closed it. I'm sure Jennifer wouldn't have minded if I'd been up to greet them, but van Niekerk had all these theories about the amount of sleep I required which needed humouring. I'm certain that my father also had no idea of the frequency with which both Jennifer and I spent the hours between four and six sitting in front of Kilminster's fire eating toast. So I shrugged and said to him, "I suppose so. But I don't want to live in a Victorian house, what-ever you say. I don't care about the insides, they all look ugly from the outside."

And so the conversation picked up and we re-established the harmony that was to last for a further twenty-four hours.

* * * * * * *

They have arrested Bernadette for conspiring to murder my father. This is insane. Bernadette couldn't murder a flea. She's too stupid for one thing. For another, she had no need to murder him. She didn't need to murder him for his money, because he gave her as much as she could possibly spend. I simply cannot understand it.

She didn't do it. I happen to know she didn't do it.

We got the letter yesterday. It was from Jennifer and covered in extra stamps and express delivery stickers; not that that makes any difference around here. Mail comes to the island when the ferry comes to the island. If there's a storm or the ferry company decides to send the boat somewhere else, you gets no mail, stickers or no stickers. There had been a warm, wet wind blowing from the south for the previous four or five days—apparently it was the tail end of the sirocco, which, although it may have had all the warmth of Africa in general and the Sahara in particular, meant that the fishermen down at the harbour suddenly found themselves on a weather shore, while on our side of the island the beach below the taverna lay tranquil and sheltered. The fishermen retreated into the cafés, drinking coffee and brandy in small shot glasses, their nets and lines in need of repair in wicker baskets in front of them. They sat, mending their nets like old women darning, muttering about the weather, while outside the café's windows the waves piled up on the unprotected wharf. The smaller boats were pulled across the expanse of tarmac that serves as both waterfront and village square, to lie under the eaves of the couple of shops and cafés that cater to the needs of the port. Kilminster and I were down there a few days ago when the winds were at their height. There was a strong sun shining and the wind itself was hardly chill, but the seas were breaking right across the water-front. The bigger fishing boats, the ones that are anchored just off shore, were tossing at their moorings, the water breaking over their decks. In the sunlight the water was a deep iron grey-blue, the white, broken waves almost phosphorescent. We had to dodge an incoming wave to reach the café. With weather like that the island is effectively cut off from the mainland. No one can leave, no one comes, there is no mail.

So we hadn't had a ferry for over a week. Then yesterday the wind shifted to the north and it began to snow. The temperature fell and the winter came down out of northern Europe full of the cold and ice that has been "crippling" (as they say on the English language news) England and northern France. It's snowing now. From my window I can watch the drifts sliding down between me and the mountains, falling into the choppy waters of the bay. Kilminster has been trying to remember the final paragraph of Joyce's *Dubliners*, the bit about snow being general all over Ireland and falling on the living and the dead and on Michael Furey's grave and further westward into the dark, mutinous Shannon waves. He's worked it up into a fine, dramatic piece although I doubt that it's anything like word perfect. He does a good Irish accent, old K. He says he spoke with one as a child (which is nonsense, he spoke with a Scouse one, like everybody else born in Liverpool). We've got the paraffin heater turned up full blast. Kilminster is kneeling by it, brewing coffee and taking the mickey out of Joyce. It now appears that the snow is falling on Rupert's grave and into the dark, mutinous waves of the Aegean. As indeed it is. From where I sit, a number of tele-phone lines cross the view—they rather spoil the effect, but they provide something for the wind to whistle and moan in. I love the sound of wind in wires or rigging or whatever. It's one of the things I have in common with Jean-Claude. Half the reason why a channel crossing is not really worth calling a crossing if there's less than a force-eight blowing is the absence of proper wire-moaning. One of the great things about Jean-Claude's Renault is its sun-roof. Even in winter, if you turn the alpine heater up full blast, you can open the roof and have this stream of hot air coming up from around your ankles and out of the gap above your head. But if you do this with the empty roof-rack screwed down over the opening the effect is like every typhoon that ever wrecked a ship. The damn thing howls, moans, screams, and whistles. It's the only way to drive down an autoroute.

I digress. But there is little else to do. The situation is overwhelmingly frustrating. Jennifer's elaborately enveloped letter had very little of substance to it, apart from the information that Inspector Michaels had rung her to say that they'd arrested Bernadette and charged her with conspiring with a person or persons unknown to murder van Niekerk. As Jennifer said, "We are all stunned by the news". Indeed. But why? How? With whom? What for? Kilminster and I sat up half the night inventing one crazed explanation after another. The only one that seems to have any possibility of being true is that although Bernadette was receiving all the money she could spend from van Niekerk, she wished to leave him for someone else, but taking the money with her. So she decided to bump him off before he cut her off (as Kilminster insisted on formulating the theory).

We went to the telephone office this morning and after an enormous amount of frigging around got through to the château. The only person at home was Philippe and he could tell us nothing much more than the scanty news we'd already gathered from Jennifer's letter. There have been no new developments; the committal proceedings start in a week or so's time. Bernadette is out on bail, but her whereabouts is unknown. Michaels rang the other day wanting to know when I was coming home. He'd like to speak to me. I'd certainly like to speak to him.

We leave early next week, God, the weather and the ferry company permitting. We should be in Paris three days after that, assuming that Europe isn't so damned crippled by snow that we can't get through.

[End of entry: Taverna notebooks.]

THE BOTHY NOTEBOOKS

In the meantime I'm going to write it all down, write about our bungled kidnap plot. I have bought this notebook down from the bothy. I should be writing up there, but it's far too cold. It's still snowing. I'll sit in my room with the paraffin stove stinking up the place and spin a rope for my own neck. Hang the consequences.

That last phrase just slipped out. The demands of literary style decree that I strike it from the record. This might be the place for gallows humour, but not of the feeble double-entendre variety.

I'll leave it on the page. This is what happened. Kilminster and I took turns driving the truck up the motorways. We reached the side track on the road above Llan Ffestiniog two hours before dawn. I switched off the radio and the truck's engine. It was very quiet. In a clear sky, half a moon hung just above the line of mountains on the horizon. The waters of the little lake shone black and silver.

We put on the balaclavas and stockings. Kilminster picked up the soda syphon and the tape recorder and we made our way to the back of the truck and climbed in.

There it was—the box. We stood looking down at it. My father was inside, quite conscious again.

The night was very quiet, very still. We just stood there for about a minute, not doing anything. Then Kilminster held the tape recorder's speaker above the holes in the top of the box. There was a click and then a few seconds of hissing tape before a voice with a thick, muffled, foreign accent (Kilminster's own voice, actually, distorted by both pronunciation and electronic wizardry) started to inform van Niekerk that he had been kidnapped and that if he wanted out he should start talking. Kilminster switched the machine to record and stuffed the small microphone into one of the larger holes in the lid. There was a certain amount of kicking and shuffling from inside the box and then my father started to speak. I couldn't hear very clearly what he was saying. I didn't want to hear. I jumped down from the truck and walked a few metres towards the little lake. My hands were shaking. Far away, towards the ridge that stood between us and the quarry, some sort of nocturnal bird began to honk—a lonely, clear sound that had nothing to do with me or what I was doing. I turned towards the truck; Kilminster's dark, hooded figure motioned to me. I climbed back inside.

Kilminster squirted a blast of ether through the ventilation holes and we waited for half a minute and then undid the bolts that held the lid in place. My father lay like Dracula in his coffin, the stench of ether was overpowering. Again I sat with my left hand over my father's eyes, the soda syphon in my right. Kilminster produced the hypodermic needle and injected the anaesthetic. There was enough moonlight in the back of the truck for us to see what we were doing without using the torch, I could even read the *For Animal Use Only* sign on the bottle (it's a lot easier to obtain illegal veterinary supplies than it is to get the same stuff if it's designed for humans). Kilminster, however, is now not clear if he managed to get the full amount into the vein. In any case, van Niekerk stayed sleeping peacefully and we manhandled him out of the coffin and set off across the ridges for the quarry, Kilminster carrying my father over his shoulder like a fireman rescuing someone from a burning building. We stopped twice for Kilminster to rest and change shoulders. I carried the airline bag with the soda syphon and torch. We reached the quarry entrance and I switched on the torch; Kilminster swore and almost dropped van Niekerk; I jumped, quite literally jumped, backwards at least a foot. Thirty or forty eyes regarded us from the depths of the cavern, shining like marbles.

"Sheep," we both said.

"No talking," we both said.

We entered the tunnel, the sheep retreated to the wall which prevented further access, and then, as we approached, stampeded past us in single file. Kilminster laid my father on the wall. We both climbed over and carried him between us the remaining fifty feet, the torch dangling from my wrist by its lanyard. We laid him on the ground about ten feet from the low wall around the mouth of the vertical shaft. To leave my hands free I left the torch propped on a stone on the tunnel floor. We retrieved the tripod from the place behind the fallen rock where we had hidden it on the supply run two days earlier. We erected it over the shaft and as I was fixing the block and tackle to the apex, Kilminster returned to the fallen rock for the slings.

There was a sudden crack and a flash of flame from the corner of the cavern. Kilminster yelled "Christ!" and appeared to fall to the floor. Another explosion, and a chunk of wood was torn from the strut of the tripod above my hand. For the second time in five minutes I jumped convulsively backwards. For an instant I thought there must be some fourth person in the cavern. From where I crouched the torch and my father were obscured by the retaining wall. Then I saw the shadow of his head and shoulders on the ceiling, enormously large, distorted by the irregularities of the rock. The shadow suddenly grew to encompass the whole cavern as my father reached for the torch. Darkness.

"Stay where you are, Dino," van Niekerk said groggily, "I have a gun."

He didn't sound very compos, he must have been still sitting down.

Dead silence. Jesus, I must think. I needed to be cold, to be rational. My father thought we were Dino and friend. My father had a gun. He had the torch. Kilminster might have been hit. Kilminster might be dead. Jesus, no, please, no. If van Niekerk thought I was Dino, or Kilminster was Dino, anyway if he thought one of us was Dino, he would expect us to have a gun. Or guns. Yes guns. Only we weren't Dino and we didn't have guns. Yes we did. Of course we did. I did. I must think. Time was running out, with every second van Niekerk was gaining sense. Why hadn't we checked his pockets? It didn't matter now. He had a gun, but he couldn't use it without turning on the torch. He wouldn't turn on the torch if he thought this would make him a target for our guns. Or gun. My gun. Get the fucking thing out of your pocket for Christ's sake.

"Stay where you are," Kilminster hissed. It wasn't clear to me who he was talking to, but I had no intention of moving from behind the retaining wall anyway.

"Kilminster?" said my father.

Silence.

"I know it's you, Kilminster. And you, Anasuya."

Silence.

"You are filth, Kilminster."

Silence.

"Anasuya, come here."

For thirty seconds nothing happened.

"I am going to shoot that dog, Anasuya. Come here out of the way."

I *was* out of the way. Kilminster was a good twenty feet from me. My father was going to shoot James.

And then I became very cold. In the lake of ice every possibility, every move and counter-move, were clear before me. Van Niekerk was not yet convinced we were unarmed, otherwise he would switch on the torch. He might have guessed we had the gun from his briefcase in our possession. He could probably be induced to turn on the torch if he thought we were unarmed, thus presenting me with a target. But he might shoot James before I prevented him from doing so. I had never fired any sort of firearm before. I would probably miss at anything but point-blank range. I believed that if I pushed the catch below the butt so that the word *safe* was obscured, all I would then need to do would be to pull the trigger. This might not be the case. I had heard of the process of cocking a gun. Did this gun need cocking? I didn't know what was entailed in the process. There was a small semicircle of moonlight at the end of the tunnel, anyone who crossed it would present a target of sorts. Kilminster did not know I had a gun.

I moved a few paces to my left, not leaving the squatting position I had adopted. I now believed I had an unimpeded line of fire to the point where my father was. There was a sudden scuffling from Kilminster's direction. He had now put the retaining wall between himself and van Niekerk. He was about five feet from me, breathing hard. Van Niekerk said, "Come here, Anasuya."

Kilminster said, "Turn that torch on, van Niekerk and you're dead. I'm armed."

"Come here, Anasuya. I'm not going to harm you. This is not your fault. You've been led into this by that dog, Kilminster. Come here, Anasuya."

I decided to walk up to my father and shoot him.

"Daddy, I'm coming over to...."

There was a violent bright white explosion behind my father. He stood, silhouetted by the flame, a statue in an overcoat holding a gun in one hand and a torch in the other. The light disappeared, but not its after-image; I could see nothing but the cut-out statue against the light whichever way I turned my head. Through the singing in my ears I heard and felt Kilminster rush towards van Niekerk, brushing against the gun in my hand in the process. There were cries from both men as they collided, then the sound of scuffling. I heard my father say "filth" and then some words in Afrikaans. I was powerless. I walked slowly forward, holding the gun in both hands. I stopped a few yards from the sounds of fighting and heavy breathing. I could see nothing. My father's gun exploded with a thin flash of flame. There was a grunt, a scream, another random shot from the gun. Suddenly one man rolled across the floor to my feet. I jumped backwards. The sound of running footsteps pounded down the tunnel away from us.

"Who's that?" I said.

"Anasuya," the figure at my feet grunted.

"James."

"Ansu, are you all right?"

The figure now clambering over the sheep wall was my father. The upper part of his body came into view against the dim semi-circle of moonlight. The after-image of the explosion still superimposed itself on my field of vision. I struggled to see only the figure now swinging one leg over the wall. I fired, holding the pistol in both hands at arm's length. I fired until all the bullets in the gun were spent. Each time the gun gave a little kick, I brought it back into line. I could not actually see the barrel of the gun itself, just the black mass of my two hands and the gun, obscuring and then revealing the figure sitting on the wall.

"Don't do it, Anasuya! Stop!" Kilminster shouted from the ground at my feet.

Then there were no more bullets. And the wall had no figure sitting on it. I just stood where I was, holding the gun, entranced.

"Anasuya," Kilminster whispered.

"Yes," I said.

"Come over here, behind the wall."

I made my way to the retaining wall, almost tripping over one of the tripod's legs. A hand touched my arm. I sat down beside Kilminster, the wall between our backs and the tunnel entrance. For a while neither of us said anything. Then I said, "Are you all right?"

"My arm's hurt. I think a bullet hit it. You?"

"I'm fine."

"How did you get hold of his gun?"

"I didn't. This is another one. I found it in the car."

It took some time for this to sink in. Kilminster wasn't thinking very clearly. I couldn't remember why I hadn't told him about the gun.

"Christ," Kilminster said after a pause, "It means he might still have his. He might be sitting there at the entrance waiting for us to come out. Are there any more bullets in that one?"

"I don't think so. It just stopped working, it must be empty."

"Do you think you hit him?"

"I've no idea. First he was on the wall and then he wasn't. That's all I saw."

"That's all I saw too. He stayed there a long time. He just sat there. Maybe you did hit him, maybe that was why he didn't dive over."

"I don't know."

We just sat there behind the wall of the shaft for an hour. It grew slowly lighter at the entrance to the cave. We said little, we both shivered from time to time. At one point I whispered, "What was that explosion?"

"The ether in the syphon. I threw it at him."

When it was light enough for a dull greyness to illuminate our surroundings, I peered around the side of the wall. The sheep-wall cut a clear, unbroken silhouette across the mouth of the tunnel. In the place where the struggle had been I could easily make out the yellow plastic shape of the torch and what could possibly be the other pistol.

"I think I can see the gun," I said.

"I'll crawl over and see."

"No you stay here. It's safer for me."

I crawled on my stomach to the object. It was the gun. It was exactly the same sort as the one I'd found in the briefcase. I took the gun in both hands again and walked slowly down the tunnel to the sheep-wall. I looked over.

My father lay on the ground.

There was a small amount of blood on his overcoat.

I walked back to Kilminster.

"He's dead, James."

We both walked to the wall and looked over.

"Yeah, he's dead."

And then, saying almost nothing to each other, we continued with the plan we had decided upon when we envisaged van Niekerk as being alive. We carried him back to the shaft and lowered him gently down into the black rock. We jiggled the ropes holding the tackle until the hook cleared the slings. We cleaned up the cavern and dropped both guns, the bits and pieces of the soda syphon and all the spent cartridges we could find, down the shaft after my father's body; but carefully, we dropped them carefully so that they wouldn't hit the body of the man lying below. We hid the tripod and block and tackle behind the rock.

We returned to the truck, took off our overalls, boots and gloves, placed them together with the wig and beard and our balaclavas in the crate, added three large rocks and very loosely secured the lid. We floated the crate on the chill waters of the little lake and pushed it away from the shore, a slight breeze carried it a further six or seven metres before it slowly turned over and began to fill. Then it sank.

We returned to Bootle where the truck had been hired. As it had been planned that only Kilminster would have dealings with the hire company, I got out a block away and Kilminster drove the last couple of hundred yards using only his right arm. I picked him up in the station-wagon and drove straight to the university. We were seen by a number of people eating breakfast in the cafeteria. Then, in Kilminster's room, we made a copy of the tape which we put in a padded envelope addressed to the diamond company to whom we had already sent the written ransom demand. The original cassette we put in a water-tight plastic container that Kilminster pilfered from a laboratory store-room at the end of his corridor. I rang Ivan, told him I'd been unwell all night and would not be coming in to the museum, left Kilminster to his academic duties, and spent the middle part of the day driving to Manchester and back. I posted the padded envelope in Manchester's central post office and stopped for five minutes on the return journey to bury the original cassette in a nondescript little copse by the side of a minor road. With luck we'd not need it, but if the diamond company was slow to react we had plans for further demands on various other companies and banks.

Then I went home and lay on my bed and looked at the ceiling and murmured, "Now what?"

* * * * * * *

It's still early in the day, but I can't write any more. It has stopped snowing. I am going for a walk. I half wish I drank; if I did, I'd get drunk.

* * * * * * *

I've been re-reading the results of the last few day's writing. Tawdry little tale of bungling, isn't it? Dialogue very weak. Characterisation poor. Too much fussy detail. Plot barely credible. Jennifer could have written it better. Jennifer could have *done* it better.

Look, that's what we did. That's how we did it. That's what we said to each other. All right?

I'm sorry about the aggressive tone of the last remark.

I'm really not feeling very sane at the moment.

* * * * * * *

The phone call from Scotland Yard came towards evening. It was a relief of sorts. Once I'd been "told" about my father's disappearance, I had a legitimate excuse for the depression and anxiety that had overwhelmed me. After the initial incident in the quarry, I suppose I was in that "shock" condition that I've talked about before; I was in a state of mind in which nothing really seemed to impinge on my feelings, in which I had no feelings, just thoughts and perceptions. And, of course, there had been all the action of carrying through the rest of the plan. The action had alleviated the necessity of feeling. Now, lying on my bed in the attic, there was nothing to do except feel and brood. I felt the protective layers of shock slipping away. I couldn't name my condition; I couldn't remember if the word was *parri-*

cide or *patricide*. I couldn't separate the action from the actor. Maybe the act of patricide is committed by a parricide. Maybe it's the other way around. From where I was lying on my bed I could see my copy of the *Concise Oxford*, its blue, green, and red dust-jacket so tattered that it had almost parted along one edge of the spine. I love dictionaries. Kilminster once called me a dictionary freak; for a birthday present one time, he gave me the photo-reduced edition of the whole thirteen-volume OED. It sits on my table in my room in the château in its blue Oxford University Press box with a small drawer above the two heavy tomes for the magnifying glass. But in Liverpool I had a *Concise*, a *Webster's*, the *Penguin* dictionary, a *Larousse* and a couple of volumes of *Harrap*. I have little pretence to scholarship, I'll never be an academic, I might never even finish my degree, but dictionaries I know and love. I sometimes read them as other people read cookery books, thumbing through, looking for a good word, something tasty for dinner. *Stamina* is the plural of *stamen* and was used as a plural rather than a singular noun until quite recently. In the middle of the eighteenth century Fielding wrote, "I am convinced there are good stamina in the Nature of this very Man." (OED) Pedants and other moth-eaten hysterics who object to the English language's adoption of *media* as a singular collective, rather than an ordinary plural noun ought to take heed of this. There is something satisfying and consoling about the columns of print in a dictionary; the ordered marshalling of the language, the sober precision of the definitions is almost loving. So I lay on my bed looking at the covers of my dictionaries, the *Concise Oxford* and *Webster's* in particular, knowing that sooner or later I would reach across the three feet of space between my bed and the bookshelf and see in the calm, ordered prose the label that now applied to me. But for the time being I just lay feeling the realisation ebb and flow.

Daddy I killed you.

I am a murderer.

My father who played with me when I was a child, who walked with me around Lloyd Square, who loved me more than anyone else, is dead. Is no more. Will never be again.

I shot the rapist, Pieter van Niekerk. With luck I will have exchanged the rapist's life for the liberty of Albert John Mbumbira. And if ever an end is justified by a means, this one is.

Just less than ten hours ago it hadn't happened. Just less than twenty hours ago Kilminster and I could have called the whole project off and no one would have been the wiser.

Time moves in only one direction. Time moves away from events that have occurred. This time tomorrow it will be just less than thirty-four hours since it happened. It will be just less than forty-four hours since Kilminster and I could have called the whole project off and no one been the wiser. The numbers of hours will increase with the passing of time. They will always increase. There will be no count-down to a point at which the effect of my actions will be reversed.

I am not dreaming; therefore I cannot wake up.

What has happened is fixed.

And there is no mystery about the sudden disappearance of the banker, swindler and arms dealer, Pieter van Niekerk.

I shot him.

Stone dead.

I shot my father with a pistol, killing him.

I am a murderer. I am guilty of murder. Also of kidnapping. Also of demanding ransom against an already expired life. Add fraud to my crimes.

The sudden release, the explosion of sensation that just writing these words has produced, is electrifying. I have been sitting for five minutes looking at the above paragraph. My handwriting is normally very neat, very controlled. That paragraph is scratched into the paper with an ugly, decisive power. If I write these words often in this exercise book, it will be to permit myself the clarity, the knowledge that I can name absolutely the actions I have committed, the sober, dictionary joy of definition.

I shot my father. Daddy, I killed you.

What is it about the written word, that it holds this extraordinary power? It is not that I have been prevented from speaking these phrases—I've done so often, alone, and when talking to Kilminster—but the spoken word evaporates into the air that gives it life. These ink marks on paper are at once outside myself and the material products of my own volition. They are both object and subject.

I am a murderer.

Kilminster says not. He says it's a pity we killed van Niekerk, but we could not have continued with our plan once he had recognised us. Albert's freedom (and indeed our own) is worth more in the scale of things than van Niekerk's life. We were forced to exchange one for the other. If van Niekerk hadn't had all those dealings with Pretoria, we wouldn't have been in a position to make our ransom demand. The South African régime deals in murder, consistent, institutionalised murder; the money that van Niekerk made from his shares in the diamond and gold mines alone, was made at the expense of a definite number of African lives. To make that sort of money in that way, is to forfeit any claim to an inviolate right to one's own life. Kilminster can be very persuasive when he is using these arguments. "We killed van Niekerk, but we didn't murder him, Anasuya, don't ever say we murdered him. In this sort of struggle, necessary killing isn't murder." I know these arguments backwards; they are the ones that I used when I was recruiting Kilminster to my scheme. He was a very reluctant recruit, he was very unimpressed with these self-same arguments, he thought phrases like "in this sort of struggle" sounded as unnatural on my lips as they now sound to me on his. I think the argument that really won him over on that night in his kitchen when I harangued him across the Formica table, was simply that without his help I might fail. Well now we are both failed kidnappers. After a fashion. We are what we are. We have done what we have done.

I reached over from my bed for my dictionaries. Both *parricide* and *patricide* exist in the language, although *parricide* has a wider scope and may be used in any case in which the killer and the killed are related. In my case, *patricide* is the word to be preferred, since the child-father relationship is the only one permissible. There is no distinction between the action and the actor.

I am a patricide. I have committed patricide.

Oh, Daddy, I wish I wasn't and I wish I hadn't. Daddy, it wasn't you who raped me, it was someone else. It wasn't me who shot you. It was someone else. Show me the houses in Lloyd Square again, show me the importance of proportion on the back of an envelope.

It was you all right, Pieter van Niekerk. And you'll never do that or anything else again. And I am cold, as cold as the lake of ice into which you threw me. And I was so very, very cold in that quarry this morning. I held the gun so steadily. Every time it kicked with the departure of a bullet, I brought it back into line so very steadily, so very, very coldly. That's why you're dead.

But it is not why I tremble. I do not tremble for the cold. I tremble because I shall never walk with you in Lloyd Square. Never, ever again.

* * * * * * *

I heard the telephone ring. Clara called up the stairs. "Anasuya, for you. Long distance."

Scotland Yard said there was no real cause for alarm at this stage, there was almost certainly a perfectly good explanation for my father's disappearance, but Mrs van Niekerk was worried and so they were making some routine enquiries. Did I know my father's whereabouts or anything that might help locate him?

No I didn't.

Was my father a homely sort of person?

Homely?

Did he often spend a good deal of time away from home?

He travelled a great deal.

But in London?

To the best of my knowledge he did not have a mistress. But my knowledge could have been at fault. I had not seen very much of him lately.

Scotland Yard repeated that I should not worry unduly at this stage. They would let me know if there was any news.

I thanked them.

"Anasuya, what is it?" Clara said, "You're as white as a sheet."

"My father is missing. Someone might have kidnapped him."

Clara put down the book she was holding. She embraced me, comforted me with words. I clung to her, trembling. She made me sit down. Spoke more comforting words, made me tell her what Scotland Yard had actually said. Clara was sensible and concerned. She repeated Scotland Yard's point about not worrying unduly. He had, after all, only been missing since last night. He would probably turn up very soon.

"Yes," I mumbled, "Don't talk to me, Clara. Just hold me. There's nothing to say, just hold me."

Clara held me. She held me while I trembled and shivered. After a few minutes she said, "Honestly, Anasuya, I'm sure he'll turn up. He might have just lost his memory or something.…"

"Don't talk, please Clara, don't talk. Sing me something."

"What shall I sing you?"

"That Silkie song."

Clara sat with one arm around me and sang, accompanied only by the hissing of the gas fire and the occasional noise of a passing car outside.

> And he has taken a purse of gold,
> And he has placed it upon her knee,
> Saying "Give to me my little young son
> And take thee of thy nurse's fee."

I kissed her and made my way upstairs and lay on my bed again. As it was getting dark, Kilminster arrived. He closed the door to my room and sat down next to me.

"Scotland Yard rang," I said.

"Clara just told me."

"They don't seem to know anything."

"Good. Listen, about my arm, I've worked out a possible accident, but it needs your help."

Kilminster was very efficient. His manner had lost none of the purpose of those hours of planning and rehearsal. The wound in his arm, so the story went, had been caused by his electric saw. I had been using it when we were making the benches for his kitchen; Kilminster had been screwing down one of the legs at the other end of the bench. We had both stood up at the same time; the saw had nicked his arm. He made me get off the bed and together we acted out the manoeuvre using an imaginary saw and an imaginary bench. The accident seemed to fit the wound exactly.

We both sat on the bed. For a few minutes the movement and purpose of the little play we had enacted lifted my depression slightly. Kilminster said, "The only thing to do now is sit tight and wait for news of Albert."

"And then what?"

"We'll know we have succeeded, that it wasn't all in vain."

"Do you think they'll try to hit back at Albert when they get no news about Daddy?"

"If Albert's got his wits about him, he won't stay around London. He'll probably take off for Tanzania or Moscow or wherever."

"What if he goes straight to Tanzania without contacting the papers?"

In our letter to the diamond company we had specified that Albert was to be put on a plane to London. He was to be told to contact Walter Black of the *Guardian* with a story about conditions in South African gaols or anything else that would be newsworthy and would include his name as informant. We'd stressed that Black had no knowledge of the ransom demand, that we had chosen him simply because he was a reputable journalist with a wide knowledge of African affairs. We had hinted that Black knew Albert personally and could not be fooled by a pseudo-informant claiming to be Albert. This last might have been true, but probably wasn't. Walter Black certainly knew a vast number of people in African political life—he had stayed the night at the château once and he and Jean-Claude had bored the rest of us silly with detailed political discussions which included a lot of unpronounceable names of which Mbumbira might have been one. The story that Albert would give Black when he arrived in London would be the signal for van Niekerk's release. Now it would be the signal for nothing; or rather, as Kilminster said, it would be the signal that the whole exercise had not been completely in vain.

"There's a certain inelegance to it," Kilminster said, "Now it doesn't really matter if Albert contacts Black or not."

"Inelegance?"

"The plan is now not so neat, it ends raggedly."

"James. Please. I'm very depressed. I've just killed my father."

"I know you have. We both have. I was there just as much as you. It's immaterial that it was you who had the gun."

"You were yelling at me to stop."

"I'd completely lost my head. If you hadn't kept your wits, we'd both be in gaol now and Albert would have no chance of escape."

"And Daddy would be alive."

"Anasuya!" Kilminster hissed at me, "That man raped you. It's past the time when you can carry on about him having been your father. You shot a rapist. And now we are waiting to see if we've got a genuine revolutionary out of South Africa. Do you understand? We can't afford to be sentimental about a rapist, about a man who owned shares in slave labour camps. You can't afford it. We can't afford it."

I looked at Kilminster. The poor bastard was trying so hard. Kilminster the hard man, steam-rolling through the slush of sentiment with a curt nod to the brute realities of our present position. He was doing a good job, but I knew him too well. He was ten years older than me, but we'd grown up together, I knew what he was really feeling and thinking. And I knew that he had no cold centre; that it was me, not him, who'd been thrown into that lake of ice.

"Listen, James, I'm not going to crack up. I'm not going to confess everything to the police at the first opportunity. I've probably got more reserves than you have. But I'm also going to be very depressed for a while, and you are going to be the only person I will be able to talk to openly, so you'll have to listen to my talk about Daddy, see. It's no good being the hard man; that's not what I want or need."

"Yeah, you're right. Sorry."

"And *I'm* going to be the only person you can talk to as well."

"True."

We sat in silence for a while and then Kilminster said, "What about Jennifer?"

"What about her?"

"Should we tell her?"

"What good would that do?"

"We could talk to her. You could talk to her; I may not be sufficient support for you."

"And I may not be for you?"

"I don't know."

"She's still your great Mother Confessor, isn't she, James? She's still the ultimate recipient of your fears and anxieties."

"Yes. Isn't she that for you as well?"

"I didn't tell her about the rape."

"That's true. I never understood why not."

"I didn't need to. I talked to you, made love to you. And I talked to myself, I came to know I could contain ice and fire at once and still stay whole. Do you see?"

"Sort of."

"What do you think I was feeling when I was shooting? Do you think I felt nothing but blind hatred and white-hot anger, or that I'd totally panicked?"

"I don't really know. Something like that, I felt something like that myself."

"Ice. I felt like ice. I was as clear and as cold and rational as one of your calculations about neutrinos. If not shooting had been the right thing to do—tactically—I wouldn't have shot."

"And you don't need to talk to Jennifer?"

"You'll do."

There was a knock and Magpie put his head round the door. He was wearing a second-hand homburg hat with a badge pinned to it which read *Stamp out silly badges.*

"Hi," he said, "You lot eating here tonight?"

"Am I invited?" Kilminster said.

"Of course not."

"Then I'm pleased not to accept. Cider or beer?"

"Either or both."

Magpie disappeared. Kilminster looked at me and shrugged. "Life goes on," he said. "Come for a walk to the off-licence."

I love cities at night. I like walking through them, even if it's raining, especially if it's raining. The ink is blacker and the gold more golden. I put my arm through Kilminster's.

"Shit!" he said.

"Sorry."

I changed sides and with my arm linked to Kilminster's good one, we walked through the ink and gold to the Irish off-licence. I began to tell Kilminster about the planned opening of our Liverpool Docks exhibition. Within a fortnight I would be unemployed.

* * * * * * *

For eleven days I scanned the pages of the *Guardian*. Four times there were stories under Black's by-line. Each time they had nothing to do with South Africa or Albert. Kilminster and I were starting to talk of digging up the tape and sending new ransom demands to van Niekerk's other concerns. All the stuff about the Hong Kong bank collapsing was beginning to fill the front pages of the dailies. It was hard to estimate what effect, if any, this would have on our South African excursion. The press started pestering me for reactions to it all. The last-minute preparations for the exhibition's opening kept me up half of most nights. Life was becoming just a leetle bit wearing.

Then, on the twelfth day, there it was: *New Allegations of S. African Torture. In London yesterday Mr Albert John Mbumbira said....*

We'd done it. We'd got him out. An hour after I'd rung Kilminster with the news, Scotland Yard rang me again. An Inspector Michaels would like to talk to me. So I arranged to meet him, and later I talked to him as I've already described.

* * * * * * *

And that's what happened. That's the end of the story. There is nothing more to say. Except that they have arrested Bernadette for murder. For *conspiracy* to murder.

[Greek notebooks, both Bothy
and Taverna series, end of last entry.]

THE CHÂTEAU
NOTEBOOKS

La France. Oise. Château. My own bedroom. Home. Family. Jennifer *et al. C'est bon. C'est très bon.*

Old habits die hard. I've decided to continue my Greek practice of keeping a journal, although I can't be bothered keeping two sets: the incriminating and the non-incriminating. Indeed the way things are at the moment I'm none too sure I can make the distinction.

I've found a place in the château where I can hide the notebooks. It's in the loft, between the fibreglass insulation batts and the slates of the roof itself. It's easy to reach and quite impossible to stumble on accidentally. I'm not going to write in the loft, it's as cold as the North Pole up there, I'd only draw attention to myself and die of pneumonia.

I'll write in my room where it's warm and secrete the notebooks in their hiding place at my leisure.

* * * * * * *

So what the hell is going on? The theory that Kilminster and I almost convinced ourselves was correct when we first discussed Bernadette's arrest on the island was that Michaels was playing an elaborate game to induce me to confess. That is to say, Michaels knows that Bernadette didn't do it. He knows or suspects that I did do it. He believes that I am decent enough not to let an innocent party take the rap for something I did.

Therefore if it looks as if Bernadette will be lumbered with the crime, I can be expected to make a clean breast of it.

That can't be right, can it? Sitting around our paraffin stove late at night with the Aegean crashing on the beach and the wind howling in the telephone wires outside our room it seemed feasible. At least Kilminster thought so, but he's not met Michaels. I can't see Michaels playing that sort of game. He's too decent to let an innocent party suffer the agony of thinking they might be convicted of a murder they didn't commit. Unless, of course, Bernadette is in on the act, unless she's a willing accomplice. But Bernadette is even less likely to play that sort of game than Michaels. Also, while that sort of elaborate cat-and-mouse game-playing may make rattling good Le Carré reading, it's not actually *British*, it's not how the common English fuzz work.

"Tell that to the IRA," Kilminster said. Kilminster doesn't exactly love the IRA, but he's got the good old working-class Liverpool Irish opinion of the English police so deeply ingrained that he'd suspect them of anything but decent and intelligent behaviour. So would I normally, but not Michaels.

The committal proceedings provided some enlightenment, but not a lot. They were held while Kilminster and I were driving gingerly up through Yugoslavia on roads about as wide as toboggan runs and twice as slippery. When we reached the château, Kilminster stayed the night and then left for Liverpool. He rang me as soon as he'd read all the relevant English newspapers. The prosecution had called Dino Torri of all people as their star witness. It seems he's turned Queen's Evidence, which means that if he helps the fuzz shop Bernadette, they'll let him go free on whatever they might hold against him.

"What did I tell you, Ansu? The buggers'll stop at nothing. They'd sell their own grandmothers to get a conviction."

"All right, James, all right. What did Dino say he'd done?"

"He claims Bernadette approached him with a plan to murder van Niekerk. He wouldn't touch it, of course. Wouldn't touch it with a ten-foot barge pole. I mean, it's wrong, isn't it? Murder, it's against the law, it's not right.…"

"Get on with it, Kilminster."

"But a spot of blackmail. Well, she was asking for it, wasn't she? I mean, it serves her right, doesn't it? Thinking up a nasty plan for a nice man like that."

"So he blackmailed Bernadette?"

"Yeah. He told her he was prepared to go ahead with her plan, but he wanted it in writing that he, Dino, would be paid a million quid for it."

"She didn't? The twit. She didn't put it in writing?"

"No, not according to the prosecution. She can't be completely stupid. She and Dino had a long argument about it in some seedy hangout Dino had invited her to; Dino insisting that he wanted it in writing, Bernadette insisting that her word was as good as her deed. In the end Dino finished the argument by declaring he'd never had any intention of going ahead with the plan, but suggested that a thousand pounds a month from now to eternity might keep the tape-recording of the conversation they'd just had from ever reaching his old friend, van Niekerk's, ears. Cunning eh?"

"Kilminster, do you think she actually *did* this?"

"That's what the papers say the prosecution says she did."

Which was all Kilminster was prepared to say over the phone. I shouldn't have asked him; we'd agreed not to say anything out of the ordinary over the wires. Still, there was no harm done, it was a perfectly reasonable question.

For the benefit of anybody tapping the wires, I said, "So who actually did it, if Dino didn't? She can't have done it all by herself."

"Either the prosecution aren't laying all their cards on the table at this point or they don't know. The charge is only conspiracy after all. Maybe your friend Michaels will be more informative next week."

I've arranged to see Michaels in four day's time in London. Kilminster and I talked for a bit longer as if we knew nothing more than the general public and then Kilminster rang off pleading the high cost of international calls.

And that is all I know.

So my dilemma is this: regardless of whether or not Michaels is playing some fiendishly cunning game (which is highly unlikely) what do I do if it really looks as if Bernadette is to be convicted for what I, in fact, did? Say she was utterly innocent, that Dino's tape was a complete hoax; then obviously I'd have to confess.

Wouldn't I?

I think I would. I *think* I'd have the courage to do it.

But it seems unlikely that Dino's tape is a hoax. Bernadette really must have been trying to murder my father, she must have been doing it for money. I beat her to the punch, but I did it under duress, in order to save an altruistic kidnap plan from failure. I also did it to save myself and Kilminster from arrest and imprisonment. I also did it as an act of revenge for what van Niekerk did to me. So even though, by the mere accident of timing, it was me who did the deed, it is right and proper that Bernadette takes the blame and I go scot free while she cools her heels in gaol for a few years.

Very neat, Anasuya, very neat. Amazing how things work out in your favour, isn't it?

So what do I do now? Nothing for the time being; see what Michaels has to say in London next week; hope to hell the prosecution fudge their case, that Bernadette gets let off and we both go free—that all *three* of us go free. There is no way I could confess without implicating Kilminster. I recruited him, I can't act merely in accord with my own wishes.

Jesus, Jesus, Jesus.

* * * * * * *

Back in the bosom of my family. And it is good to be so. It's good to be able to talk in English or French to more than one person. I love Kilminster. Having spent four and a half months on that island with him, I know him and love him more than I ever did. But there were times, there were times when the constant conjunction did become just a bit trying. I think I came to understand very clearly, not only how Jennifer fell head over heels in love with him when she first met him, but also why she eventually left him for Jean-Claude. There are times when Kilminster's presence becomes too much; you want to dilute him. Kilminster is too intense and too feeble at the same time. If the intensity of his preoccupations could be somehow diluted by the feebleness of his convictions, he'd be much easier to live with. It would have been better, also, if our party had contained more than just the two of us. The islanders were friendly, the islanders were quite stunningly generous and entertaining, but there's a limit to the amount of real communication that can take place between northern European intellectuals and southern European peasants through the medium of pidgin Greek. Especially if, as in my case, one doesn't drink retsina.

There are only eight people living in the château at the moment; it is almost empty and yet it feels like a modest hotel in high and festive season. Philippe has given up his wheel-chair entirely, he lurches around the place on crutches in a mad French version of Long John Silver. Jennifer's latest novel has won some prize. Bernard is refusing to learn English, or rather he is refusing to speak it. Jennifer and I religiously only talk to him in English, but he answers only in French. Jean-Claude says it doesn't matter. I could go on, but I'd rather live my family than write about it. I've got enough other stuff to write as it is.

* * * * * * *

I went to England last week and saw Michaels at Scotland Yard. I was shown into another of those comfortable, anonymous interview rooms. Michaels was just as affable as before. He called for tea and biscuits again, asked how my holiday had been, made a few appropriate comments about the weather and then said, "Well, I don't suppose you'd expected events to take the turn they have."

"Frankly no. I can't believe she did it."

"It's hard to credit, I know. Of course in cases like this we always suspect anybody who stands to gain considerably from the deceased's estate. Just as a matter of routine, you understand. And we always suspect spouses of murdering each other. The majority of murders are committed by the husband or wife—it is the most domestic of crimes and one of the most easily solved."

"But those sorts of murders are done out of passion, aren't they, as part of a fight, out of jealousy? The husband strangles his wife and then rings up the local police, who come round and take him away."

"Most. But some are done out of greed, to speed up the inheritance process."

"But that's what I can't understand. My father wasn't mean, he wasn't ungenerous, he kept showering presents and money on the people he liked, loved. He would have given Bernadette anything she wanted. She probably had one of those Bottomless Pit bank accounts like I did."

"A joint account with your father? She did; she still has. That's how she can afford Grearson."

"Who?"

"Grearson Q.C., her barrister."

"Good grief, is that his name? How odd. Do you know where he went to school?"

"Who?"

"Grearson."

"Well, no. Why?"

"Oh it doesn't matter, it's irrelevant. My mother has a character who appears in a few of her stories called Grearson. She pinched the name from one of her brother's school-friends. It might be him. It doesn't matter."

"Well it could be, how interesting." Michaels was clearly intrigued. "Of course," he said, "Grearson carries the footless soldier in that funny little parable or fable or whatever it is."

"He also turns up in *Pig Fat and Chapatties* as a blundering British subaltern."

"The one who keeps singing *God Save the Queen*?"

"That's right. How much of my mother's stuff have you been reading?"

"Well, quite a lot actually. I 'discovered' her after I started work on this case. I thought I'd have a quick dip into one of her books to see if there was anything that might give a hint or two about your father's character. Well...actually, I don't suppose that was the real reason. I interviewed your mother as you know. She, err, fascinated me. I hope you don't mind me saying this, I'd never met anyone quite like her."

The scene was becoming quite cosy. Michaels had assumed the demeanour of one of those English country parsons who write to *The Times* about the first cuckoo of spring. All we needed was for the interview room to become a book-lined study and for the functional radiator against the wall to become a cheery coal fire and the pair of us could have spent a jolly afternoon really getting to the bottom of this little problem in literary detective work. As it was, Michaels solved the problem in two minutes flat, but I'll swear he actually rattled his tea cup as he said, "Just a minute, Miss Tamar, I think your old friend *Who's Who* should be able to tell us." He left the room and returned with the fat book in question. Grearson, Q.C., LL.B., etc. etc. and Goldstein M.B., B.Ch., F.R.C.S., etc. etc. were of an age and had both risen from the ranks of the same undistinguished little boarding school. "That's them, all right," Michaels said with satisfaction, snapping the book shut. The first cuckoo of spring had been positively identified, it only remained to reach for a sheet of the vicarage's notepaper and to pen the message to Printing House Square. There is a difference, I told myself, there is a very big difference, between a literary vicar playing detective and a detective playing literary vicar. One's in the job of saving souls, the other is in league with Jack Ketch in dispatching them smartly back to their maker. Well, not exactly; in England they've retired Jack for the time being at least. But the stakes were high; becoming cosy with Inspector Michaels wasn't really where it was at. I said, "Have you read *The Tides of Winter?*"

"Oh indeed. I thought it was much better, much more subtle than the Mutiny novel."

"I'm not Anna."

"Oh, good heavens," Michaels said, "I never thought you were, not for a moment."

The vicar was quite perturbed at the thought. It hadn't crossed his mind. The vicar lied with the practised ease of the trained detective.

"Well," I said, "You must be one of the few people who've met me and not made that connection."

"Well, perhaps it's the similarity of names that causes it. Your mother should really have called her Felicity or something."

"Perhaps," I said.

With reluctance the vicar brought the conversation back to the grim matters in hand. "When we last spoke, you said that Mrs van Niekerk had been actively trying to reconcile you with your father. Do you think you could elaborate on this, please?"

"Well...I don't know what there is to say. She sent me a couple of letters trying to convince me I ought to re-establish contact with my father. She came to see me about this once; drove all the way up to Liverpool to do so. I'm sure I told you about her visit last time we spoke—we arranged a little reception party for her. She went on and on about how much my father missed me and how upset he was."

"Do you still have her letters?"

"I don't think so. When I left the Huskisson Street house I threw out everything that wasn't essential. Bernadette's letters aren't really essential documents."

"Well they may be. Are you sure you don't have them?"

"How could they be important? They're the most empty-headed ravings imaginable."

"You're quite certain you didn't keep them along with other more important papers and things?"

"Hell, I don't know. If I did keep them, I know where they'd be; in some boxes of my stuff I left in Kilminster's garage. But why?"

"Can you remember how Mrs van Niekerk wished you to meet your father? What she specifically suggested?"

Michaels obviously wasn't going to answer my questions about the letters' importance, at least until I'd answered his about their contents. I stared at my feet, as if trying hard to remember the exact wording of the letters, trying very, very hard to work out why they were important.

"Christ!" I said.

I was still holding the saucer and now-empty cup in one hand. There was no play-acting about the sudden rattle of one against the other.

"Bernadette wasn't going to.... She wasn't thinking of killing me as well?"

Michaels said nothing for a while. He just looked at me, very seriously, and then said softly, "Do you suspect that she might have been planning this?"

"Well, no. At least not until just now. Do you want to know what she suggested in her letters because you think she was trying to get me and Daddy in one place so that she, or Dino... or whoever she recruited after she'd failed with Dino, could... could murder us both at once?"

"Miss Tamar, I know all this is very disturbing for you," Michaels smiled, gravely, understandingly, "but do you mind if I insist on following the protocols of my profession? At this stage, I'm afraid, I can't really answer all your questions, much as I'd like to. But I would be very grateful if you'd answer mine."

"I still can't believe it of that woman. She's such a twit. She's so empty-headed...I'm sorry. As far as I can remember, the first letter invited me to a weekend party at some place in Sussex. Bernadette was going on ahead, but if I liked to come to London.... No sorry, that's wrong. Bernadette was going to remain at the Sussex place for a few extra days, but I would be able to drive back with my father on the Sunday night.... Oh, Christ! Is that what she was planning? Was she going to put a bomb in the car?"

"Do you think you could remember as exactly as possible the wording of the letters?"

I spent the rest of the afternoon trying to reproduce the contents of both Bernadette's letters and the conversation we'd had in my attic. At one point, after the stenographer who'd taken down my formal deposition had left the room, I said to Michaels, "Look, can you tell me one thing? Can you tell me the provisions of my father's will?"

"As we haven't been able to locate the body, your father isn't officially dead; so his will is still a private document in the hands of his solicitors."

"But you obviously know what's in it."

"I think it would be fair to say that the will contains the provisions your father told you it contained."

"He never told me anything."

"Oh," Michaels said, "Oh, I see. We thought...." He seemed just slightly flustered.

"Why did you think I'd been told about the will?" I said. And then, just to push home my advantage, I said, "You must have reasons."

"Look, Miss Tamar, I'm afraid that among the documents we have been studying is a complete file of your father's correspondence with you."

"Including my letters to him?"

"I'm afraid that is the case. Of course under normal circumstances...."

"Yes, yes, of course. These aren't normal circumstances. But what's this got to do with his will?"

"In one of his letters to you he outlines the broad provisions of his will."

"Must have thrown it away unopened. I threw a lot of his letters away.... But what was in this one?"

"Well, umm, I suppose you have a right to know. We'd assumed you'd already read it. I take it I can rely on your strictest confidence?"

"Of course."

"In complete confidence then, in your father's will you receive the lion's share of the wealth. You are virtually his sole heir."

"You mean I own all those crashed banks and diamond mines and shit like that?"

"There will be enormous legal complications. It will take years; and as we have not yet found your father...."

"Did he leave nothing to anybody else?"

"There are provisions for various other people and for bequests to a number of charities—the National Trust, a school of architecture, the Courtauld, etc.—but these were all fixed amounts and quite small."

"Who were—are—these other people?"

"Your mother receives the largest single amount, two million pounds."

"Oh, as you say, quite small. Peanuts. Poor old Jennifer. What about Bernadette?"

"The Kensington house and a half a million."

"Look, Mr Michaels, what happens if I'm eliminated? Wouldn't my next of kin, Jennifer, get it all?"

"You will keep all this quiet, won't you? From our point of view, from the prosecution's point of view, it is essential that our friend Grearson Q.C. does not learn how much we know or suspect."

"Yes, of course. I won't tell a mouse. Although Bernadette must have been told about the will...."

"We believe she was. She probably knew the specific provisions for disposing of the estate if you or your mother are unable or *unwilling* to accept it. It's not normal practice to allow for an inheritance to be refused...."

"Daddy was no fool. What actually happens if we're unwilling?"

"It's complicated, but Mrs van Niekerk's share increases dramatically, very dramatically."

"And the same thing happens if I'm *unable*, if I'm dead?"

"Yes."

I sat for a moment, trying to work out the ramifications of all this. Then I said, "But I wouldn't have accepted a penny of van Niekerk's money. I would have been unwilling. I am unwilling. So what's in it for Bernadette? Why this alleged attempt to bump me off?"

"If you were faced with a decision between accepting a fortune that you could then dispose of in any manner you wished, say by writing cheques out to organisations like Amnesty International...."

"Or Rasta Action...."

"...or Rasta Action, and allowing control of the money to pass into the hands of Mrs van Niekerk and a few others...."

"Yes, of course, I see. Sorry to have been so thick. All this has come as a bit of a surprise to me; I'm not thinking very clearly."

As I was standing up to leave I thought I'd try Michaels for a few more details. I said, "Look, after Dino Torri refused to do the job, Bernadette must have recruited somebody else."

"A person or persons unknown."

"Are they really unknown? Do you have no suspects?"

Michaels suddenly looked very tired. He took off his glasses, rubbed his eyes, cleaned the lenses, and replaced them. For a moment I wondered if it would be over-familiar to kiss him when we eventually parted; I suppressed the idea. I said, "Look, she must have been wanting to leave my father for someone else, for a lover, maybe the person unknown is her lover."

"Do you know if she had a lover?"

"No."

"I assure you we've looked for one. With no success."

I was suddenly overcome with a sense of utter disbelief. I couldn't credit Bernadette with anything other than worrying about her make-up. I said to Michaels, "Do you really, honestly, think Bernadette or someone was going to put a bomb in my father's car?"

"Strictly speaking I shouldn't tell you this. But the opposition are well aware that we know it; and it will all come out at the trial before you take the stand. There was a bomb in your father's car. There were bombs in both the Rover and the Bentley."

"What?"

"All wired up and good to go."

"What?"

"When we were examining the car we discovered in Fulham we found an unexploded bomb hidden in the upholstery of the driver's seat. It was very well hidden, and was a very sophisticated device. It had a switch, which only had to be thrown to activate the system. Once switched on, the device would have remained inactive until about twenty minutes after the car had been started. Then it would have exploded. There was a similar bomb in the Bentley. They could both have been in position for months—your father's bodyguard says he could easily have cleaned the interiors of the cars half a dozen times without discovering them."

"Bodyguard?"

"Martin."

"Who?"

"Brian Martin, he...."

"Oh, Brian. He's the chauffeur."

"Well I believe he had a number of duties."

This was all becoming a bit much. I sat down again. I felt very cold inside. I looked at the policeman, he wasn't smiling. I said, "So these bombs could have been switched on at the first opportune time? That is to say, just before my father and I set out somewhere alone in one of his cars?"

"Possibly. That's a quite possible scenario."

"Well there must be at least one person unknown. Bernadette could not have manufactured and installed bombs like that. There are some things I am simply not going to believe about that woman."

And here the policeman smiled. "No, Miss Tamar, I don't think you will ever be asked to believe in Mrs van Niekerk the mechanic."

I left Scotland Yard in a daze. I walked to Marble Arch and then took the tube to Joseph's place. I spent the night with him. He said he'd heard that Albert had been in town, but was now believed to be in Dar es Salaam, but the news was a few months old, he could be anywhere by now. In the morning I took the train to Liverpool. I'd promised Michaels I'd go through my stuff in Kilminster's garage to see if I could find Bernadette's letters. I'd told him I'd mention nothing of what he'd said to anyone.

Kilminster and I walked by the docks. The weather had improved and the dirty snow had melted. The Mersey surged, brown and sluggish, under a weak winter sun. Kilminster said, "I'd say they don't know very much, that all their investigations have come up against brick walls. If all they are doing is charging Bernadette with conspiracy, it means they don't think they've got much hope of pinning the actual murder on her, and they don't think they've got much chance of finding her accomplices. They probably think that if they can get a conviction for conspiracy they can play some sort of Queen's Evidence trick again. Promise her no further prosecution and an early release if she tells all and leads them to the people who actually murdered van Niekerk."

"About whom she knows nothing."

"Quite so. But she knows who put the bombs in the cars, she knows who would have murdered van Niekerk, if they hadn't been beaten to the punch."

We walked in silence for a few minutes and then Kilminster said, "I wonder why Michaels told you about the bombs and the will."

"Daddy had already written to me about the will...."

"Yes, yes, I know. But Michaels still didn't *have* to tell you. He can only have told you because he thought it would be good for his investigations. Or perhaps he thinks it will affect the way you give evidence, make your evidence stronger, give you more conviction."

"Oh don't be paranoid, James. He told me because I asked him. I've a perfect right to know, and anyway Michaels and I have a sort of rapport...."

"The fuzz, Ansu, are after results and nothing else—even your precious Michaels. He probably wanted to shore up your conviction that Bernadette was out to get you. You are going to be the star prosecution witness. Nobody in their right minds would believe a word that lying hound Dino Torri says, but van Niekerk's innocent young daughter.... That's what it's all about, Michaels just wants to make damn sure he shops Bernadette."

"So what do we do?"

"Nothing. She's a murderer, albeit a failed one."

I felt unimpressed by Kilminster's assertions, but I didn't wish for an argument. I murmured something like assent.

I took a train straight to Heathrow and a plane to Paris. On the way I solved the whole case. It's quite simple. Michaels can't find Bernadette's lover because there is no evidence that she was ever seen in the consistent company of another man (or woman for that matter) whom she could possibly want to leave van Niekerk for. Well of course she'd never been seen in his company, or at least only riding around in the back of his car. Bernadette had contracted a liaison with Brian. Right under van Niekerk's nose. Brian, to put the matter bluntly, had done a Kilminster. Of course Brian the chauffeur and loyal body-guard hadn't "discovered" the bombs while cleaning the cars, he'd put the bloody things there in the first place. It was all so clear, it couldn't have been otherwise. There was that time when Bernadette had come to visit me in Liverpool. Bernadette had alighted from the front seat of the Bentley. She'd been sitting *next to Brian.*

I can just imagine myself telling that to a judge and jury. Grearson Q.C. would have a field day. You can't convict people for murder because they sit next to the drivers of cars.

But do I want to convict Bernadette? Or Brian? Kilminster thinks we ought. Kilminster's a moralising old papist. God, in

Kilminster's court, wears a black robe and has a silly wig on his balding pate. I dunno, I dunno. I'll play it by ear.

* * * * * * *

The charges against Bernadette have been increased. She is now formally charged with having conspired to murder me as well as van Niekerk.

* * * * * * *

I'd been expecting some sort of gothic horror show: stained glass, dark panelling, Dickensian clerks on high stools, the dimly heard clanking of chains from the dungeons below. All reasonable expectations, if you ask me, this was the Old Bailey after all, not some tuppenny-halfpenny magistrates' court where they process shop-lifters and drunks by the score. But not all the Old Bailey is actually old at all. Number Seven Court where Bernadette was facing her Nemesis was a modified sauna bath. I was very unimpressed. The walls were panelled in blond Norwegian pine or something similar. The chairs, tables, and dividing partitions were all made of the same wood. Above the panelling the walls were white. There was no glass, stained or otherwise, for there were no windows, just filtered fluorescent light that threw no shadows. In this setting, Grearson, Mutimer the prosecutor, and Millard the beak all looked a bit silly; their robes, wigs, and bifurcated bibs contrasted none too well with the sauna bath décor. To change the metaphor—they looked like broken-down old public-school masters who'd strayed into a secondary modern by mistake. Above Millard's head was a cheap plaster coat of arms, *Honi Soit Qui Mal y Pense*. Shame on him who evil thinks. It became apparent soon enough that if the amount of thought evident in Millard's handling of the trial were anything to go by, we were well insulated from shame and evil, both. At first it wasn't clear to me who was Grearson and who was Mutimer. I was, of course, very interested in clapping eyes on Simon's old school-friend. The man was one of the great anti-heroes of my childhood. It was as if I had suddenly been given the opportunity of meeting Batman or Donald Duck. I had half a mind to ask him for his autograph. But before I could make positive identification a clerk handed me a copy of the Christians' bible and a card carrying some guff about swearing by Almighty God. I swore by Almighty God and settled down to the serious business of perjuring myself to hell. Mutimer got to his feet (thereby indicating that the other black-robed gent was Grearson) and began a series of tomfool questions about how long I'd known Mrs van Niekerk and what my relations with her had been like and so forth.

I said I'd known her for years and regarded her with considerable affection and was sure that this conspiracy to murder nonsense was all a terrible mistake. Mutimer looked a bit put out by this. I was, of course, *his* witness. My testimony was meant to put Bernadette behind bars, not hand her acquittal to Grearson on a plate. Millard woke up from his doze on the bench and told me to stick to answering counsel's questions and to refrain from expressing generalised opinions as to Mrs van Niekerk's innocence or otherwise.

"But look here, it's me she is meant to have been bumping off. Surely my views should carry some weight."

"Miss Tamar, you are here as a witness for the prosecution. Just answer those questions that are put to you."

"Oh, all right."

As all this was going on, I looked around the courtroom. The dock ran along the back wall. It had seating for a dozen or so accused, but contained only Bernadette and a policewoman. Bernadette sat very still. She looked a bit lost. From where I leant against the witness box's lectern I couldn't see her hands, but I knew what she was up to. Kilminster had been in the public gallery the previous day and had been able to look straight down on her. If nothing else, the trial would prove a godsend to the manufacturers of pale grey kid gloves. I smiled at her, poor, idiot, bungling twit. She managed a shadow of a smile in return. High up, to my right, was the public gallery. Packed. Ghouls and sensation seekers: tourists, Americans and Japanese, Kilminster. In a box across the room, a dozen good citizens and true were keenly following the argument, writing with practised ease on the pads in front of them—the fourth estate, Jean-Claude's lot. Not a word will I hear against them. In their own compartment the jury sat like stunned mullets, their court-issued pads as innocent of the written word as the tabula rasa itself. I watched one of them come slowly to life, prod one of his fellows with a pencil, and subside into his original torpor.

The afternoon proceeded. Mutimer abandoned his line of questioning me about my relations with Bernadette and got down to the serious stuff about the content of her letters and her attempts to get me alone in the car with van Niekerk. I was, I'm afraid, a bit vague. It was all some time ago. By this stage I'd decided quite definitely to call a halt to the proceedings. In fact from the moment I'd entered the court and clapped eyes on the dove grey and alabaster figure of Bernadette throttling her gloves in the dock, the dozy mound of black cloth and dirty white wool that was Millard, the jury nodding and gawping, the ghouls in the gallery, from the moment the whole absurd ritual had attempted to claim *me*, I'd decided enough was simply enough. It was now almost a year since I'd decided to kidnap van Niekerk in a quick in-out operation which should have been completed in a week, and still the crazed consequences of that exercise plagued me. It was in my powers to stop it all, and stop it I would. But first, Grearson QC.

Grearson, to put the matter bluntly, was a trifle aggressive. Whatever else the much-vaunted old-boy network does, it clearly doesn't afford much protection to one's old classmates' nieces. And Grearson must have known perfectly well that I was his old friend, Goldstein's sister's daughter. But, I suppose, being as he was pig-ignorant as to the state of the case, knowing nothing about the trial's imminent disruption, nothing about my feelings concerning the conviction of Bernadette, probably convinced at the back of his mind that his client had, in fact, murdered her husband, he could not really be blamed for trying so hard and so stridently. He presumably thought his manner and comportment were necessary in order to reduce my evidence to tatters. All the same, I doubt that Batman or Donald Duck would have proceeded with such lack of chivalry. Anyway, it soon became apparent that I couldn't really be sure that the statement I'd made to Michaels about the content of Bernadette's letters was very accurate, or indeed accurate, or even slightly accurate. Grearson postured and probed, declaimed and submitted, peered down his bifocals at the record of my statement to Michaels, tugged at the lapels of his gown with his well-manicured hands and generally earned his Bottomless Pit cheque. At one point Mutimer tried to stem the rout.

"Millard! I submit that my learned friend's questions are being put in a spirit of hostility. There is no need to browbeat the witness."

Millard started to mumble something incoherent, but I cut in smartly with, "It's quite all right, Millard, really it is. I don't find the questions overly hostile. It's probably just Mr Grearson's normal manner; the poor man can't help it any more than he can do anything about his feet."

Everyone started to speak at once. Millard almost woke up. I don't think he had understood my remark about Grearson's feet; he didn't look the widely-read type, snappy literary allusions were almost certainly beyond him. In his confusion all he could do was drag out a few more tired clichés about me being only a humble witness and it not being my job to decide whether counsel was being hostile or not. I subsided into docile silence. Millard told Grearson to get on with it, but to bear in mind the proprieties of courtroom procedure; for all her attempts to take over the running of the court, the witness was, in fact, being extremely co-operative. Grearson said, "Thank you, Millard," and continued with his questions, being just as aggressive as before. For the first time in my life I began to develop an understanding of, if not a sympathy for, Old Soames-Pritchard. By late afternoon my evidence lay in shreds and I was dismissed from the stand.

I found my way out into the street. There was a lot of traffic about. A large number of cops were standing on corners and lurking in parked cars. I asked one what was going on and was politely informed that the trial of some IRA bombers was proceeding in Number Six Court. I wandered round into Newgate Street, to what was obviously the genuinely *old* part of the Old Bailey, the gothic horror show part. A door bore a small sign, *Public Galleries*. I went inside, surrendered my handbag, had a metal detector run over me, and climbed the stairs. There were only a few ghouls and tourists in the gallery of the court I selected at random. I sat in the front row, leaning my head on the brass rail. This was a proper court—pregnant with hopeless doom. The panelling was dark, the lion and the unicorn fought for the crown in dark timber relief, the seats were worn, the leather cracked. The late afternoon light fought its way down from arched skylights. The murderer sat directly below me in the dock, hunched, broken, indifferent. In the dark witness box a man in a dark suit answered technical questions about internal bleeding caused by violent and prolonged shaking. In front of each juror, counsel, judge, and the murderer himself, was a folder of large glossy photographs of the murderer's baby. The baby looked up, battered, blackened, dead. And I looked down from the gallery at the face of the child. I looked down over the shoulders of the child's father to the photograph that lay cradled on his knees, and I wept. Quietly, softly, I wept. I wept for all the battered, blackened, dead children. I wept for all the murderers in all the docks of the world, and I wept for that strange and special sort of murderer who takes her stand, not in the dock, but in the witness box. And the man in the dark, dark suit spoke on about bruising both external and internal. And an attendant tapped me on the shoulder and led me gently from the gallery. And in the corridor I fainted.

* * * * * * *

The next morning I took the train to Liverpool. I bought the day's papers at the station. The fourth estate had done a passable job. My own evidence had been summarised neatly in half a dozen short sentences, there was a picture of Dino Torri entering the court—he looked even more like a weasel than I remembered from the night club—but the body of the report was given over to a verbatim transcription of Dino's tape which had been played in the morning, before I had taken the stand. Apparently there had been an aggressive attempt by Grearson to have the tape declared inadmissible. Mutimer had argued that as his client was about to tell the court the substance of his conversation with Mrs van Niekerk, there was perhaps some point to actually hearing the conversation itself. Wonder of wonders, Millard had agreed. Perhaps I've been a bit too harsh about poor old Millard, perhaps a modicum of sentience lurks behind his bleary eyes. I read through the transcript slowly, although I knew pretty well what was in it. Kilminster had heard it from the gallery and had supplied me with a spirited rendition. When I'd finished reading, I looked out of the window; the countryside screamed silently past at slightly over a hundred miles per hour, green, ordered; the clouds were grey and tattered like a worn-out Salvation Army blanket.

So who is Bernadette? What is she really like? As far as I can see, there can be no serious doubt that she intended to kill both van Niekerk and myself. In cold blood. For money. With malice aforethought.

And yet the woman is a twit. Can twits also be murderers? Why not?

I have always regarded her as empty-headed, foolish, stupid, preoccupied with small things. Being like this she cannot also possess the executive with necessary for the task of murder. Is her entire manner, then, a façade, a cover for a cold and rational intelligence? Does she ever drop the gushing, overemphasised, hand-clapping, ingenuous, upper-class-twit demeanour? Is there ever a time when she speaks, if only to herself, with the tones of a clear-sighted competence? I don't know, I can't imagine her like that. Kilminster says that when they played the tape, even though the quality of the recording was bad, the tones, the rising and falling inflections of Bernadette's delivery, came over loud and clear. Sitting in the train, I took a red ballpoint and went through the transcript in the newspaper, inserting the emphases and exclamation marks that the reporter had felt constrained to omit:

Mrs van Niekerk: Oh, but Mr Torri, you must do it! There is so much at stake! And you would be able to pay back Pieter for the *horrible* way he has treated you. It is all *so unfair.* And I am Pieter's wife! And yet he is leaving it all to Anasuya who has *heartlessly* cut herself *off* from him *completely!* He's even left more to that horrible writer woman who made his life absolute *hell* than he has to me. And she must make pots and *pots* of money from all those *dreadful* paperbacks she writes. And she hasn't even *been* to see him in ten years.

Mr Torri: Now look, let's get this straight, you want me to do in van Niekerk and his kid for a million quid, right?

Mrs van Niekerk: Oh yes, that's what I just *said!*

Mr Torri: I'd still prefer the agreement in writing, if it's all the same to you.

Mrs van Niekerk: But, oh my goodness, one can't put that sort of thing in *writing.* It just isn't *done!*

Kilminster says that at this point he and some of the other ghouls giggled. Millard banged his mallet, instructed the clerk of court to stop the machine, admonished those who had laughed, threatened to clear the court if there was a repeat performance, instructed the clerk to rewind the tape and subsided into his normal doze. The clerk spun the reels for a few seconds and began again, but of course he'd backed up a lot further than was required. Again the court listened to Bernadette raving about how *unfair* it all was. This time the entire court was anticipating the "It just isn't *done!*" remark. Kilminster says that no one actually burst into outright laughter this time, but the foot-shuffling, smile-suppressing tension in the room rose and subsided with a physical presence greater, if anything, than the previous audible laughter. But the tape rolled on.

> But Mr Torri, a million pounds is all I can *afford!* I know it isn't a *fortune.* But for only a few days work....

Kilminster watched Bernadette throughout the playing of the tape. He says she sat very still, not even twisting her gloves, like a mourner at a funeral, keeping her grief to herself. Will Grearson call her as a witness? Kilminster thinks not. Obviously Mutimer would like to get her into the witness box for a spot of cross-questioning, but for some reason he isn't allowed to call her. People charged with murder, apparently, very rarely become subject to question and cross-question. I know what I'd do if I were Grearson, however. I'd allege that the tape was a clever forgery put together by Torri and an unknown actress. Then I'd quietly hire a crooked elocution teacher (a weird concept, I know, but there must be out of work actors or starving drama teachers whose services and confidentiality can be bought) who would teach Bernadette not to gush, not to end her sentences on those idiot rising inflections, not to stress every tenth word for no reason at all. Then I'd put her in the witness box; obviously the voice on the tape could not be hers. Brilliant! When I grow up I'm going to become a QC.

It has just occurred to me that perhaps this is what did happen. Perhaps the tape really is a forgery, perhaps the quality is bad for just that reason. If it were made by an actress, she must have done a good job, but accurate mimicry is not beyond the competence of good actresses. If Torri and associates had suddenly presented Bernadette with a tape allegedly implicating her in an attempt to murder her husband and his highly beloved daughter, would Bernadette have been so completely sure of van Niekerk's faith in her that she would have allowed the tape to come into his possession? Or would she have simply syphoned off a thousand pounds of van Niekerk's endless supplies of money once a month to keep even the possibility of his suspecting her at bay? A thousand pounds is very reasonable, after all, it is not a sum that Bernadette would have missed, or van Niekerk either. (Given, that is, slightly more sophisticated laundering techniques than the one I used on behalf of Rasta Action *et al*.) And it seems quite plausible that Dino Torri would have taken a delight in that sort of action; van Niekerk certainly regarded him as capable of harmful acts against him. The man has a criminal record; he is only co-operating because of this Queen's Evidence lunacy, he's only spilling the beans in order to gain protection from the results of acts of blackmail he openly admits to having committed. Which is more likely? Dino concocting a false tape in order to engage in a bit of blackmail, or Bernadette plotting to murder both van Niekerk and myself?

But where does all this leave the question of the bombs? And Brian? Perhaps Brian and Dino were in league with each other, organising Bernadette to syphon off the money, with the bombs in the cars as an alibi. If Bernadette had gone to van Niekerk claiming to be the victim of a dreadful frame-up by that horrible, *horrible* little man, Dino, Brian could have suddenly "discovered" the bombs, thereby undercutting her story that the tape was a fake. Oh Christ, that's absurd. The whole bloody world is absurd. Who knows what the truth is? I don't. And I don't care. I've had enough of the whole bloody mess. I'm going to bring the trial to a halt, throw a spanner in the legal works.

* * * * * * *

So I did it. I did it by myself, without consulting Kilminster. I did it out of pity. I did it out of a sense of fair play, I did it because I was sick of the whole thing. I did it because someone else was being blamed for my deed. I did it because someone else was being *credited* with my deed.

In Liverpool I bought a small gardening trowel in an ironmongers, put it in my shoulder bag and took a bus out of town to the village near where I'd buried the tape. I walked along the bridle path to the copse, dug up the tape, threw away the trowel, and returned to London by bus and train. The next day at Tamar's I waited until everybody was out of the house and then played the tape on Ivan's expensive tape-deck. At first I used the earphones so that no one could overhear what was being said, if they happened upon me. But I felt claustrophobic. I didn't want to hear my father's voice, but I especially didn't want to hear it a couple of centimetres from my ears. So I played the tape normally. Why not? No one was around, if anybody had come to the door I'd have turned it off.

Van Niekerk pleaded for his liberty. My father, long dead, spoke of his desire for life. Daddy's voice was tinged with fear, but he wasn't babbling, he was well in control.

I wasn't in control. I freaked. I freaked as completely and assuredly as it is possible for a human being to freak. I shook. I shook so badly I would not have been able to turn the tape off had I wanted to. My father's voice hit me, stunned me. My father, long dead, spoke of his desire for life. I sat and shook. This was it, this was the point at which words, my words, gave out. All those thousands and thousands of words in my note-books, all the verbal therapy, all the exorcism of confession and analysis, might have been a preparation, a circling in towards the centre, towards a confrontation with the act itself. But this was the act.

My father had spoken into the microphone in the box, and now he spoke to me from the twin speakers in Ivan's living room. I had stopped that voice. That's what I had done: stopped the words.

The story I have been telling in these notebooks deserted me. Until that time all the extraneous story line—my child-hood, Philippe's broken back, Kilminster and Jennifer, all the words that surround those few mundane narrative sentences that describe my father's death at my hands, even the words that described the rape—had been insulation, padding, a verbal sea in which the murder had taken its place as one small island, an insignificant island in an archipelago of incidents, happenings, doings. Now that one act was the world itself.

My father had been alive and had spoken the words I now heard. But he was now dead. The words had no owner. I shook and shook, sitting helpless on the floor. I shook while the remaining half-hour of blank tape hissed meaninglessly and clicked into oblivion. What was the use? What is the use? What is the use of all those exercise books of so-called exorcism if I cannot now write down what I felt? I can say that I shook. I can describe how I finally stood up and rewound the tape and played my father's words again. How again I shook and trembled. I can say that I played that tape at least a dozen times until I shook no longer. Those indeed were my actions. But having described my actions, how can I describe my soul, my state of mind? I have used the idiom of my generation, I have said that I freaked. Well so I did, but what does that mean? I have used my limited literary powers to construct an elegant analogy for the transition in significance that the killing suddenly had for me, but what can clever talk of islands and archipelagos tell me or you about the reality of the transition itself? I have failed completely in the telling of my story. It could not be otherwise.

Kilminster once quoted Wittgenstein at me "Whereof we cannot speak, thereof we must be silent." I have never read the book from which this quotation comes. I doubt that I would understand it if I did, but I have only now, as I have been struggling to write the above paragraphs, seen what it means. I had taken the quote as a wise injunction: "You would be well advised not to run off at the mouth about things you know nothing about," or maybe: "Intelligent people do not assume they know more than they do." That's not what the quotation means at all. There is a frontier at which words fail, a line beyond which they have no dominion. We may sometimes cross this frontier, but having done so, silence is imposed absolutely upon us, whether we like it or not. Being wise or judicious in speech has nothing to do with it.

Still, in the sure knowledge that I will fail absolutely, I will proceed with this third-person case study. Thus:

> During the afternoon on which Anasuya continually
> played the tape recording of her father's voice she ex-
> perienced a severe existential crisis, an overwhelming
> feeling of angst, despair and, for the first time, the full
> and complete realisation of the consequences of her
> own actions. This state of mind was accompanied by
> strong physical symptoms of distress, of which shak-
> ing, rapid shallow breathing, and the continual oscil-
> lation between a clammy coldness and a feverish high
> temperature were the most pronounced. At times she
> dug her fingernails into the palms of her hands with
> almost enough force to draw blood. With the repeated
> playing of the tape these symptoms subsided, until, on
> about the twelfth playing she was sitting almost com-
> pletely still with temperature, pulse, and breathing all
> at a normal rate. She appeared drained of energy, but
> otherwise in good health.

See what I mean?

I rewound the tape again and made two copies of the speech—
this time using Ivan's portable tape-recorder connected to the
deck by a jack. I kept the speakers switched off. I played a
portion of both copies on the portable to make sure the machines
had been correctly engaged and then wiped the outsides of all
three cassettes clean of finger prints and placed them in padded
post office bags. I took the tube to a pawnshop I know in Kensal
Green, bought the cheapest second-hand typewriter I could
find, and came home.

I wrote to Mutimer at the department of Public Prosecutions
telling him that he was barking up the wrong tree and the
people to investigate were the diamond company to whom a
ransom demand had been made some time ago. I said copies
of the tape were being sent to Grearson and the press. Using
the typewriter I prepared three label addresses. Grearson's bag

I addressed to his club, the other I addressed to the *Glasgow Herald*. On Mutimer's bag I typed "Urgent and Confidential". I posted all three at the General Post Office, sending Mutimer his by express delivery; I wanted the police to have time to act before the others got their copies, but I wanted the knowledge that they did not have a monopoly of the evidence to spur them into action.

I took a bus to Notting Hill and hocked the typewriter under a fictitious name for eleven pounds less than I'd paid for it. Then I rang Kilminster from a public phone box.

"James? It's me."

"Hi."

"Listen, there are going to be unexpected developments in the case, but don't be alarmed by them, see? I just thought I'd let you know."

There were a few moments while Kilminster ummed and erred and then he said, "I see, like that is it? Have you been doing a bit of gardening?"

"That sort of thing."

"Can't say I blame you. I expected you might. We'll talk about it later. Okay?"

"Okay."

"Be loved."

"Same to you."

We rang off and I went to a cinema and watched *Casablanca* for the third or fourth time. It's a fine film. There isn't a word or a scene out of place and like Bogey says, the problems of two little people in this world don't amount to a hill of beans.

* * * * * * *

I met Kilminster outside the Old Bailey. He'd only been in the public gallery for half an hour. There had been a general commotion in the place when Mutimer had asked for the case to be adjourned for the time being, pending the investigation of important new evidence that had just come to light. Grearson hadn't seemed surprised and hadn't objected. Millard had grumbled and moaned and finally allowed himself to be led away to his chambers where Mutimer had a few words with him in private. He re-entered the court, adjourned the case for a month and left again. Hubbub.

I kissed Kilminster in Newgate Street and then made my way back to Tamar's. Kilminster left for Liverpool. After lunch I rang Michaels.

"What the hell's happening?"

"Miss Tamar, I'm not at liberty to say at the moment, but our investigations have unearthed some evidence that throws the whole case into doubt."

Our investigations! Jesus, Michaels.

"What a bore," I said, "Do you mind if I go back to France for a while?"

"No. Not at all. I don't think we'll need to talk to you again. If we do I can ring you, or maybe organise myself another trip to Paris. I'd quite like to meet your mother again, now that I've read all her books. My superiors might just foot the bill if I put the screws on. I tried to arrange a trip to Athens to talk to you when you were in Greece, but they wouldn't come at it. We've some frightfully mean people in Scotland Yard. Anyway, I'm sorry about all this. You've been a great help. We've been thrown into a complete tizzy at this end by these developments, I don't know what's going to happen. I wish I could tell you more, but I'm afraid...."

"Yeah, I know, don't worry about it Mr Michaels. The protocols of your profession and all that...."

"Quite. Well, all the best. I'll let you know what's happening the moment I'm allowed to."

So I left Michaels the vicar-sleuth to his complete tizzy and came back to France. And I felt good. The omens were right: the crossing was the roughest I've ever encountered. It was superb, the ferry rolled and pitched, the waves broke clear over the bridge. The wind screamed in the wires. Force ten and the barometer falling. We left Dover at midnight, straight into the teeth of it. There were very few people on board and the lounge was almost deserted. The blackjack girl sat at her table playing patience. A group of routiers played dice and drank cognac. I drank coffee standing at the bar and talked to some *marginaux* going home from a rock concert. They passed me a joint from which I took a few puffs to be sociable. The water streamed down the glass of the windows. The loudspeakers crackled and stuttered and informed all aboard that it was too rough to proceed into Calais harbour in the dark; we would steam up and down until daylight. The *marginaux* cheered and rolled another joint. They had a van, did I want a lift? Certainly, and what's more, if they cared to diverge fifteen kilometres at Rissons I'd promise them breakfast. So the ferry rolled and pitched and in the grey first light we entered Calais harbour. Two and a half hours later the *marginaux*'s van careered up the château's drive.

The month slid by. I heard nothing from anybody. The only communication of any importance was from Ivan. He had tendered for, and won, a contract to stage an exhibition of early trade guilds for the Nottingham City Council, due to be ready in six months' time. Did I want a job? What could be better? One evening I sat on the sofa with Jennifer after everyone else had gone to bed. She had her feet on the coffee table in front of her. Her soles turned to the fire. There was a hole in the big toe of one of her socks. She said, "How much did you actually write in Greece?"

"Dozens of exercise books."

"Can I read them?"

"I don't know. There's lots about you in them."

"I'm sure I can handle anything you might say about me."

So I gave her all the taverna notebooks. Three days later she gave them back. We talked for a while about what I had written, then she said, "Well, you've done a good job, they're quite convincing."

I looked at her. She said, "You know, they're a convincing picture of you and your relations with us all."

But that's not what she had meant. I said, "You never stopped being Kilminster's great Mother Confessor did you?"

"No," she said, "And I never will, but I appear to have fallen from that role with you."

I looked at the flames of the fire for a while and then I said, "No, Jennifer dear, I'll tell you anything you like. I can take you or leave you."

So I gave her all the rest of the notebooks. When she returned them she said very little, just kissed me and held me for a long time. We went for a walk around the orchard with our arms around each other.

Then all the charges against Bernadette were dropped. Immediately the case was no longer *sub judice* a newspaper, the *Glasgow Herald* of all things, unleashed a sensational story about a mysterious tape-recording and a daylight raid on the premises of a diamond company by forty detectives from Scotland Yard that had produced evidence that the missing businessman, Pieter van Niekerk, had been held to ransom against the freedom of a captured black guerrilla leader in South Africa. I rang Michaels.

"What on earth is happening?"

"We really don't know anything more than the newspapers."

"Bernadette is the last person in the world to ransom my father for a guerrilla."

"Which is why the charges have been dropped. We'd never prove a connection there."

"Do you think it could have been one of those groups I sent dud cheques to? You know, our old Rasta Action theory?"

"We just don't know, Miss Tamar. We have no real leads at the moment, although our investigations are proceeding."

"The trail must be pretty cold by now."

"I'm afraid so. It would be misleading of me to hold out much hope of solving the case or finding your father now. We will continue looking, of course, but don't be too hopeful."

You can't tell with Michaels, especially over the phone, but my impression is that he was telling the truth.

So that's it. What more is there to be said? I'm sick of writing in notebooks. I'm sick of writing about myself—it has all started to become a bit self-regarding. But it's worked. I know who I am and I know what I did and I sleep very easy at night and I laugh a lot during the day. In a fortnight I'm going to Nottingham to work on early trade guilds and all that they entail. When that's over I'm going to start a proper novel. Dunno what about. Wild scenes in the early trade guilds possibly. Or maybe a Trouble-at-Pit novel, or one about court life in Mandarin China. I'll have to think about it. I'll have to learn to touch-type.

But something happened the other day; a small incident, but significant. The telling of it will finish this notebook very neatly. Then I'll bury it and its friends deep in the woods or under the floorboards and write no more about my past.

Jean-Claude came back from Nigeria where he had been doing a series of articles on the restoration of "democracy". Jennifer and I took the Renault to Charles de Gaulle to meet him. As we were churning back up the autoroute Jean-Claude said, "I met Walter Black from the *Guardian* in Lagos."

"Oh yes," I said.

"He had a message for you."

"For me? But I hardly know him. I've only met him once, that time he stayed the night."

"It was from someone else, someone he'd been talking to in Dar es Salaam. Walter didn't give his name, he said you'd know who he was. He sends his regards."

"Anything else?"

"Not that Walter could remember, just his regards."

So I've an anonymous well-wisher in Dar es Salaam, have I? Ho hum.

[Anasuya's notebooks: End of final entry.]

ABOUT THE AUTHOR

Rory Barnes was born in London in 1946, but was immediately transported to Africa, where he learned to walk and talk in a mud hut in a tribal village (the standard infancy for the children of anthropologists). By the time he was ten, his family had moved to Sydney, and he has lived in Australia ever since. He studied Philosophy at Monash University, where he met Damien Broderick. Over the years these two have written seven or eight novels together, the lastest joint production being *Human's Burden*, published by Borgo Press (2010). By himself Barnes has written another seven novels for both adults and teenagers. He can claim the usual list of writers' other jobs: teacher, farmhand, journalist, builder's laborer, book reviewer, publisher's reader, lecturer, etc., etc. He once delivered a baby. Once, when hitchhiking, he was given a lift in a hearse. On another occasion he walked from Jerusalem to the Dead Sea without getting shot. A widower with two adult suns, he lives in Adelaide. His website can be found at:

http://members.optusnet.com.au/~rory.barnes